A CALL FROM JERSEY

ALSO BY P.F. KLUGE

Eddie and the Cruisers

Gone Tomorrow

Biggest Elvis

Final Exam

Alma Mater

The Edge of Paradise

A Season for War

McArthur's Ghost

The Day I Die

COMING SOON

The Master Blaster

A CALL FROM JERSEY

P.F. KLUGE

THE OVERLOOK PRESS
NEW YORK, NY

To the people who watched me
grow up in New Jersey—
the Ensslens, Fuchses, Bruders,
Gerediens, Kochs—and
the Kluges, my parents
Maria and Walter, and my brother
Jim, who still keeps an eye on me.

This edition first published in paperback in the United States in 2011 by
The Overlook Press, Peter Mayer Publishers, Inc.
141 Wooster Street
New York, NY 10012

Cataloging-in-Publication Data is available from the Library of Congress

Book design and typeformatting by Bernard Schleifer & Jerry Kelly
Manufactured in the United States of America
FIRST PAPERBACL EDITION
2 4 6 8 10 9 7 6 5 3 1
ISBN 978-1-59020-687-4

Some are in prison, some are dead;
And none has read my books,
And yet my thought turns back to them …

From "The Chums" by Theodore Roethke

PART ONE

I.

You couldn't not like Max Schmeling. I know that sounds strange, considering the millions who hated him. But if you knew him the way I did, you knew better. Der Max. "The Black Uhlan." Heavyweight champion of the world, 1930-1932. Still alive, as far as I know. I don't think I read about him dying, but then again, he is old and some days I skip the newspapers. Everyone remembers that great upset in 1936 when, already past his prime, Max right-handed Joe Louis half to death, knocking him out in the twelfth. And, since everything involving Germans and Americans has to be a confrontation between Good and Evil, they move quickly to The Brown Bomber's dramatic night of revenge, two years later, when he stopped old Max in the first round. One step backward for the master race, which Schmeling represented, one step forward for the human race, which Joe Louis was a credit to.

Heinz—that was my brother—was the one who brought me to Schmeling. They'd been friends on the other side and whenever Schmeling came over for a fight, Heinz walked away from his job, bartending on 86th Street in New York, and he joined Max's entourage. Heinz was always a charmer, the life of the party. He was a big gambler, not just fights, but horses, baseball—which he hardly understood—and how many inches of snow and what time, exactly would the Hindenburg be crossing over the island of Manhattan? It wasn't about money. Gambling was my brother's way of making life more interesting. Every event that had money riding on it was a drama. It was exciting. It had meaning. His definition of 100% happiness would have been to bet everything on anything, every day. Impossible dream, but he came close a time or two. He called it "action." And that's what drew him to Max Schmeling. Schmeling was action. Plus, they were friends.

Heinz came over a few years ahead of me, in 1925. He was bigger than me, he grew up faster. Though I was older I was always "brüderchen," the little brother. Heinz was a headache, at school, at work, at home. I'm not sure there wasn't a girl he got in trouble, right before he left. He was always taking chances. By the time I arrived, in 1928, Heinz was already set up on 86th Street. I came across on a second-class ticket—that was Heinz's doing—so I was able to avoid a night on Ellis Island and go straight to Battery Park, where Heinz met me, looking like a million dollars, wearing a fedora, a camel hair coat, a three piece suit, new shoes. He'd stepped out of a movie poster: tall, dark, handsome. Standing next to him—actually a little behind, as if waiting to be properly introduced—was an older German who had to be Otto Hofer, so-called Onkel Otto, my father's friend and my sponsor in America. He'd come over in 1898. He remembered the Spanish-American War. He lived through World War I, when they stopped teaching German in schools, they looked at German-speakers as spies, they closed shops and re-named streets. Sauerkraut was liberty cabbage, hamburger was Salisbury steak. We were a race of bull-necked, baby-murdering, nun-raping monsters. Otto got through that. And, starting in the 1920's, Otto and Hilde Hofer sponsored one greenhorn a year, giving them a place to stay—and work—in the apartment buildings where he was superintendent, on the West Side, from Harlem to Morningside Heights. I was the latest in that line of greenhorns.

Years later, we put together a party for the Hofers. This must have been in the 1950's. Much later, Otto was dead and couldn't attend. 1952, say. They were both in their eighties then. We rented a room in a restaurant, the *Deutsche Hof* out near Flemington, New Jersey—the town they railroaded Hauptmann in, if you remember the Lindbergh kidnapping. The restaurant's still there, doing good: deer heads and cuckoo clocks on the wall, beer steins and Hummel figurines on shelves, a *lederhosen* wearing oom-pah band on weekends. "*Ist das nicht ein Schnitzelbank?*" But that night was something. Fifteen greenhorns and their wives and kids, fifteen out of sixteen they brought over. And it was mostly a real nice time, going way into the night, dancing and singing, Otto and Hilde sitting at the table, stern and proper as ever, until at the very end, the two of them got up and danced and, I swear, there wasn't a dry eye. What a night. Some of us had never met, because the deal was, you worked a year for Otto, then you moved on and made room for the next one off the boat. But we all got up, one by one and thanked them, funny little speeches about how green and young we'd been. It turned out none of us had been able to resist retrieving things out of the trash, perfectly good things that came down the dumbwaiter, shirts with lots of wear left in them, shoes that were fine for us to walk around in. We all slept between the luggage room and the boiler—we talked about that—and the looks from Otto when we came home a little tipsy and the way Hilde would serve us corn on the cob for our first American meal and more than half of us bit into it like it was a hot dog. We recalled the sound of operetta—Tauber singing Lehar—on Saturday nights and how other old-timers came over, bringing records to play, these were the Hofers' contemporaries, some of them had even known Carl Schurz. They weren't so sure about us newcomers, whether we had what it took to make it in America. They nodded at us, we nodded at them, and they kept their opinions to themselves. We were still on probation. But by 1952, there was no doubt, we were all successes, us with our fat-finned 1950's cars and our suburban homes and Florida vacations, wives and wunderkinder. *Look at us* we seemed to say, *aren't we something*. American success stories. Sure, we had to admit it, we were lucky. We came to the country at the right time. We had trades. We were willing to work—that leaves out a lot of people in this country, let's face it—and we knew how to work—and that leaves out a lot of the rest. The Depression? We worked. The War? We worked overtime. And after the war—the forties and now, fifties—best time a working man ever saw. We owned nice houses. We had televisions, soon as they came out. We weren't so sure about unions anymore. We were sending our kids to college so they could have the chances we'd never had. We were doing good. Some of us were even doing fine. But, as the speeches rolled on, when we got to the year 1925, it was awkward. That was Heinz' year. The room got quiet and I felt that they were all looking at me, as if I knew something they didn't, which I didn't, and I was looking at my wife, wondering if *she* knew something I didn't. Everybody in the room was waiting for something from me. Whatever they knew about Heinz, it wasn't enough. They'd all found themselves wondering about him, every one of them, and now it was as if we ought to raise a glass or have a moment of silence. But what for? War criminal? War hero, good German, bad German, who knew? Then I saw Otto Hofer smiling at me for the first time. "Well," he said. "Nobody's perfect."

That was all in the future. At the start, Otto Hofer was a proper old man standing behind Heinz. I'd heard so much about him but in real life, as they say, he was disappointing, especially when you compared him to the fine figure Heinz cut that morning. Even his handshake, it's the way I pictured the Germans surrendering in that railroad car in Versailles, after World War I. Everything was muted and polite. Except maybe his eyes. He had curious eyes. I felt him watching me while Heinz spun me around in welcome. Who are you? What are you? Are you like your brother? His house was my official address in America, he explained. I was his responsibility. "That is the arrangement," he said in German. "I hope you like it. And I hope that I like it too." Normally, he would take me home but he understood my brother—a stiff nod at Heinz—had made other arrangements. He expected me at work the next morning, at seven a.m. Another look at Heinz. Make it six a.m. he said. Then he left.

Heinz was in a rush to show me the town. I said no. I wanted to just stand there for a while, there where my ship came in. I wanted to remember the moment. The arrival hall was huge, filled with the dusty yellowish light that you see in train stations and factories, the sun shining through windows that hadn't been washed in years, that the rain streaks but never cleans. It's the yellow light that makes every day seem like afternoon and every season autumn, even on a bright spring morning. There were birds inside the building, pigeons way up high, sitting on the roof beams. Down below, it felt like the floor of a cathedral. I watched the passengers come out from behind the immigration barriers. A furniture maker from Ulm, a pair of sisters from Heilbrunn, some Jewish department store people from Stuttgart. Out they stepped, some of them carrying a suitcase and nothing more, traveling light like me, others leading a couple of porters who'd wrestled their trunks onto carts. Steamer trunks. I was seeing something I would never see again, people stepping out into a new world. I told George, the future travel writer, about it once, that is I tried to. I said I felt like I was standing between my past and my future. My son looked at me and rolled his eyes, the way he did when he felt he'd heard something dumb. It made me want to clip him, when he did that.

"Pop," he said, oh-so-wearily. "If you could only listen to yourself."

I never did hit him, not then, not ever, though I gave him some looks that scared him. "I heard myself," I said. He was home from college, reading out on the back porch. Whenever you got near him, he turned over the book, so that we wouldn't see the title. Then he wouldn't have to talk to us about what he was reading, which was over our heads of course.

"Every minute you're alive, you're standing between the past and the future," he informed me. "That's what the present *is*."

"Yeah, well," I said, turning away. "You weren't there that morning."

"But Pop, if you want to talk about it ..."

"You were in the future," I said, heading out the side door to the garden. Mom had patience, not me. She'd cut him plenty slack, ever since we got called into school when he was in the seventh grade. We stopped into the principal's office wondering what kind of mess our George had stepped in. We had no idea. As a kid, he wasn't up to much, just reading. Even then, he asked permission to keep the light on late, would you believe it, the good little boy, sometimes if we were playing pinochle on Saturday night at somebody's house, he'd even *call* and ask permission, could he stay up and read a little more. This was the kind of boy, when his mom baked cookies "specially for you" and they came out a little burned, like charcoal, he'd ask for more, just to please her. That kind of kid. In summer we let him play under a hose, he'd always make sure to find a brown spot on the lawn, so the grass would get the benefit. What could the trouble be? Then they told us that they'd given tests and he was—here comes a nickname we used for years—"college material." I swear, that was the start of what's happening today, wherever in the world he's eating for nothing at the moment. College material. Like that, a sweet dreamy kid—a real klutz around tools and nothing special in sports—became our wunderkind. Mom tried keeping up with him, but, hey, did Werner von Braun tell his mom about Peenemunde? Our rocket scientist kept his V-1s to himself. When George was in high school, I'd see mom trying to read what he read. Then she'd try to discuss these books with college material. Herman Hesse. She was scared, so she'd watch for him to be in just the right mood and still he'd sniff—annoyed at being interrupted—and say, "Mom, I'd have to start with the invention of the wheel." I learned early, not to make that mistake. In the garden, by myself among the red currants and the gooseberries, I remembered that thick yellow light, gold dust almost, and that wooden floor, scuffed and polished the way wood gets, almost oiled, like the deck of a sailing ship or the banister in an old house. I could see groups of people coming out the gate, some rushing out, like kids into a schoolyard, others scared, holding onto pieces of paper with relatives' addresses. This was the beginning of something. Part of me was in a rush, anxious to begin, tired of waiting, aching—after ten days at sea—to walk for miles. But another part just took in what was happening. Those people. The birds in the rafters. The sunlight coming in. I wished I had the words.

I was happy from the first day. It was the time of oranges for me, for all of us. That's how I think of it, to this day. I didn't have much money but I had enough for small things and just seeing those piles of oranges in grocery stores—sometimes out on the sidewalk—I couldn't have been more excited if I'd come across a pot of gold. An orange meant a lot to a young man who'd spent the winter of 1917 eating turnips so that the sight, the smell—the very idea—of a turnip all these years later, makes me gag. Those oranges meant more to me than any car I ever bought. And barbershop shaves! Oh my God! Those were the days of hot towels and warm shaving lather, talcum powder and bay rum and when I stretched out in the chair, I could see an overhead fan turning and a stamped tin ceiling and on the radio they'd be talking about the Yankees. I learned English fast. Already, I was ahead of the Italians who were shaving me, already I understood about the Yankees. Every time I picked up a newspaper, I learned new words. You could look at a photograph, you studied the caption, you learned. So, I was young and green and happy those long ago Sundays. Most of my life I was happy, but that was the happiness with other people around me, with Mom and later George. Back then I was just happy by myself. Now that I'm alone again, I wish I could get that kind of happiness back.

I'd leave the barbershop and enter the park at 110th Street, by the lake. I'm shaved, I smell of talcum powder. I've got a new suit and a straw hat, I'm a Yankee Doodle Dandy, headed to Eighty-Sixth Street to visit my brother, and there are kids and nannies, German nannies, lots of them, on the benches along the lake. I leave the park behind and stroll down Fifth Avenue, past mansions. Call it May, 1932. A left off Fifth brings me onto 86th Street, crossing Madison, Park, Lexington, the city that belongs to people who were here before us. At Lexington, though, it changes. Yorkville. Little Germany. Land of Greenhorns. Some of them got to Yorkville and never left, the ones who had to have German food, movies and newspapers and would rather worry about a soccer game that happened three weeks ago than a pennant race with the Yankees in it and two Germans, Ruth and Gehrig, leading the team. But that's where Heinz's place was: the Restaurant Germania. Food in front and a back room … knock … knock … that was a speakeasy, with bad beer and my brother in charge.

"Pass auf," he shouted as I came in that first time. "Here comes the greenhorn." This was all in German, everyone at the table was German, recently arrived. The women were housekeepers and nannies—a few secretaries. The men were printers, machinists, carpenters, electricians, skilled blue-collar types who—they didn't know it—were a little too young for World War I and a little too old for World War II. They caught it just right, coming to a country that would enrich them beyond their dreams. If they stayed. Already, they had a kind of rakish style, just like I was acquiring, a kind of cockiness, because it usually didn't take more than one day on the job for them to know that the competition was nothing to worry about. So they were all at that point when New World money and Old World style were mingling evenly. Later, they had more money. And less character. But that was later.

Heinz introduced me to his crowd. Already, I felt nervous around all these Germans. Nice people, but why cross the Atlantic to surround yourself with *Landsmänner?* Heinz had been talking about me, before I came, I could see from the way they looked at me, wondering if I was another Heinz. Also, I was a newcomer and the newest arrivals made these people feel that much more experienced. We reminded them of home. We repeated the same greenhorn mistakes, getting lost in Queens, trying to walk to Schutzen Park in Jersey City through the Holland Tunnel. We showed them how far they'd come.

I was distracted, all the introducing and teasing, trying to remember names. I shook hands with the men and nodded to a tableful of German nannies, a kind of ladies auxiliary to Heinz' *stammtisch.* The woman I married was there that day, it turned out. She saw me then, the first time. She saw me and noticed me. I knew nothing. I noticed nothing, except this. I thought she ... that's Maria ... was with him, with my brother. It was just a little flicker, a glimpse of something that came and went, that's all. But it was there. He was so popular. Everybody liked him, even the ones who regretted it. Maybe she'd heard about me, on the nannies' network. The latest of Hofer greenhorns is arriving, another one sleeping in the basement. He's not so tall, not so dark, not so handsome. Smaller than Heinz. A soccer player, not a boxer. Also—not like Heinz—he's shy. He blushes when they talk about women. He looks like a worker, not like that Heinz. He's not a gypsy, not a gambler. Anyway, Mom knew about me before I knew about her. But that afternoon, she was in the future. That's how college material would put it. Just as now, in 1984, she's in my past. He'd say that too, I guess. A lot, he knows.

"*Post aus Deutschland!*" Heinz was waving an envelope, standing in the middle of the room, between the two greenhorn tables.

"So," someone asked in German. "Is it a boy or a girl?" I heard snickers but, by the time I turned, I couldn't tell who had made the joke.

"Nothing like that," Heinz said, embarrassed I was there to hear this.

"Is it money from home, Heinz?"

"The money goes one way," he answered. "From here to there." That was true, I learned. We never lost sight of the people on the other side. The time we spent in America, even if it stretched into years, was nothing against the time we'd spent in Germany. We'd left a lot behind there. If we had to choose, we knew what the choice would be. Or thought we did. And then, when the question finally arose, the contest was over and America had won.

"My friend is coming to America," Heinz said. "My special friend. Leaving next week from Bremerhaven."

"Schmeling?"

"Der Max."

"This time he wins standing up?"

"This time," Heinz said, glaring, "he makes it official."

Max Schmeling had won the title from Jack Sharkey the year before. But it wasn't much of a victory. Sharkey had fouled Schmeling, hit him below the belt. Max had gone to the canvas. The foul was real, Heinz insisted—he'd been there—but some newspapers said Schmeling was acting. Anyway, he was the first boxer to win the title on the floor of the ring, clutching his groin and looking up at the referee. So this second fight had a lot riding on it. It would shut up the people who said that Max was the best German actor since Emil Jannings.

"You'll be at the fight?" I asked Heinz.

"Yes," Heinz said. "And before that. At training." Already he was in his glory. "We'll all go. I'll set it up." Then he included me. "You come too."

Well, Max Schmeling's upcoming fight against Jack Sharkey took over my life. Remember, I was new in America and America was new to me, in the time of oranges. I was open to whatever came my way, those long walks up and down Manhattan, sticking my nose into all kinds of neighborhoods, taking the ferry to Staten Island and over to Jersey City. And then there were the blacks. I'd seen maybe six in all my life, all sailors, always from a distance. In New York, they were all around. I still would have been shy about meeting them except that there were two who worked for Otto Hofer. Cleveland and Billy.

The first time I saw them they were standing outside my room, down in the basement, one man coal-black and big, the other brown and thin. If Otto hadn't been standing behind them, I'd have jumped and run.

"What's this?" the big man—who was Billy—asked. He wore blue overalls and his hair was turning white. I stared at his skin, black as could be but polished, it seemed, almost shining. "Another kin of yours, Mr. Otto?"

"He's the brother from Heinz," Otto said. He wore dark

pants with suspenders, a white shirt. In his hand, he held a morning cigar, short and stubby. "You're remembering Heinz?"

The two men traded a glance, Billy and the thin one, Cleveland. "We remember him alright," Billy said. "There's people all up and down this street remembering Heinz."

"Well," Otto said with a nod. "Maybe this one is different. He looks like a worker. We'll see." Then he turned to me. "You do what they say."

It wasn't much of a trade for a trained metal worker and I wasn't at it for long but I learned about New York buildings from Cleve and Billy, from tarring the roof to feeding the furnace to washing windows, waxing floors, vacuuming carpets, polishing woodwork, hauling garbage. They'd broken in a bunch of greenhorns already, so they mixed jokes with lessons, which meant letting me do things my own way, then showing me how to do it, just as well, in half the time.

A lot of people in Otto's building were German Jews. Harlem wasn't always a black neighborhood. The blocks just north of the park stayed white into the 1930's. Look at the names on New York hospitals and music halls, department stores and newspapers and those were the names whose garbage came down the dumbwaiter: Lewisohn, Frankfurter, Bamberger, Bloomingdale, Klingenstein, Ochs, Damrosch. These people knew I was German the minute they saw me and I was the one they'd talk to first, in German. I noticed that. When they wanted something done, they'd talk to me. They weren't all like that. Some made a point of knowing Cleve and Billy. These were good people, good for a slice of cake when we worked in their apartment and some apples and peaches, when they came in from their country places: Teitelbaum 10-G, Elmann 7-A, Rudofsky 5-B. But it bothered me a lot, when people who spoke to me ignored them. I tried to tell them as much. Sometimes, in good weather, we took lunch together at a bench by the lake in

Central Park. The way we talked! Cleve and Billy had been working around Germans so long that German expressions showed up in what they spoke. So when they came into the basement at dawn to wake me up, it was *"zeit for aufgettin."* At the end of the day it was, *"Hans, wir heading knock house."* We got along fine. But I wanted them to know what was bothering me.

"Hans, what you complaining for?" Cleve asked. "You're doin' alright, nick war?"

"But you are my seniors!"

"Maybe so ... but your seniors aren't complaining either."

"Was dis?" Billy said, digging around the basket Hilde Hofer had given us. "We got three kinds of sandwiches." He lifted the bread to see what was in between. "Knock worse, liver worse, blood worse." He offered me first choice. I waved him off, I was giving them the respect they deserved. Cleve and Billy made their choices. I got the knockwurst.

"This liver worse," Cleve said. "Not the stuff you see in the stores. Hey, Hans, what you call this kind?"

Coarse liverwurst, it was, with diced skin, pimentos, onions, flecks of fat. *"Grobe,"* I said. And that was all I said. My thoughtfulness was wasted on people who did so little on their own behalf.

"Listen here," Cleve said. "What you say is you wish folks would respect Billy and me more because we been working for years around here." He gestured across the lake. Seen from inside the park, beyond a line of sycamore trees, it looked like something from Hamburg. "Well," Cleve continued. "How come you don't respect us?"

"I don't?"

"Me and Billy been around a long time. You just came. You're telling us you don't like the way they treat us. We're asking—we're telling—you to leave it alone. And you ain't listening."

"We're staying," Billy said. "Not you. You move on out.

And up. We ain't going no place. Your uncle don't mess us around. Your *tante's* nice people. As for the other, it don't matter. You complain, it'll come back on us. Just leave it alone, Hans. You just got here. Takes time to figure a country out."

"*Gones be stimmed,*" Cleve added. *Ganz bestimmt.* Damn straight.

Smelling, they both pronounced it, the way Joe Louis said it a few years later. You wondered whether he meant an insult. Louis seemed to like saying it that way. But black people do have a problem with S-C-H. I leave it at that. Cleve and Billy knew of Heinz and his connection with Schmeling. Smelling. They saw me reading the papers, the sports pages, as if it were homework for an examination I was going to take. I lived and breathed that fight. I talked like an expert, the fine points of Max's style, compared with Sharkey's. They knew I didn't know a thing. And one day they decided to do me a favor.

They didn't speak to me directly. Instead they talked to each other, while I sat alongside. They talked about black boxers who'd spent whole careers and never had a chance at the title—Sam Langford and Harry Wills—or were made to wait until they were over the hill. About what it was like to spend your whole career on the road, in front of crowds who wanted you beaten and officials who went out of their way to assure a loss and if you happened to win—usually it took a knockout—you fled like a thief. They guessed that being white was worth three rounds, any day.

"Smelling is white," Billy said. "You've got to give him that."

"White for sure," Cleve granted. "But he's not an American. Makes him ... off-white."

"I wouldn't bet my money on Smelling. Not if it was money I needed."

"Any money you don't need?"

"Not if it was money I worked for."

"Don't you work for all your money?"

"You know anybody got money they don't work for?"

"Used to," Cleve said. "But I ain't seen that fellow lately. He don't come around. I been looking for him. But I don't reckon he's looking for me."

That was Heinz they were talking about, I was sure.

Back in the 1930's, you didn't have suburbs like you do today, all the way from Boston to Washington. Half an hour out of New York, in any direction, you were in the sticks. That's where fighters had their training camps, up in Greenwood Lake, in the mountains, the Poconos, the Catskills. A few years later, Joe Louis went to Lakewood to get ready for Schmeling. To prepare for Sharkey, Max went to Summit, New Jersey, to a place called Madame Bey's. That first time, I took the train out from the city, hitched a ride, hiked up a driveway into a collection of sheds, barn, boxing ring and heavy bags, bunk houses and kitchens and cabins, a kind of mess hall where they served ham and eggs in the morning, which is why bum fighters are called ham-and-eggers. I walked right in on a sparring session my brother was watching, so intent he hardly said hello. I got more of a greeting from Max, who nodded my way, even as he hooked a right at the belly of a much smaller man. The punch missed.

"He looks big," I said to Heinz.

"The other man is a light-heavyweight," Heinz answered, all his attention on the ring. "Paulie Costello. We want someone fast. Hard to hit."

Well, I watched Max work three rounds and I've got to say he proved my brother's point. Paulie Costello was very hard—for Max—to hit. He connected three or four times a round, not more, not enough to slow Costello down. Meanwhile, Costello threw jabs by the dozen, meaningless little punches, but he looked good, flurrying, dancing out of danger, posing. If Costello gave him this kind of problem, what would Sharkey do? I felt my wallet settling deeper in my pocket.

After it was over, people at ringside applauded politely, but they weren't impressed. Even I could tell. And Max stayed in the ring a moment, chatting with Costello. It was hard to believe, but it seemed he was coaching Costello, trying to show him something that would make him even harder to hit and when his English failed him, he waved my brother through the ropes so he could continue the lesson.

"You believe that?" someone asked. I turned around and it was a newspaperman, talking to another gentleman. Maybe another newspaperman, or a gambler, or a spy from Sharkey's camp. Training camps were open in those days and just far enough out of New York to make pleasant drives for sporting types, politicians, bootleggers, gamblers and their women.

"Believe?" said the second man. "Believe in what?"

"Taking the sparring partner to school. It looked the other way around, to me."

"Next time, little Paulie only gets hit two times, not four."

They walked off, deep in conference, adjusting the odds, and headed down the hill to where the cars were parked across the street, in an apple orchard no one looked after, though the trees were blossoming. The smoke from their cigars mixed with the smell of grass and flowers. I saw women with lipstick and perfume and good legs and no wedding rings, shoes that were meant for nightclubs and sidewalks, so they took their time going down the hill. When Heinz got back to me—Max had gone for a rubdown—I asked who those people were. Heinz shrugged, he couldn't keep track.

"Mayor Hague was here last week," he said. "And Gene Fowler. And Bugs Baer, the columnist."

"Mayor of ..."

"Jersey City. That's nothing. Last week comes Gentleman Jimmy Walker."

"Who is he?"

"New York City. Former mayor." He gave me a look that said I was a little thick. "You meet a lot of people here. You make connections. They know me. Walker, he said I should run for Mayor of Yorkville. Of course he was only joking ..."

His voice trailed off into a silence I didn't interrupt. I heard a last car pulling out of the orchard, onto the road that led out of the valley where the training camp was located, already falling into darkness, while the sun just caught the top of the trees, beech and oak and maple. This was the first I'd seen of the country outside New York. It was different from Germany, where every inch of ground, field, forest was spoken for. America was untended. Uncared for. The woods were full of fallen trees and branches that no one collected, all that firewood going to waste. I liked it in New Jersey. But not Heinz. He reminded me of how someone sits next to a car that's broken down, waiting for the mechanic to come.

"You stay here tonight," he said. "It's taken care of." He said it in a grand way as if it were his treat, he was paying. I nodded my thanks. I could smell dinner, steaks grilling, and onions. A radio was playing and some of the hanger-ons were sitting out, end of the day for them, too. I liked being there, now that it had quieted down. The visitors were gone, Heinz had to go back to New York. No getting out of work behind the bar, when he was off, the place went flat. But now, in New Jersey, crickets were starting up. And I felt at home.

"I saw the sparring," I said.

"Well? So?"

"He didn't look so good."

"Don't worry," Heinz said. "Max will find him. Max wins

this fight. It's money in the bank." He laughed. This was at a time when banks were failing. "It's better than money in the bank." I felt him looking at me, appraising, deciding not to do something: to place money on the fight. Then he walked towards the car that was taking him back to Yorkville, riding with new friends.

Five minutes later, Max Schmeling emerged from a cabin. He stood and considered the evening coming on. Then he did something I never forgot. He walked by, giving me a little wave, but you sensed he wanted to be alone. He walked to the edge of the yard, where the land sloped steeply down to River Road. A tree was there with a swing hanging down, a child's swing that he tested carefully, respecting property, and found it was sturdy enough to carry a heavyweight. He sat still, studying the ground. The greatest athlete Germany had produced, a few weeks away from a packed arena, he regarded that bare patch that children make, dragging their feet across the ground as they swing back and forth. Then he tilted back in the swing and looked up at a sky turned pink and purple, the sun long gone, he himself not much more than a silhouette. He started moving, pushing off with his feet. Then he put his weight into it, pushing forward, pulling back, and the swing was creaking, creaking, creaking like an animal in the woods. To this day, that's how I picture him, swinging back and forth in the dark. That is how I picture all of us, up and down, high and low, daylight turning dark. Anyway, I never forgot that moment.

"Who the hell are you?" someone asked. I turned around and saw an older man in a suit. He'd come up behind me, he'd watched me watching Max. The way he shouted scared me. This man was like the police.

"Well ... who the hell are you?" he repeated. I saw a tall, thin man with slicked back hair, prominent nose, sharp eyes, a Jewish face, I guessed. He smelled of barbershop and gymnasium, of beer, liniment and tobacco. He piled smell on smell the same way, I soon learned, he piled one language onto another, English and American, Yiddish and German.

"*Ich bin* ... I am ... der brother ... von Heinz," I managed.

Now he let go and stepped back. "Well, tell me, der Bruder von Heinz. Anybody come for sparring this afternoon?"

"Yes. Quite many."

"And your bozo brother, did he remember to charge them admission?"

"Charge?"

"Take money. *Gelt nehmen.*"

"No sir. I did not see that."

"What I thought. Anybody drops by to see the champ work out, it's fine with Heinz. It's on the house. What's your name, der brother von Heinz?"

"Hans Greifinger," I said. After a minute, I stuck out my hand, which he took and shook.

"Joe Jacobs," he said. I recognized the name. Schmeling's manager. He pointed at some round metal cans he'd put on the grass when he arrested me. "Grab that stuff, will you Hansel." I obeyed and followed him towards the cabin they used as a dining room. They were singing German songs in there. It felt like they were camping out in a strange land, singing to keep from feeling lonely.

"Alright, time for movies," Jacobs announced.

Ten minutes later, two figures circled around a ring, as if they were copying each other. The first one crouched, bobbed, moved sideways, the second did the same. Anything you can do, I can do better. The first was the Basque heavy-weight Paulino Uzcudun. The second—he sat at the table watching himself—was Max Schmeling. The Uzcudun fight, three years before, was just before Schmeling's first fight with Jack Sharkey. And it was a gamble. Uzcudun was an awkward fighter with a cast-iron chin. He could make anybody look bad—including, later, Joe Louis. He didn't punch hard but he could embarrass you to death. At one point, when there was a problem with the projector, I wandered into the kitchen for coffee. It was that kind of fight, that went with coffee better than beer. And there was Madame Bey, who ran the place. A French-Armenian woman, the wife of a Turkish diplomat who became an American, she spoke half a dozen languages, cooked international food, sang opera. She'd sung the national anthem in Buffalo when President McKinley made a speech there and was standing next to the president when he was shot. Years later, I attended her funeral. She's buried over in Chatham.

"I never watch my fighters fight," she told me. "Even on film ..."

"In the case of this film," I said, "I can't blame you."

"Paulino trained here," she said. "And Max ..." Her voice trailed off. Then she added something I never forgot, looking me in the eyes when she said two words I remembered and shared with her. "My Max ..."

Well, boxing in real life is nothing like in Hollywood. In Hollywood, you have a war every round. In movies, every punch lands right on target. You watch the real thing, you see elbows, clinches, punches missing and, careful as you are, you wouldn't want to have to say who won that last round. That explains why, all those years I watched Friday Night Fights, the future travel writer wanted to switch to wrestling.

"Pop," he'd say. "This is boring."

"Wrestlers are clowns," I'd snap back. George loved them, though. Ricky Starr, the ballet-type wrestler, Antonino Rocco, the inventor of the flying drop kick, and his particular hero, Tony Martinelli, the Clifton (New Jersey) Cutie. Now I think about it, the difference between the writer I'd hoped he'd be and what he actually became was the difference between boxing and wrestling. I wanted a Schmeling, I got a Gorgeous George.

"You know what?" George complained again. "Boxing's fixed."

"I see," I said. "And that's why we should switch to wrestling."

He shrugged and went upstairs to read, another father-and-son moment, up in smoke. I watched the fights alone. I'd learned what to watch for and it went back to that shaky black and white film I saw at Madame Bey's. Joe Jacobs was one of the first to use films. Through the early rounds, Max mirrored Uzcudun. Not much of a fight you'd say. George would vote again for wrestling. But then you saw what was happening. Max had Uzcudun timed. He started firing uppercuts that landed, if not on the jaw, then on the forearms and biceps. By the tenth round, poor Uzcudun couldn't keep his arms up.

"See, Max," Jacobs said. "Like taking the shell off the crab. Get past that shell and ..."

"Joe," Schmeling said. His English was like mine. Polite, guarded, careful. I heard that kind of English again in the newscasts, where Hauptmann pleaded for his life, before they electrocuted him in Trenton. His English wasn't good enough. "I remember that fight fine, Joe," Max said. "I was there. That's me."

"Okay, Max. Good that you remember. Because now comes the main attraction. Which you remember also. Only not so fondly."

The next film was Sharkey versus Schmeling. I knew Max had won the title on a foul but I had no idea how ugly and disappointing the whole fight had been. The famous low blow came near the end of the fourth round. Max had just caught Sharkey with a nice right and Sharkey came back with a punch that was low, no doubt about it. Max collapsed on the floor, the referee called time, Joe Jacobs jumped into the ring, other people followed and they asked Max to continue, which he said he couldn't. All this, with eighty thousand customers trying to figure out what the hell went on, which wasn't finally decided until they declared Schmeling the champion a week later.

We watched the foul again and I watched Max watch the foul. Some people didn't see it … but it was there alright. The next question was harder. How much did it hurt? Only Max could answer that. Was he acting? Another heavy-weight, the Englishman "Phainting Phil Scott," had made a medium-successful career out of getting fouled. Is that was Max was doing? And what made the question harder was that, up to the fourth round, he was losing the fight. He wasn't going down, he wasn't hurt, but it was slipping away. When he wanted to, Jack Sharkey could fight and when he didn't feel like fighting, he could box. That's what Joe Jacobs was trying to say.

"Max, you dance with him, you lose. You follow him around the ring, you lose. *Kein tanzen*, this time."

Max listened, waved away the worry. But Jacobs wasn't done yet.

"Max, listen, you're an *Auslander* here, *Verstehs*? An outsider. Take it from a Jew. *Amerikaner ist du nicht*. They gave you the title on a foul. That surprised me. But listen, Max. I say this in front of your *freunds* from the old country. Every champion, every—every white champion—gets a few rounds. That's the tradition. A tip of the hat to the man who owns the title. *Verstehs?*"

Max nodded yes. Everyone knew that, for a challenger to win the title, he had to take it decisively.

"Well, Max, you don't get that edge. It's better you think about it the other way. Sharkey starts the night three rounds ahead."

Max nodded again.

The next morning, Max and Heinz and three sparring

partners went out for roadwork. I watched them leave, standing next to Mr. Jacobs. I couldn't have put it in English yet, but I was moved by the sight of them running down the hill, turning right on River Road, disappearing in the direction of the little town of New Providence. And I know why. We were innocent, all of us, in my time of oranges. That goes for me, for Heinz, for Max most of all. We had a lot left to learn and some of it wasn't so good. So excuse me if I look back at that training camp, that bunch of shacks and bunkhouses and the sound of German voices after visitors cleared out, the gathering darkness of a spring night in New Jersey, the sight of a champion on a child's swing—a decent man with no idea what history was cooking up for him—and I choke up a little. To this day. Anyway, it was touching. It was touching, seeing them run, as though each step would make them stronger, as if preparation were everything, even though I knew Jack Sharkey was running too, even though Joe Jacobs had delivered a warning that scared me the night before, whether or not it scared Max.

"Max is always in shape," Joe Jacobs said. There was no one else nearby. That meant he was talking to me. "Not like some guys I've had, come into the camp thirty pounds over and a ring of hickeys around their neck. You know what is a hickey, Hansel?" He took one look and knew I didn't. "Christ. A love *küss*. From a *fraulein*. To say thank you for a nice time."

"I see."

"Come on, Hansel, we'll get some breakfast." Why so nice to me, I wondered, because he wasn't necessarily a nice man. He'd maneuvered Schmeling's original manager, Arthur Bulow, out of a contract. He was a terror at the boxing commission and negotiating with promoters. Still, he couldn't stand to be alone. He'd rather have an argument than take a nap.

Food from the city, bagels and farmer's cheese he shared with me, guaranteeing that I'd remember him the rest of my life when I saw that food again. He ate fast, like someone might take it away from him. He never faced a meal that lasted more than two rounds. But after he drank his first cup of coffee—boiling hot—he relaxed.

"You know how Max got started?" he asked. "You remember Jack Dempsey?"

"Everybody remembers Dempsey," I said.

"Hell of a fighter. When he fought. Which wasn't much, once he had the championship. You could look it up. Years went by, he fought stiffs, he fought exhibitions. It was enough letting people see him. So, 1925, Dempsey comes to Deutschland. Max is fighting middleweight. Doing okay, but it's still Germany, you know what I mean? Maybe you don't. So listen. You brew good beer. You make music. You make war. Cuckoo clocks. What else? Chocolate? That's Switzerland. Well, Hansel, I hate to be the one to tell you this, but Max could've been the middleweight champ for years and nobody would care. Local hero, that's all. Well, Dempsey sees him. They go a few rounds, nothing serious, but Dempsey likes what he sees. Not just in the ring. In the mirror. He sees his younger self. He mentions it in the papers. He comes home, he mentions it to me. So when Max comes to America I went after him. A little bit of this, a little bit of that and I'm his manager."

Just then, the runners came back, heading into the showers. Half an hour later, Joe Jacobs was driving me back to New York City. He had to see the Boxing Commission. He wasn't happy with the officials, especially the referee, a former heavyweight, Ed "Gunboat" Smith. He suspected Smith wanted to see the title back in America. He talked all the way to the Holland Tunnel, and then he drove me all the way back to 125th Street, pulling up in front of Otto Hofer's building.

"You live here, Hansel?" He was impressed. "High society."

"*Ja*," I said. "In the downstairs. I also work here."

"At what?"

"Apprentice janitor."

He laughed, slapped me on the back, wished me luck and pulled away. I'd enjoyed my time with him. An hour from now he'd have another audience. If I met him again—even tomorrow—he'd have forgotten all about me. So I thought. But I was wrong.

The afternoon of the fight we met at the Restaurant Germania. Heinz wasn't there: he was with Schmeling, coming in from Summit. The men I joined to go to Schmeling-Sharkey were mostly Heinz's friends, some greenhorns, some a few years off the boat, out to cheer our *landsmann.* Who all was in the bunch? Heinie Strasser was there and Otto Jacobus and Lorenz Schroeder and some others, I forget their names, mostly all died or moved to Florida by now. We were working men, not your sporting types, but a heavyweight title fight—an international title fight at that—was something special back then, the way the World Series used to be special, and a presidential election.

I remember it all, like it was yesterday. Better than yesterday. More to remember. The fight was out in Long Island City. We arrived hours early to beat the crowd, but the crowd was there, sixty thousand plus, sweeping in past cops and vendors, everybody talking fight, so that you could feel it in your chest, in your calves, in the palms of your hands. Tremendous excitement. You knew that something was going to happen. But you didn't know what. So two things came together—certainty and mystery. Usually, they don't mix. One cancels out the other. But this—oh my God—it made me shiver. Then came the moment when they turned down the lights and a spotlight reached across the audience to a far corner where the fighter came out, stepping into the spotlight, which guided him into the ring, Sharkey first, then Schmeling, dark robes, dark trunks. No nonsense. I studied Schmeling when he came into the ring. Tall, muscular, heavily bearded, swarthy, Max had the 1930's barbershop handsomeness of a Gable or a Dempsey or a Hemingway. Or—for what it was worth—a Heinz Greifinger. Sharkey looked like a rum runner, shifty and mean and sneaky smart. I didn't hate him. I just never liked him, a Lithuanian or someone who took an Irish name. I didn't hold with name-changing, then or now.

Next came an odd moment. At the time, I thought nothing of it. Later, when it seemed important, I wished I'd studied it more closely—but I was excited—the fight was so close—and it was only the national anthems. Two of them. First, "*Deutschland Über Alles.*" There were scattered boos. We stood, all of us, though the people around us stayed in their seats and elbowed each other as if to say, get a load of this. We sang, some of us, and the rest moved their lips. It sounded good, a rousing national anthem, say what you will, and it made me feel good, just then, to think of all the people back in Germany. Then came "The Star Spangled Banner." We stayed on our feet and some of us sang the words to that one, too. It tickled us to be part of both places. That's all. Maybe we should have felt silly or awkward or disloyal. You couldn't have two national anthems, any more than you could root for Schmeling and for Sharkey. I guess we didn't think about it. It wasn't a war. It was a fight. And now the fight was starting.

Bum or not, Jack Sharkey was smart, you could see right off, a jabbing, jumpy, dodging kind of fighter who made our Max miss badly during the first couple rounds. "Plodding" and "methodical"—those were the words that always came up when they wrote about Max Schmeling. What they meant, of course, was: GERMAN. Long on effort, low on imagination, disciplined and dull. The world always thought of us that way and for a while I thought this night was going to confirm it—goose step losing out to Irish jig. It was what I'd seen at the training camp, when Paulie Costello made Max look clumsy. Only this wasn't just sparring. This was in front of 60,000 people.

The men I came with made it worse. "That was close," one would say after Max missed a right. "Any minute now," another added hopefully. "It's coming soon." But not yet. One bad round led to another. "Those jabs don't count," they said. But they were landing, those Sharkey jabs, and I was sitting with a bunch of *landsmänner* who made me feel like a greenhorn all over again. By the fourth, though, Max Schmeling started to beat Jack Sharkey. He pressed forward, took charge, started landing. One of his rights spun Sharkey half way around, and it was all proof of what we all believed in, hard work and being on time and that stuff. We looked at each other, us greenhorns, as if to say, *now we'll see what's what*. Or, as Lorenz Schroeder put it, "*Jetzt gibts wurst*," now the meat comes on the table. Our sense of justice was restored. Max was winning, and that was right, not because he was German, oh certainly not that, but because he was solid and deep where Sharkey was flimsy and shallow. Schmeling came to fight, Sharkey came to avoid fighting. What was happening—though it wasn't the most exciting thing to watch—was correct. That was what it was, that was all it was, and please, being German had nothing to do with it, and if the situation were reversed ... and so forth. So we thought. But then, Sharkey came back at Schmeling. Sharkey recovered in the middle rounds and—if you could call back-pedaling fighting—he fought well, his kind of fight, give credit where credit is due. He was talented—"a regular fancy Dan"—someone said, a German using the phrase for the first time, sounding like Germans do in war movies, when they try to sound like Americans. Sharkey's surge lasted for a round or two. Not longer. After the eighth round it was all Schmeling. Nothing spectacular, not Dempsey and Tunney. But it was solid, steady and—no getting away from it—German. Late in the fight, the sting drained out of Sharkey's punches, his face puffed up and, a time or two, Schmeling had him wobbling. But that was where another German thing came into play: caution. He never risked that last shot which would have landed Sharkey on the canvas. Oh, how we talked about it later, Sharkey just hanging there, so ready to go! One good Schmeling right would have ended all the arguments! Why, oh why, did he not throw that punch? Was it something German? Something good or bad? Was it charity towards a beaten opponent? Or an unwillingness to depart from a plan that was working? Later that night, Lorenz Schroeder summed things up nicely. Last year, I had a card from him in Sebring, Florida. "The way he fought," Lorenz said, "it was as if he thought people would be disappointed if he did not give them fifteen rounds."

Still, when it ended we were feeling fine. I looked around at my pals and we nodded approval. You only had to look at the ring where Sharkey was draped over the ring ropes, like a passenger being seasick over the railing of a ship, he was the picture of a beaten fighter. No, no doubt about it. We felt the way we felt when we got up from the table after one of those hot, heavy German meals, roast pork, dumplings and gravy. No strange fixings, no fancy sauces, just solid stick-between-the-ribs cooking. Or boxing. A victory, no doubt about it. Our kind. Later, they said two thirds of the reporters at ringside gave it to Schmeling. The Times reporter, Dawson, gave it to Schmeling nine rounds to five, one even. Mayor Walker gave it to Schmeling. The crowd gave it to Schmeling.

The judges gave it to Sharkey.

Split decision. The worst in history. Don't take my word for it. You could look it up. The last I saw, among all the booing, the nose holding, the throwing of stuff into the ring, was old Max walking across the ring, rushing to shake Jack Sharkey's hand, even though he'd just been robbed. We all were robbed. A so-so fight is bad enough. A wrong decision is worse. The taste in your mouth won't go away, every time you swallow, you gag all over again. We stayed in our seats after the fighters had gone back to the dressing rooms. I pictured Schmeling as I'd seen him on that swing, up and down, back and forth, as darkness came.

On the ride home that night, Lorenz Schroeder went on about appeals to authorities, protests, setting things right, honesty and fair play, the way Germans go on when the world puts one over on them. Heinie Strasser, too. A rematch was a foregone conclusion, the public would demand it. And Otto Jacobus saying, over and over again, there must have been an error somewhere, as though our Max got robbed by mistake. Inventing excuses for thieves. I doubt I kept my mouth shut, but all I remember is looking out the window of the car as we moved through Queens, as we passed all the apartment houses and cemeteries, the factories along the East River. A strange country, America. It disappointed me that night. It was a disappointment I was determined to put behind me. You couldn't stake everything on a fight, I told myself. That's what gamblers did and I wasn't a gambler.

We were on the park bench by the lake, sometime the next week, Cleveland and Billy and I. It was the first hot day. We hadn't discussed "Smelling." Another bum decision. Add it to the list. My list was new and short. Theirs went back forever. Already, Max had returned to Germany, confident about a rematch. For me, it was as if a fever were passing. I closed my eyes and felt the sun on my face and wondered if I could make a trip to New Jersey sometime. Maybe look in on Madame Bey. Then I sensed someone standing in front of me, blocking the sun. I opened my eyes and my brother was there.

"Boys," he said to Cleve and Billy. "I'd like to speak to my brother." Then came what sounded like an insult. "About business."

Cleve and Billy looked at each other and laughed. They got up, but they took their time about it, stretching and yawning.

"Well, Billy," said Cleve, "I guess that's alright with us, isn't it. The man wants to speak to his brother ..."

"Yessir. About business"

"It's better than alright. These business talks cost money." They walked slowly away and I wished that I were walking with them.

"You shouldn't ..."

"Alright," Heinz said. "I'm sorry. Can we talk?"

"I can listen," I said, making room on the bench. He'd been out all night, it looked like. He hadn't shaved and his clothes were wrinkled. There was beer in his sweat: you could smell it, on a hot day like this.

"No song and dance for you," he said. "You saw what happened. They robbed him."

I nodded. That was undeniable.

"But all they took from Max was his title. For the fight, he was paid. In full. For me, it was different. They reached right in my pocket. So ..."

He smiled at me. He shrugged. We were still brothers. We both knew what was coming. And that, turned it around, Heinz would give me everything he had. We also knew that such a turn-around would never happen because he was who he was and I was different.

"How much?" I asked.

"How much do you have?" he asked. Fifty dollars, I said. That was everything. I walked with him towards Otto's building. He waited across the street, in the park, while I got the money. He nodded, gave me a longer look than usual. No thanks, no promise to repay, nothing like that. Then I watched him walk away. And so, from across 110th, did Otto Hofer. He was, as I have already told, a stern man. He went out of his way to counter the immigrant notion that America was a wonderland, the streets were paved with gold, everyone got rich. He rarely spoke to me, only watched me work. But now he signaled for me to stay a while.

"How much?" he asked.

"Everything. Fifty."

"Fifty." He was impressed. "You save. But now it's gone." He puffed his cigar. He always wore a suit out of doors, always with a vest. He had that old world dignity. "Now you start all over again. Are you sorry, what you just did?"

"No," I said after thinking about it. I was sorry what had happened. I missed my money. But I wasn't sorry about giving it to Heinz. And I was a little proud that I said as much to Otto, who maybe expected a different answer.

"And," he continued, "if he came to you again, your brother, after the next Max Schmeling fight and if he asked for money again, would you give again?"

I glanced into the park where my brother had gone. I thumbed through my collection of moments in America. Heinz and Otto at the pier. Schmeling on the swing in New Jersey. Two national anthems.

"Well?" he pressed. Not like a lawyer presses, more like someone who was offering you another drink.

"No," I answered. And that was that. He patted my shoulder and padded up the street to buy his afternoon paper, the *Journal-American*.

Now it's fifty years later and I'm in Berkeley Heights, New Jersey, sitting out after supper-for-one, liver and onions I cooked myself, watching cars full of Little Leaguers go up the street, an hour to go before Wheel of Fortune comes on and what I'm realizing is that June night in 1932 was a milestone for me. I think about that night. Even though I was there, it's like a newsreel I'm watching, black and white, historical, the men with cigars and hats, the women with lipstick and furs and stockings with a seam up the back. Everybody looks like actors in a movie. I mull over what became of them all in the time between now and then. Just consider the mayors sitting down at ringside. And Bruno Richard Hauptmann—he was there that night, a carpenter in the cheap seats—as we later learned. Mayor Walker wound up an exiled playboy, Mayor Hague went to prison, Mayor Cermak got shot in Miami while he was with Roosevelt, and some say he took a bullet meant for Roosevelt, others say, hell no, it was meant for Cermak. That poor Hauptmann got framed and fried for the Lindbergh kidnapping; lucky for Max Schmeling he wasn't in the neighborhood that night or they'd have nailed him too. *A strange country, America.* It keeps coming back to me. Getting stranger all the time and me a stranger in it. Watching tv almost any night has become an act of treason because, in my heart, I was rooting for the Vietnamese, the outsiders, the underdogs, the way I pulled for Max Schmeling. I rooted for those Cubans who got steamrollered on Grenada. And during the Olympics ... well, that's the worst of all. Here you had the whole world coming to Los Angeles, coming to our country, and night after night, whether it's javelin throwing or wrestling, gymnastics or whatever, the camera pans row after row of those blonde cocky people, finger in the air, booing foreigners far from home, booing officials, chanting "We're number one, we're number one," and "USA! USA!" And don't take my word for it, watch the films, read the books, and I swear you'll find the crowd at the 1936 Olympics, the Hitler Olympics in Berlin, had better manners than those golden-haired super-fans in sunny California.

This used to be a neighborhood, out here. I don't want to make too much of that—we didn't loan money and we didn't swap bed partners—but each morning the women had coffee together and sometimes in the winter, when the snow plows didn't come, we shoveled the streets ourselves. Summer nights we sat out and listened to the Dodgers on the radio and when the first television came—a ten-inch Dumont with a magnifying glass that stood in front—we all watched Uncle Miltie. Not a commune, not a kibbutz. A neighborhood. I'm the last one left. My new neighbors, I hardly know; that's close enough. People who say we've got to teach the Japs a lesson one more time and me, I ask what the lesson would be and they can't tell me. People who say they can't believe all the brave men who died in Vietnam and me, I ask them which brave men they mean, the Americans or those others. They can't believe men die for nothing. I tell them it happens all the time. Take it from a German.

Well, nobody beats the clock. But we try. We try to leave something of ourselves behind. A tree, a garden, a house with memories, a bird feeding station. Or you have a son. Mom and I believed in him, the way parents do, the way poor people do, the way immigrants do. Add it up, it's a triple whammy, a whole lot of believing. Our golden boy, our college material, our first generation German-American scholarship winner. It wasn't just Mom and me. We all believed it, the whole bunch of us. Our kids were our religion, our nod in the general direction of eternity. Maybe there's no way they could have lived up to all the hopes we had for them. There were some hits and misses, that's for sure. Heini Strasser's daughter ended up a research scientist at Rockefeller, working on cancer. Lorenz Schroeder's Teddy who they spent thousands of dollars on, sending him from school to school, lives in a trailer in Maine and when they went to visit, he weighed three hundred pounds and they didn't stay for supper, the place wasn't clean. Hits and misses, breathers and breeders, in-betweeners. Disappointments, kind of. You pick up things, reading in between the lines of Christmas letters. "Our Pete is still with Maytag. He got married again. This one seems like a nice girl." Sometimes, they're bragging and brave for the record, their kid owns a boat, real busy, travels around a lot on business. And never calls. Sometimes the prides-

and-joys visit once a year, maybe, and the failures show up every weekend messing around in the refrigerator. So what's the moral of the story? You tell me. I have a son. I come back to him, again and again, to the fellow who calls himself George Griffin. The well-known travel writer.

PART TWO

I. Faraway Places, Backyard Adventures

by George Griffin

It's odd, how countries begin. In a boat on the Mekong, wide and turbid, right at the tip of the legendary Golden Triangle, I see the first and last of three countries. Behind me, in Thailand, sun glints off gold-leafed pagodas. Hawkers' stalls line the river's edge, smoke from cooking fires drifts upward into lazy, spice-laden air. Upstream, forbidden Burma begins in a field of reeds and cat-tails, beyond which stands a wall of mountains, green-gray and formidable, reserving judgment on a world that wants to visit. Much nearer—I could wade ashore in a minute—Laos is a bunch of kids sliding down a red-clay riverbank, splashing towards us, waving cheerfully, then pulling away at the last minute. Off to one side a woman, topless, a sarong wrapped around her middle, washes slowly in muddy water. Across closed borders, our eyes meet …

Bangkok, 1984. Welcome to my world. Bangkok as seen from a penthouse suite, high, roomy and free, Bangkok at dusk, with the neon twinkle kindling down below, the nightly magic that turned one of the world's ugliest sprawls into a festering wonderland of food and sex. There I sat roughing out my column, just in from a day in the field, turning life into art. Or trying to.

I liked the opening riff—"it's odd, how countries begin" —but after that it was not more than competent: sun glinting on Buddhist temples. Your first temple was spectacular, the first one stopped your heart: the gold leaf, the inlaid porcelain, saffron-robed monks—always outnumbered by tourists— and then the big man himself, seated, reclining, reposing. After that, they were franchises. So, for that matter, was the Golden Triangle, complete with a golden arch, not unlike McDonald's so many million served. Narco-tourists posed for pictures with a quartet of mountain tribe kids, aboriginally attired, embroidered and beaded. "Take picture, ten baht, okay, take picture, ten baht, okay" they pleaded. Then there was the "turbid" Mekong: a word right out of Somerset Maugham. Whenever a Maugham character sat on a colonial porch, reading a months-old newspaper underneath a fan, a dusky mistress out back, a neurotic wife due on the next boat, he'd glance out at an invariably turbid river: thick, opaque, filled with sediment. The river hadn't changed. The reading public had. Delete turbid. That business with the topless woman wouldn't last either. It would take too long to explain that she wasn't welcoming, she wasn't voluptuous, she wasn't interested. But in a world of ready welcome, I welcomed indifference. I liked people who didn't smile at strangers, countries that had nothing to sell. There weren't many left. Close shop for a while, throw around that magic word *forbidden* and watch the lines form.

A bus trip to the infamous Golden Triangle, three countries in view at once, then, a boat ride on the fabled Mekong, after that, a visit to five, count 'em, five primitive hill tribes: believe it or not, I had been virtuous that day, gathering ingredients, cooking my column from scratch. Sometimes I decided to lose myself in the tourist crowd, slip in among those slow-moving gaggles who wore name tags, rallied around flags, laughed at guides' jokes, and obediently went shopping, wherever they were told. One temple, one shop, that was the pattern, one stop for culture, one for souvenirs. And I sat in a van, watching a tour guide earn his pay, chasing a family of Indians who disappeared down a knick-knack alley, hustling after a Singaporean who knelt down to look at a pile of gems, some Germans posing with mountain kids, a couple of Aussies drawn toward a Carlsberg sign. The money pouches the tourists wore in front, dangling below their navels, looked like jockstraps, stuffed with bills. Back on the road, a little later, the van couldn't handle hills and air-conditioning at the same time. Cold air leaked an inch out of overhead nozzles, then retreated. Passengers grew torpid and indifferent. If someone had the nerve to suggest it, we'd have voted to bag the hill tribes. Half of us were sleeping, missing a whole range of mountains, jagged, unclimbable slopes. In Thailand, most mountains had long since been stripped; bamboo grew where hardwoods once stood. Replanted trees grew in straight lines, staying where they'd been put, like hair transplants I remembered on Senator Proxmire. Here and there, you could see traces of the original forest, though, a glorious tangle, trees like ship masts, trailing vines, leaves and flowers all around, but only on unprofitable slopes, in hard to get at places, like hairs around a wart, too risky to shave. Twenty minutes ago, the guide had informed us that they grew two crops of rice per year around here. Any questions. No? Then he zoned out. I studied our human cargo: heads tilted back, eyes closed, mouths open, no pretense of interest in the land we passed through. Tourists. After fifteen years, I still wondered what to make of them. Early on, I'd been excited that they were there for me, that I had an audience which my agent put in "the low millions." Sometimes he stressed the *millions*, sometimes he emphasized the *low*. It was the real estate business writ large. What realtors in yellow jackets said about houses, I said about vacations: a good starter trip, needs TLC, dates from colonial times, river frontage, don't curb appraise, won't last long. After that, after friendship, after cynicism, there was something else, a *Miss Lonelyhearts* kind of feeling, compassion for people who went so tamely, so gamely into a world that greeted them with uniform cynicism. Now, when the driver honked at a three wheeler crossing in front of us, I saw tourist eyes fight open, then close. After lunch they were finished, photographers without cameras, cameras out of film. Only so many pictures in a roll, only so much insight in a day.

The van turned off the highway. The guide revived, the needle fell back in groove. We learned that with government encouragement and international aid, hill tribes had been induced to abandon their border-crossing poppy-growing ways and move to permanent settlements, in reach of schools, clinics and tourists. I guessed what was coming and it wasn't going to be pretty. Aborigineland. We came to the end of the road and what looked like a yard sale on the edge of a pit mine: baked brown dirt, dusty leaves, rickety huts. Sunken-chested, cataract-clouded old men shuffled between stalls. Old women, all knees and cheekbones, waved us on, as if towards communion: this is my culture, broken for you. Babies crawled along in the dust trafficking with dogs bound for the cook pots, dogs so red-skinned, pocked and mangy that they looked half-cooked already. My companions gamely exited and wandered up the road, 200 lb. men and 180 lb. women, picking over hats and belts and shawls and quilts, hard-bargaining a tribe of starving locals while the Chinese guide pattered about "these people." And I leaned against the window, struck by the dead-end sadness of it all. I guess what got me was the idea that anyone who was watching me watch the tourists would include me in the scene, as much a part of it as the tour guide and the driver. The travel writer. There he sits, like a playwright, watching his work being performed. George Griffin, proprietor of *Faraway Places, Backyard Adventures*. The whole world's his stage, you'd better believe it.

Returning to Bangkok, I confined myself to the Dusit Thani, with television and room service, early swims, late breakfasts and no apologies to anybody. I worked on my column, getting the tone right, turning jadedness into savvy, familiarity into geniality and despair—stark shuddering despair—into enlightenment. What I accomplished, I thought, was an account of a world-worth-visiting. If that took perjury, it was alright with me. Lying, when you came right down to it, was a heroic act: you faced up to the difference between what was and wasn't. You met the world as it was, on its own terms, and then you did the best you could. But now, after a Thai meal, an Irish coffee, a Cuban cigar, life was fine. Once more I resembled the man whose photograph perched atop my column, shrewd but approachable, good company. Hey, you from Jersey? I'm from Jersey too! And it was in Bangkok, right there, right then that Jersey found me. The envelope marked "CONFIDENTIAL," it came from my agent, a pile of recent columns and a second envelope with handwriting I knew. A crucial moment. Looking back I picture myself as an oncologist, holding a chest x-ray against a wall of neon lights, frowning at some shadowy inoperable mass. A letter from my father. From a return address I once called home. That would be New Jersey.

Well, I said to myself, he's still alive. So it can't be that kind of bad news. Or maybe it was. It might be a letter he'd written a while ago, when he sensed the end coming, leaving instructions and—no doubt—postage on the table beside his deathbed. That was his kind of stunt. He'd die, knowing he had the last word. I was nervous when I opened the envelope. DON'T WORRY ABOUT ANSWERING THIS ONE, SON. YOU'RE OFF THE HOOK. I'M DEAD. SO LONG.

It was a printed notice. Dear Classmate, it began, but someone had crossed out the classmate and scribbled in: George! My high school class—1964—was organizing its twentieth reunion, scheduled for three months ahead, in November. I scanned the names of the reunion committee. Dan Cerruti, Sandy Parks Cowan, Emil Russo, Warren Flieger, Vivian Amadeo Torres. We'd gone to a big regional high school, four hundred seniors from five New Jersey towns that ranged from upper-class suburban estates parked along the ridges of the Watchung Mountains to aging factory-refinery towns in the flatlands outside of Newark and Perth Amboy. Kitty Scarpato Jackson, Leslie Levin Baum. The girls had all dusted off their maiden names, as if pleading to be pictured as they used to be, before they met the guy they'd be standing next to. Beckoning from out of the past; hey, remember me? And that, it turned out, was the gist of my father's message as well.

> George—
> I'm okay. These high school people called to find out where you were. I told them I only know what I read in the papers—and I don't believe much of that—but I would try to get this to you. George, it's none of my business but I think it's nice that your old friends remember you. Come on out, why don't you? You can stay with me. Also, George, there's some things we need to talk about that can't wait much longer. Call

me back when you get back from doing whatever it is you are doing wherever it is you do it. Come visit me *and* see about the reunion. That way, you can kill one bird with two stones.

Your Pop

Rereading the old man's note, I pictured him, sitting at the table in the kitchen nook, putting pencil to paper. It felt like a childhood memory, even though his note was only two weeks old. You come to a time—like an airplane's point of no return—when your parents, even if alive and well, become figures out of the past. They aren't part of your life anymore, your today and your tomorrow. It was unlikely that we had anything new to say to each other. "Things we need to talk about that can't wait much longer." It was probably what did I want him to do with my sash of Boy Scout merit badges, my stamp collection, that pile of 45 rpm records with my name written on the labels.

That night, I walked along Patpong Road, the nightclub strip that everyone in Bangkok finds, sooner or later. No place for a son to be thinking of his father, but I did. In a way, I was shopping for him. The road was closed to traffic at night and stalls filled the thorough-fare, pens, copy watches, lighters, scarves, shirts, socks, silk, compact discs, videos, belts and purses. Thai shills worked the sidewalk, shoving little books in front of tourists, laminated pages that were menus for sex shows that visitors could pay to watch or join. Everybody could star in his—or her—porn movie. "I always wanted to direct." On either side, the nightclubs were getting busy. They made a stunning first impression, no doubt about it, a beery epiphany, beloved of Australians. You could sit on a bar stool, hug a Carlsberg and watch the street parade, into the wee hours. Or you could ponder what was on display inside. The music was as loud as you liked it, the lights changed color, as if moving to the music, slow, fast, hot and cold, hard and soft. The way those rich pink and green and orange lollipop lights covered those bikinis, those legs, that long black hair, those bored high-cheeked boned faces, oh God, how could a situation be so tragic *and* so tantalizing. Even now, in the plague years, those bars could take your breath away. Even now? Make that, especially now. The bars caught you in the way the deep green of a baseball field transfixes you before a different kind of night game.

Out on Silom Road I found what I was looking for, on a rack of postcards, sunrise at Wat Arun, the Royal Palace, the floating markets, and Thai boxers. The boxers were for Pop. He'd always liked boxing, Friday nights, all through my childhood, he'd watched the television fights, Jimmy Powers and the Gillette Cavalcade of Sports. I could still sing the commercial, "to look sharp and be on the ball." After that, "Greatest Fights of the Century." Newsreel footage of the great ones, La Motta and Robinson, Ross and Armstrong, Zale and Graziano, Louis and Schmeling. I doubted he'd ever seen a live boxing match, but he always watched the fights. Back at the Dusit Thani, I filled the postcard out.

> Dear Pop:
>
> Hello from Thailand. I got your message. I'll be home soon.
>
> Love, George

There, I thought, short and sweet. That should hold him. I'd visit him in Jersey and, when I needed to get away from him, I'd check on the reunion. That appealed. Killing one bird with two stones, the old man said. He sometimes got things backwards. And sometimes he got them exactly right.

II.

"HELLO?" NEW YORK CITY, 1 A.M. JET LAGGED, just in from Bangkok, I'd been lying in bed, improbably restless, waiting to catch a wave of sleep that wouldn't come.

"You took your time about it, sonny boy. Hoping I'd hang up?"

"Pop?"

"It's me alright."

The old man had always hated phones. I could call him with any news, a marriage announcement, a diagnosis of leukemia—his or mine—and he'd say "yup" or "nope" and then: "Put it in a letter son." And then, always: "a letter is as good as a visit."

Maybe better.

"Are you alright, Pop?"

"I'm still here."

The last time he called, three years before, was to report my mother's death. He called collect, claiming he was in a hospital booth with not enough change. "Well, she's gone," he'd said, as if a plane had just taken off on time.

An old-timer who called a stereo a "hi-fi," a refrigerator an "icebox," and himself "the last of the Mohicans," he was, in many ways, quite a guy. But when we met, he always seemed to get away from me. I was in a business that required a certain amount of interviewing. Granted, most of my subjects were soft targets. Getting a food-and-beverage guy to define what on earth was meant by "Pacific Rim Cuisine" wasn't exactly like nailing Robert Vesco. Still, the old man escaped me, especially since Mom's death. I used to wonder what it would take to reach him. Subpoena power and a syringe of sodium pentothal?

"What's up?" I asked.

"I've been thinking."

"And so you called me? At one in the morning?"

"I wanted to make sure the rates were down."

"From Jersey?"

"Did you get my note?" he asked.

"Yes. And I sent you a postcard back."

"It hasn't arrived. Did you put a stamp?"

"Yes."

"Well, thanks in advance." Now, a silence on the line, which always signaled a change in tone.

"I want you to come home. Can you come home tomorrow?"

"Pop!" I protested. "I just got back from Thailand. I haven't unpacked yet." Another silence. "I've got to earn a living, you know." More silence. *I know how you earn a living*, it said. *No one needs you tomorrow. You're not a doctor. Or a baker. You don't drive a school bus.*

"The day after tomorrow," I said. "Promise."

"Okay. I can probably make it that long."

People from New Jersey can't kid themselves: It occurred to me, two days later, while the bus boomed through Secaucus along the Turnpike. On one side there were refineries, warehouses, factories, mostly old and abandoned, railroad sidings, the poisoned Passaic River ("Piss-ache," we used to say). There were garbage mountains, chemical holding ponds, salt marshes and drive-in movies that stretched all the way to Port Elizabeth, where behemoth freighters deposited Japanese cars by the thousands, like a parody of some World War II island beachhead, except here the defense was shot and the natives were lining up to surrender. *People from New Jersey can't kid themselves.* Radio transmitters that had toppled into salt marshes, piles of used tires, stacks of crunched up auto chassis, walls of hubcaps and Welcome to Newark, "next to the biggest city on earth." A new football stadium in the Meadowlands and a new prison near Newark Airport, and whenever I passed by here, I couldn't help looking for what wasn't there anymore, the landmark and logo of my childhood, the three-ring Ballantine Ale sign hovering over the brewery where my father worked for forty years. *People from New Jersey can't kid themselves.* Onward and upward, build we must, you can't stop progress. Now, Route 22 through Hillside, Union, Springfield, one of America's great junk highways. The un-zoned land of anything goes: Greek diners, discount shoe stores, Channel Lumber, carpet remnants, u-paint-it furniture, Cohen Fashion Optical. Then, in Mountainside, things opened up. You got archery ranges, landscapers' nurseries, miniature golf courses. You got to look into people's backyards, at above-ground swimming pools, aluminum utility sheds. You got garden apartments and nursing homes and it scared me, knowing that you could live and die here. You could never leave.

The ritual of homecoming hadn't changed since I'd come back from college. The old man parked in the same corner of the Snuffy's Restaurant parking lot, in the aging green Plymouth which, he insisted, would "last me out." I pictured him on the last day of his life, trembling and gasping for air, driving a belching, lurching car with bald tires, smoking muffler and an eighth of a tank of gas to the entrance of a hospital emergency room where they'd expire—"conk out," was his quaint way of putting it—simultaneously.

I took my time crossing the lot. It was important to take him in now, before we opened our mouths and things fell apart. We'd had a hard time with each other, since Mom died. She'd been gentle and loving and smart. More important, she was patient. She'd believed in me. Everything I'd written, she clipped and saved, even the mediocre stuff was forward motion. She'd died just when my first book came out: *NO WRONG TURNS*, all about family travel possibilities within a dozen miles of interstate highways. She'd had time to see the book, but not read it. Perfect timing, the old man said.

There he stood, a sturdy bandy-legged guy, six inches shorter than I was. If it hadn't been for food rationing during World War I, he'd say, he'd stand six feet. He had a broad chest, muscular arms, callused hands and gnarled fingers. He combed his hair straight back, more white than black now, but plenty of it. His face was a German face, his nose the most prominent feature, not hooked or broad or broken or pugged, not aquiline or Roman or any of those words, just big and there. If everything else was working class—look for the union label—his eyes were different. Those eyes made me feel like a target, coming into range.

"Hi, Pop," I said. It was awkward, putting my arms around and drawing him in.

"Sonny boy," he answered. Into the car. Close quarters.

"You see this?" he said as I tossed an overnight bag in the back seat. He pointed at the sports pages.

It was a sports-talk column and today most of the talk was about the Hall of Fame's continued denial of Yankee shortstop Phil Rizzuto's admission into the ranks of the immortals.

"A marginal candidate, Pop. There are better men out and worse men in."

"Well, I don't like it."

"It's the announcing that keeps him out," I suggested. In recent years as a Yankee announcer, Rizzuto had been shilling for enterprises of the sort that crowded Route 22: Italian restaurants, tire stores, household mortgage operations.

"A walking billboard," the old man agreed. "They announce the Rizzuto vote and every Italian restaurant owner in North Jersey goes into mourning."

"The Veteran's Committee will vote him in eventually," I offered.

"Not this veteran!" He laughed, he clapped me on the knee. "Boy, did we used to have fun hating the Yankees! More than we loved the Dodgers, we hated the Yankees. It felt like we were guerilla fighters out here in Jersey. Viet Cong!"

Now we were driving up into the first ridge of the Watchung Mountains, and I sensed I was inside that net of roads that extends outward from home, like light from a campfire, those roads whose bumps and turns are imprinted on us forever, from the time they bring you home from the hospital, maybe, through childhood rides, sleeping on laps, and on through your own first drives, coming home from dates, radio pumping heartbreak music: "I'm Mr. Blue," "It's Almost Tomorrow," "Since I Don't Have You." Roads that become part of you so you feel you could find your way along them in the dark forever, just as I knew you could walk, eyes closed, through every room of the house to which I was now returning.

"You look ... I don't know ... washed out ... washed up," he said.

"You don't look so bad, " I said, "considering ..." And so it began, our rough-and-ready. Human relations are way overrated. At least that's the way we'd been behaving. Father-son, husband-wife, brother-brother: the magic went out of them so quickly. They lasted no longer, really, than Santa or the Easter Bunny, but it took longer to shake them, to see how death and divorce and distance canceled life's big deals. Sometimes I wondered if maybe we shouldn't take a chance with each other, only which one of us was going first, who would take that chance, and what then? There were no gamblers in our family that I knew about.

"So what about death, sonny boy?" the old man asked. "Where's it rank? As a travel experience, I mean. Would you say it's a *Backyard Adventure?* Or is it a *Faraway Place?*

Old joke. My father knew how I shuffled my columns around, so that a piece on the Delaware Water Gap, say, would be a *Backyard Adventure* for New Jersey readers but a *Faraway Place* when it showed up in a California outlet.

"I know what you're going to say," the old man said. "It depends on where you die, right?"

"Sure. You die in Florida, it's a *Backyard Adventure*. Conk out in Colorado—*Faraway Place.*"

"And what about New Jersey? What about your old neighborhood? Suppose I die here? What do you say then?"

"I say ..." It came to me. *"He's gone to a better place."*

A mile away from home now. Almost every house we passed, I'd been inside, down in cellars, even, wrapping bundles of newspapers and magazines for Boy Scout paper drives. I'd shoveled snow off most of the driveways along here, I'd cut grass in the summer and I still knew where there were above-ground roots that could wreck a rotary blade. Berkeley Heights was the name of the place. Berkeley Heights, New Jersey. It wasn't a rural village, giving out onto cornfields and orchards, and it wasn't a city block with gossip and laundry and corner bars where you could watch generations roll. Berkeley Heights was a gathering of lawns and houses, streets and trees. Though there wasn't the least hint of autumn yet, the trees—oaks, tulips, beeches—were darkly, terminally green, a fullness that could go no further, and the lawns too, were past the madness of watering and mowing. They were full, fat and tired. So were the people we passed; their hot weather enthusiasm behind them, swimming pools and barbecues and yard sales, another year rolling by, a year that aged them while adding to the value of their houses, people going down with real estate going up.

"I read somewhere, twenty percent of this country moves every year," the old man remarked as he turned into the street we lived on. "Works out to a complete change every five years. A brand new America. What do you think of that?"

"It makes me wonder why you stayed."

"What am I going to do, George? Die? Move to Florida?"

So he stayed, re-reading the Hornblower novels, writing an occasional letter-to-the-editor, and putting out poisoned peanut butter for the grackles, starlings and other "junk birds." He'd been in the same house since before I was born, an old timer in a neighborhood where time didn't count.

"Well here we are, son," he said, "how's it feel?"

And as I listened to the familiar, unforgettable crunch of gravel in my father's driveway, I felt something inside, a shudder or a tremble of the heart.

III.

I KNOW THAT PARENTS AREN'T SUPPOSED TO fiddle with their kids' lives, beyond a certain point. Every job they take is a great opportunity, every move they make is a promotion, every transfer is to California. And everyone they marry, you're supposed to love. Or else. But this is my son we're talking about, our son, college material, our magic boy. And in these last years, it's gone sour. I can see it in his eyes, no matter how much money he makes.

His mother was George's fan club, and even she knew something was wrong. That book about Sunday drives for families. She hardly had the strength to hold it. She looked at the book, which is not the kind of book you read through, you just use it like the yellow pages. She studied his photo. I could tell she was disappointed. I took it from her and saw our son on the back cover, wearing a Hawaii shirt and his special I'm-having-fun-for-free look. She loved him a lot. It was frightening.

"It says here," I remarked, "that he's an intrepid author."

"Intrepid ..." She came back to life a little. She was always looking up words. "He takes chances. He gambles with his life ..." Suddenly she turned away, hiding tears, but her voice came to me for the other side of the pillow. "Things came too easy for him."

IV.

When I came downstairs from my room, I found Pop in the kitchen nook, looking at the morning newspaper, which I knew he'd finished while he was waiting for me at the bus stop. He held that newspaper the way I used to put a book in front of my face, when I wanted people to know that I had better things to do. Now he was up to my old tricks. I cleared my throat. We were behind schedule. Home twenty minutes and no argument yet.

"Well, Pop, what can I do for you?" I decided the sooner we got started, the better. "Is this about your will?"

"My gosh, no," he replied. "I'm still torn between the Boy Scouts of America and the Berkeley Heights Public Library. Don't you worry about my will, son. Around here, anyway, you'll never have to worry about another library fine. And if you want to go on any camping trips … just say the word. I don't guess it bothers you, but it still bothers me, you never made Eagle. How many more merit badges do you need, anyway?"

"Five, I think."

"That's not much."

"Pop, I'm too old! And they still require Physical Fitness merit badge. They want chin ups!"

"Oh," he said. "That's too bad."

"How are you feeling these days?"

"I haven't lost a step," he said. "Never better!" But then, just as I expected him to launch into more of the heavy kidding that passed for emotional life, he looked out the window, then back at me, and his face was grim. "Could we cut this out, just for a minute?" he asked, sounding angry. "This Katzenjammer act?"

You started it, I wanted to shout. "Sure," I said. And then, when he hesitated, I got really worried. "My God, what is it Pop?" I hadn't heard him speak this way before. I wasn't sure he had it in him. "Is there—something from the doctor?"

"Your trouble is, you think dying's the only problem, when you get to be my age. It's all just biopsies. You think that's why I wrote you in ..."

"Bangkok," I supplied.

"... that place? Dying? You wouldn't hear it from me. Not a peep. Millions of people on earth, not one has failed at dying yet."

"That's a prepared line, Pop."

He smiled. Me criticizing him for lack of originality! The adventurer who hired a car and driver to the top of an Indonesian volcano and headlined the resulting column "Bali High."

"Living ... that's my problem," he said. He got up and walked towards the kitchen. When he reached the doorway, he turned back to me. "I'm the oldest man in the neighborhood. I'm the pioneer. I shot at deer to keep them out of your mother's tulip bulbs, remember? I said hello to the Italians, the ones just off the boat, carrying flats of tomatoes on their heads while they walked down Plainfield Avenue. I remember when we used to get snowed in. I remember when there were ice storms, you could hear the frozen branches snapping, it sounded like an army was out there in the woods. Nobody knows this place like I do. So the question is—you don't have to answer it now. George, just think about it—how come I feel like a stranger?"

I heard him opening the refrigerator door, taking out some beers. I heard him try the radio that sat on top of what he called "the ice box." And I wondered what to tell him. Sooner or later, every child plays the game, guessing which of his parents will be the first to die. I had picked him. He was a rough and hectic worker who threw himself into every task, the Saturday garden, the Sunday walk. I knew how he worked, sweating and storming. I knew how he ate, wiping gravy off a plate while other people were still cutting meat. Whatever life had in store for him, he was bound to finish it first. My mother seemed longer-lived, a quiet and contemplative sort, dreams and pains deep inside her. An apple, a piece of Nestle's chocolate, and an article in the Reader's Digest—that was her nightly ritual. But cancer, that wild card of a disease, upset my forecast and stranded the old man. I almost wished he'd marry again. But I knew what his response would be; he'd used the line for years, patting my mother's hand after she burned a cake or misplayed a hand of pinochle: "That's alright, Mom. Germans are like pumas. We mate for life."

"Mom died," I said, "and you're left. But you're not the first. You have two people, they're both going to die, but chances are they won't die together. One of them is going to live on and ..."

"And what ... ?"

"Maybe make new friends. Get to know the new neighbors, I don't know. Stop sitting around the house feeling sorry for yourself."

"I'm not just feeling sorry for myself," the old man corrected me. "You got it backwards. I feel sorry for them too."

"Them?"

"What you call the new neighbors. Because the town I lived was a better place than what they've got now."

"Come on, Pop. You're not going to be another senior citizen cranking up a speech about the good old days."

"Good old days, bad old days," he shrugged. Then he got out of his chair and walked over to the kitchen window. "Will you look at it?" He pulled back the curtain and stood there, beer stein in hand, as though he were an artist offering a full-view of the just-completed canvas. He gestured for me to behold the world outside, out beyond his apple tree and lawn chairs, out beyond the picnic table where the old Germans came together for his famous beer parties, out beyond his chicken coop, empty now, and his vegetable garden where, beside bell peppers and tomatoes, he grew kale and Swiss chard and radishes that were the size of apples, out beyond the hemlocks that marked the edge of our property. Three generations of family dogs were buried there and that was where he'd scattered my mother's ashes too, a handful at a time, like 5-10-5 fertilizer.

I kept looking at that old picnic table. If any place attracted ghosts, this was it. They came to me now, all the old timers sitting there. The driveway full of cars from three states. New Jersey was a country drive back then. "The sticks," they called it. They showed up late in the morning and I was always out front, watching for company coming, at least until the years I didn't care; then I'd be upstairs reading and didn't appear until they asked for me. When I pictured them now, aunts and uncles and a scattering of cousins, I saw them at the table, smiling in the direction of the camera, and what registered the most was their certainty, self confidence, their pleasure in the way things had turned out for them, from Germany and World War I to America in the 1950's, the finest, fattest place of all. And now another couple of decades had passed and the table was out there in the rain.

"Pop." I put my arm around him and at least he didn't move away. Still, it felt odd. I held onto him, knowing he couldn't wait to be let go of. We were both glad nobody was watching.

"Pop, if I had an answer ..."

"I know you don't." Like that, he turned on me. That stab

at human intimacy, father and son style, had set off an alarm in him. Now we re-entered the zone of argument. Familiar territory for us. "You know what's wrong with you, son?"

"I was just wondering. Let's hear it."

"Skip it."

"No, Pop, let's hear it. Let's get it off your chest. You'll feel better then." What an enormous subtraction Mom had made. Let him have his say, I thought. And swallow your tongue, for Mom's sake.

"You don't want to hear this," the old man said.

"I've heard it before, that's all."

"It didn't do any good then, I guess," the old man said. "But that doesn't mean I'm wrong. The stuff you write, George. Honest to God! I mean this thing out of Florida ..."

He shuffled through the mess on the table he kept next to his easy chair, junk mail, a Horatio Hornblower novel, U.S. News and World Reports.

"Here we go," he said. He showed me the column before he read it. It was old, he'd been saving it for years. For what? I was in for it but this wasn't the main agenda. Those were warm-up tosses. He read it aloud. My words coming back at me:

FARAWAY PLACES

By George Griffin

> Blown out truck tires, black-top highways, palmettos and peanut brittle. Were those your best memories of Central Florida? Well look again, traveler. The mouse that roared—We're talking Mickey—has wrought some hefty magic down South ...

"Alright! Enough! Halt!" I waved the napkin that had come with the Ritz crackers as a white flag. I couldn't help laughing but the old man shook his head as if to say, *this ain't funny*.

"George, I used to cut out your clips to save them, so you could have them all in a scrapbook someday. Now I take my scissors down to the library and cut your articles out to save myself embarrassment. Everybody's complaining about stuff missing out of the Sunday travel section ..."

"Then there's at least one thing you must feel good about," I said.

"Yeah? What's that?"

"The name thing."

"Oh my God!" I stopped him cold. *Nom de plume* sounds high flown, so I don't know what you'd call "George Griffin." An alias, maybe. The fact is that my father's name is Hans Greifinger and my name was, and for some purposes still is, George Hans Greifinger.

"You got your nerve, George," the old man said, swallowing a mouthful of Becks as though to get rid of a bad taste in his mouth. "What a battle that was. A humdinger."

A humdinger indeed. I had a whole list of agents, publishers, magazine editors who'd say I was right. A German-American from New Jersey named Greifinger stood as much chance of being accepted as a travel writer as an Indian named Two Mules stood of prospering as a wine critic. Writing was hard enough, at least at the start. Why go around sounding like you'd come to a Club Med opening in a loden jacket and lederhosen? Greifinger had to go or I'd never get past the Trapp Family Resort in New England.

"I see better writing in my Burpee seed catalog," the old man groused. I'd heard that before, too. We repeated ourselves a lot. No new material in our act.

"I'm still young, Pop"

"That so?" he retorted. He stopped for a moment and looked at me, appraisingly, as though it was time to march me out to the garage where, right next to the wall covered with New

Jersey license plates, a new one for every year from 1931 to the early sixties, when the state stopped issuing plates and started with tags, there was a two by four which he'd stood me up against while I was growing up, marking and dating my height. The way he was looking at me, though, he might take me out to the garage this minute and find I'd lost an inch or two off what I'd been.

So I decided to try and get an inch back. I sat him down in a chair, saying I needed his advice, needed it badly and I told him, when he spoke—please, after letting me finish without interruption—he should remember that he wasn't just speaking for himself. He was speaking for Mom too. That got his attention. It took twenty minutes to get it all out. The way I had come to feel about my work. I described my struggles with "serious" projects, novels that never got past outlines, serious nonfiction that expired in a single sample chapter. To recall was to ache. My proposed comparison of Florida and California, reality and myth in America's two dreamlands. "The Duel of Oranges," my agent called it. The Edward Wilcox project: profile of an aged planter, hanging on at a rubber plantation in Malaysia, which he still called Malaya. This proposal had it all, racism, poetry, brutality, nostalgia, the petty rituals of a dying world, servants, clubs, teas, tennis, sex and torpor and endless, bitchy gossip. "Staying On, II" was my agent's shorthand: it sounded like a sequel to Paul Scott's fine novel of India. I took the project back when he mentioned, offhand, that we might shop it around to university presses.

The old man listened carefully to a story that kept getting worse. When a frown crossed his face, I hoped he was sharing my disappointment, my frustration at being locked into a hack reputation. "Phil Rizzuto," he sighed, not without sympathy.

"Yeah, Pop. If he makes it, maybe I will."

Now, there was nothing left except to find out what he

wanted—whatever had prompted that letter to Bangkok, the late call from Jersey. Then I'd leave. There was nothing here for me, nothing and no one. No one home.

"I got a favor to ask," he said. "Not for me."

"Yes?" I hated how he added, *not for me*, as if that would make me more likely to oblige.

"Pauline Kennedy's been asking for you."

V.

—baseball doubleheaders
—barbers who could shave
—free suet for birds, free bones for dogs
—free slices of wurst for kids, from the butcher
—road maps at gas stations

THOSE ARE THINGS I MISS. I'VE BEEN MAKING LISTS, THESE last years. Every night after Vanna White waves "bye-bye" I sit down and make new lists or add to old ones. Food I used to like but can't find anymore. People who I'm sorry they died young. My favorite American roads. There's nothing you can't make a list out of. Here's one: When I Knew This Country Was Past Ripe:

—when banks started giving away gifts like televisions and rotisseries to attract savings accounts

—when people started drinking water that got shipped all the way from France

—soap on a rope

—tanning salons
—light beer

George would think I'm being silly. He takes a dim view of anybody writing something he doesn't get paid for. When he was out in college and no mail came and his mother's heart was breaking, I made a deal that I'd pay him ten dollars per letter and boy, you should have seen him stuff the mailbox. Even his mother smelled a rat.

"Dear folks, a lot has happened since yesterday, and more than I can put in just one letter ..." A money-writer from the start.

VI.

THE OLD MAN SAID HE'D MET PAULINE Kennedy—where else?—in the Berkeley Heights Public Library. They were both people who loved a place you could get books for free. I supposed their meeting was a coincidence. But the idea of their talking, even if by chance, made my ears burn. "You went from Lowell Thomas to Robin Leach," my father said. I hoped he hadn't shared that opinion with Pauline Kennedy. She'd been my high school English teacher. Now she wanted me to visit.

I crossed over Route 22, which looked like an airport landing strip, convoys streaming east and west, and I drove into North Plainfield on Watchung Avenue, past stately Victorians with porches and attics and room to spare, hard-to-heat and slow to sell. Whenever you saw one that still impressed, it turned out to be lawyers offices or a funeral parlor. Downtown Plainfield was boarded store fronts, closed-down movie theaters. These days, Thursday night shopping and Saturday night dates were transacted elsewhere, someplace on the highway. It wasn't communism that gutted America's towns and despoiled its countryside: it was shopping malls.

Out through South Plainfield, left turn through Iselin and I climbed onto New Jersey's primal artery, the Garden State Parkway, a nostalgic, sensual conduit that transported generations of Jersey youths to tacky, heartbreaking beach towns where they lost their virginity in sandy, funky boardwalk places and then, three or four decades later, took them to the tidy, manageable retirement communities where they gave up their lives. At Exit 88, I turned off the mainstream coursing towards Atlantic City and came down a quiet eddy that led into what was left of the pine barrens.

Cedar Glen West was where I was headed. Following directions, I got as far as the community itself. Then I was lost. The streets were named after birds. Oriole, Heron, Robin, Dove and the whole settlement had the air of an elderly, orderly aviary. The posted speed limit was 15 miles but just to make sure no motorcycle gangs missed the point, municipal signs were supplemented by private warnings: SLOW, THIS MEANS YOU. I could sense people watching me as I drove in, vigilante oldsters, quick on the draw with flashlights and garden hoses.

Pauline Kennedy had been sitting out in her patio keeping an eye out for company. Little kids and old people are like that. In the prime of life, you're fashionably late, but not at the edges. She popped out of her chair and walked towards me as I got out of the car.

"Thanks for coming, George," she said. I had given her my hand because it didn't feel right hugging a teacher, but she pulled me towards her into a hug. "I know you've interrupted your schedule."

"It's high time I came, Mrs. Kennedy." I had expected someone ancient. I foresaw a visit that was one step up from a call at a nursing home. A pat on the hand, some shared memories and parting endearments: how much she meant to me, how much I meant to her. But Pauline Kennedy surprised me:

dressed for tennis, brisk and vigorous, she looked about the same as I remembered her. And the arithmetic was humbling: the woman I remembered might not have been any older than I was now.

"Listen, George," she said. "I'm going to say this whether you like it or not. You have no idea how happy your visit makes me."

"Well," I said. "That's good ..." I meant it, too. Weeks could pass, I realized, before I saw anyone brighten at the sight of me, anyone who wasn't interested in money or publicity.

She took me by my elbow and walked me across the patio, into her quarters, which were exactly that: one fourth of a building that had three more apartments in its other corners. Sitting room, living room, kitchen, bedroom and bath: nice and tidy. I did what I always did, when I found myself in offices with lots of identical desks, a bank or an airlines office. I looked for personal traces, a raunchy calendar, a kid's finger painting, anything that was different. I noticed a wooden typing table with an ancient portable Underwood and a whole wall of the living room that was covered with maps, maps of the world, continents, and state maps: New Jersey was covered with notes and circles and underlines. Two or three decades of high school yearbooks were piled in a corner, along with books and what might have been some papers she'd never gotten around to grading.

"Do you see anything interesting?" she asked. She was in the kitchen pouring coffee into mugs.

"I hate to snoop."

"I can't believe that, George. Snooping is a sign of an inquiring mind. I go into people's medicine cabinets, wherever I visit."

"No television. That impresses me."

"Don't be so impressed," she said, laughing. "It's in my bedroom." She came out with cake and coffee. "Save your compliments. I didn't bake this."

Juicy plums set like cobblestones in a crust that was just a minute away from turning to charcoal: it was right out of childhood. Sometimes I worry about keeping recipes alive. Not those breathless fashions, ginger and mango topping mahi-mahi, tofu and pears accompanying free-range chicken. I'm talking about potato pancakes fried in a pan that made potato pancakes for twenty-five years, about combinations of strawberry and rhubarb that no one but me seems to have heard of.

"My mother made this," I replied.

"Brings back memories to you?" she asked.

"Yes ..."

"*You* bring back memories to *me*," she said. Something in her voice warned me that this wasn't going to be about pulling out old yearbooks and getting nostalgic. I've learned that those inner signals—those premonitory twinges—are hardly ever wrong. They come off an envelope before you open it, out of a phone on the first ring. You know you're in for something.

"See those books over next to my chair?" she asked. "That stack? That's what I've been doing. I decided I would read a biography of the U.S. presidents, each and every one. It was a job just to put together a list, but I found a man in the history department at Rutgers."

"How far along are you?"

"I'm closing in. Caro's book on Lyndon Johnson." She stubbed her cigarette on the edge of her coffee saucer. It wasn't the sort of gesture I'd expected from her. I wondered if she was doing this so I'd put aside my memories of her as a schoolteacher, dedicated, formidable, ascetic. I wondered what else there was in her life. There were pictures on an upper shelf, framed black-and-whites. Some of them were of men in uniform, soldiers and sailors, but there was no way of knowing whether they were brothers, fathers, lovers. And no offsetting snapshots of kids, no technicolor smilers wanting to be remembered on their birthdays. She knew a lot more about me than I did about her.

"I made a mistake," Pauline Kennedy was saying. "My mistake was that I started at the beginning. I started with George Washington."

"What's wrong with that? You start at the beginning."

"That's what I thought. But now I see I should have started with the incumbent gentleman and worked my way back to the beginning. Reading it in order as I've done, there's a ghastly, sinking feeling. It's as though I were walking down a ladder. Not that all the steps are evenly spaced. But you compare the founding fathers with today's leaders ... compare education, ethics, what they read, what they wrote, how they wrote. Compare, for that matter, the houses they lived in. It doesn't make you feel too buoyant. Want some more coffee, George? Am I depressing you?"

"No."

"No to coffee? Or no, I'm not depressing you?"

"You're not depressing me. I arrived that way."

"From talking to your father?"

"You guessed it," I answered, wondering how much she knew. Had the old man set up a one-two punch? A paternal left, a pedagogical right? Immigrant parent and high school teacher: no way I'd go free. But something new accompanied my irritation. It was their belief in me. Touching. And I realized something that pleased me. It was about teachers. Not all of them, but a few. You think, when you leave school, when you escape, you're beyond their reach. They must not think about you, you think. Why bother? There's a new crop of kids every fall. It's over. But some of them don't let go. Pauline Kennedy was one of them.

"Yes to coffee," I said. "It's nice seeing you."

"I've been thinking about you," she said, staring at me. I remembered the way she used her eyes, the way other teachers used their voice, or hands, to reprimand. "I've received an invitation to your high school class reunion. When I called to confirm that I'd attend, I asked about you. They said you'd declined. Or at least, you hadn't accepted. I want you to reconsider."

"Why?" Is that all it is? I asked myself. She just wanted to see me with the others at the reunion? No deeper interrogation? What a relief! What a disappointment! "What's so important about reunions?"

"I get invited all the time. It's a retirement benefit, I suppose. I'm a connoisseur of reunions. And a believer in them."

"I didn't know you'd be there," I answered weakly.

"You *never* know who'll be there. That's part of the charm. Or what they'll be like. Reunions, George, are potluck dinners. You take what's there ..." She relaxed and smiled. "And there are some remarkable covered dishes. Shall I stop this metaphor now or do I continue?"

"More. Please. I love metaphors. I'm the man who called Big Sur 'Mother Nature's Maginot Line.'"

"Well, then. You stand by the door watching people come in and you think, well, there's a tuna casserole, there's a macaroni and cheese salad and, oh, my, tortellini and pesto! Sushi! Who could have known? Ah! Meat loaf. Once a meat loaf, always a meat loaf."

"Terrific. What kind of dish would I make?"

"That's what I've been thinking about," she said. No more jocular metaphor now. No fun deciding whether I was a pineapple upside down cake or a cotton candy cone. "Let's take a walk."

"*Ein Platz fur alles und Alles in Sein Platz*," the old man used to say: a place for everything and everything in its place. And this was the place for people who placed cleanliness next to godliness, or maybe ahead of it. They weeded seriously here, they mowed and clipped and raked yards the size of carpets. I didn't need to look at mailboxes to see German names: the ceramic elves and dwarves and deers and mushrooms gave the game away.

It was hard to picture Pauline Kennedy fitting in. She wasn't the type, I thought.

"I didn't think you'd stay around the Garden State after you retired," I said. "I thought you'd be in the Berkshires someplace."

"I wanted to travel," she said. "I needed a house that I could lock up and walk away from and not worry about."

"Do you travel?"

"Oh, my, yes!"

"You must know my work," I said, trying again to put a comic edge on what was mostly a feeling of dread, as though she were about to grade a very shaky paper that I'd just handed in.

"Yes," she answered tersely. "I do know your work."

"Lots of people find it useful," I said. "Some would say —I'm quoting *Auto Life*'s review of my first book—'close to indispensable.'" Keep it light, George, I told myself. Turn on the charm.

"I'm not that kind of traveler," she responded. "Or reader."

Okay, so I was in for it. I decided to just keep walking, let her decide on the time and place of execution. I took a lively interest in the neighborhood, especially the yards, which were revealing as the medicine cabinets Mrs. Kennedy said she snooped around in. Some yards reflected surging happy retirement, second childhood. Sunflowers, pinwheels, rock gardens, waterfalls. Wooden cut-outs of bending-over women in polka dot bloomers. Elsewhere there was only lawn, bare lawn, and a dripping air conditioner and the sense of life winding down behind drawn shades.

"Your father found this place for me, you know," she said. "He helped me move in."

"I didn't know," I said. I'd no idea that the old man had that kind of contact with Mrs. Kennedy.

"He's a remarkable man. When I met him first … that's when I had you of course …"

What was happening? I asked myself. *When I had you*. That

was a mother's language, about an inch away from "when I was carrying you."

"… well, my first impression was wrong. That's odd, George, because in general I credit first impressions. I don't believe that there have been more than two times in life when I've had to say, well, I got that person wrong. Your father was first. And you … you may be the second."

It's coming now, I thought. Brace yourself. You pass judgments all the time. Bed-and-breakfasts live or die on your comments. If you say a drive is scenic, that's the way traffic will turn. So now: be judged.

"I thought that your father was a lot like other foreign immigrants." She stopped and caught herself. "*Foreign* immigrants? That's redundant isn't it? Well, I thought here's another earnest hard-working newcomer who won't give his wife or child a moment of peace until his son has made his first million. Getting rich in America, such a tiresome scenario! And we were implicated in it, because education was the ticket to money and good grades were a mark of education. Oh my. They didn't understand education, they didn't understand grades, they didn't understand …"

"What?"

"I was going to say they didn't understand America either. But maybe the joke's on me. Maybe they did."

"I think they did." Let's talk about America, Mrs. Kennedy, I thought, making notes for my defense. The America she taught, Emerson-Thoreau-Melville, the New England America she was born in, had nothing to do with New Jersey. When those transcendental traditions were forming and flowering, New Jersey's future citizens were making traditions of their own in Sicily and Odessa, Warsaw and Dublin. To New Jersey, New England was a national park they drove through when they couldn't find a summer rental on the Shore. The House of Seven Gables was a shoe store, Moby Dick a seafood place somewhere between Wildwood and Cape May.

And those driving, inarticulate immigrants who came in for consultations about their kids' grades were dreaming of an America that meant low margin, high volume along Route 22 and a pastel Tara in the hills beyond.

"Maybe they were right, maybe I was right," she countered briskly. "But I was talking about your father. And your mother. They were different. They thought you were going to be a writer. I warned them. I warned them you might not get rich. That was alright, they said. Money wasn't everything.

"I've done alright," I said, "money-wise."

"Don't use wise as a suffix," she snapped. "It's barbaric."

"Sorry," I said, and she nodded her acceptance. We walked some more, passing senior citizen strollers, men in baggy shorts and ace bandages, women in slacks and tennis shoes, stepping out briskly.

"The point is that your parents were prepared to look past the money. Do you have any idea how unusual that was? They sat there in my office and your mother as much as told me that money didn't matter so much. Being a writer was special. A writer was a good thing to be."

"Well, that was my mom," I said. Then I couldn't resist a question. "How did my father take the news?"

"He nodded his head. He was all for it. I was amazed. I'd been condescending to them. Your parents realized—if only instinctively—that it wasn't just about how well you made out, George. 'Money-wise.' I find it interesting that you asked about your father. You have doubts about him?"

"Nothing compared to his doubts about me, Mrs. Kennedy," I fired back.

"He came to me a while ago with a question. He asked me what I thought of your work. Writing wasn't his line, he said, and although he reads a lot, he wasn't, he said, 'what you call educated.' So he came to me and asked me to confirm—or contradict—an impression that he had that your work was … second rate. I told him that it was hard getting started as a writer and that many good writers had to do things they weren't proud of, especially at the start of their careers. Because it *is* a hard trade and I suspect it's getting harder. My reading of presidential biographies suggests as much. But at the end of it all …"

"You agreed?"

"Yes." She looked right at me. "Second rate."

"Maybe …" This was hard for me to say. I was shaky. "Maybe we'd all be better off if they hadn't taken the chance, on a writer. If they'd settled for a …"

"A what?" she challenged me. Maybe she sniffed my weakness. The fact is, whenever I'd tried to identify a trade that I could practice, other than writing, something that I could get paid for, I ended up working as a night watchman.

"A little knowledge is a dangerous thing," I said.

"Alexander Pope," she snapped. "The point?"

"Well, so is a little talent," I said. "That's dangerous too." Then I supplied the source of my quotation. "George Griffin."

We passed a community house where oldsters were playing cards and walked down to a pond where there were benches near the water's edge. She was deciding how to respond to what I'd just said, about a little talent being a dangerous thing. Sometimes, back in high school, I'd seen her pause like that, usually when someone had said something unusual, something that was startlingly bright or shockingly dumb. When she turned towards me, I could see I hadn't said anything bright.

"If there were corporal punishment …" she began.

"You'd hit me?"

"I'd shake you up some, that's for sure. Honest to God, George!" I felt I was back in school. Humiliated. "Sit down," she commanded. I obeyed. "It's been a long time since I saw you, George, and there's every chance I may not see you again."

"I slipped up and from here on out ..." She raised her hand for silence. I was speaking out of turn.

"Now I see you again for the first time in ever so many years. I compare the boy I knew to the man who's visiting me today."

"Don't," I said. "Please. I don't need this."

"That bright, cocky, callow, virginal, bookish boy ..." She stopped for breath and smiled at me, or the memory of me.

"That covers it," I said.

"And now ... this hangdog, equivocal, charming lost man. Trapped by his own success. Resigned to it. As if life's a prison and failure is a meal that gets slipped through the bars of a cage. Oh, George! There's so much depending on you! You mean a lot. And what happens to you matters. So ten minutes of talk from me, uninterrupted talk, shouldn't be unbearable. What does it come to, if you average it out? Half a minute per year? You used to sit still for much longer than that for me, every day. After I'm done, you're excused, and let's face it, there's nothing I can do about what happens to you. So I'm going to give you a bit of a lecture and after that you're free to go on your merry way. Or not so merry."

"That's fine," I said. "And ... thank you."

"Thank you? You haven't heard me yet."

"Thank you for caring."

"Caring is the theme, George. Caring about your work. Remember how I used to break that down in class? You had to care about your subject matter and you had to care about your audience and you had to care about yourself. 'The big three.' And my difficulty or ... to put it more precisely ... my disappointment with you is that your work had come to show remarkable indifference to all three."

She paused to light another cigarette but I could tell she wasn't done yet, though I wished she was. Possibly, I could defend myself. I could explain things. Indifference to subject matter? You bet. These days, traveling around America got old fast. I wished I could make her see that. And my audience, my too-faithful readers? They were tourists, crowding and contaminating whatever they touched. And what about myself, not caring about myself? I could tell her about my plans, my projects. I decided not to. It was the difference between "guilty" and "guilty with an explanation." No difference at all.

"When you left your father's home, when you left my classroom, we thought you'd make us proud. That's the investment a parent makes in a child, the same kind of investment a teacher makes in a student, except that we have so many more children. So many. But you live for the ones that are special, George. All my life, there were a dozen like that, which is large for a family, I admit, but very small for a career. A tiny percentage, out of thousands. I never wrote off anybody. I turned them into careful writers, maybe, or better readers, or maybe better people. And I hear from them, George, some of the worst thugs in school remember me. But it's the special ones that I recall. The ones you send out into the world like arrows, like missiles, like … I don't know … knights. Good lord, I'm losing it."

She turned away from me, shuddering or maybe crying and part of me wanted to jump up and hug her, but she was my teacher and I stayed put and when she freed me she was dry-eyed.

"The special students," she resumed. "You were one of them. I care about you. I don't want you to fall into a trap, George, even if it's of your own making. Most traps are. You were special. Promise me you won't forget that."

"Okay," I said. But my agreement had come too quickly. It was suspect.

"I haven't even gotten to the heart of it, George. I'm not close to finishing."

"I figured …"

"Wrong. Listen. What's next is difficult because I have to begin by admitting that I might be wrong. I don't think I am, though. Here's what it comes to. Those first years, that are so hard on everybody, have been easy for you. You took off. You saw your name in print. You were paid. You prospered. And all of us who were watching you—and there are more of us than you might think—were thrilled. I know your parents were. And a lot of those people who'll be showing up for the reunion, I'll wager many of them were watching you too. They recognized your name."

"Not my name," I corrected her, although it felt like I was doing the old man's job for him. "My face, at the top of every column."

"Fair enough. We pictured you at large, working, writing, making your way in the world. Now here's the question. While we were thinking of you … did you think of us?"

"Often," I admitted. "All the time."

"How?" she pressed.

"I even called it my if-they-could-see-me-now feeling. You know what I mean. You must. In Hong Kong. In Hawaii. In Kenya or Vienna. Just anywhere. Whenever I felt … excuse me … hot shit."

"You'd look back to New Jersey."

"Not in anger. Just … wow … here I am. Here! And getting paid for it!"

"So … we were your audience."

"Not my only audience, Mrs. Kennedy. You know that. Eighty newspapers. More or less." Not bad, not bad at all. "But when I pictured the faces I wrote for … they were Jersey faces, that's for sure."

"That if-they-could-see-me-now-feeling. Do you still have it?"

"Yes," I said. "Only … it's not the way it was before. The fun's gone out of it. I don't know what it is, whether it's harder for me to imagine them or them imagining me."

"That settles it, George. You come to that reunion. You *need* to come. To see the ones you wish could see you."

"Alright," I said.

"Alright?"

"I mean, yes, of course."

"Good." I felt her slip her arm through mine and turn us back in the direction we'd come. Late summer evening crept into the Pine Barrens, with the whoosh of lawn sprinklers, the murmur of senior citizen voices on front porches, the glow of televisions bringing reports of disaster in the world they'd retired from. They sat around televisions the way people once sat around fires, watching flames. Pauline Kennedy walked beside me, matching my stride. We were done talking and it felt good. She was thinking things over, I sensed, and that was my excuse not to think at all. I remembered those tubes in radios and early televisions, the way they glowed awhile, fading slowly after you turned them off, and the old man saying he guessed dying would be like that, not an immediately black out but a gradual dwindling. When we got to where my car was parked—the old man's car, I should say—Pauline leaned against the door.

"It wasn't so bad, was it?" she asked.

"It could have been worse."

"You've had some success … of a certain kind. Too much success … of a certain kind. There are worse things than failure, George. Think about it on the way home." She tossed her cigarette into the grass and stepped on it. "There," she said. "You're excused. For now."

VII.

I'M SITTING HERE WITH MY LISTS AND WITH some old photo albums, calling roll, marking people absent. I've got pictures of beer parties we used to have in the back yard, a half dozen couples at a picnic table covered with steins and wurst. I've got pictures of us dancing out in the garage, Ernst Muller playing the accordion. I've got pictures of horseshoe games and fishing trips and vacations from Cadillac Mountain to Key West, folks leaning against cars, the '51 Mercury is the one I remember best, and pictures of dogs and gardens and pictures of Christmas trees with packages spread underneath, the Wildroot Cream Oil I got every year and the neckties they gave me for a joke. There's pictures that we mailed back to Germany, to show folks what kind of country we were living in and how well we were all doing over here in America. We're grinning from behind twenty-five pound turkeys, dangling bananas and pineapples in front of the camera. There's pictures from further back, between the wars, hammering away on each other's houses, or camping in the Catskills, or lounging outside those tents we used to rent for the summer on Jamaica Bay. Plum Beach was the name of the place. There's pictures of me and Mom before we met, me working as a janitor for Otto Hofer, her standing guard over baby carriages in Riverside Park, working as a nanny. There's Eighty-Sixth Street and the Steuben Day Parade and the Turnverein and Nature Friends and *Sängerbundhalle*. There's pictures of me as a kid with a bunch of others, wading in the Elbe, a dozen of us in bathing suits, boys and girls, arm in arm, and out behind us you can see the ships—some of them still had masts—that were going to be carrying us away. And a picture of Mom just before she left Stuttgart, leaning against some Swabian apple tree, looking like she'd been crying. Sentimental, she was. I remember there was a song years later, in the fifties, maybe, "throw momma from the train a kiss, a kiss throw momma from the train a goodbye," a real can of corn, but she was sobbing in the kitchen nook, remembering the last time she saw her mother. Goodbyes meant something then: the ocean was wider, before Peoples Express and those other cheapo airlines.

VIII.

PAST THE PERTH AMBOY TOLLBOOTHS, I came into a zone that would challenge any travel writer: essence of New Jersey. Check it out. Tired looking tar-paper-sided houses, motels and gas stations, a fourteen-screen movie theater next to a place that offered clowns and pizza and then, up onto the Raritan Bridge, arching over a sprawl of chemical plants and ponds, rotting wharves, factory parking lots, high-tension wires, oil refineries where smokestacks, burning off gas, looked like giant pilot lights, flaming day and night, marking a shoreline that asphyxiated fish shared with washed up medical syringes. But I was happy, happier than I'd been in years, because Pauline Kennedy still had hopes for me and now—this is all it took—the Drifters were on the radio, singing "Save the Last Dance for Me."

Suddenly I felt that I hadn't returned from high school to the present at all. I was still back there somewhere, young and promising, a writer-to-be, driving a car in the dark and listening to a heart-capturing song, and sometimes when I think of God, I picture him as a kind of disc jockey, a sort of Wolfman

Jack, plugged into a mega transmitter that can send music wherever it wants and, if you were lucky, God the disc jockey sent out the perfect music to match your mood. The Drifters, the Silhouettes, the Moonglows, all the bird groups, Meadowlarks, Robins, Orioles, those eerie doo-wop harmonies, and Jesse Belvin singing "Goodnight, My Love" while we danced the last dance in the high school gym, crepe paper trailing off basketball hoops, coats piled on classroom desks, cars parked outside, waiting for us to match the mood with the road. It all came back: the ache, the awkwardness, the whispers and, after saying goodnight, the ride home, the loosened tie, the rolled-down window, the rolled up sleeves, turning Saturday night into Sunday morning.

Failure, not success, was what used to bring me to Irene's. When my dates ended earlier than I had hoped, as they always did, I would come into Irene's for a sausage-and-peppers sandwich. I would sit at a counter with people who always looked like they'd made out better than I had. Some of the guys had their dates with them, mussed up, pawed-over women in whom horniness had yielded to hunger. God, how I wanted to join them! Pauline Kennedy was right. They were my audience, those Jersey people parked along the counter, those couples tucked in booths, the guys in gym class, the girls in the bleachers at basketball games, they and their parents too, they were the ones I pictured when I sat down to write. There were classier audiences out there, but I performed for Jersey people. I performed for years too long, never deciding whether I was thumbing my nose at them or blowing a kiss, celebrating where I had come from or how far away I'd gotten. You'd think I'd have figured that out by now. That, I guessed, was why Pauline Kennedy wanted me at that reunion.

As soon as I stepped inside, I was sorry. There was no mistaking it, the place was owned by Greeks now. You developed an instinct for this: the whorehouse carpeting, the black Naugahyde booths, the wood-veneered plastic paneling, the oil painting of the Parthenon, the shiny black pants and wrinkled white shirt on a tired looking waiter emptying a can of beans into a bowl on the salad bar, with all the style of a mechanic popping a can of Quaker State into a clunker that had started burning oil. But the hostess said they still made sausage and peppers sandwiches, so I let her lead me to a booth and, declining adventure at the salad bar, I stepped over to the juke box, and someone tapped me on the shoulder.

"Hey, dipstick, the reunion's three weeks from now." Someone from high school? Whoever he was, he'd gotten old fast: big had gone to heavy, blonde had gone to mostly bald.

"You don't know me?"

"Wait a minute, it'll come." But I doubted it would and he looked like he doubted it too, daring me, as though he was wearing a disguise I'd never be able to penetrate. Then, to my surprise, I had him.

"Gooker Cerruti," I said, offering my hand. Dan Cerruti, nicknamed "Gooker" for his habit of tramping through brooks and swamps, rolling in mud, hunting frogs. "Not a nice boy," Mom said. Still, we'd been friends once.

"Still in the neighborhood?" I asked.

"You don't think I'd drive from out of state to eat here, do you? No, George, I'm staying close to the scene of the crime."

"How are you doing, Gooker?"

"Come on over and sit with us. I'll tell you." He led me to a booth which looked out on Route 22. Dining-with-a-view: all that separated sixty miles per hour west from sixty miles per hour east was a concrete divider and a cloud of poisonous exhaust. It was a miracle that they could grow the best tomatoes in the world in this state. Or make sausage and pepper sandwiches they'd never manage in Colorado.

"The girls are in the john," Gooker explained.

"Wife and daughter?"

"Wife and wife's friend," he responded, glancing towards a ladies room door that had a cut-out figure of a Greek peasant woman with a basket of melons on her head. I couldn't see what was on the men's room door. A guy at a deep-fryer?

"You know both of them," Gooker said.

And so I did, instantly. There was Kate Kramer, "Kiss Me, Kate," a game, spunky cheerleader whom Gooker had dated all through high school. And the woman who followed her—who stared at me and then, God knows why, blushed—was Joan Simmons and now I was sure I was back twenty plus years, that I'd never left town at all, because my heart was in my throat.

"Hello, George," she said, reaching for my hand which—thank God—hadn't even had time to break into the clammy sweat they used to produce whenever she was in the vicinity.

"Hi, Joan," I said, stepping aside as she slid into the booth, right next to me. She'd been a year behind me, when those things mattered, when a senior who dated a junior would be kidded about "robbing the cradle." Yet we had dated, a dozen times at least, and nothing was robbed. By junior year, Joan Simmons had the sort of figure boys cartooned in schoolbooks. "She won't *do* anything," the word was, and I never proved otherwise. Still, it could make you feel grown up, just walking with her. She was game about going into New York and once she got me to acquiesce in her policy that there would be no sex between us—our mutual understanding that her body was something that could harm us both, so we'd better not arouse it—she was good company. After high school, we'd lost touch. The world was full of women I hadn't met. Still, I wondered about her sometimes. What became of high school beauties anyway?

After the hellos, the hugs, the stares, Gooker took charge, which was alright with me. I'd talked about myself enough today. And what do you say to the likes of Joan Simmons after half a lifetime? "What's new?" "How you doing?" Besides, my life got tracked through newspapers, my columns were like letters to the mildly interested, and there was that photo that I changed every couple of years, so people could watch me grow older. But Gooker was an unknown. Kate and Gooker. And Joan. Gooker was easy. It all came tumbling out: the tire business on Route 22, the equestrian estate in Basking Ridge, the time share in the Poconos, the age of his kids, the cost of his home, the prospect of retirement, Gooker favoring Florida while Kate had thoughts of Charleston. His many excellences, his memorable errors, his secret pleasures. Europeans denounce us for this full, unforced disclosure; Japanese are appalled by our lack of restraint. I loved it. So little time, so much catching up to do! That's what it was, catching up, and underlying it—what foreigners miss—the notion that we were in life together and catching up brought us back in formation, back where we belonged and we could move forward not as a generation—that was too literary—not as a gang—that made us closer than we were—but as what the old man called "a bunch." That's what we were. A bunch.

"So," Gooker said when he'd finished his adventures in cocoa futures. "What about you, hotshot?"

"You see the column, don't you?"

"Sure we do, but ..."

"I cut out the article about castles you can stay in around Austria and Germany," Kate interjected, appealing to Gooker. "That sounded like something we might do."

"Anyway, you married or something?" Gooker asked. He wasn't into castles. "Or you just dial room service?"

"I was married. No more."

"What'd she ..." Gooker's expression darkened. "She didn't die?"

"Oh no. She lived."

"Kids?"

"No."

"That's nothing, then," Kate said. "Getting married and having no kids is like going steady, is all."

"A divorce like yours doesn't mean dippity," Gooker declared. "If it were a car accident it would be a fender-bender. Just drive away from it."

I sensed that my story was going flat. Ho-hum. It needed punching up.

"She was a stewardess, actually," I said. That got their interest.

"A stewardess?" asked Kate. "Isn't that kind of a … cliché?"

"Well, it happened."

"Hey, listen, George," Gooker asked. "Is it true what they say about those girls …"

"You mean, a man in every country? Like sailors?"

"No, not that."

"The mile-high club?" Kate asked. She was a game woman, give her credit, hanging in with Gooker, smirk for smirk. An oddly companionable couple, in an x-rated pop-some-popcorn-and-put-on-a-porn-film way.

"What I hear is that stewardesses have an unlimited supply of those little weenie cocktail bottles they wheel around on carts. They got closets full of them, I hear."

"Not that I saw."

"Well, shit! First they took away Santa Claus and the Easter Bunny …"

"Who'd she fly for?" Joan asked.

"Thai."

"She was …"

"Yes."

"George, old buddy," Gooker said. Now he was really

impressed. "We've got to talk. What happened?"

"She was someone who wanted to come to the U.S. badly. A green card kind of thing."

"I heard about those cases," Gooker said. "Arrangements of convenience."

"I was doing a favor," I said.

"Yeah, right," Gooker said. "Did you put the blocks to her?"

"Gooker!" Kate protested.

"Excuuuuse me," he said. "Like you weren't wondering."

"I thought it might … develop … once we got to New York. This was someone I'd have done anything for. But what I did was all she wanted."

"The perfect husband!" Kate said. "It's … in a way … romantic. It's noble!"

"I still think you should've put the blocks to her," Gooker said. "It's not like you were asking for the moon."

"You were always a nice guy," Joan offered. "I'm not surprised."

"What have you been up to, Joan?"

"Oh …" she stubbed out a cigarette, looked up, and for the first time our eyes met. "I've been busy fucking up my life."

"I'm sorry," I said. I felt as though she were accusing me; it sounded as though I were apologizing to her, as if it were my fault.

"Hey," Gooker said. "If yours was a fender-bender, Joan's was … boy … it was a head-on collision. Total."

"We should've never been on the road," Joan said. She looked out at Route 22. There was a break in traffic and I noticed the garbage that collected along the divider, blown out tires, beer cans, chunks of styrofoam. She looked at me. "One kid."

"You're skipping something," Kate prodded.

"What's that?"

"Who you married."

"Oh." She turned to me. "You knew, didn't you? I always thought you must've heard, some way."

"No."

"I married Kenny Hauser."

"Kenny," I said. "You married Kenny? You're kidding!" We were friends, Kenny and I. We were rivals. We were budding writers, co-winners of the I-Speak-For-Democracy contest, the Ruth and Gehrig of the National Forensic League. He edited the yearbook, I honchoed the school newspaper. We were going to be great, of course. It happened all the time, I guessed. How great? How soon? Those were just details. Catch me in Hollywood or Paris, my book in Scribner's window, that gorgeous woman on my arm, making a speech, accepting an award. You might say these things pass, these youthful boasts and ententes. Maybe not. If I hadn't been in touch with Kenny Hauser, or he with me, it was only because we weren't ready to come to the table yet. Meanwhile, the years slipped by.

"Tell me something," Gooker said. "You ever do any travel pieces on Israel?"

"Not much."

"Come to Israel, come stay with friends?" he pressed. "All that bullshit?"

"No."

"Because that's who your old friend Kenny Hauser works for these days."

"I didn't know," I said, glancing at Joan and, once again, sorry that I hadn't kept in better touch … in any touch at all, really. It was odd how we cluttered our lives and avoided going back to the subjects of our true wonder. "What about the insurance business? His father's outfit? Hauser Agency?"

"Oh sure," Gooker answered, "he fills out a form, what's your occupation, he puts down insurance. Beats writing down, agent of a foreign government. But the insurance is on automatic pilot. Bunch of women running it. Israel is what your old buddy lives and dies for. He's on TV all the time."

I glanced at Joan, waiting to see how she reacted to Gooker's denunciation of her ex-husband. Was she one of those divorced people who sifted the past, picking out the good parts? Or did she repudiate it all? I found, when I looked, that she was staring at me.

"I always thought you knew about us," she said. "I assumed you knew."

I shrugged. "News to me."

"Hey, come on Joan. It wasn't in the newspapers. How's George going to find out? Flying Thai!"

Kate gave her husband a look. He made Thai sound like *thigh*. And he made it sound dirty. Meanwhile, Joan was still giving me a look as though—somehow—she was upset that I hadn't heard about her and Kenny.

"I don't know," she said. "It's just that …"

"What?" Gooker pressed, but not unkindly. I think he was intrigued.

"Well, when you grow up together, the way we did …" She threw up her hands. "Never mind. It's … you figure that word gets around. One way or another."

Gooker shook his head and held his tongue. He gave me a look—half shudder, half shrug—which implies that things didn't work that way. People weren't connected.

"Not that it would have made any difference," Joan added, in a way that suggested maybe it would have.

"What I hope," I said, "for your sake and Kenny's … is that it wasn't all always bad. I hope it was good first."

"Oh, sure," she replied. "We had some good times in there, someplace."

"Well, hell, who doesn't have memories," Gooker declared. "I dropped dead tomorrow, Kate would have a lifetime of memories to live on."

"Oh really?" Kate deadpanned.

"Oh Christ ..."

"I mean, is there a specific occasion you have in mind?"

"Geez, I'm tired of that Jewish stuff," Gooker said, returning to familiar ground. Kate rolled her eyes. I guessed she'd heard it all before. "I'm tired of that shit. Okay? Sue me! Never forget and never again and all that. They think they're turning me on. I got news, babe. They're turning me off. Push comes to shove, I'm telling you ... What ever gave him the right to preach?"

Gooker made me uncomfortable. The oldies but goodies mood that had carried me up from Lakehurst was gone, replaced by transmissions from another station, an abrasive all-talk all-news operation. I tried to change things.

"So ... how's the reunion?" I asked.

"You wouldn't believe it," Gooker said. "The work."

"I wish he never started," Kate said. "People don't appreciate it."

"Hey! If I don't do it, who will? If I don't make those phone calls, they don't get made. And there's no reunion."

"Well? Is that such a tragedy? If you want to see people, you see them. So why bring together a bunch of people you don't care about, you barely even remember?"

"The fifth and the tenth were snaps," Gooker said. "Everybody's still around or if they're not, then their parents are. Like your old man. I want to get in touch with you, I call him ... bingo. But now, oh baby, we're out beyond the reef."

"People moved away?"

"Parents are going, going, gone. Once they're not around, it's a whole different ballgame. One local phone call turns into four, long distance. Ex-wives, former employers, realtors, landlords, hell, a parole officer for Ronny Filippo. And Carol Saunders. I called a booking agent in Vegas. Unbelievable."

"I still don't know why you do it," Kate said. "No one even

thanks you."

"I told you. It doesn't happen without me."

"My point," Kate said. "Exactly."

"Christ," Gooker said. He turned to me. "This was an accident," he said, "meeting you here, right?"

"I came out to see my father," I granted.

"Well, let me tell you this. From a guy who knew you in gym class. We've got this reunion coming up. Don't even think about missing it."

"He's been kind of telling people you'll be there," Kate said. "Everybody."

"Who cares?"

"You're an attraction," Kate said. "Your column and all." The way she smiled at me, I knew she had delivered a compliment, a plain compliment, and it made me cringe. Right then, I wished I'd done more. Or, failing that, that the work I'd done had been less successful, that I was a writer's writer, cruelly neglected. A poet, even.

"We're out of here," Gooker said.

"It's gotten late," Kate agreed. Then, on our way out the door, I saw one of those transactions—wordless question, silent answer—which took me right back to high school. Kate to Joan: *Who's taking you home*?

"I'll give you a lift," I said.

"If it's not out of your way."

"Even if it is. How often do I get to talk to you?"

We watched Kate and Gooker pull out onto the highway we all lived on, the way people used to live on rivers; if you didn't get out into the current you were becalmed, landlocked, dead. When I turned to face her, she had curled up in the seat, tucking her feet beneath her, the way women used to pose for calendars, tossing her hair a little as she moved.

"So what's he really into?" I asked.

"You mean Gooker?"

"Yes. I mean Gooker." And I did, but Gooker was just a warm up.

"What about him?" she asked. "What exactly?"

"Come on, Joan."

"Women," she said. "That's what Gooker is into these days."

"And Kate?"

"She lives with it."

"That so? How well does she live with it?"

"You and your questions, George. Sometimes we used to go out, you asked more questions than my parents did when I got home. Kate evens the score, George. Now I told you, I'm trusting you not to ..."

"Who am I going to tell?"'

"The thing of it is, they've stayed together. That's something. And you know what? Gooker? He's always there. And he never changes."

"That's good news? Gooker forever?" It sounded like a life sentence. "I'm sorry about you and Kenny."

"He changed. Not like Gooker. Lots of people change, right?"

"Except Gooker."

"Yeah," she said. "Kenny changed alright."

"What happened?"

"I liked what you asked back there, did we have good times before the bad? It was ... thoughtful."

"And you said yes."

"A lot of good times. How well did you know him?"

"We were best friends once. I thought we were, anyway. I knew him as well as I knew you." Something in that last line made me wince, as soon as I said it. This return to New Jersey was rough on tenses. Maybe it was wishful thinking, but I corrected myself. "As well as I know you ..." It sounded clumsy too. I hadn't seen Joan or Kenny for twenty years.

Know or knew?

"If you had to describe him to a stranger, what would you say?" she asked.

"There was always something up with Kenny. You know? A project, a plan, a trip, a phone call. Things he couldn't wait to share. The next big idea. It was always something. You wanted a word? One word? I'd say … restless."

"You got that right."

"Read the great books. Folk music in the village. Walk into a black bar in Newark. Take over student government."

"Catch up with Joan Simmons," she said.

"That too, I guess."

"But with Kenny, it's never enough … one thing. He's always looking for something else. The insurance … Gooker wasn't wrong … it runs on its own. And he has all this energy. Even his hobbies. Golf one year, tennis the next, we had a boat in Atlantic Highlands for a while. He was always on the lookout for something special that would take over his life. Something he could put himself into totally."

"And then he remembered he was Jewish."

"He knew that all along. But Israel … that was what he was looking for."

"But … that didn't have to mean divorce …"

"Yeah, it did. You have to see it his way. There's a kind of logic. If it were the kind of commitment he was looking for … total … I was a goner. Anything I could come along on would be … near beer."

"Now I get it," I said. And I did. That would be Kenny, over-the-top and all-out. No trailing spouse, no next of kin. The only question—which I decided to save—was whether Kenny gave up his old life to find a new one or choose a new one to lose the old.

"How about you, George," Joan asked. "Have you changed?"

"There's a difference of opinion," I began. "Some say, yes

I've changed. Others say, no." It surprised me how easily this talk came to us, this resumption of intimacy after years of not knowing. "It goes on from there. One school of thought says I've changed too much. The other says, too little."

"Sounds like you've got people talking about you, at least."

"Maybe. But it's nothing that I hadn't thought of myself. What about you?"

"Post-Kenny, you mean?"

"Yeah. What now?"

"Beats me. I spend a lot of time wondering how to get from here ... to there."

"Where's *there*?"

"Out ... away ... gone. Any suggestions? You've been all over."

"Let me think about it," I said. I doubted an answer would come to me soon. She was New Jersey. She was on the inside looking out and I was on the outside looking in and what it came to was what the old man liked to call "the same difference."

"Well, if you think of something," she said, sitting up, looking ready to leave, "put it in a letter. Or call me. I'm in the book."

"You know what I'd like to do?" I said. "Tonight?"

She didn't say yes, she didn't say no, but she listened for what was coming and that made me feel like I was back in high school with her, not certain if I was asking too much, which was wrong, or too little, which was also wrong. Poised between two kinds of regret, I tried to ask for something that was just right.

"I'd like us to take a ride. Just around."

"You're on," she said. She smiled.

Cruising past shopping centers and drive-ins that were almost as old as we were, she took control of the radio without being asked to—I liked that take charge touch—and stopped turning when she ran across Frankie Valli keening "Big Girls

Don't Cry." I told her about God-the-D.J.

"That's what I like about New Year's Eve," she said. "The only thing I like. The way they play old songs, counting down through the years."

"It's a little too soon to give up," I said, echoing what Pauline Kennedy told me. "You were always smart. You still are. And you're still looking good."

"Tell me about it."

"You're looking better, actually."

"Are you hitting on me, George?"

"I don't know," I said.

"Well, when you decide … tell me, okay?" She laughed and curled up on the seat, like we'd been going steady for awhile. "Same old George," she said.

We turned off the highway and drove up into the Watchung Mountains through Mountainside, New Providence, Berkeley Heights, past houses where people we used to know used to live, where their parents—one or both—still sometimes lingered, but most had turned over, houses devouring generations, so that the realtors' signs seemed to say *fill me*, *feed me*, *next!* We talked about everyone we knew and when we got to the end of that, silence came, but it wasn't empty silence, because the open window gave us the summer night, full, heavy, just at the edge of turning, and the radio kept pumping out oldies but goodies, so the silence was alright, it was better than okay, because there was no place else we would rather be than in a car, driving around, with Buddy Holly singing "True Love Ways."

"You know where to, now?" I asked and I expected her to tense, guessing whether I wanted to take her to a motel or something, but that wasn't what I had in mind.

"Yes," she said. "I know."

"Where?" I challenged, feeling in control. "I'll bet you don't."

"The thirteen bumps."

"Jesus!" I said. "You got it."

Five minutes later I turned up onto Johnson's Drive for the first time in twenty years. This was memory lane time, jolting over the 13 speed bumps that led up to the main part of the road, which ran along a ridge right above Route 22. Memory Lane? Lovers Lane, too. This was where we used to park. There were other places, better maybe, dark and secret sites all over Watchung Reservation, but they didn't have the view from Johnson's Drive. From here you could look down at the river of highways, the shopping malls, where search lights panned the skies when new stores opened. You could sight across the sprinkled lights of the suburbs all the way to where Goethals Bridge arched over to Staten Island. And—though it took a clear night—sometimes, beyond the salt meadows, beyond Jersey City's humping shoulder, you could spot the topmost stories of Manhattan's tallest buildings. It was a wonderful place to feel romantic: an aching, yearning, promontory place. I could feel it now, an enormous surge of memory, a whole wave of wanting, when New York City was in the direction of my dreams, so that I could sit for hours with Joan or sometimes Kenny and see my future on the horizon, twenty miles east. That was high school, senior year.

"Does anybody come here anymore?" I asked. There were new houses on both sides of the road.

"Are you kidding? Kids don't park in cars anymore. They've got vans. They've got summer places. They've got their parents' permission."

"Oh." I felt silly. Parking up here now, I wasn't acting my age, I wasn't even acting like a kid. I was acting like the sort of kid who didn't exist anymore.

"Are you surprised, George? Disappointed?"

"I don't know." But I did know. I knew as soon as I came

around a curve and found a little road that led to a clearing, a cul de sac we shared with some beer cans and a tipped over shopping cart. Unbuildable lot, unbeatable view. When I snapped off the headlights, it felt like I was turning off a bedroom light, not to sleep but to dream, dream of a boil of lights that stretched out forever, highway lights and refinery beacons and planes circling over Newark Airport and the far touch of the Manhattan skyline, like a first glimpse of Oz.

"Wow," I said. "I'd almost forgotten."

"Not me," she said. "We used to come up here and … let's face it … as far as sex goes …" She laughed. "You weren't about to … I mean, even if I was willing … You weren't going to …"

"Pathetic."

"All I'm saying is that I loved sitting up here and looking out and talking. I loved talking to you. You bubbled over with things. And I wished …" She turned away. "I wished that I could hang in there with you a little more. That's what you never knew. You were going places. And I wished I could've come with. I missed out."

"We both missed out, maybe."

"And if we'd connected, that wouldn't have changed things, would it? Should it? You'd have gone anyway. You were headed out, it was written all over you. And I was staying."

"And here we sit."

"Yeah." I ran my thumb, then the side of my hand over the tip of her cheek, feeling for tears and finding them and she watched me do this, eyes-wide. "You must think I'm such a mope, George. I'm not. I do lots of things. Read. Take classes. Ordinarily, I'm okay, considering. Really. But seeing you at the diner tonight … and coming up here now … it makes me thoughtful."

Now she fished in her purse for some Kleenex to dab her face with, then a cigarette. The tears were gone now. I sensed a change in her, a shift of gears. She looked at me as if she hadn't decided what to do with me. Or as though she wanted me to decide what to do with her.

"So," she said. "Did you ever get to your big three?"

"What?"

"You used to go around saying there were three places you had to see before you die. You wanted to see Tahiti because it was the most opposite from New Jersey. Remember?"

"What were the others?"

"Mount Kilimanjaro, because of some Hemingway short story. We even went to see the movie they made out of it at the Strand, down in Plainfield. I remember you said it was nothing like the story."

"That I remember."

"And you were already doing research. You told me that the thing about Kilimanjaro was you could walk to the top of the mountain. No ropes or pitons needed. Did you ever make it?"

"Not quite to the top," I confessed, uncomfortable with the implication that I hadn't scaled the peak. "You can walk it alright. But the altitude gets to you and there's no way of knowing about that until you try it."

"The thin air got you."

"Yes," I said. "The air."

"What about Tahiti?"

"Easy. I've been there a half dozen times."

"God, you used to get excited about Tahiti. You said it right here. You said it was as far away as you could get from New Jersey."

"It's gotten closer."

"And Tibet?"

"Soon."

"You don't sound so excited about it."

"Because ..." I leaned back in the seat, hands behind my neck, and stretched. She was good at asking questions; in no time she was hitting the same sore point the old man had been pounding at for years. "By the time I get to a place, the game's already over, Joan. It's on the circuit. Airlines, hotels, tours, the whole drill. I'm the leader of the pack. I travel alone, but there are plane loads and busloads behind me, which is something I don't always feel good about."

"So tell me something about Bangkok. You mentioned Thailand and Gooker started to go into orbit."

"It might have been a great city once," I said. "Or pleasant, anyway. You still see traces, canals and temples. The people are still there and the food. But it's cars and traffic and smog. Gooker might still get turned on. There's plenty of action, that's for sure. But I don't like to write about the place."

"Why not?"

"Because I started out discovering the world as it is. But these days, I sell the world as it's not. Anyway, don't rush off to Bangkok. It's a Buddhist Los Angeles."

I heard an intake of breath, in, not out, as if I'd jabbed her.

"What's wrong?" She was looking out the window now, struggling with herself.

"George?"

"Yes?"

"I haven't even been to Los Angeles. Las Vegas is as close as I got."

I turned towards her. I touched her forehead, ran a finger over her face, turned it my way. I pulled her towards me and we kissed and in a moment we had gotten as far as we had ever gone. Our catching up. And what started as sympathy started turning. She was still something. I felt her nestling against me. I drew her closer. Joan Simmons! Gentlemen, start your engines!

"My God!" she said. She went with it awhile. Now she

stopped. "We're necking! We're parking on Johnson's Drive and necking." She glanced towards my hands. "You're feeling me up!"

"If the cops come by and shine a light in here ..."

"You'd better take me home, George."

These days she lived in an apartment just off the highway in Scotch Plains. It was the sort of red-brick, fifty-unit complex that used to be called a garden apartment, mostly because the developer tucked a few Japanese yew trees onto a patch of crab grass and left just enough room for a tripped-over tricycle and a Korean-made hibachi. We parked in front. I switched off the ignition, pushed in the headlight switch and wondered what would happen next.

"I've got a confession to make," she said. Oh no, I thought, here it comes: a younger boy toy stretched out in front of the television, a hard-body stud-muffin with a remote tuner in one hand, a beer in the other, please don't tell Kate and Gooker. She took her time about it, though, lit a cigarette and inhaled slowly, the way they do in the movies, only *after* they've had sex. The smoke trailed out the open window, out towards the highway. I tried picturing what life was like in these garden apartments. Joan and her boyfriend. What would their program be? What would *our* program be? Rent a couple movies at Video Shack? Watch *Blue Velvet*? Surf-and-turf specials at the Bull and Barrel? Take a place down on the shore next summer, sand in your shoes, steaks on the grill, Springsteen on the radio?

"I always thought of you as the chance I'd missed," she said. It jolted me, the timing and the content. It wasn't about a boyfriend. It was me. Holy shit, it was me! "The chance I wish I'd taken. Swear to God. I thought about you plenty. Once a week, anyway. Then I saw you sitting there in Irene's when Kate and I stepped out of the ladies' room, where she'd been telling me about this guy ... and I saw you and I said, oh my God, is this my reward or punishment?"

"That's for you to decide."

"What I've decided, is that it wouldn't feel right for us to go inside tonight and ..."

"So it's just like the old times after all. I drop you off and drive home."

"I don't like the picture. You walk into a diner and I'm there like I never left—which let's face it, I haven't—and you pick me up and drive me around and we go home to this ..."

"I understand," I said, cursing myself. If not now, when? If not me ... who? Somewhere over in Basking Ridge I heard Gooker laughing at me. You idiot, he shouted. Go for it! What's your strategy George? Wait another twenty years and tackle her in the old folks home? Unwrap those ace bandages and party on down? Go for it!

"It seems tacky." Case closed. She reached for the door, opened it, stepped outside and walked around the front of the car.

"Open the door," she said, when she reached my side. I obeyed. I started to move.

"No," she said. "Don't get out." With that, she leaned down and moved in towards me and her lips were on mine, lingering, not like the chaste pecks—kiss offs—I remembered. Our mouths opened.

"So ... good night."

"Good night, Joan." I flipped on the headlights, turned the key, found reverse and started backing away.

"George?" she called out.

"Yes?"

"You're still a good kid."

I nodded and wondered what she'd meant by that, all the way home. Then I pulled into the driveway, that crunch of gravel, so familiar, signaling safe return, journey over, not getting laid again. "You're still a good kid." Walking across the grass—dew soaking my shoes and socks—I found my way into the zone of ghosts, the picnic table, home of uncles with suspenders and beer steins, sweaty, smothering *tantes*. The grass underneath the table was still tentative, after all these years, rutted from where they put their feet while they sat and ate.

IX.

I HAD TO GET UP LAST NIGHT AND GET A blanket. My old bones can tell: autumn just around the corner. *Herbst*, in German. Autumn sounds better, fall better still. I have to admit it. German is damn awkward. I could start a list. There's this little insect that flits around flowers in summertime. Now in English, they call it a butterfly. That's cute. You picture yellow wings and pure food and dairy cows munching through green pastures. The French call it *papillon* and that's nice too: lacy, fragile wings catching every little breeze. So what do Germans come up with? We call it a *schmetterling!* Can you believe it! *Schmetterling.* Like a combination of Schmeling, heavyweight boxer and Messerschmitt, World War II fighter plane. The German language turns a butterfly into something that you'd expect to drop out of a cloud bank and strafe a column of refugees.

Schmetterling. Schnitzelbank. Schmeling. My brother's friend and hero. They shared fights together, Young Stribling, Steve Hamas, Mickey Walker, Max Baer, Jack Sharkey, Paulino Uzcudun, Joe Louis. That's a lot of fights. And one more after that, a humdinger! World War II. I never thought so much about my brother as I did during the war, when I worked hard on the tanks that might kill him. The cannon, the machine gun mounts and—what made me shudder—the treads that might flatten his body. And oh, those pictures they loved printing. Dead Germans, dangling out of charred tanks in Africa, frozen solid in Russian winter. How could he not be among them, dying while the world cheered? Dying in newspapers, newsreels, comic strips and movies. And then, those incredible columns of prisoners marched away from Stalingrad, long dark columns like skid marks on the snow, off into white nothingness. Dying. Like Max Schmeling was supposed to have died. Back in 1942, Max was in the paratroopers. Somewhere in the Mediterranean … was it Crete? … he made a jump. And a report surfaced that he'd been killed in battle and there was a cartoon that showed him with his hand raised in a boxing ring and next to that, in uniform, on the ground, bleeding. That was what was supposed to happen to him. And to my brother.

I wrote Max Schmeling after the war. I asked Max Schmeling, did he know what happened to his old friend Heinz Greifinger. Schmeling was scuffling around for fights then, the newspapers said, trying a comeback that led no place. I wrote him care of the mayor's office in Hamburg, one of a million such letters that went around Europe after the war, addressed to bombed out houses and people who were gone forever. Dead letters, alright. But I heard back. Max remembered me. And he'd seen Heinz in 1943, he said, home from the Russian front—good news—wounded, but lightly—good news—and headed back. Bad news. The worst.

Anyway, autumn. All my life, I've tried imagining if my life were a single year, what season am I in. When I was thirty, was that summer? When I was fifty, was that autumn? Now, no doubt about it, I'm in winter, killing frosts behind me, ground hard-packed. And you know what else I wonder? Take a piece of the time remaining, a week say, and ask yourself how much of your life that's left that week is. A tenth? A half? But there's a problem with these guessing games, because you assume you'll have a full year, you can count on getting to see all the seasons roll. It doesn't work that way. Take my wife. Cancer didn't wait for winter.

X.

"GOOD MORNING, POP." I FOUND HIM IN THE CELLAR, wrapping newspapers. We'd been through this before: the Boy Scouts were too lazy to come in the house and tie things up anymore. They stuck a notice under the door, announcing the truck would go up and down the street and after that it was up to you.

"It's afternoon," he said. "Lend me your finger, will you, George." I placed a finger on the string, holding it tight while he tied a knot. He was wiry and deft. He was still strong.

"Now the magazines." A pile of *Consumer Reports, U.S. News, Travel and Leisures*. Not the *National Geographics*: he still kept them on a shelf, next to the same dark closet where he kept beer, apples, and herring, rollmops he made himself. I wondered why he kept them: to me, they ranked with those rows of *Readers' Digest Condensed* books that were the pride of otherwise print-less households. But he held onto them the way he held onto old license plates.

"You used to make wine down here, didn't you Pop?"

"A time or two. We bought the grapes in south Jersey, an old Italian over in Millville. Applesauce we made too, when you were little."

"I remember the wine. Whenever you had parties, you gave me a couple glasses, so I'd get sleepy. I remember falling to sleep, like I was in a boat that was rocking, and I'd hear all of you outside singing those German songs."

"During the war, someone called the cops on us. Figured we were having a Nazi rally or something, like maybe we were toasting some spies who'd just landed off of Sandy Hook. But it was just a beer party. We sang the Horst Wessel song. The International, too. Anything we knew, we sang. Home on the Range …"

"I remember."

He kneeled beside a pile of old magazines, lifting it up, squaring and smoothing the edges to make an orderly bundle. "They run down these eighty-year-old Latvians or something they say were Nazis. What are they going to do when all the Nazis are dead? The world will be an empty place. The way I see it, they made a mistake at Nuremberg, hanging what was it? Thirteen? They should have stretched it out. Start with the oldest, a trial every four years, like the Olympics. Make it last."

He stood by his workbench, everything neatly sorted, coffee cans full of nails and screws, hammers, pliers, screwdrivers, files and chisels along the wall. Everything was in order. It got on my nerves, this German thing about control, self-control, the illusion of control. And now this aria on Nazi-hunting. Maybe he was just in a mood.

"Pop …" I stood in front of him. "What did you want to talk about?"

"This house is as old as you are, George, just about. A few years older."

"It's a nice house," I responded. It sounded flat, but I didn't know what else to say.

"Nice," he said. "Yup. Only I never thought it would end so quickly. Be over so fast. The thing of it is, I thought a house was different from a car that you wore out or traded in. I thought a house was where your life continued, sort of, after you were gone. That's not the way it works, is it? Not in this country."

He leaned towards me, staring hard. A watery stare, though, diluted by old age and old feelings. "Not the way it works in this neighborhood. No sir."

"Pop," I pleaded. "What do you want from me? You want me to tell you it's not Germany, it's America?"

"I know that."

"That it's not the twenties? It's the eighties?"

"Know that too," he said, turning away. "I know something else, too. An old saying. *Kein Haus, keine Heimat.* Know what that means? No house, no homeland."

"I suppose you're talking about me."

"If the shoe fits," he said, pausing at the bottom of the cellar steps.

"You want me to take the house?"

"I offered."

"With you in it?"

"Now that you mention it, I'm just wondering. When did it become such an all-of-a-sudden bad idea, parents and kids in the same house? Your generation, George, you guys changed things. You put your kids in day care and your parents in nursing homes. Congratulations, to you. You're free as a bird. How much do you think I'll be able to sell this place for?" With that, he turned and headed upstairs. So that was it! He was selling the house! He'd said what he had to say and now he left me in the cellar, as if I needed to be left alone to consider his disclosure. I decided to play along, the way people do when they call for a moment of silence in memory of someone who's died. You tilt your head down. Maybe you close your eyes. It's like kissing, that way. Usually you're wondering what's for dinner and what are other people thinking and is a *moment* of silence the same as a *minute* of silence. But I gave the old man his minute.

I looked around the cellar. Furnace and tool bench, laundry

sinks and cool closet, smelling of apples, onions, herring-in-brine. In my mind I traveled upstairs, into the kitchen nook, then the dining room, where they played pinochle, the bedroom where my mother had died, the living room, where on chilly days Pop and I napped on the floor, butts against a radiator. I paused at the mantel, row and row of pictures of somber-faced Germans. Then I went upstairs, a converted attic with two rooms. One was a guest room. For a while it belonged to a grandfather—on Mom's side or Pop's, I couldn't remember. He stayed a few years and then he went back over there. We played a card game on his bed, which was covered by a billowing feather quilt. War, the Americans called that game. Germans called it *Auf Leben Und Tot*: of life and death. My grandfather. I hadn't thought about that old man in years. There was something wrong about that. Something was wrong with me. I made my way up the steps and found my old man in the kitchen nook, waiting for me to disappoint him.

"It's a seller's market, George," he said. "You'd better believe it. The place is in good shape and the location ... well you know what they say. Or maybe you don't. But the three most important things in real estate are location, location, and location. And you know something else?" He was piling it on, real estate talk, rubbing it in. "All these offices that are moving out of New York—corporate headquarters, clean industry they call it—they're making people rich out here. I can name my price and there's no reason I can't get it. Everybody else has."

"I don't know Pop ..." I held up my hands, shook my head, looked around the place, which had been our only place, and our place only, and I realized how I'd gotten used to knowing that he was here, at home. Gooker was right. As long as parents lived at home, the center held. We were still in it together. Once they left, it was all kaput.

"Why keep it?" he asked. "Why save it? Am I saving it for you? Just say the word ... say yes."

There was nothing to say. Was I supposed to argue about family, when I had none? Or about the importance of roots? In the suburbs? Of traditions? In New Jersey?! Should I pretend that I could see myself living in this house?

"I'm selling your home, George. I just told you that. And I take it you've got nothing to say."

"Where will your home be, Pop?"

"Where's yours?"

"Pop ... why are you doing this to me?"

"To you? I'm not doing anything to you. I just wanted you to come out and answer me and you have. Now, I guess you'll want to be heading back to the city." He started running water over some plates in the sink. "You'll want to beat the rush hour traffic."

"Rush hour traffic goes the other way, Pop."

"You could sit outside the Holland Tunnel for hours. Or the Lincoln."

"On Sunday?"

"And I guess you've got lots of stuff to do there."

"Pop, I'm asking you ... where are you going?"

"I've been asking you the same question for years, George. You tell me."

"Pop!"

"I asked first." He stood by the front door, ready to drop me off at Two Guys from Sicily. For years we joked about how unsubtle he could be. When we were visiting somewhere, he'd suddenly get up out of his chair and start pacing, while I rushed dessert and Mom made excuses for him. Some people thought he was restless, some thought he was rude. It's how he was. Now it was time for me to go. Looking at him, I could see I made him uncomfortable.

"Could we talk about this some more, Pop?"

"Sure we can," he said. "Sure we can talk. Better yet, write me a letter. You know how much I like getting mail."

PART THREE

I.

Faraway Places, Backyard Adventures

by George Griffin

> What are we to make of the fact that New England's finest, richest harvest is not of fish or lumber, not of blueberries or maple syrup, but of leaves …

Don't forget those factory outlets, an inner voice heckled. I'd been re-reading a series of columns I'd started a year before, a series interrupted by an unexpected junket to Antarctica. Now I returned to the unfinished project. The idea was to cover the turning of the leaves, north to south, Maine to Florida. Now I planned to resume. And no one, I was sure, would complain that two autumns had been combined into one. Autumn wasn't exactly breaking news.

I glanced up from my typewriter, out onto the street. Summer lasted longer in New York. Leaves on sidewalk gingko trees, green as ever, hung limp and listless, pleading for the first frost to put them out of their misery. But it was still warm enough for the Puerto Ricans to brown bag it on the stoop across the way, tossing poptops and bottle caps into the street. And it was still warm enough for traffic to pound the stuff into the pavement, which was as close as anybody would get to the immigrants' dream of streets paved with gold. Summer in New York. But, like a model forced to wear fur coats in August, I conjured dreams of seasons yet to come.

> ... and, if only it were possible to position oneself on Maine's northernmost border, a sentinel against a change in the weather, eyes out for the forest, the tree, the very leaf that would be the first to change. The first, the very first sign of a death and glory beyond counting ...

Leaf peepers, they called them, and they came up by the busload from the south, as if to meet the invasion from the north. Autumn in New England was death like it ought to be, full and flaming, every year. That was the rub. Trees were perennial. People were annuals: one growth, one death. Maybe that's what was bothering the old man.

> ... a fascinating process, days growing shorter intimations of mortality, photosynthesis—the life process itself—slowly faltering, chlorophyll withdrawing, carotenoids, unleashing oranges, anthocyncnins exploding into blazing reds and lustrous lacquered browns ...

The oldest, corniest story in the world, maybe. It reminded me of the essays we wrote in grade school, when we were encouraged to be creative: Mother Nature skipping through a forest wonderland, palette can in one hand, brush in the other, daubing every leaf a different color.

> ... a blend of summer rains and autumn winds, warm days and cold nights. No death the same, no life identical, each season inevitable and unique ...

Could we put this to music? I wondered. What a cliché! I guessed I was drawn to these hackneyed stories, just to see if I could make them work, one more time. Virtuosity and cynicism came together on jobs like this, like a gourmet chef re-inventing meat loaf.

I switched on the television, flipping from channel to channel, MTV, sports, pornography, news, we'd come a long way from the days when everybody watched the same shows. And there, plain as day, was my old friend, Kenny Hauser, sitting with an Englishman, an Arab, a couple newspapermen, and an Oriental woman moderator, a low-rent Connie Chung. I knew him right away, before his name flashed on the screen. Smart, funny Kenny Hauser, still overweight, still disorganized, a half inch of calf flashing between cuff and socks. I backed to the kitchen, eyes still on the screen and pulled out a beer, not wanting to miss a second. It was odd, I knew it even then. Not miss a second? I'd missed twenty plus years of Kenny. Now, something had hooked me and was reeling me in. I sat on a hassock a yard from the screen. Kenny! Kenny on a local panel show dealing with Israeli settlements on the West Bank, Kenny on the side of the settlers. The show was well along, and the Arab must have mangled his English badly, because everyone disregarded him. But the Englishman was taking up his part, asking Kenny some hard questions.

"Now let me see if I have it straight, Mr. Hauser," he said, all full of snotty English politeness. "When Hitler takes territory—'Lebensraum'—from Poles and Czechs and calls it his '*Drang Nach Osten*,' that's perfectly deplorable. The world protests. And when American pioneers take land from the Indians and call this process 'Manifest Destiny' that, too is deplorable ... or, at least, regrettable. Now, when Israel plants its settlements on the conquered West Bank and by way of justification refers to the Old Testament concept of 'Yretz Ysrael,' then that is not deplorable, and not regrettable."

I admit it tickled me to see Kenny put on the spot. And yet, though I had every reason to relish seeing Kenny Hauser nailed by the hard-charging Englishman, I found myself waiting for him to pull off the kind of wacky off-the-wall gambit he used to come up with in student council or debate club or Boys State, the last minute launching of a secret weapon that sometimes shot into orbit, sometimes toppled over at the launching pad, but always made things interesting and fun.

He didn't even try! Or so, at first, it seemed. Sure, he made some kind of response, impressive enough, but only if you didn't know what Kenny could do. I heard him mention some U.N. Resolutions, and the Balfour Declaration, and the Old Testament, but it was plodding and mechanical. He sounded the way I used to sound, when we debated together, when he pleaded with me to insert some "snap, crackle, and pop" into my presentation. And the British antagonist, the Oxford Union style debater, dripping irony, kept hammering away, arching eyebrows, sighing heavily, playing to the cameras and claiming victory. That was when Kenny got him.

"It seems that we don't agree," Kenny said, a flabbergasting simplicity which stopped the Brit cold. "I guess that's why we're here."

"True," he said.

"Too bad. Smart men arguing. I'm smart and our Palestinian friend is smart and you're smart. Maybe even as smart as you think you are. How old are you, anyway?"

"I don't see what ..."

"Just asking," he said. Something was up. Kenny sounded

like a Jewish uncle on early television show, echoes of George Jessel, Danny Kaye. That wasn't his way of speaking. "Of course, if it's a sensitive point."

"Thirty two," the Brit snapped. His father had been a celebrated iconoclast, back home. The son had transplanted that persona to a richer market. An Oxford Union hit-man. So I was rooting for Kenny, after all.

"Thirty two," Kenny repeated. "And … you don't mind my asking … you're not from this country?"

"This is absurd," the Brit asked, turning to the host. But she was intrigued as well. Even the PLO guy seemed amused. "I don't see what this contributes, Mr. Hauser, but it should be perfectly clear where I'm from."

"England, I guess. If not, I've got to hand it to you, you sure do have the accent down."

"It's not an accent, Mr. Hauser. It's the way the English language sounds."

"Well, thanks. That's an extra treat. My last question, I promise. You've been a citizen here, for how many years?"

I loved it. The taxi driver manner, the yenta inquisition, the ruptured, tacked-on clauses. Go, Kenny!

"I'm a British subject …"

"Okay," Kenny said, "enough already. Too much, maybe. I apologize. I hope I haven't gone too far. Forgive me."

Enough already! Earlier they'd been thrashing about dual loyalty, conflict of interest—American Jews, Jewish Americans, the whole drill. Now Kenny had exposed his adversary as a stateless talking head with dual loyalties of his own. Maybe, no loyalties at all. A global ambulance chaser.

"Forgive *you*?" the Brit said. He was fast on his feet, it turned out. "I can forgive all sorts of things, Mr. Hauser, including your kitschy, pandering persona. There are other things at stake here and more lives than your own, which remain at gravest risk as long as you defend the policies of a belligerent, theocratic garrison state, zealous at home and manipulative ... endlessly manipulative ... abroad."

"Back to Israel," Kenny said with a sigh. "Not Syria or Libya. Garrison, belligerent, zealous et cetera, et cetera. No, not those. Israel. And manipulative. That clinches it. Israel for sure. So let me say my piece and I'll be brief, because we've been here a long time now and I'd like Mr. Massawi to have a moment before we close, okay, it only seems fair."

The moderator nodded agreement. Well done, Kenny, I thought. He'd determined closure. He'd speak, then the PLO representative. The Brit was history.

"You look in from the outside," Kenny said, facing the camera. "And it seems to you that lots of outrageous, unfair things go on over there. My friend, the British subject, has given you the list. Part of it, at least. Matters of land and law, employment, education, political power at home. Military action nearby. Manipulation abroad. Here, especially. Lobbying, propagandizing, you only have to read the newspapers, even the ones my friend says are slanted in Israel's favor. No end of problems. Granted. My problem is this. With all my best efforts—my cleverest manipulations—I still worry. I worry that, given a chance, even half a chance to destroy Israel—make that, destroy *and get away with it*—their neighbors would take it. That's my problem."

"You're part of the problem!" the Brit interrupted.

"Better a problem I know," Kenny retorted, "than a solution I don't."

It was time for the Palestinian to have his say. Then the credits flitted across and the names of the foundations that paid for the show and I saw Kenny leaning forward, chatting with the Palestinian, kibitzing even, while the British fellow sat rigid and angry. Then he was gone—Joan's husband. My old friend.

I thought things over for a while, some of the connections between then and now. Then I called New Jersey.

Looking out my window, I saw a Land Rover with Jersey plates moving slowly down the street, heading for a parking garage I'd recommended, proceeding cautiously, like an army patrol car in a newly-captured city where snipers lurked on rooftops. Five minutes later, I saw them on the sidewalk. They dressed like Jersey. In Joan's case, it wasn't unappealing: black slacks, shiny, maybe leather, maybe not, and a yellow blouse, frilly and silky, that made me hope she was spending the night. Kate had dressed somberly, in a suit-like thing that suggested she was visiting a kid who'd gotten into trouble at college.

I buzzed them in and waiting for them at the elevator. Kate was the first out the door.

"Welcome to New York," I said. While I hugged her, she looked over my shoulder at the room behind me, curious about what she had gotten herself into. I motioned her inside and faced Joan.

"I didn't know exactly what kind of clothing ..."

"You're fine," I reassured her. I held her hands, smiling at her, trying to run off her worries, though I had some worries of my own about this evening. "My house is your house."

A few words about my place. Costly. That would be the first word. Tenth and top floor, view of the park. Like all apartments, it started out empty. In a room off the kitchen—the maid's room, once—I made my original nest: a Sears card table, a typewriter and a hard chair. Poet's corner, monk's cell, whore's crib, this area where I worked. Bit by bit the place filled up and now I could look around and see trips I took, various Backyard Adventures and Faraway Places. A temple door from Thailand, a pair of hardwood-and-wicker chairs from the

Philippines, a wall full of batiks from Bali, some oversized book ends—ceramic cherubs—from Hong Kong, a kitchen loaded with state of the art Italian pots and pans and an espresso machine that, with all its valves and knobs, resembled the control panel of a submarine, Captain Nemo in command. The place disoriented people. And the group from New Jersey were no exceptions.

"How you doing, buddy?" Gooker asked when he arrived. Maroon jacket, wine-colored pants, blue-shirt open at the collar. "How long you lived here?"

"Years. Who's counting?"

"Oh." And then. "You planning on staying?"

"I'm not planning on leaving. Put it that way."

"I'll be damned," Gooker said. He studied an elaborate five-foot tall birdcage, a copy of a Victorian house, all porches and gables, I'd brought home from Sri Lanka, that sat between an Elvis lamp and a teak humidor. "Geez. The loot. Hell of a yard sale, you could have."

"People say, they can't tell if I'm just moving in or just moving out."

"Do you entertain much?"

"Mostly on the road," I said. "Or I go out."

"I figured, when I didn't smell anything cooking," Gooker said. "I guess all you need is a place to empty out your suitcase. And anyway, you got the city all around you."

"All around," I said, concentrating on opening a bottle of champagne that Iberia Air had sent over.

"You own this place, or what?" Gooker asked.

"I own it."

"You and the bank, huh?"

"No, just me."

"What's it ... a condo?"

"Co-op," I said, pouring into four long-stemmed champagne glasses. One of them had some packer's straw in the bottom. That would be my glass. "It's almost the same thing. Co-ops are a little fussier about who they take."

"I could do things with this," Kate said, looking around constructively. "It has possibilities."

"George doesn't need any hanging plants," Gooker argued. "It's a bachelor pad, is all. Okay if I explore?" I nodded and he headed down the hall, glass in hand. Sitting in the living room with Kate and Joan, half listening to Kate's remodeling schemes, something about how certain paints and papers could "bring the sunlight" into my room.

"What's the program?" Gooker shouted from down the hall.

"I thought we'd look around the neighborhood some, before we eat."

"I just parked ..." he protested.

"That's okay," I said. "We'll walk."

"Walk?"

"To the park. It's nice."

"Central Park!?"

"Relax," Joan said.

"Okay," I said. I appreciated her advice. In the few hundred yards we'd covered on Columbus Avenue, I'd commented on yuppies and gentrification. I'd chatted our way through a gamut of boutiques, chocolate chip cookie shops, ice-cream parlors and Korean fruit stands. Walking towards the park, I'd pointed out where Ed Bradley lived and Kiri te Kanawa, where John Lennon died, where Paul Simon and Carrie Fisher had wed. And, like a tour guide who wasn't sure of his customers' tastes—did they want to photograph? shop? meet natives?—I'd been hoping something, anything, would impress them.

"I just wanted this to work out," I said.

"It will or it won't," she shrugged. "Don't worry about them."

"I'm not worried about them," I said. "I was worried about you."

She smiled at that. "I'm glad you're worried ... that you care, I mean. But I don't want you to worry about me, George. Ever. That's a ground rule. Okay?"

"Okay," I said, sounding nonchalant, but my heart leapt. Ground rule, she said. Ground rule! Ground rules were what you established at the beginning of a game. Before you *played!* Did that mean we'd be playing a game? That night? A night game, yet! Is that what ground rule meant? Or did all of this over-calculation, this will-she-or-won't-she mean that I was back in high school?

Once you got them moving, Kate and Gooker were game. It wasn't the skyline that impressed them. It was the sight of a dog owner picking up his pet's turds with a glad-bag he'd put over his hand, then reversing the bag and depositing the package in a garbage can.

"I love it," he said. "Hey, George. It's like baseball or fly casting. It's all in the wrist."

"Fifty bucks if you don't pick it up and they catch you," I said.

"What's it for people?"

"Huh?"

"No kidding. On the way to your place, the block between your place and the parking garage, there's these two cars, a station wagon with Connecticut plates and Porsche and there's a bum taking a dump—Jee ... sus ... right on your doorstep, practically. They won't believe me at work."

"You sure?" The fact was the guys at Gooker's tire place would love this story, because for them New York existed as confirmation, not as reproach. They fed off bag ladies, rapes, muggings. The way kids built an imaginary world around their Lionel trains, they dreamed about what could happen on subways, and shuddered with pleasure when their dreams—other peoples' nightmares—came true.

"This reminds me of when we used to come into the City on class trips," Gooker remarked. We'd arrived at the Sheep Meadow. People were sunning themselves on the grass, flying kites, listening to the pennant race on the radio. There were musicians all over the park, playing for change, a Dixieland band near the bowling green, a guitarist doing Beatles stuff at Strawberry Fields and, right where we were, four black guys, puppeteers who moved bird-like figures to the dips and glides of 1950's doo-wop. The Moonglows' "Ten Commandments of Love." There was no getting away from those old songs. While Kate and Joan listened to the music, Gooker and I sat on a park bench. "We went to the United Nations, I remember. And the Statue of Liberty. What else?"

"The Museum of Natural History," I said. "That's right up the street."

"Oh yeah. They still got the dinosaurs? I guess so. It's not like you have to bring in next year's model, when you're talking dinosaurs. It's funny. Milk cartons! Whenever I think of class trips, I think of milk cartons." Gooker fell silent, trying to figure out his memory. Then he shrugged and gave it up. He noticed some women who came walking by, a couple sassy Latinas, sharp-featured, cocky, the f-word peppering their talk, their laughter.

"Wow!" Gooker said. "The hits just keep on coming! What I'd give for a shot at one of those. Both!"

"Hey," I said, gesturing at his wife and high school sweetheart, not ten feet ahead, arm in arm with Joan.

"Let me tell you something, George. Okay? You're not

married and I, as you just pointed out, am. You with me so far?"

"Yes."

"Try staying married to the same woman for a couple decades, and no time off for good behavior. Every time you climb on board, you know that's the same ride you'll be taking forever. Try it, George. You marry them ... well, you get laid before you marry ... and it's like driving a sports car, brand new, mint condition. Man, you're speeding, you're downshifting, you're laying rubber 'round corners, a Grand Prix driver. Shit! Couple years pass, kid or two comes along, she's something else, something Detroit-made, heavier, more power under the hood, more room in the trunk. Solid. Holds the road. Good mileage. Sort of car you can take for long trips and not worry about breakdowns, not if you've been giving her regular maintenance."

I nodded, awed by the ugly vitality of Gooker's metaphor. Which wasn't over yet.

"And then, more years, and you're one year older after every one of them, and you can't kid yourself anymore. If it drives like a truck, and steers like a truck, if it groans going uphill and runs over you going down ... it's a truck. And you, my friend, are a teamster."

"Jesus," I said. But he still wasn't done. Gooker was on a roll, the sort of effortless roll I used to think writing was like. Before I wrote. Gooker was a natural. Put a pencil in his hand, nothing would happen. Shove a tape-recorder on the table, silence would reign. But walking around the world, he was something else again.

"Which is where I am now. Teamster. But I see what's next. I see what I'll be climbing into. A slow-moving black limo that goes through traffic with the lights on. We're talking hearse. So there you have it. Every now and then I go joy riding. I take a spin in one of the sporty new models, foreign-made."

Gooker took over after that. He kibitzed with the taxi driver who took us down Fifth Avenue. He bantered with the drug dealers in Washington Square, high-fiving someone who'd offered him a nickel bag. "I could operate in this burg," he said, and it seemed he was saying it especially to me. In Soho, he feigned serious interested in an over-sized oil of an anorexic woman, something that would go good in his showroom. And, though Kate admonished him sometimes, whispering, tugging at him, rolling her eyes in what was supposed to be despair, I could see that she was loving it.

"Jersey comes to New York," Joan whispered.

"Does it ever," I said. "Gooker's a piece of work. A free-range chicken."

"You got that right."

"How about you, George? It's none of my business. You were married. You're single. What's it like? What are you like?"

"My old man says Germans are like pumas. We mate for life."

"That's your answer?"

"I've had affairs," I said. "Plus ... especially at the beginning ... a lot of room service."

"You sounded like you could be talking about visiting the dentist, 'Had my checkups.'"

"Had my checkups too. 'Look ma, no cavities.'"

"Why do I feel like I didn't get the whole story on Miss Thailand?"

"You didn't. It was a heart-breaker. We started out as friends She was in a jam. A government guy ... a Mr. Big ... was after her. Impossible for her to say no and keep her job. I helped her out. And we were lovers. I thought we were. But as soon as she arrived here, she was gone. I never even told my old man about her. Thank God."

"Are you still friends?"

"She's in town. She imports art. Has a shop on the east side. I stopped by once, just to see. I guess I remind her of bad times. It was complicated."

"Does that mean ..." I could feel her bristle. "Usually when people say, it's complicated, it means, I'll tell you, if you insist, but there's no way you'll understand it. Is that what you're saying to me, George?"

"No," I said quickly. She could be touchy. Jersey girl, sneaky smart, her intelligence a concealed weapon. "No. Complicated means I'm still figuring it out myself. Obviously."

"Another thing. *Obviously*. When people say obviously at the start of a sentence, in that certain way, well obviously, it's as plain as day, they think you should know it already."

"Okay," I said, holding up my hands in surrender. "Okay."

"It doesn't sound like a marriage at all."

"Not like my parents had," I said. Suddenly Mom and Pop seemed like people out of another time. They were still-lifes. When I pictured them, I saw old photographs, almost like the ones on Pauline Kennedy's book shelf. And it was odd, walking down a street in Soho, being reproached by the memory of them.

A stamped tin ceiling, white walls, dark booths crowded with slow, serious eaters: by New Jersey standards, the place I took them to was dingy. No barroom and the bathrooms were downstairs in the basement. The place didn't even have a parking lot. The most I hoped for was that my guests would find it "charming." And that they'd like the food. Italian food didn't travel well. Too far outside the Lincoln Tunnel, life went out of pasta, crust came off bread, tomato sauce was catsup and espresso was something you used when the package absolutely, positively had to be there overnight. But it had gone well.

"Hell of a feed," Gooker said, leaning back in his chair. "New York's great!"

"Well, happy birthday."

"Don't sing it, don't even think it," he protested, shaking his head. "No point trying to kid this group about my age. If I told you I'd been skipping grades on account I was brighter-than-average, I don't reckon you'd believe that one either."

"No," Joan. "You cheated off me."

"Count me in," Kate added.

"Well, come on! The stuff they taught us in high school. Latin? Would you believe it? Algebra. Anybody around this table used any algebra lately? Algebra help you do your income tax return?"

"What they were doing," Kate said, "what they were trying to do, was teach you how to *think*."

"Well you know what I *think*? I think spending six weeks on *Paradise Lost* at Rutgers was a joke. What were they afraid of? A shortage of poets? What'd I need that for? Was it gonna help us catch up with the Russians? You know how I know it's poetry? It's got a raggedy right hand margin. Other than that ..."

"What can I do with him?" asked Kate, mostly for my benefit. "No poetry in that man."

Boy are you wrong, lady, I thought, remembering how Gooker compared her to three kinds of moving vehicles.

"Poetry!" Gooker cried. "Don't start. Have I got poetry. That old bitch Kennedy pumped me full of it.

'When the values go up, up, up
And the prices go down, down, down
Robert Hall this season
Will show you the reason
Low overhead!
Low overhead!'"

That last bit, a clothing store jingle we all remembered, Gooker had sung. Now he subsided, triumphant. He'd gotten loud and people were looking our way, though not unkindly. That was Gooker. A pain in many ways, yet somehow it mattered how he was feeling.

"Well, she wasn't a bitch," Kate said after a while. "She was a role model."

"Yeah? Just what role was she trying out for? Wicked Witch of the West?"

"It couldn't have been easy, facing us every day," Kate persisted. "Plus she was a single woman. A professional. I always thought she cared."

"But what good was it?" Gooker pleaded.

"What do you think was good? Shop class?"

"Driver education! Donut runs! Plus, it helped you get your license and, if you passed, they cut a little off your insurance. That's useful. Later people buy cars. The cars need tires. They come to me. See?"

Kate threw up her hands. "I give up."

"Did you like the food?" I asked. "Really?"

"Dynamite!" Gooker exclaimed, bouncing right back. "Best meal I ever had."

"If you get in the habit of coming in, there's lots of other places we can try," I said. "Not just on your birthday." I caught an amused smile on Joan's face, as if to say, are you a sucker for punishment? But, I'd enjoyed this evening. Gooker swarmed with gambits, jokes, pretensions. Kate's pattern was subtler—sneakier, almost—but I sensed she was watching, calculating possibilities, risks, costs. With their kids almost grown, she might not be willing to sit in Basking Ridge, thumbing through *Architectural Digests* while Gooker "worked late" at the tire store. She might have a few surprises left in her.

"So," I continued, "let me say it before you say it. A great place to visit but you wouldn't want to live here."

"The thing of it is," Gooker said, "I've got obligations you don't have." He sounded like a general discoursing on command responsibility, a pilot navigating turbulent skies while heedless passengers picked at food trays.

"Kids?"

"It's a dirty job, but somebody's got to do it." He made it seem important that the twenty-first century not miss out on the next version of Kate and himself.

"Could you bring up a family here?" Kate asked. "I'm sure some people do … but maybe I'm old fashioned, I don't see my kids growing up in an apartment."

"Lawns and sprinklers in the summer, leaves in the fall—I still burn 'em, just for old times sake," Gooker said. "In the winter there's snow and snow men and shoveling snow. In the spring, mud and daffodils poking out from underneath."

I was flabbergasted. Gooker's version of the four seasons, delivered with absolute conviction. As though I had challenged him and he needed to defend himself.

"And sure, it would be easy to say it's for the kids, we live this way …"

"It is for the kids!" Kate interrupted.

"That's what we *say*" Gooker retorted. "But it's for the kids in us. All of it. The Little League, the Boy Scouts, Halloween and Christmas, the whole thing. Otherwise … let's face it … they're in college. What used to be home is just a stop-off now. A laundry. A bank. They're gone. But I don't see us moving anywhere …"

"Maybe we should," Kate said. "I like those lofts that George was pointing out."

"Yeah," Gooker said. "Sure. That'll be the day. We sell Basking Ridge and move into Fun City. Some place that's about the size of my tire showroom, only on the eighth floor, up a freight elevator, and I'll rent a porto-san we can put in a corner, behind a curtain. That appeal to you?"

"It kind of does, actually."

"Why?"

"Never mind. You wouldn't understand."

"Wouldn't understand, huh?" Gooker was annoyed. "The whole world moves out to the suburbs, am I right, on account of the schools and air and room. It's the American dream out there and I could make money betting that most of the people eating in this here restaurant and *all* of the people working in it would give their left nut to have what we have and here you are saying, oh honey, let's bag it all and move to town. Well, try me. I'll put on my thinking cap. Tell me why we have to move."

"It's nothing," Kate replied, jaws tight. "We'll talk about it later."

"Sorry, honey." He glanced at me. The hearse. "What's logic got to do with it?" He shrugged and turned to me, brightening. "I almost forgot," he said. "You need a reunion update." He reached inside his back pocket and pulled out a notebook. "We had 409 graduates in our class ..."

"George doesn't want to hear this," Kate said. "He's got another life here."

"He does *so* want to hear it," Gooker fired back, pleading with me not to correct him. "We have 180 deposits already, fifty bucks per head, covers room rental, dinner with wine and the D.J. I'll be telling you about in a minute. We got a cash bar ..."

Kate escaped with Joan to the lady's room. It was past the kitchen and downstairs. They'd be a while. Grateful, Gooker watched them go.

"She just doesn't get it," he said. "Where was I?"

"Deposits. One hundred and eighty so far."

"And a couple more in the mail, every day. And phone calls. Remember Bobby Eastman? His father worked for Korvettes, in sporting goods? Bobby calls and says for fifty bucks he should get some drinks. It shouldn't be a cash bar. Like I'm making a profit."

"Tell him I'll buy him a drink." The class clown. Imitations of Myron Cohen, Shelley Berman. A generation too late for the Catskills. "What's he up to?"

"Dogs."

"Pet shops?"

"Kennels. A franchise deal. Dog Heaven. Sounds more like a pet cemetery. But he's worth a fortune. Screw him. More important. Remember Carla Cordero?"

"Sure." Pleasant memory. In the days when you could call someone nice, she was nice. Too nice to date. But we'd talk for hours at the back of the school bus and I went over to her house sometimes. And I hadn't thought about her for years. But now, just picturing her made me feel good about the reunion. Her inscription in my yearbook had run to half a page. Now I wanted to go to the reunion, just to hug Carla Cordero.

"Dead," Gooker said. "Years already."

"Carla?"

"I spoke to her mother, retired down the shore. Spring Lake. Some kind of female cancer." He glanced up and saw his wife approaching, with a look that said she'd wait to use another restroom.

"You were going to tell me about the disc jockey," I said. Carla Cordero. I wondered how far she'd gotten beyond her picture in the yearbook, if she'd had time to grow into anything else or was that as far as she got. After years of absence, she'd come back to mind, flared right up, only to flicker out.

"The guy's a genius," Gooker said. "He's a young punk, name's Eugene Moretti, and I figure, that young, what does he know about when the music was good? This is for the class of 1964, I say. I don't want any folk music, protest music, psychedelic disco, rappity-hop-hip bullshit. He says, pick a week, any week, so I say, November 22, 1963, when Kennedy bites it, who remembers the music? And he rattles off the top ten, like that. Garnett Mims and the Chanters, 'Cry Baby.' You believe it? Got any requests, get 'em in now. I'm in. The Skyliners 'Since I Don't Have You.'"

"I liked 'This I Swear' better. The flip side."

"Also, 'Stay,' 'Silhouettes,' 'Tragedy.' Quick, who sang that one? His one and only?"

"Thomas Wayne," I answered. "Who do you think you're dealing with?"

"Sonofabitch!" Gooker cried and we started singing, on the way out of the restaurant. I thought we sounded good. I was sending it out to Carla Cordero.

At the end came one of those moments that gives you goose bumps. The taxi dropped us in front of the garage where Gooker had parked, a couple blocks from my apartment. Kate and Joan conferred. Then I looked at Joan Simmons, not knowing whether she was going to say goodnight to me or to them. We hadn't talked about it. I didn't know. She stood by my side while the attendant brought out Gooker's Landrover, which he walked around, checking for dents. She watched them get inside. Kate handed her an overnight bag. We waved as they drove around the corner and disappeared down Amsterdam Avenue.

"Wow!" I shouted as we headed across Broadway. I damn near jumped for joy.

"What is it?" she asked.

"You had me going there. I didn't know whether it would be a thank-you-for-the-lovely evening and you'd climb in the back seat of the Gooker-mobile. Or this."

"Well ... it's this," she said. "For the weekend."

As soon as we entered the apartment, I had her in my arms, right in the darkened foyer, like there were parents somewhere inside and we didn't want to wake them. I took her hand and led her down the hall towards the bedroom. She saw the mosquito netting, a muslin curtain hanging from the ceiling, draped over the edges of the bed.

"That," she said, "turns me on."

"Just come along." I led her to the side of the bedroom. "Close your eyes." I pulled back the curtains, slid back a glass panel, and led her out on to the terrace. I'd been saving it for her, for now. I guided her to the railing and, moving behind, put my head next to hers, let her back fit against my front. Then I told her to open her eyes.

"Oh my God, George." She was looking down at Columbus Avenue, traffic moving through staggered lights that you could watch changing, turning off onto cross streets, passing through the west side and curling into the dark rectangle of Central Park. Fifth Avenue was a line of battlements. Harlem was north. Ominous and dangerous. But the south side was spectacular, the way it caught the sun in the morning, pink and tentative, and lit up at night like the sky itself, a wall of stars. That never stopped pleasing me. It got to her, too, seeing it for the first time. She fell back against me, relaxed, folding into me. I heard her saying something, whispering. "God, god, god," it sounded like, "all the things I've missed." She leaned over the railing, like a kid at the edge of a wishing well. "It makes me thoughtful," she said, finally turning to me. "Wonder if there are kids out there tonight. In Jersey. Dreaming. Big city and all … ?"

"I hope they are."

"Yeah, well …" She turned and looked at me and the look said *now*. "Hey, George. This is the kind of talking people do in between stuff."

She disappeared into the bathroom. I sat on a chair and waited for her, wondering what was coming. Then I sensed someone standing behind me. She moved in front. She'd showered. She was wearing an old shirt of mine.

"I want this to be perfect," she said, taking a last drag on a cigarette. She moved towards me, took my hands and pulled me towards her. "But that would put the pressure on. With perfect there'd be nothing to top. So, slow dance, fast dance. Whatever."

We spent the weekend together, even Sunday night. It was funny, going around New York with her—street fairs, the park, Lincoln Center, a delicious afternoon nap followed by espresso in a backyard garden on a brownstone street. In the old days, when we'd come to New York together, it was as though we were discovering a magic city. We went to off Broadway plays I read about in the New Yorker, fun things like "The Fantasticks" and "Little Mary Sunshine," hip shows like "The Connection," terrifying ones like "The Blacks," when glaring black people lured sweaty-palmed ticket purchasers on stage to be baited and humiliated. We'd ridden hansoms through Central Park and, taking the wrong subway, gotten lost in Brooklyn, and we'd bought Ferlinghetti's *A Coney Island of the Mind* at the Sheridan Square bookstore. There was music at Gerde's Folk City or the Half Note Club. We were right back there, the nights we'd walk the streets off Washington Square, headed for Little Italy, singing songs from "West Side Story."

It couldn't last. I should have known, from seeing those mood shifts, how she could stop in mid-sentence to follow the trail of a thought. Monday found her in my kitchen, trying to make coffee. She was standing by the stove, wearing one of my shirts. The look on her face suggested something had just occurred to her: she was staring off, into the air shaft, following a thought.

"What is it?"

"This coffee machine of yours, I've been trying to figure it out." She confronted a device that cost $2,000 in Milan.

"Me too. I used to have an instruction booklet."

"You mean …"

"I call up the place, they hook it up and check me out on it. They train me. But I haven't gotten around to it."

"You've never gotten a cup of coffee out of this thing?"

"Not yet."

"How long have you had it?"

"Two years," I confessed, wondering whether the warranty began at the date of purchase or of first use.

"God!" She turned away from me and walked back into the bedroom. I followed and found her sitting at the edge of the mattress, her face in her hands, and from the way she was moving, something was happening under there, but I couldn't tell whether she was laughing or crying.

"Actually … I eat breakfast out."

"Yeah," she said, taking her hands away. "I guess you do." She looked around the bedroom: travel brochures and laundry bag and pieces of cardboard that came out of my shirts when they came back from the laundry. "What do you do with yourself, George?"

"Well, I'm on the road a lot …"

"No. Not then. Now. Days like today. If I weren't here today. Would someone else be here?"

"No. I'd be by myself. There are people I could call who'd be glad to hear from me. For dinner. Or a movie. Some of them I could sleep with. But not here …"

"What are you aiming for?" she pressed. "So you saw Kilimanjaro, Tahiti and maybe you'll see Tibet. But what do you want?"

"Whoa …" I said, raising my hand. "Could we have breakfast first?"

"I wasn't expecting … a house beautiful," she said. "You're alone. And I know you travel a lot. But this …"

"Okay. Maybe this won't make sense to you. The reason this apartment doesn't look like home is because it isn't. And the reason for that is that I've always believed I would find a place I'd know was the right place for me and that's when the books would come out of the boxes and the garden go in the ground and yes there'd be real coffee in the morning."

"And it's not here? The view and all?"

"I used to think it was. You bet. I spent most of my life thinking once I got here … that was it. An apartment with a view of the park. That was making it. That was happiness. But there's more to it than that. It's about the work I do and how I feel about myself. It's complicated."

"Complicated …" She nodded like she understood, like she was willing to leave things at that. She'd asked, I'd answered. But it didn't feel like the right answer. Things went downhill from there. A too quiet breakfast at Sarabeth's Kitchen. A quick return to the apartment to pick up her bag. A taxi ride to the Port Authority Bus Terminal. Whatever we'd had was slipping away. When we faced each other, we were almost strangers.

"See you," she said, heading up the escalator. Another of the rushed, nonchalant, noncommittal farewells she specialized in.

"Joan!" I called out after her, followed up the escalator. I hated seeing her walk up the escalator, helping the machine along, getting the weekend over with. "This is all wrong," I said. "The way you're going. Like we stepped out into the parking lot at the reunion and had a quickie in the car, for the hell of it."

"Do you think there'll be an awful lot of that going on?" she asked.

"Don't do this," I pleaded. "Don't joke."

"I've got to get back, George. You know that."

"I know."

"Okay." Now we were at the base of a second set of escalators that led up to the bus loading docks. Her expression softened as she came back to me. "I make this mistake sometimes that lots of women make. Men, too, maybe. I don't know. For a while there, I thought that you were someplace I'd never gone to. A place I'd never been. A place I wasn't sure I'd reach. I thought of you as a place. You know the old joke. *You can't get there from here*. You had. And I thought maybe I could too. With you. Follow?"

"Yes."

"I saw you at lrene's, I said, well there's a script for this movie after all. It's a movie, not an old scrapbook falling apart. But I put too much on you, George. You've got problems. You're lost too." She smiled at me. "Too bad."

"Come with me. Anywhere. You name it."

"Not possible." She had way of talking that was getting on my nerves. Those short non-sentences, as if language itself wasn't worth using now.

"I'll call you."

"Call. Write. Sure. Anything." And, turning away from me, towards the line of passengers: "Bye."

II.

Another one checked out. Overlook Hospital, age of 71, long illness—cancer, that means—leaving a son in Portland, Oregon, a daughter in Raleigh, North Carolina, a brother on the Jersey Shore. "Predeceased" by wife. Cliff, our old milkman, a nice fellow, even if he was a Yankee fan. The Italians I could always forgive for rooting for the Yankees, what with DiMaggio and Crosetti, Berra, Rizzuto and the rest. Milk and cream he carried in a wire basket and when he retired nobody replaced him. That son who's now in Portland didn't want to be a milkman, that's for sure. So that was the end of it. Well, I started a list of people who used to come up the sidewalk. The paperboy. First on foot, then on bikes, now their parents drive them on the route, end of story. A guy who sold cheese and another sold fruit and vegetables, a man who brought ice when you called and others who brought coal, all kinds of salesmen—not just Fuller Brush—and television repairmen in the days they tried to fix it on the spot. Doctors too, a million years ago. These days, the sidewalk waits a long time for the feel of feet, the front steps are mostly a place where I sit, waiting while the last and maybe the only person who made house calls comes up the sidewalk with a smile old Cliff would have envied. The realtor. The realtor still makes house calls.

"Putting it on the market" is how he expressed it. "Turning it over" was another phrase he used. He said the smart thing was to set a price that was high, a price that you were hoping for, but in the back of your mind you had a price that you'd be willing to take. I walked him through the house which he said was solid but choppy. Some walls would be coming out, he guessed. The yard impressed him—the rock garden, the rose arbor, the hemlocks along the edge of the property, the blue spruce in front. And the size, a double lot by today's standards. And the location. No problem in turning this one over, he said, and I wondered if I should tell him it's not houses that are turning over, it's people. Turning over and trading up, that's what he was about, as though this was God's plan for us, onwards and upwards forever. Would someone please straighten me out? What's the goal? A nation of 200 million people living in castles? I told him he'd be hearing from me, maybe. He gave me his card, he gave me half a dozen of them, raised letters on good stock, which I can use for book marks or to pick my teeth with. As soon as he left, I went into the cellar and made a sign. Three signs, actually, connected by a cord that runs through holes I drilled. I planted it right out by the mailbox and, sitting here this last half hour, I'd already seen a half dozen cars slow down and stop, the drivers fishing for pen and pencil. FOR SALE says the top part of the sign. BY OWNER says the middle. And there's a phone number on the bottom. George's number in New York, business and home. Me, I hate telephones.

III.

"Look homeward, angel and ..." The voice at the other end of the phone paused and waited for my reply.

"Melt with Sue!" I fired back. Sue Hoover, the Mansfield/Dors/Loren of our high school class. "Hello, Kenny."

"Ever wonder what happened to Sue Hoover?"

"Never," I said. "Or maybe once in a long while."

"Yeah," he said. "I know what you mean. Nightly."

"I like the idea of second chances."

"So I hear," he said. I guessed he knew that I'd seen Joan. I sensed tension. He had no grounds to attack me. They were separated. I was single. But a whiff of bird-dogging was in the air, of *she's mine, no mine, I saw her first, the hell you did, now it's my turn.* The phone silence stretched out. Two guys too smart to say what they were thinking. Not smart enough to have other thoughts.

"You want to get together?" I asked.

"Sure."

"So where do you want to eat?"

"I'll give you a hint. Did you see 'Marathon Man?'"

Perhaps Kenny thought that 86th Street was enemy territory, little Germany, a place where people kept quiet about their war records. He'd be disappointed. New York's melting pot may not have worked on people but it played hell with neighborhoods. I'd watched it happen here, the Gimbels, the RKO movie twins, the running shoe shops, Mexican restaurants, Korean fruit stands, salsa nightclubs. The place had been hit by more bombs and torpedoes than the *Bismarck*.

I came to the Heidelberg once in a while, just to confirm that it was still there, so that if the old man ever came to visit, I'd have a place to take him to. He'd knocked around here some when he was young, I recalled, and he'd had a brother who was a bartender, the one who went back to Germany just in time for World War II. Shrewd move. You had to wonder, sometimes, why more people didn't see things coming. Heinz. That was his name. His picture sat out on a wall-shelf in the living room, all the time I was growing up, this uncle in a snappy uniform, my mother in his arms. She'd gone back to visit, a year or two before the war. The grandparents sent the ticket, so that they could see her one more time, before all hell broke loose. I guess some people saw it coming after all.

Kenny was late. I ordered another Dortmunder and found myself thinking about the Nazi uncle. He was something of a sore point, or if he wasn't, the picture was. It was at the center of the only argument I'd ever heard my parents have. And I started it. It was around the fourth grade. I went out with neighborhood kids to build forts and tree huts. There were still woods in town then. We played softball and told dirty jokes. Some of us collected baseball cards, others had graduated to skin magazines. "Stroke books," Gooker called them. In no way was I the leader of the pack. But I did have an ace up my sleeve, and that was the German stuff. In a gang of nondescript Americans, that made me a little interesting, that blood connection to dark-uniformed villains. What were Indians, after all, compared to snappy Nazis? Playmates asked to come in the house and "see that picture," to see a woman recognizably my mother flanked by four men in enemy uniforms, their arms around her, everybody smiling. My friends would look—dumbstruck—and I'd usher them out. For a little while, I'd be something special. Now, here's the poignant part. My mother greeted the crew as they came in, tickled to death that her George was getting company. She'd be at the sink, up to her elbows in suds, she'd be doing something with swiss chard, she'd drop everything and offer milk and cookies to the bunch, as if every minute they were in the house, every bite and swallow, added to my popularity. And, watching them leave, she'd hope they'd come over again, anytime, we even had a badminton set we could put up in the backyard. On her own, God bless her, she'd never have figured it out. But the old man did.

"What's this parade into the house?" he asked one Saturday. He'd been working in the garden when a bunch of friends arrived —a special tour, including somebody's cousin from Connecticut. Now he was sitting on the stoop at the side door, in shorts and socks that curled up against an old pair of shoes. He was bare-chested, covered with sweat, the sweat dusted with peat moss he'd been spreading. And, as usual, he was drinking a Ballantine Ale.

"Maria," he shouted. "Come out here." It was the voice he used when something was wrong, a cut finger, a wasp sting, snails on the tomatoes. My mother rushed out. "You noticed the parade a while ago?"

"Those are George's friends," she answered proudly. "They come to play."

"Play what?" he asked her. Then me. "Play what, George?

"The picture," I confessed. "They want to see it."

"Which picture? Narrow it down for me a little. They were wondering what you looked like when you were a baby?"

"The one ..." I hesitated. I looked at my mother, certain this was the last second she would ever love me. "Mom's."

"Mom and me and you at the Catskill Game Farm?

"Mom ..." My eyes filled the way they always did when I screwed up.

"Hans ..." My mother said, but it was too late. My father had his hands on me, not to punish me, but to steady me while I told the truth.

"Mom and those soldier guys," I said. "The ... uh ... Germans. The kids want to see it. I don't know. They think it's neat. They think I'm neat, a little bit."

"Okay," he said. "Go inside." I did, up the steps, through the kitchen and into the nook, where I listened to every word they said, still blurry and sniffling.

"Take it down," he said. But it wasn't an order. The commanding tone was gone. It was a plea.

"*Du warst doch sein Bruder*," she said. I used to understand German, in a rough and ready way. "You were his brother, after all."

"*Ja*." the old man acknowledged. "*Das war Ich*." That I was.

"*Und sein Freund*." And his friend.

After a minute. "*Das war Ich auch.*" That too.

"He brought you over. He helped. Don't forget that." This, in English. And that was it. The next thing my mother came inside so fast, she caught me in the kitchen nook before I could sneak upstairs or even make it to the icebox, pretending to search for a snack. "No more parades," she said, returning to the sink.

"That looks tasty," a voice behind me told the bartender. "I'll have one. And this gentleman will pay ... and pay."

"Hello, Kenny," I said, shaking his hand. Crew cut, blue

eyes, overweight, a scuffed-up valise under his arm, a sense of deadlines and projects barely under control. Kenny. "It's good to see you."

"It's been about half a lifetime," he said, studying me closely. "You take me back."

"You do the same for me," I said. It was funny. Or sad. Of all my friends, he was the one I would have guessed would be with me forever. "When … I've been asking myself … was the last time we met?"

"Don't know," he said. He thought about it a moment. "Got me. For guys who take each other back, the way we always say we do, you'd think we could remember our historic last meeting."

"During college, it must have been. That first Christmas vacation, I couldn't wait to get home and compare notes. We even wrote some letters back and forth. But there was one vacation—spring break—you went away. The Caribbean. And it wasn't so important anymore, getting together. Once we missed a turn, we were off the track forever."

"I went to Jamaica," Kenny said. A pleased look crossed his face: a chance to score a point. "Joan went with me. We were both at Bucknell, remember? And I was chasing her. Had been. God! I won't say it was the only important thing I wanted to do in life. But it was the first. And Jamaica. George! That's where it happened. Big time!"

Was I going to hear about it, in detail? Was I going to listen? He might want to trade. I had to stop it. "Why are you telling me this?"

"Life's little ironies. If she'd gone to that place you went, you might have been the lucky man."

"I went to an all-male school. In Ohio! Remember?" And like that, we were past the rough spot. We both laughed and the beer—my third, his first—arrived. We toasted, no hard feelings.

I let Kenny decide what we would talk about. It was easy to do. Old patterns reasserted themselves. I remembered those dozens of tests we used to take, running neck in neck for the head of the class. I won Pauline Kennedy's A, but Kenny edged me everywhere else. The master test-taker of all time, murder on multiple choice exams, he unerringly detected the right answer, distinguishing the true from the not quite true from the palpably false. I was slower. Considering all the possibilities, I imagined situations in which the false answer might be true and the true, not quite. Important situations that needed to be pointed out, even to the people who devised the tests. While Kenny was circling answers, I wrote notes in margins, notes that would never be read, explaining things the teachers might have missed. My imagination cost me time, and points. But it also nudged me towards writing. Kenny was into choices. Now the word was that he'd chosen Israel. Lobbying, letter-writing, fund-raising, not for the government, but for orthodox, irredentist never-againers—the Gush Emmunim—who settled the West Bank.

Pigs knuckles for him, veal shank for me, sides of creamed spinach and red cabbage, double order of potato pancakes, the food was on the table. The waitress called us over. Kenny hefted himself off his stool, grabbing his briefcase off the floor. Man and briefcase, both overweight and out of shape and stuffed with plans. He held it out towards me.

"A million stories in here," he said. "Incredible. Things you wouldn't believe. Know any good writers?" He was needling me. But there was more. Joan had told me Kenny always wanted to write, he'd tried a couple things that were—Joan at her most succinct—"no-go." And then, with an absolute certainty that surprised me, as if she were giving me his weight or waist size, she added, "Kenny can't write."

"So, what do you think of her?" he asked.

"Fine," I said. "Terrific."

"Come on, George. It's not like we can't talk about her. We go back forever."

"I'm thinking about going forward."

"Whoa! We're playing it close to the chest this evening, aren't we?"

"My chest."

"Fair enough ... I'm not here to ... you know ... I've got no feelings of rancor."

"Why'd you marry her in the first place? That's what I can't figure out."

"What's to figure?" he flipped back at me. "Are you kidding? Joan Simmons! The gorgeous? The untouchable. And smart, besides? You're asking me why? What's wrong with you? She was your fantasy too."

"Okay," I said. "Yeah. She was." The beers were catching up to me and it was too bad, because I wanted to be sharp.

"Something I want to tell you," Kenny said. "I never told anybody this before. I'm sure Joan knows. Sooner or later she figures things out. Maybe you noticed."

"I noticed."

"Yeah, she packs it in, the highs and lows. She had better grades than I did, until she got pregnant and quit. Never got back. Sat there, in maternity clothes, typing my papers. Sucks, when I look back. We didn't know much, did we? About women, I mean. Could be, women didn't know much about themselves."

"Sure," I agreed. "We had a lot to learn. Was there something specific?"

"Yes," he said. "This. We thought we were learning about women when we were out chasing them, trying to get laid. Did you ever, by the way?"

"Damn it! Yes! Lots of times!"

"Okay, okay. Touchy, aren't we?"

"People keep asking. First Gooker, then you. Same question."

"Me and Gooker. That's a frightening alliance. Anyway, about women ... the sex we were after ... that was a lesson, no doubt. But it was only lesson one. Which we kept repeating because it was so much fun. More sex with this one. Different sex with other ones. It's like we were choosing to stay in kindergarten. 'Sure, teacher, just let us keep playing with these nice toys and we'll be alright.' That's arrested development, George. It kept us from moving on to the next lessons. Such as all the ways they're smarter than we are. Wiser, shrewder, savvier. We were hot shots, George, we really were. But we missed a lot. Anyway, the reason I went to Bucknell. Not Dartmouth or Connecticut Wesleyan. She was it."

"So what happened?"

Kenny reflected for a minute, poured himself beer, poured me some too. Then I caught him studying me and I guessed what he was thinking: why am I telling you this? You of all people? And then—I could see the grin when the thought came to him—why not you? Who else?

"Maybe it would have happened anyway," Kenny began. "You know me. A lot of ability and no clear calling. I tried some other things."

"Such as?" I'd had some answers from Joan but I wondered if he'd mention writing, if he'd take that chance with me, risking a confession of failure.

"Stuff ..." he said, shrugging. "Anyway ... what made it worse was ... I always saw what I was doing through her eyes. And what I saw looked second rate. She never criticized me, that way. I did it myself. I knew what she was thinking."

"So then ... Israel ... you discovered there was a war going on and you enlisted ..."

"Yeah," he said, sounding annoyed. "Maybe you're being funny. I don't know how seriously to take you these days. It comes from reading your column, I guess. I'd like to think that you're turning out that crap tongue-in-cheek. I'd like to give you that much credit at least. But yeah ... Israel. And a war."

"Okay," I said. "Sorry. How'd it happen?"

"Remember when we used to make a list of 'great Jewish athletes.' That bit of schtick we used to do? The comically short list?

"Let me see," I said. "Benny Leonard, Hank Greenberg, Sandy Koufax and ..." I shrugged and raised my hands. Kenny loved Jewish jokes. He invented them. Once, when we were sitting in a Broadway delicatessen where all the sandwiches were named after show business celebrities—you could order an Eddie Cantor, say, or a Jack Benny—he proposed a menu built around notorious Jewish criminals. Order a Julius Rosenberg, say, or a Bernard Goldfine, a Lepke Buchhalter, or Abba Dabba Berman. We were like that once. Diaspora humor, I guessed. We figured it should go both ways, that we should tell German jokes as well. Only there weren't any. "Did you hear about the German who invaded Russia every thirty years?" "How many Nazis does it take to ..." Not funny.

"Well, I got me some more Jewish athletes," Kenny said. "Munich, 1972. That turned everything around for me. Being a citizen of New Jersey wasn't so important anymore."

"Israel?"

"Israel," he confirmed. "Or, as our classmate Mr. Cerrutti puts it, 'fuckin' Israel.'" He leaned over towards me, pushing plates aside, as though we had to clear the table for some further transaction, playing cards maybe, or arm wrestling. "Remember he used to show dirty movies on a sheet in his father's rec room? Remember?"

Of course I remembered. A knotty-pine paneled den, a six pack of beer and Candy Barr—or so we were told—serving the man in black socks. She really knew how to throw one, Gooker said, commenting expertly, as though he had the experience to tell. What he had was the experience of watching the film before.

"He was a sleazy kid and now he's a sleazy adult," Kenny said. "Puts a move on Joan as soon as we split up. You'd think he'd be careful, moving on his wife's best friend. A little discreet, at least, so close to home."

"I think he's better than that. Sometimes ..."

"Is he? When?"

"He's alive ..."

"He's a fat, restless, hypocrite ... if that's what you mean by being alive, you've gotten softer than your column, which is plenty soft already. God, George, what ever happened to you? What's it like spending your life writing about what people should do on vacation?"

"I'm gathering material," I said, with a partial irony that made me feel foolish. "Seeing the world."

"Like the guys who join the Navy, huh?" he asked, eyebrows lifted.

"I saw one of your television shows," I said. "Some panel thing about the West Bank."

"What do you think of that?" he asked. "That's what I want to know. I've been wondering ... how it all looks to you."

"What do I think of ... what?"

"Oh, come on George," He leaned back, shaking his head. "Don't make me do all the work. You know the stuff. The special relationship. The military aid, the lobbying, the begging, the borrowing, the stealing ..."

"Stealing?" I asked.

"Oh, sure. Fissionable material out of a place in Pennsylvania. Patents. Nuclear fuses. The Pollard case. The political affairs committees, the letters to the editor of the 'Jew York Times,' Ed Koch, Ivan Boesky. Nine hour holocaust movies. It's no secret. We've all been keeping lists on this one. Want me to say it for you? You wonder about Israel. Hey, is it the sixth borough of New York? Is it the 51st state? What goes on here, right?"

"Alright, it's occurred to me ..."

"And that's not all I bet," he continued, relishing the role. It was fun almost, it was ... delectable ... succulent as pork, sustaining as dumplings, quenching as beer. "It's not so much Israel, you say to yourself. It's Jews. Or rather check me if I'm wrong, George, but I don't think I am, it's people like me. Are we Jewish Americans or American Jews? Dual citizens? Double agents? What? And then you ask yourself, what am I? An anti-Semite? Perish the thought! Just wondering. That dual citizen charge is hoary, ancient. But why not call it venerable? Recurrent? Archetypal? Okay ... I won't put all this on you. I'll put it on me."

He paused, setting me up the way he used to set up debate judges, back when we had argued for and against world government. "This is between us. In public, I'll talk the usual talk. Only friend in the Middle East, only democracy, loyal ally, what's good for them is good for us. New York Times stuff. But my heart is there, not here. I wanted you to know that. That's the difference between us, George. You traveled everywhere and nowhere. I went ... and I stayed."

"But you're here," I said. "Right across the river from Jersey. Twenty miles from where you grew up ... where we grew up ... together. Remember?"

"Because this is where my work is. The speeches, the fundraising, the arm bending. I'm not so good at picking oranges. Or driving a tank. I'm not on the first team, George, and I know it. I do cable TV shtick, tricks we learned in debate club. I'm outrageous, provocative. Expendable. I know. It's alright with me. I'm an opening act. I warm up the crowd. Plus I'm cheap. I work for nothing. I do it for love."

"Christ, Kenny!" I looked at him, embarrassed, maybe touched by a confession I wasn't entitled to. "I don't know what to say."

"Don't say anything," he countered. "You don't have to agree or disagree. I just wanted you to know."

"Why? It's not as if we were close anymore."

"We used to be …" he said. "So say it's for old times' sake. For Joan's sake. And yours."

He pushed back his chair, ready to leave. The audience was over but I wasn't ready to let go of him. It was our old story, Kenny whipping through the exam, ready to turn in his paper, and me just starting out on the essay section.

"Don't go yet," I said.

"I'm late," he said. "I can't get shit-faced with you, George."

"Just one question. Are you happy?"

"Of course I'm not happy." He sat back, waiting for me to follow up, next question please. It was pure oneupmanship.

"Come on," I said. "Give."

"Well, let's face it, George, we're neither of us exactly first rate, are we? Your column, my TV appearances and letters to the editor, it's not what we pictured when we started out. So no, hell no, I'm not happy. I look in the mirror in the morning and I say this is not what I had in mind. But here's the difference between us, George. I'm part of something larger. There's a war on."

"You needed that war," I said. It slipped out and I regretted it, even though it was true. "I can't imagine what you'd do without it. And I don't think you can either."

"I'm out of here." I could tell he was angry. Controlled anger but anger nonetheless.

"No. Not yet. There's another question. It's not about me or Joan or you. It's about … America."

"America, huh?"

"How it's turning out."

"Let's see," he said. He was enjoying himself again. "A broad topic, that's for sure. Let's see if I know what you're thinking. That's to say, let's see if I still know you. I bet I do." He sat still a moment, the way someone does when they're about to recite or sing, getting back to a place we used to share, enjoying the challenge of it. Of reading my mind.

"Okay," he said. "Let's try this on for size. You travel around this country and, though it doesn't show in your work, you think about this place. You probably even describe yourself as an American writer since you are an American and you do write. You find yourself wondering what's become of America and I don't doubt that your recent contacts with the home of Walt Whitman and Joyce Kilmer have raised the stakes. *Quo vadis?* All of us kids, different backgrounds, all those hopeful parents. What's become of it? Is that it?"

I nodded. "Right on the mark."

"You're the writer. But from where I stand it looks ... I'll put this in language you can understand ... it looks *kaput*. Loss of momentum, fall out of orbit, settling of foundations. I don't know. Entropy? That's how it looks to me. But I've got to go." He stood up and offered his hand. "Good to see you."

"I liked seeing you," I told him. But I couldn't suggest we meet again: our old friendship got us only so far. "You're going to the reunion?"

"Hah!" He picked up his briefcase. "Hey! I just remembered. How's your dad?"

"Hanging in there."

"Tell him I said hello. I always liked your old man. Don't know if he knew it. But anyway ... say hello for me."

"He wants to sell the house," I blurted out. "Or says he does."

"He's not the first. My parents are in Florida now. A place near Boca Raton."

"The thing is, it's as though he's rubbing my nose in it.

He's referring all callers to me. If you don't want the house, son, you be the one to sell it. It's on you."

"So sell it. What's the issue here? It's only a house."

"The issue is continuity. He's got this vision of the house passing from generation to generation. Me growing old in the house he built. You and me growing old. And not just you and me but a whole community that stays put and hangs in there and grows up and grows old and passes on and leaves something behind that people remember. It's community. It's continuity."

"In New Jersey? He must be kidding. He wants continuity, tell him to visit Jerusalem."

"No. He wants it in New Jersey."

"Well, that's sad." Kenny arose. "Continuity in New Jersey? That's a joke. That's a sign at McDonald's, says five billion served."

IV.

The taxi driver does a double take when I climb in outside the Port Authority and give him the address: Seventh Avenue and 110th Street. What's an old white man want up there, he wonders. That's asking for it, he says. I used to live there, I tell him. How long ago was that, he asks? It was me and the Indians, I reply. It's changed, he says. We drive uptown along the park. At a stoplight in the seventies, some women cross in front of us, black women pushing white babies and talking with a British accent. From Jamaica, I guess, and headed for a bench and I wonder whether some young fellow will be meeting them there, some greenhorn who'll see his future in their eyes. Heading up Central Park West, I see myself stepping into the park in the spring of 1932. Riverside Park, it was. I knew where the nannies pointed their carriages and I could make it look like an accident, the Hofers' greenhorn out for a walk, probably lost, but she'd be there with a bunch of others. I stopped in front of them, looking across the Hudson at New Jersey. I'd made my first trip there the week before, out to Summit, and I felt connected to the place, that first ridge of hills west of New York. Then I glanced around, I pretended to be surprised.

"I'm Heinz's brother," I said. Me in my one suit, my hat in hand, a fine fellow. The other brother. The little brother. Older but smaller.

"I know who you are," she said. She always did. Looking back, it amazes me how wrong people were about us, how everyone, future travel writer included, got fooled. Because I was talkative, because I argued and teased, because I wanted dinner, six on the dot, and got it, because I slammed down cards at pinochle and won, because when I sat on the stoop after weeding the garden, I had my beer without asking, because I read the newspaper first and had opinions that no one contradicted, at least until college material hit his stride, they thought that I was the boss. But Mom was the one. She ran things, just with a look that said, let's go, or stay a while, keep it up or cut it out, enough already. A look was all it took to handle me.

At the end of the park the taxi turns right. 110th Street is called Duke Ellington Drive, I notice, and when we get to Seventh Avenue, it's called Adam Clayton Powell Boulevard, just the way the streets got re-named after Germany got conquered, Adolph Hitler Platz became Adenauer Plaza. Now I see the building. It's a ruin. They re-named the streets and lost the buildings. Go figure. Otto Hofer's place looks like something you'd find in Hamburg after the bombings and fire storms of 1944. The lower windows are sealed up with concrete blocks, like a rush-job mausoleum. The windows on the upper stories are knocked out, empty as the openings to a cave. I walk into the foyer, through puddles of water, maybe pee, and broken glass crunches underfoot. The door is covered with metal sheets that someone has partially peeled back, the way you open a sardine can, room enough for someone to squeeze inside, God knows why. I look through the opening and I can see broken plaster, pieces of wood with nails sticking out, electrical wiring hanging from the ceiling, and I can just make out the door across from the elevator, where steps go down to the cellar where I spent my first night. No point in going further. It's the difference between visiting a grave and climbing into it.

I cross the street and enter the park, the same route I took with Cleve and Billy. The park hasn't changed much and if where I sit isn't the same park bench, it's close. One of the wooden pieces is missing, so it's narrower than it ought to be, and not so comfortable, but I can still sit on it. I kick myself, I don't know what became of those two guys. I never knew their last names, even. We were going to go fishing sometime, Billy said, and I was eager for it. Sheepshead Bay. We talked about it plenty. Maybe they were playing with me. Instead, they brought a bunch of fish—bluefish—in to work as if they were doing me a favor, saving me the trouble of spending a day with them. "All cleaned and ready to cook," they said.

Okay. My first home in America is a ruin. My last home is for sale. What to make of that? Maybe nothing. Did I expect that this place across the street would be a historical landmark, like the birthplace of a President? Hell, if I look at it just in terms of myself, I did okay in America. I made it. I'm an immigrant success story. I was a greenhorn, I worked and saved, I built myself up, I married and had a family (if that's what you call George) and now, I've got a $150,000 house for sale. And here's what really gripes me. The realtor I talked to, he was polite, he had a line of talk. He loved the property, gawked at the garden, and the oversized lot. And of course he yammered about location, location, location. But when we're in the house, he used words like cozy, quaint, tidy, charming and it was there between the lines. If the place sells, it's for the land. The house is a tear down and up goes a lawyer's mansion. That's what happens to our home. Our stay here is erased, we were just keeping a place warm for a rich man and I get the feeling that something has gone wrong. Looking back, I see there was an argument being fought here years ago. I took a side and never looked back, until lately. And the battle was fought right across the street, between Heinz Greifinger and Otto Hofer, back in the thirties.

"*We wuz robbed!*" Heinz shouted. Sunday dinner from Hilde Hofer. Roast chicken, dumplings, spinach. Heinz didn't come often—his relations with Otto were strained—but Hilde insisted on holding things together. Women are more forgiving. Also, more unforgiving. Anyway, there we sat, shortly after the Sharkey fight, sometime in the summer of 1932.

"We wuz robbed!" He repeated the line a second time. He was quoting what Max's manager, Joe Jacobs, said about the fight—a colorful saying that's become part of the language, though nobody who uses it knows where the expression came from. Heinz kept talking about the fight and I could see Otto Hofer was getting uncomfortable. He loved a quiet dinner; he was a slow, careful eater, not like Heinz and me, who cleaned our plates in no time. Otto took his time with a glass of wine he bought from some Italians. Heinz drank beer that he picked up someplace. And kept talking about the damn fight.

"What kind of a country is this?" he asked. This was all in German, except for *we wuz robbed.* No translating a man like Joe Jacobs. Then Heinz wondered about America, where corrupt judges robbed an honest sportsman, and so forth. He was winding down now, shaking his head, puzzled. But Otto had heard enough. He finished his coffee, dabbed the corners of his mouth with a cloth napkin which he neatly folded and restored to a corner of the table.

"*Du,*" Otto said. "*Hör zu.*" You … listen. It was unusually direct for him. Hofer was an old-world gentleman, stern-mannered and soft-spoken, more German than American, and more of the Kaiser's Germany than what came later. A lot of Germans in America stayed German in a way that Germany itself did not: the manners, the recipes, the way of working. They carried in them a country that didn't exist any more. They were the last generation of Germans who could go out into the world without apologizing.

"I'll tell you something," Otto said. There were things about America he didn't like, he said. The way people worked—that left a lot to be desired. The way they ate, rushing their food. That meant Heinz and me. And the way they behaved during World War I, when they shut down schools and breweries and renamed streets. There was a lot to complain about in America, a lot more than a boxing match. Still, he had stayed. People saw him on the street and they said—he knew it—old man, old world. But he loved how the world kept coming to America and—*hör zu*—how the Germans kept coming too, after the war. He was bringing them, one at a time, year by year, because he wanted Germans to be here, to be part of this so that after he was gone, his people would be here. Then he got up and came around to the back of Heinz's chair. He leaned forward, like a servant whispering a message to a king.

"Everyone who comes," Otto said, "I say the same thing. I said it to you, the first day off of the boat. I said it to your brother. Hans ..."

"Yes," I said. I wanted to save Heinz, if I could. He sat rigid, red in the face, just the way he sat when he was in trouble with our father. "I remember."

"What did I tell you?"

"You said, 'I hope you like it. And I hope *I* like it.'"

"Now Heinz. You can be an American or a German. You can't be both. If you don't like it, the ship sails both ways."

Heinz got out of his chair, stood in front of Otto. "*Ich hab mich vergessen*," he said, nodding. I forgot myself. And then, he bowed to Hilde, thanked them both, and left the room. I walked him to the door, out through the lobby, onto the sidewalk. He nodded at me—not more than that—and headed home to

Yorkville. He'd be walking fast, considering the money he put on Schmeling.

Otto was carrying dirty plates into the kitchen when I came back inside. He always cleared the table. Now he drew a leather case out of his pocket, a cigar out of the case. He went to his desk and found a cigar cutter. He clipped the end and examined it as he walked towards me. In a minute, he'd be out on the stoop, watching people come in and out of Central Park, fielding complaints from tenants, bidding people a fine good evening.

"So, Hans," he asked. "Tell me. Did Schmeling really win that boxing match?"

"Yes," I said. "I think so."

He lit the cigar with a wooden match, holding the end of the cigar half an inch away from the flame, toasting before lighting, then drawing the flame in while turning the cigar. Those old-timers, everything they did, everything that looked like a routine, same old thing, caught in a rut, a predictable race, they did with a kind of ceremony. I liked that about them, the love of work and life. Combined with, I admit, a fear of surprise.

"You are sure?"

"Schmeling won."

"*Schweinerei*," he said. Piggish business. He shook his head. "We wuz robbed," he said.

V.

"YOUR FATHER'S HERE," THE DOORMAN SAID, calling me from the lobby.

"No way!"

"You mean he's dead, sir?"

"No. Put him on."

"Hello, son," he said.

"Pop … What's wrong?"

"Can I come up?"

I stood by the front door, watching the lights above the elevator door go from 1 to PH. I'd invited him into the city a dozen times after Mom died, till he made clear that I could come to New Jersey if I wanted to see him. Mom could have gotten him to come. She cared about where I lived. But, by the time I asked her, she was sick. I told her it was a penthouse with a view of the world. I told her about the morning sun, the evening skyline. She asked about the kitchen. Now the door opened and there he was. He nodded, walked past me and stepped inside. I heard him walking from room to room. In a few minutes, he found me in the kitchen.

"So," I said, when he returned from his tour of inspection. "You were in the neighborhood and you dropped by for a beer …"

"I tried calling," he said, peeking into the refrigerator, unabashedly nosey about my six pack of Ballantine ales and some

Colby cheese and a box of Triscuits. “But I only get your answering machine.”

“So ... did you leave a message? That’s what the machine is for.”

“No. That was me hanging up. I guess I was hoping they wouldn’t charge me for the call. They do anyway, don’t they?”

“I’ve had a ton of messages,” I said, handing him a beer can. “Thanks to you. House buyers.”

“In a glass, son,” he reminded me gently. He was fussy about the aroma being part of the pleasure of a brew and after he poured the beer into the glass, slowly, tilting the side, he raised it to his nose and whiffed it. “Not bad,” he said, “not good.”

“Well, anyway,” I said. “Welcome.”

“What a place.”

“People say I need a warehouse,” I allowed.

“You got a warehouse,” he shot back. Then he corrected himself. “Sorry. No arguments tonight. Let’s go out back. I see you have a porch.”

I followed him through the bedroom, out onto the terrace. I stood next to him against the railing. For a minute, we felt like passengers on a ship. And the land below, bridges and airports, avenues and parks, those were places we lived, chunks of time, like ports of call.

“Up north,” he said, pointing towards the dark end of the park, “that was my first home in this country. Your uncle’s place. You heard of him.”

“The one in the army, you mean?”

“No. That was Heinz. My brother. Otto was an older gentleman. A great-uncle to you. My uncle. He was my sponsor, when I came in. He was super in a building up there, right across from Central Park. I went there a few hours ago. Just to see what it looked like today.”

“And?”

"Kaput." Kenny Hauser's epitaph for America. The old man repeated it. "I knew Central Park pretty good. I walked all over on Sundays. People do that anymore?"

"You've got to be careful. Not at night."

"Could we sit down, out here?"

"Sure."

"You could spare your Pop another beer?"

"Coming right up."

"Some food, maybe. Crackers? Cheese?"

"You want to eat out?" I asked.

"Not if you've got crackers and cheese."

While I spread some Triscuits and cheese on a plate, I wondered what he was up to, talking to me like he'd never done before. No baiting, no joking, none of the tired father-and-son routines. I opened some sardines.

"So," he said when I came back out. "Germany on one side and Jersey on the other."

"Right."

"Turn out the lights, will you son." I stepped inside and turned out the terrace and bedroom lights. Now I sat beside him in darkness. The lights beyond were lots brighter now.

"Well, there's something I got to tell you," he said. He was quiet, almost apologetic and that was awkward for a man who never apologized. "It's hard to explain. You'll think it's something I'm doing to you or because of you and the trouble is you might not even be wrong but I don't want you to think that, even if it might be true. You shouldn't blame yourself ..."

All I could do was look at him and wonder what was coming after a preface which, for its casual distribution of guilt, was a small mind-game masterpiece.

"I'm moving," he said.

"I figured you would," I said. Take a step at a time, I tell myself, the smallest possible step. "I didn't suppose you'd hang around New Jersey after you sold the house."

"To Germany, George," he said. "I'm going back. I decided."

"To Germany?"

"Yup." He nodded his head. Perhaps he was hoping I'd take it nonchalantly. Small world, open borders, oceans easily crossed: like that. Not Florida, not Arizona. Germany. An off-beat option, Pop, a surprise, but now that I think about it, about hospitals and retirement homes and socialized medicine, it all makes sense. Still, I shuddered. He was going back. It was as though he'd decided that the whole adventure of his life—the great experiment—was a failure. America was over.

"Just tell me why."

"Why?" He shook his head. "You don't want to hear it, George. We'll only wind up arguing."

"No argument." It was my turn to promise.

"Well … since Mom died, I've been out in New Jersey on my own and it's not such a good place to be when you're alone. But I figured maybe someday you'd want the place. I'd pass it on to you. It's silly, when I think about it. It's kind of an old fashioned way of looking at things. It's not a castle, not even a farm, it's just a house on a lot in Jersey … and you're not coming home. You made that clear enough …" He raised his hands to ward off my protest. "You promised … no arguments."

"Okay."

"So it's going to be sold sooner or later. Why not sell it now … turn it into money … and be a citizen of the world, like yourself?"

"You didn't say *world*, Pop. You said Germany."

"I'll tell you, George …" He drank his beer and smacked his lips. "There's a place along the Elbe … Blankenese … and you sit at a table, out of doors in a beer garden, and you watch the ships come down the river, in off of the North Sea. From all around the world, they come … and they play the national anthem of every ship as it passes and … I don't know how to put it … but that pleases me an awful lot. It makes sense. That's the same harbor I left from."

Now he looked at me, to see if I still wanted to protest, but the fight had gone out of me. His comments had been so gentle ... though I didn't doubt he'd rehearsed every word of it ... that it felt as though he'd already gone. And that sickened me. It was like the news of death. He wouldn't be here anymore, he wouldn't be sitting out in New Jersey, feeding birds and hating Yankees. He'd be in another country. I'd be alone.

"Listen, George," he said. "I criticize you plenty. Too much. Because your mother loved you too much, if that's possible, which I think it is."

"So if Mom loved me less ..."

"I'd have loved you more? Well, I think I loved you. But I'd have showed it more."

"Mom's been gone a while, Pop. I haven't noticed any particular ... upswelling ... of emotion from you ..."

"Maybe not," he said. That stopped him. Other nights, one of us would have walked out. Now he waited and tried again. "But I saw you drive home the other night. You didn't come into the house right away. You sat outside on the table. That table from the old days."

"You were watching me?"

"Yes. And it brought tears to my eyes. Seeing you there."

"I felt you were watching."

"Maybe that's love. Watching you ..."

Down on the street, there was a commotion of horn-blowing and shouting. Someone double-parked, blocking traffic. People cursing. Then people in buildings got into the act. Someone whose sleep had been disturbed must have lobbed something on the hood of the complaining car. Now I saw the roof lights of a police car lighting up the scene.

"When are you leaving?" I asked.

"No rush," he said. And I thought I saw a little opening. Maybe he left it there for me to find.

"Good," I said. "There's something I want you to do before you go. Remember all those trips we used to take?"

"You bet I do," he responded. Trips to Florida and up to Maine and at least two cross-country outings. He liked those memories, I knew: trips that begin with the two of us inside the car while Mom walked through the house one more time, making sure that windows were down, doors were locked, the gas was off. She'd already lost an argument about packing a breakfast to eat along the way, all that "perfectly good food" going to waste. Now she walked from room to room until the old man finally agreed to let me pound the horn. That brought her out fast … and ornery. "Who did that?" she'd ask. The old man would point at me and I'd point at him and my mother would get in the car.

"What say we take another trip before you go?"

"Where …"

"Down to Florida, Pop. Memory Lane."

"By car?" he asked. I knew what he was thinking. It was one thing to bring up a son, live with him and even—in a German sort of way—love him. But it was something else again, agreeing to spend all those hours and miles sitting next to him.

"Hey, Pop," I said, enjoying having him cornered. "You've never traveled with me since I was grown. It'll be a treat, watching me work." Now I went into my column-writing voice. "Ah, in America, there are morning roads and evening roads, straight shots and scenic routes. There are open roads and dead ends, happy roads and heartbreakers, honeymoon roads and killer highways, lovers lanes and miracle miles …"

"Okay, alright already," he held up his hands in protest. "Stop, please."

"Well? What do you say?" I filled him in on my leaf-peeping odyssey. He listened, just barely. The magic escaped him. His mind was someplace else.

"I don't think so," he said.

VI.

I DRIVE SLOWLY DOWN HILLTOP AVENUE and turn into the driveway of a house that has a for-sale sign in front of it, which reminds me of quarantine signs the Board of Health used to put up when a kid had measles inside. This house is condemned. There's sickness here. Death. This is what it feels like coming home to a house that's empty, walking through it room by room, knowing that nothing's changed and a pile of junk mail is your only welcome back.

The house is quiet. It knows I'm a lame duck. It's waiting for a changing of the guard. New blood. Kids tracking mud and making noise. Meals being cooked for more than one. What strikes me tonight is the German-ness of the house. Not just the objects, though there are plenty of those. There's the herring crock, the Hummel figurines, the carved wooden plates on the wall, the collection of beer steins, the pine-scented Badedas bath oil next to the tub. And, of course, there's those pictures. Old black and white. My parents. Mom's. Various dogs. And the picture Mom brought back from a trip she took in 1938, she and my brother and some buddies, all in uniform.

But it's not what we have in this house so much as the way we live, or lived. Never leave dirty dishes in the sink overnight, even if our guests didn't leave until midnight. The way we saved. The piggy bank, the pinochle kitty, the Christmas club. The way we bought. Cash for refrigerator, cash for a new car. We opened presents on Christmas Eve. Americans waited till morning, eating breakfast among piles of torn up wrapping paper. Dummies. We were Germans. We spent dollars, paid cash, and couldn't sleep with an unpaid bill in the house. We believed that work was good, the more work the better and it never hurt to do a little extra. Maybe *we* were the dummies. We got up early, to work during the week, to garden on weekends. Oh how we gardened! Rock gardens and rose gardens outside, African violets and Jerusalem cherries inside, and vegetables you never find in markets: gooseberries, currants, kale, Swiss chard. We believed that weeds—"*unkraut*"—were morally bad. We found that dirt washed off, we didn't mind getting dirty. I loved it. And Mom with me. Alright. Okay. I can hear it now. A typical *frau*, dominated and docile, working like a man. Teutonic stock. What can you do? Watch her now: the husband takes a break and she rushes inside to bring him a beer which he drinks, sitting on the front stoop, bare-chested on a Sunday, and then she checks on the afternoon roast inside, fresh ham with the rind still on it. We were like that, maybe. Germans. She wore ancient house dresses and ankle socks and old shoes and I sat on the stoop in shorts that were never long enough to cover that last inch of boxer underwear, waving cheerfully to neighbors driving home from church. Germans.

Well, it meant being out of fashion. You say "Gallic" and it means something snappy, elegant, maybe a little rude but stylish enough to pull the rudeness off. You say German or—my God, Teutonic—and the roof falls in. I've checked the New York yellow pages. Manhattan has more Cambodian restaurants than

German. It has French places by the dozen, Mexican, Italian, Japanese. But propose a German place and listen for the groans of pain. It's that way down the line, books, language, clothing. Everything but weapons and uniforms. Well, we had some good times of our own. A keg of Ballantine Ale out in the garage and a driveway full of cars and someone playing an accordion, and the kids sleeping upstairs. Another kind of good time was coffee, coffee with cake. Stollen would do, and cookies were accepted, but serious baking was from New York *konditoreis*, providers of *sachertorte*, *schwarzwalders*, pistachio, marzipan, brandy, butter-cream. And we were all charter members of the clean-plate club.

We were Germans. We walked a lot, especially after meals. Me and any number of neighborhood *onkels* would step out into the best and worst of weather, congratulating ourselves on how good or bad it was. We walked miles on Sundays, passed by convoys of Sunday drivers. The simple pleasures were ours. George, do you remember our Florida room? In mid-winter, snow on the ground, icicles hanging off the rafters, we'd wheel chaise lounges out of the garage, onto the concrete slab in front, and lie down under a blanket, basking in the sun, one-up on Miami.

We were Germans. I plead guilty. The language was everywhere. No Katzenjammer stuff. We never said "*dummkopf*" or "*schweinhund.*" But Yale was Jail. We sat on the table. And we ate our plates. We were Germans, hooked on schedule, detail, routine. It was annoying, I grant, always arriving on time. I figured that if a grown-up human being said seven o'clock, seven o'clock was what the person meant. Any sane person who wanted guests to arrive later was free to say 7:15 or 7:20 and, hell, I'd've been there just when they said. I never budged on that one, because you start caving into that stuff, the world goes to hell in no time. I never budged, no matter how many people came stumbling to the door in bathrobes, with soap in their ears. Maybe all this going-by-the-book shows a lack of imagination. Maybe so. But we believed in rules, for ourselves and for others. Promises kept, work delivered, bills paid. We knew there were plenty who made out fine breaking promises, dogging work, shirking bills. But we couldn't live that way. We played by the rules, lived within our means, showed up on time, worked hard and wondered—this was the price you paid—if the world wasn't laughing at us.

I'm almost through. We were Germans. That means you can put aside all the old world work habits, the immigrant customs, the home country recipes, and you still have something else. We lived through the first world war on one side and the second on the other. We changed sides. But some things never change. And the tie remained. Christmas we sang "*Stille Nacht*" and the first presents we opened were the ones from Germany. You could spot them by the crinkly wrapping paper, the sprig of Black Forest pine that left needles all over the carpet. Pathetic presents, right after the war. Neckties. Chess pieces. The only gift we really wanted were *schnappsbohnen*, whiskey-filled pralines, which usually melted, drained and dried en route. Those were the Deutschland *pakete* and they were nothing to what we sent in the other direction, right after the war. George, do you remember when you were little, those long rolls of brown butcher paper, those neighborhood *tantes* cramming boxes full of coffee, chocolate, Crisco, socks, sewing needles, razor blades, toothpaste? Package weight was restricted. Five pounds. We contacted everyone who was Germany-bound, we cut deals with freight companies in Yorkville, sent parcels care of a New Jersey soldier who was stationed near Stuttgart with the Occupation. Once we drove to Philadelphia, a trunk full of packages, because a German crew had delivered the cruiser *Prinz Eugen* to the Americans and were willing to carry packages back home. Mom added it up, figured we spent two thousand bucks on Germany packages. I wondered then, still do, whether those people—our people—would have done the same for us, if Adolph had won. The way this country's headed, I might yet wait for packages. Maybe we'll all find out what the world thinks of America.

And now: the last of it. Being a German in America gave you a tie between then and now, between here and there, between winner and loser, good and evil. It was like watching western movies and knowing you had some Indian blood. It gave you a complicated view of things. And I confess that, like my son, and for better reasons, sometimes I rooted for the Germans. Alright? For their dedication, their cleverness. Like the Indians. And because, like the Indians and the Brooklyn Dodgers, they always lost. The bad Germans and the once-in-a-while good ones. Whether it was Maximilian Schell in "The Young Lions" or James Mason in "The Desert Fox," the Germans had to lose. I may be way off base here, but I think the experience of defeat gave us an edge on what was happening and what was going to happen in America. We were ahead of our times. We knew. That good men do bad. That lives are lost for nothing. We knew. The taste of defeat. We knew. George, I watched you go to school and they taught you America had never started a war. That was number one. And never lost a war. That was number two. What a cocky, happy nation back then, might and right together, an unbeatable combo! But we knew. We came from a place that started wars and lost them. Every one of us had traveled to a place no American had ever been, way out on that last frontier: defeat. Absolute defeat. Unconditional surrender. We knew. We know.

German stuff, you call it. And you shrug. Well, the truth is, I'd have dumped the whole kit and caboodle in a minute, every last *Stille Nacht* and *prosit* and *sauerbraten*, every package from here, every letter from there, every scrap of memory, every beer stein and Hummel statue, if it helped me become a part of something in America. That's what Otto Hofer believed and that's what my brother Heinz abandoned but never mind, because I stepped right and I sat pretty. I learned the language, took the oath. And I was loyal. We all were. We worked overtime in munitions plants, building bombs we saw in newsreels raining down on our hometowns, and we sat there watching. Saving silver foil and planting victory gardens.

Walking around the house at night in my bathrobe, not tired enough to sleep. You need less sleep as you get older. That's cruel. You should need more. It's God giving you more time to think things over. The house makes sounds during the night, sighs of wind around the windows, branches hitting against the roof, tapping out messages in code. The faucet dripping in the kitchen that I put a pot under, not wanting to waste water, but I have to listen to the dripping all night long. Creaks and hisses in the winter, when I run the furnace—not yet, not cold enough—like a ship that's running along by itself, no passengers on board, the *Marie Celeste* they called it. In the summer, the wood sighs and expands in the morning, shivers a little at night and when it rains real hard, you can sense the house enjoying itself, like a kid under a hose, water splashing off the gutters, hosing down the sidewalk. I pad around in the dark. I know this house. A pile of mail by the door. I turn on a light. Early years, mail made our day. Letters from Germany, a few real heartbreakers during the war, via Switzerland, months coming. They got here, though. News finds its way to you good or bad, Mom said. She was right. It did. Onion skin, super-light envelopes, hand printed in block letters. Inside, old style German script. Clipped obituaries. *In Russland gefallen*. Pictures of graves. Wooden crosses on the Eastern Front. Bombed out houses. Junk mail, I get plenty. Occupant. You may already have won a million dollars. Bank statements. That's it. Except for a postcard, so old it could have slipped out of a scrapbook of a trip to Florida. What's this? Picture of a motel that's right out of the fifties, before the chains took over. Flamingo Inn. "Air-cooled." Would you believe it? Is it from George in a funny mood? He travels with packs of them, no telling when they arrive. Postcards of Gallup, New Mexico, postmarked Istanbul. Drove his mom crazy, trying to keep track of him. What's he saying now, I wonder. And then, printed letters. *Herr Greifinger*. I know this handwriting. Quick, the postmark: ten days ago, from Florida. Oh God! It's Heinz. A short note. Only two words. "*Auf wiedersehen?*"

PART FOUR

I.

"You awake now, son?" I ask. He came down grouchy this morning and I left him alone. Now I'm driving carefully over the railroad tracks in Berkeley Heights, not wanting him to spill coffee on himself. That'll get to anybody. "What's up, Pop?" he asks. This isn't the way to Florida, where we're headed. I make a left off Springfield Avenue and head north, through the older part of town, used to be Italian places, maybe still. Then we're out under high tension wires where we used to pick blackberries.

"Okay," I say. "History. We built that house of ours ourselves, me and some of the uncles and we did it mostly on weekends. We had carpenters plenty and we could read a blueprint. Only outsider we hired was an electrician, some crazy Russian, lived in the woods, muttered to himself while he worked. All on weekends. The women cooked …"

"Amish barn raising," he sighs, with a stop-the-music, I've-heard-this-tune-before tone of voice.

"With beer," I reply. George doesn't respond. I'm still talking to him but I'm back more than fifty years, hearing the hammering and sawing, the way Germans work, like it's what they were put on earth to do. Weekly progress on our American home, except when my brother visited, dressed in a suit and tie and carrying cake, always, and sometimes pumpernickel bread and smoked eel he knew I loved. Heinz, come on over, we need you, we'd shout. Give him a hammer, a shovel, a saw. Not Heinz. As soon as I saw him, I knew our schedule was shot. Soon, our tools were on the ground and we were playing horseshoes. "He never changes," my wife always said. I thought she meant it as a compliment. Maybe not. He never did change. He had his ups and downs, alright, but he was always the same fellow. The rest of us, America caught up with a little at a time, sometimes almost by accident, when we laughed at some radio show or actually cared what happened in a baseball game, hard to say when we became American. Not Heinz.

Now we cross the Passaic River. Most people see it from the Pulaski Skyway, winding through those weird, polluted Jersey Meadows, a mess of chemicals by that time. Out here, it's just muddy and slow. George brought home some fish from there, all bones. His mom pretended he'd saved us from starvation. Along River Road, I park where people parked years ago. Then it was an orchard gone to seed. Now it's the building for the New Providence Rescue Squad. We get out of the car and walk to the edge of the road. I gesture towards a driveway leading to a place across the street. There's still some odd sheds and buildings scattered around, but it's hard to tell what's what, the trees are taller now and there are some hedges, planted for privacy. There's more traffic, too, on River Road these days. No chance of road work now, during rush hour. Boxers would be dodging commuters.

"No point in going any further," I say. "It's just someone's house now. But this was where I discovered America. This was Ehsan's Training Camp. Also known as Madame Bey's. That's where Max Schmeling came. And Heinz with him. While I was building my home, setting up in New Jersey, Heinz never left Yorkville, except when his friend Schmeling arrived. He never got a real job, only tending bar. He never married."

"It's like an old movie," he grouses. "One brother becomes a priest, the other goes to the electric chair."

"Not quite," I say.

"Pop? What about your brother? Why'd he go back?"

"What's this?" I say. He finds me in a weak moment. Weaker than he knows. "Is this an interview?"

"Okay," he says, backing off. "Forget I asked." But neither of us gets up to leave. And then he speaks again. "I notice you talk about him, Pop. He keeps turning up. Old days in New York. First trip to Florida. And his picture in the house all those years. It's one thing remembering the old days. But this is different. It's the difference between a scar and a wound. The wound's still hurting."

End of speech. But he doesn't move either. We're both still standing there. I can take it or leave it.

"I don't know," I say after a while. "He went back in 1938, after the second Louis fight. It was a bad business. He made a stink. Right after that, your mom made a last visit. Late 1938. Cutting it close. That's when that photo you used to show off was taken. He was already in uniform by then. Now I'm guessing. Once, I thought I knew for sure. It felt ... true. In May, 1942, there's a headline in the papers. SCHMELING KILLED IN CRETE. Max had joined the paratroopers, see? The story goes, he was wounded and captured and, when they're taking him to the hospital, he goes berserk, grabs a gun from a guard, starts in to shoot, but before he fires, someone else kills him. Well, that was too bad because I'd met Max and I thought he was a fine fellow. And that was that. Until the next day. Mistaken identity, the paper says. Someone who looked like Schmeling. And my heart stopped. Heinz. It had to be."

"You said it felt true. Why?"

"They were linked. Like a movie star and a double. It had to be him … had to be. And it stayed that way. Except after the war I wrote Schmeling, just to see what he knew. He said he'd seen Heinz in Berlin, lightly wounded, headed back to the Russian Front. And that was that. He came back to life, for a minute, and died again."

"And … so much for Heinz."

"He left in a mess. He did a lot of stupid things. Hell of a guy, though. Your mother liked him. The fact is, I've always wondered if I wasn't a second choice."

"Pop! After all these years! You're jealous!"

"Silly, no? After … like you say … all these years. God knows I loved that guy. And hated him a little too. But all the time I watched newsreels, during the war, I said to myself, not everybody dies in war, not everybody."

We head out quietly, almost reverently, as if we'd been at a ceremony ourselves. Dissolved in something great. On the way home, suddenly, George laughs.

"I used to think being German was neat," he says.

"Before you changed your name, that was?"

"Yes," he answers, ignoring my criticism. "All the other villains were born losers. Nobody came close to Germans. I always pulled for them. The first half of the movie was always the most fun."

"Well, George," I say. "I guarantee you. My brother stayed for the end of the movie." And I hand him the postcard.

"Where'd you find this?" he asks, fingering the old-time card.

"In the mail."

"Air-cooled." Then he turns it over. "*Auf wiedersehen?*"

"He means, it's been too long, it's time we got together."

"Him? Who?"

"Him!" I point up the driveway. "The brother that didn't land in the electric chair… ." Or in a fractured submarine or a charred tank or a pile of frozen snow. "He wound up in Florida."

"We're going to see him?"

"I want you to take me. Will you do that?"

'Okay," he says, handing back the postcard, shaking his head at the strangeness of it.

"If you knew him, he never did things the easy way. He was a gambler. And God knows what else."

"You don't have to do this his way, you know," he says. He can see I'm shaky. "Listen, I'm syndicated. I call one of my outlets—Tampa, St. Petersburg—and they'll make a few phone calls. Send someone over to the Flamingo Motel."

"No," I said. I opened the door. "Let's go. You drive first. An hour. We'll have a big meal in Pennsylvania. Later on, I'll tell you a story."

George sleeps with his mouth open, drooling some, and when I glance over at him, I can see what he'll look like when he gets old. A long-faced, grey-haired, sad-eyed fellow, stoop shouldered and slouchy, with only his height to save him from appearing fat. I can see it coming. You always can, if you look. Even with a young person, a baby, every now and then you get a peek of the old person that's waiting, way down the road. And when you're old—old as I am—you sometimes get a flash of what you were a half century ago, a reminder of the baby that was.

Now it's dark and we're in western Pennsylvania, and the traffic thins out, so I sometimes have the road all to myself. I like that. America was a country that I learned by car. I loved it. We'd leave early in the morning, though never early enough for me. We'd do an hour or more before breakfast, big roaring breakfasts, orange juice, waffles, sausages, you name it, breakfasts like we never had at home and never wanted, except when we were on the road. God, the diners, the dumps, the dives! And the places we'd end up sleeping. Stuffy old guest houses and firetrap hotels and that first generation of motels, cabin courts they were called, little wooden bungalows. Boy, it was fun being greenhorns, knocking around a new country with a car and a tank of gas and a wife keeping track of every penny and a little boy who made a federal case out of it if you missed a single roadside historical marker. Outside Niagara Falls, I remember, you'd see men standing along the highway with flashlights and lanterns, waving you toward their houses, where you could have a room for the night. Because there were no motels yet. It felt as if the whole country was asking you to come visit, stay awhile.

"Hey, Pop!" George snaps out of his nap, looks ahead, looks back, alarmed. "What do you think you're doing?"

"I'm just driving ..."

"It's *how* you're driving."

"I was driving before you were born!"

"Listen. Just listen. You are on the third lane of an interstate highway. That lane is for fast traffic, especially for fast traffic which wants to pass slower traffic in the other two lanes."

"Right."

"Then why are you in the fast lane?"

"I'm entitled. I'm going the legal limit ..."

"But what about that convoy of cars ... and trucks ... behind us? Didn't you notice? Honking their horns? Blinking their headlights? Hugging our bumper?"

"The legal limit, George. If they want me to pull into the slow lane it's only because they want to go faster than the law allows. That means, if I get out of the way, I help them break the law ..."

"Pop ..." He's pleading now. His voice has that frustrated tone of voice that only kids can get and only when talking to their parents. I pull out of the fast lane, find a rest stop. Anyway, it's his turn to drive, which he does for an hour or so.

"Pop," he says. "You're not sleeping."

"No, George. I'm not sleeping. Not with you driving. An accident happens, I want to see it coming."

"Would you mind if ..." His hand flicks toward the car radio. "I ... I just looked around and see who else is up tonight?"

"Sure," I say. "Go ahead."

He punches each stop on the dial and he doesn't get much. Everything sounds like transmissions from a fleet of ships that got scattered in a storm, out there in the dark somewhere. News from Detroit. Country music out of Akron. They used to build most of the tires in the world in Akron. No more. Not one. News from Plattsburgh, New York. Violins from Portland. Portland, Maine or Oregon, I don't know.

"Nothing out there, tonight," he says. "Not even a late night minister. Some of those guys are good, Pop."

"What are you looking for?" I ask.

"You never know what's out there," he says. "Especially at night. A minor league baseball game."

"At 11 p.m.?" They'd be in the twentieth inning!"

"I don't know," he says. "I spend a lot of time driving. I try my luck with the radio. Sometimes ... if it's the right song ... it picks you up. It encourages you."

"Maybe you should get one of those things ... you know what I mean ... you shove in the box of tape. Whatever you want ..."

"I thought about it," he says. "It didn't feel right." He glances over at me, to see if that was enough of an answer, but I'm still waiting for more. He stares forward. The highway has narrowed. With high beams, you can see birches and pines and hemlocks along the side. This is where our Christmas trees come from. Twenty-five years ago, for the fun of it, I'd propose pulling over and digging out a free one to take home. We'd argue back and forth, vote, and I would lose, two to one. Now I keep to myself, that stuff.

"Not right," he says. "Remember when we went off in the car, Mom would always want us to take food along?"

"'Perfectly good food,'" I repeat. "I can hear her saying it. I can hear her. Right now."

"And you insisted that the stops we made—good or bad—were part of the experience of a trip ... Well, that's how I feel about sticking with what's on the radio. It's part of the trip. Of playing fair with the trip. It's part of making yourself available to whatever's out there. You see what I mean, Pop?"

"Yes," I say. "I see."

"Pop, what about the house," he asks.

"What about it?" I snap right back. He's got his nerve. Does he think he can take me for a ride in the country and soften me up? Does he think he can *charm* me? I had one charmer too many in my life. Charmed his way all the way to the Russian front, I figure. "You're the one who's selling it? Got any live ones yet?"

"I want to talk about it, before I do anything. I want us to talk."

"Well, I don't. I didn't come along with you to talk real estate." I all of a sudden picture the house the way it must look right now. Empty. Dark. It makes me all of a sudden sad.

"It feels like I already moved out," I say.

"I've let you down, haven't I?" he says. "All sorts of ways."

I don't say yes and I don't say no. Who says we never learn? "I think maybe I asked too much of you. Maybe that's the problem. Pauline Kennedy pointed it out to me."

"When?" he asks. Nosy. "Where?"

"Stop with the questions," I say. He senses something, I can tell. "I'm not a story. And you're no reporter."

"I just was asking."

"Anyway, Pauline says those of us who came from the other side, we felt all kinds of pressures. For us, it was a matter of getting here, getting situated, getting ahead, that stuff. But there were other pressures we passed on to our kids. I mean, this was America. It didn't matter what you used to be in the old country or where you came from. This was a fresh start, an all-new ballgame. This was the moment for us to show our stuff ... in our kids. What we were made of ... in our kids. Does it sound corny?"

He's staring at me, like I was reading a will. I smile and wave my hand before he can answer.

"Sounds corny to me alright. Like all our generations were leading to you ... the first American. So what it comes to is you're off the hook. And so am I. There's a statute of limitations on this parent stuff. You get old, they take away your license. I still have my passport, though."

"I hate to spoil your party, Pop," he says, "but does it occur to you that your picture of Germany is about fifty years out of date?"

"I've been back."

"You've seen what you want to see," he snaps. "You're a homecoming old-timer. You're softer than the softest tourist. You're sentimental."

"I've got feelings, if that's what you mean ..."

"Sure. So how do you feel about the lead poisoning of the Black Forest? Or that chemical trough they call the Rhine, hell even the Lorelei holds her nose. You like soccer riots? Have you seen the way those people move along the autobahn? No speed limits and if there's a crash, no survivors. You walk around the cities, it's Turkish slaves who do the heavy lifting. Ever watch a German TV show? Read a paper over there? I'm telling you ... you'll miss New Jersey."

"Do you?"

It's story time. Our house was nearly finished, I tell him. The garden was coming along. Already, there were forsythia along the driveway, tulips and daffodils lining the sidewalk. Out back, I had apples and pears. I never had much luck with cherries. We'd get plenty blossoms and the fruit would come out—sour cherries and sweet, both kinds. And then, the birds. The word went out, hey, fly on down to Hilltop Avenue, Greifinger's treating. This was 1936, springtime. Another thing. Your Mom was pregnant. That surprises you, doesn't it? You weren't the first. She was pregnant twice, full term. Still born. RH factor. A girl and a boy. Perfectly formed. Beautiful. You were our third try. And last. Someone—Lorenz Schroeder, acting as a spokesman—came to me, when Mom was pregnant with you and he said, now, Hans, enough is enough. But it wasn't me. Your mother was the one. She wanted you bad. Well, I guess God decided that the world needed another frequent flyer and out you popped, blue in the face. You almost didn't make it. Almost.

For awhile there, after the Jack Sharkey fight, I believed things might work out for Heinz. The gambling, it never died out. But it died down. The amounts got smaller. It wasn't always all or nothing, or double or nothing, life or death. It was more like a hobby. And he talked about Florida a lot, let's go back to Florida. Florida-crazy, he was. Start a hotel, an orange grove, a date farm, you name it. Avocados. Ostriches. The idea-of-the-week. Sponges. Sea shells. Meanwhile, he still lived on

86th Street above the bar and he was there, always there, when Schmeling came over for a fight. Which Schmeling did. Win some, lose some. He had a great fight against Mickey Walker, which ended in the eighth round when Max gave the referee a sign, pointing at the Toy Bulldog, hopelessly beaten, as if to say, what am I supposed to do, kill him? Max was a sportsman in a world where sports was going out of style. Then, there was that terrible loss to Max Baer. Schmeling should have won that fight. But Baer put on the Star of David, stopped our friend in the tenth. Someone has the best night of his life, there's not much you can do. "Every time I punch Max Schmeling in the nose," Max Baer told reporters, "I'm punching Hitler in the nose." Nastiness was in the air. Schmeling seemed surprised and, as long as I live, I'll never know if he really was surprised or was acting surprised, that it wasn't sports anymore, that a boxing match became a war game. All the signs were there. They railroaded Hauptmann. They sabotaged the Hindenburg. But whatever they did to us here, it was nothing to what we were doing over there. We listened to Hitler's speeches on the radio. It was like opera, that you couldn't understand exactly, those screaming highs and whispering lows and howls of pain and sarcastic jokes and then, those huge *Sieg Heils* out of Nuremberg or Berlin, like the whole country had gathered in a cave. Anyway, we're out in the yard, the party's just getting started. I was setting up horseshoes out back, where it didn't matter if the lawn took a beating, and the women were in the kitchen, drinking coffee and working on food. It was still early. The only ones at the table were the real old timers, the *omas* and *opas* who got brought over for a visit. Not a word of English, but they watched like hawks. If they didn't like what they saw, if the house wasn't clean and I don't mean the dishes or the floor, I mean the back of the top shelf in the linen closet, the floor underneath the radiator, they might take us back to Germany for re-training. The night before, I caught Mom taking out light bulbs all around the house and wiping them with a wet rag, then drying them off before putting them back in, so some *tante* wouldn't complain, your light bulbs are filthy.

Well, the driveway filled up fast, so you had to park out on the street. I looked up from pounding horseshoe stakes and I see your uncle walking across the front lawn. Heinz was carrying a pastry box from Bauer's Bakery in Yorkville. Behind him, carrying a second box from the same place came Max Schmeling, ex-champion, a contender now and not getting any younger. When I came across the lawn to him, he smiled, shook my hand, this fellow who fought in front of sixty thousand people. It must be something, George, to have your defeats and victories happen in front of an audience like that. Then, I guess, you've got an audience of millions yourself, millions of readers.

"Thank you for letting me come," Max said in German. I nodded, though I could have said, well, to be honest, we were hoping Heinz would bring a nice girl, someone to marry. "I like your place," Schmeling said.

Maybe he was just being polite, he was as decent a man as I've ever come across, but I offered him the tour, which Mom said I should never do without permission. Max and I walked together—Heinz wasn't interested—down into the cellar, which Mom never forgave me, that the first thing I showed the important visitor was a coal bin, my tool bench, her wash sink, and the closet where we kept apples and potatoes and onions. Later, I told her I meant to give them time to prepare the upstairs, to put away the hairbrush and comb I kept on top of the toilet and replace it with some new soap. He'd think the world of us then, no doubt. Put in a new roll of toilet paper, that would impress Max a lot too. The look she gave me. That's how she operated. She gave me those looks. Those silent killers.

Max and I came up to the kitchen. You could hear them

listen to us coming, it was that quiet. They were all there, all the *tantes*, standing by like a bunch of maids waiting for orders. I introduced him and they stood there, quietly, politely. Mom denied it later, but I swear she curtseyed when he shook her hand. Max noticed how still they all were. "What's that ..." He raised his nose in the air, he sniffed " ... I smell?"

"*Zwiebelkuchen*," Mom said. That's a dish I'll never eat again. Put it simply: onion cake. The French have something like it, they call quiche, but not as good as ours. It's a springtime dish, South German, we drink it with new wine.

"*Zwiebelkuchen*," Max said. "*Kann nicht sein!*" It can't be!

"*Haus gemacht*," Mom said. Home-made. Max played the part of a little boy, sneaking over to the stove, touching the oven handle. Then he peeked over his shoulder to see if anybody was watching, the answer being ten *hausfraus*, not one of them who had been this close to anyone famous except maybe Hilde Hofer, because Otto had been super at a building up on Amsterdam Avenue and they knew the super up the block, Mr. and Mrs. Gehrig. Lou was a nice boy, Hilde always said. They watched him grow up, go to Columbia, become the Iron Horse and later they listened on the radio when he retired—"the luckiest man on the face of the earth"—and a few years later he was in the ground. Well, Schmeling studied the oven, appraised the women and calculated that if he touched the handle, his boxing career was over.

"Later, today?"

Mom nodded yes and I took him upstairs, into the room that was yours, and the guest room next to it. Max made the rooms seem tiny, the whole house like a weekend bungalow. But when he went to the window—the one where you sat to do your homework—and he saw the whole property, pine trees and chicken coop and empty fields beyond, I could see he was pleased. We'd done alright in America.

"What were you doing when we came?" he asked. "Hitting a pipe for what?"

"That's a sport," I said. "Horseshoes." I said that in English. Then I tried to figure a translation. "*Hufeisen.*" He was still puzzled. "*Hufeisen schmeissen,*" I said. To throw horseshoes. He still didn't get it. "Come on, Max," I said. "I'll show you."

It was one of the rare times when no one had a camera. I've got to count on my memory. And memory serves. All of us men—me and the others you called *Onkel*, whether or not they were related—stood around in shirts with sleeves rolled up, suspenders, trousers, pitching horseshoes. At one end, Max Schmeling and your Onkel Heinz—like the movie star and his double. I was at the other end, with Otto Hofer. In horseshoes, I was Heinz' partner, Max was Otto's. In life, it worked out otherwise. When I think back on that day, I see two men who left and two men who stayed. At horseshoes, Hofer and Schmeling got lucky. Beginner's luck.

So Max got his *zwiebelkuchen* and a little May wine. Then the men went for a walk around the neighborhood, settling our meal, Max asking about the price of land and how much did it cost to build a house. We didn't talk about boxing, the same way we didn't talk about business. And it would have stayed that way, if not for Tillie Heinrichs, your *Tante* Tillie. You remember Tillie, don't you? Big, sweet-tempered generous woman, married to Erwin, the butcher, lived in Allentown? Later you played with their son, Alfred, who moved to Carolina and went broke in the water purification business. You have to say it, Alfred was a dud.

"You have a fight soon, Mr. Schmeling?" Tillie asked.

"Yes," Max answered, stirring some. Maybe it was nice to forget, for a minute. "Always another fight."

"With that same fellow ..." Tillie turned to her husband for help.

"Jack Sharkey, *noch ein mal?*"

"No," Schmeling said. He hadn't gotten the rubber match with Sharkey, another chance at the championship. Sharkey had blown the championship to pathetic Primo Carnera who lost it to Baer who clowned around and later blew it to Jimmy Braddock, the Cinderella Man.

"Then ... who?" Tillie asked. Max could have said he was scheduled to fight Fatty Arbuckle or Tom Mix, for all the difference it would have made to Tillie.

"Joe Louis," Max replied. Around the table that day, maybe three people knew that name. Joe Louis, the unbeaten, the unbeatable, who'd cut through contenders, white and black, and just lately had been demolishing former champions, Carnera and Baer—Sharkey came later—clearing the way for a reign that would last a dozen years which ... it turned out ... was just as long as the Third Reich. Now it was Schmeling's turn, I guessed. This was hail and farewell. Max's last visit to America. It had to be.

"Louis." Now Otto Hofer had spoken. Not the sporting type, but he read two newspapers, every day of his life. "Not beaten."

"*Ja*," Max acknowledged. He met Otto Hofer's stare. Their eyes locked, the appraising and respectful nod you used to see in the middle of a boxing ring, while referees gave instructions, before all this voodoo stare-down came along.

"Not beaten," Otto repeated. I had a feeling Max had heard about Otto from my brother. The ship sails both ways. *Hin und her*. No gentle *Opa* here. "Not beatable?"

"No one is not beatable," Schmeling said. "Not me. I know that." It was as if, losing to Baer, Hamas, Gaines, even Sharkey, he'd learned a lesson that Joe Louis had left to learn. Max thought about it some more, while we all looked on. Something came to him and you sensed it was coming to him for the first time. "To be unbeatable," he said, "is not so good."

"For the other fighter?" Otto knew better. He was testing him.

"No, no," Max said. "For the fighter himself." A silence followed, just hung there, while the table divided into people who understood what he'd just said and the ones who didn't get it and never would. I saw some confusion on my friends' faces. It's better to lose? What's all this? The more you lose, the better off you are? Others understood. My wife got it. Otto, too. Heinz, I'm not so sure about.

He looked confused.

"Anyway," Max said. "When you see me fight ... or hear about it ... it was only me up there. Not Germany. Just me and ..." He put an arm around my brother, his brother, " ... and Heinz." And here was another one of those moments that stays with me forever, that just plain ambushes me, when I look back, Max standing in my backyard, beaming and at ease among us and Heinz beside him, turning towards his friend the way a flower turns toward the sun, all joy and shining. And it's in my backyard. I swore I'd hold onto that moment forever. And maybe I have. But then it was all about what we'd accomplished. Looking back now, it's about what we lost.

"He's a nice man," I said later that night. I always enjoyed helping her clean up, after one of our parties. Most of the washing and drying was done by the other women before they left, but there was always a pan or two that had been left to soak. She trusted me with that. "Do you think he enjoyed himself with us?" I asked.

"Why shouldn't he enjoy himself?" she snapped.

"Then what's the matter?" At the end of a beautiful day, something was wrong. She didn't have to turn around for me to see it. Her movements had a rushed, jerky quality, also her voice.

"Why should there be something the matter?" she asked. That clinched it.

"I'm sorry I showed the house," I said.

"It's not the house," she said. "It's your brother. He never changes."

We had a lot of rain that spring and a couple of weeks later I took a bag of asparagus—tender and white—up to where Max was training, up in the Catskills, at an old hotel. Bad luck: Max was taking a nap and I wasn't going to ask them to wake him, not for the likes of me. So I was about to leave my vegetables in the kitchen when I saw Joe Jacobs.

"Hansel!" he shouted. "Der brother von Heinz."

"Mr. Jacobs ..."

"What's in the bag?"

"Asparagus. From my own garden."

"Great. Makes your piss stink something awful, ever notice? I heard you were out here. You doing okay?"

"Fine, Mr. Jacobs." He was staring at me while I talked. It had been four years since the Sharkey fight. I'd filled out some. I owned property now, and a car. He could see that. So we talked, over coffee and some hard rolls he'd brought out from the city. He talked and I listened. He still needed an audience. And the talk came to this. Max was a ten-to-one—or should I say one-to-ten?—underdog. It was that bad. Ten to one. That meant people who knew more than I did, weren't betting about win or lose. They were betting what would be Max's last round. Round Five, even money. Joe saw I was shocked, that such a fight would even be permitted.

"Rough business, Hansel, " he said. "Besides, I like Max. He takes grief back in Deutschland. Having a Jew manager."

"Really?"

"I am Jewish, Hansel. This didn't escape you?"

"Yes," I said. "I mean no. I know you are of the Jewish."

"And I take a certain amount of grief at this end," he says. "Around the Baer fight. Traitor to my race."

"Mr. Jacobs? Does he have any chance?"

"Of course he does! Ask anybody! One chance in ten ..."

The way he said it startled me. Like a joke but not funny. I waited for him to say something—anything—more. I wanted him to say that Max would be well paid. Or it would be over quickly, that he'd tried to stop it, he'd throw in the towel if it got too bad., that life was cruel and business was business. I could see him rummaging around for something—anything—that might make me feel better. Then he leaned forward, the way he always did, and acted like he was conveying the meaning of life.

"You watch boxers, Hansel. And they look great, sometimes. Greater all the time. And this is no lie. Great they are. The fights get shorter and the odds get longer and you start hearing those words. Unbeatable. Invincible. And that's when you know somebody's getting vinced. And who does it? The number one contender? The obvious opponent? The matchup the public wants to see? No. It's some kid with no name at all, from a country nobody's heard of, some guy who's—let's face it—a little over the hill." Now Joe Jacobs leaned forward. No one was there to hear us but he liked you to think you were hearing a secret. "Louis is training down in Lakewood. The people I talk to say he's been having fun. You know what Max does for fun? He goes to the movies. The same movie, over and over again. Now, you know the star of the movie he's watching? Come here."

I leaned forward. He whispered a name into my ear.

"Joe Louis."

II.

"IS THAT STRASBURG?" THE OLD MAN ASKED. THE question jarred me. He'd been quiet a while, not sleeping, just thinking. That wasn't his style. Sure, he had thoughts, lots of them, but they came out rapid-fire, restless, fidgety, opinionated. Now he was different, oddly quiet, immersed in the past, all this about Max Schmeling and his own long-lost brother. He spoke awhile and, just when I got hooked, fell silent and the story disappeared, like a dream interrupted by a bladder with no respect for narrative. We'd run out of that day's portion of highway a little too soon. Strasburg exit, straight ahead, Strasburg, Virginia. I wanted to get back to that story, the way a sleeper tumbles back in bed, trying to locate a dream.

"Pop," I said.

"I know. I don't want to check into some place and have a lovely meal. Not yet. Keep driving."

I headed past the Strasburg turn off, into the Shenandoah Valley. We passed a cluster of motels and restaurants and whole convoys of trucks. And, across the center island, we saw headlights of traffic heading north. When I was a kid, I wondered where everybody was going. Now I know. And wonder why.

"In there," Pop said, nodding at a sign that advertised a rest stop. Rest means piss and stretch and walk the dog and that sort of stunned, moonwalky lurch that people use, after three hundred miles at sixty miles an hour. Sometimes, during the day, you saw families picnicking at rest stops. Not surprising. But then you checked the license plates on the cars they tumbled out of. They lived in the same county the rest stop was in. That always got me. "Hey, kids, what say we pack a basket and head out to the interstate?" What kind of dreams does that generate? I'm gonna be a truck driver. A state cop, that's for me. Or maybe, when I grow up I'm gonna get me a job out at the rest stop.

After dark, though, it was different and maybe a little dangerous. Trucks were more menacing, ditto truck drivers. By day, they tolerated automobiles. At night the roads—and rest stop—belonged to them. What families came along emptied furtively out of their cars, and parted reluctantly, mothers with daughters, fathers with sons, as they headed towards restrooms and an unknown fate. The old man and I headed toward a picnic table at the back of the rest stop, near a fence that separated the interstate from farmland. We sat down next to each other, on the same side of the table, facing out toward the Interstate. And after a quiet time, listening to the roar of trucks, the story telling mood returned to my old man.

III.

WHEN YOU MEET SOMEONE MORE IMPORTANT than you, someone like Max Schmeling or Joe Jacobs, you say, well, this was special. I'll always remember. What you mean is, he'll forget. Because he's more important. He's up there and I'm down here. He moves on, I stay. His life is something that happens in front of crowds, that you read about in newspapers. So I'll remember him and there's no way he remembers me. I'm not so sure about that, son. Schmeling, to this day, I'll bet he remembers horseshoes, even if he never played the game again. And *zwiebelkuchen* at our table, I'll bet he recalls that as clearly as the tea he took with Hitler at Berchtesgaden a few months later. We had better company at our table and better food, Hitler being a vegetarian. He conquered Europe and never ate meat. Go ask about that down at the health food store.

Anyway, Joe Jacobs never forgot. A week later there comes a ticket to Schmeling vs. Louis, ringside at Yankee Stadium. Better than ringside. Press. He put me down as a correspondent for a German newspaper I never heard of, the *Volkische* Something-or-Other. So I was there, the only time in my life I was at what they called a historical occasion. But ten-to-one! It felt like an invitation to an execution. I had nothing against Joe Louis, then or ever. But him I didn't know. I didn't want to see Max get beat up. And this was a fight he couldn't win. So the night of the fight I stayed home and watched it rain. The rain matched my mood, I guessed. It also cancelled the fight. So the weather gave me a chance to change my mind. The weather and the newspaper. Max had gotten a short reprieve, that was all, they claimed. Louis was still a big favorite, 8 to 1 to win, 4 to 1 by knockout, even money it would happen before the fifth round. And then this smart aleck N.Y. Times writer, John Kiernan, puts a poem in the sports section the morning after the fight got rained out.

Oh the farmer in the dell
Now the watering is done
On the crops he tills and sells
Craves a siege of sizzling sun.
But Herr Schmeling if he's sane
And he knows how Louis fights
Must be praying hard for rain
Lasting forty days and forty nights.

That did it. On June 19, 1936, I went to Yankee Stadium to pay my respects.

George, it was some night. The whole thing gave me goose bumps. It still does. Max came into the ring, cool and polite, nodding towards people at ringside. He saw me among the press and nodded, I swear he did, nice of him, considering the pain that was minutes away, that was already waiting across the ring in Joe Louis, who didn't dance or wave or do much of anything, just stood there, no particular expression, like he was standing in line for a movie instead of about to star in one.

Here's something else. Before the fight, the ring is

crowded with people. The fighters are the ones wearing robes—that's easy—but who are all those others? Then, bit by bit, it starts to empty. They introduce former and current champions ... Dempsey, Braddock, Tunney, Canzoneri ... and up-and-comers who walk across the ring, corner to corner, wishing best of luck, and slip out through the ropes of the ring because this isn't their night. Tonight, they're part of the crowd, just like me. Next to go are the well-wishers, the entourage, the hangers-on, my brother among them. The boxing commission officials. Then, after they meet with the referee in the center of the ring, managers, trainers, cut men. Finally, after all the layers of business and friendship have been peeled away, it's only three men, Joe Louis, Max Schmeling, and Arthur Donovan, the referee. The bell rings and the referee you hardly notice. Now, it's two men.

Those first rounds, I was just hoping Max would get through okay. Every minute he didn't get hurt, that was gravy, but I wasn't thinking he'd win, only he might be standing at the end. No way they'd give him a decision but everyone would know he'd gone the full fifteen with Louis, which neither of the former champs, Carnera or Baer, had done. That's what I was hoping for and sometimes I think that's all that Max was hoping for. Then it happened. They say Max saw it first in the films. "I zee something," he said. Sounds like an evil u-boat captain sighting through a periscope at a fat convoy. Well, what Max saw was some flaws. When Joe Louis threw a jab he held his arm out a while—meaning a split second—too long. You could counter off his jab. And something else. When Louis came at you, looking to throw a right, he held his left low, his whole body listed left. If you stepped to the right, you could land a right of your own. I sound like I know more than I did. I was surprised as anyone when, in the fourth round, Max threw a right and Joe Louis went down.

It wasn't a knockout, not even close. Joe got up at the count of two. I was afraid he would get up mad, that he'd come roaring after Max, like Dempsey after Firpo. That wasn't our kind of fight. What happened, though, was strange and brave and heartbreaking. It lasted another eight rounds. There were dozens, I want to say, hundreds of rights from Max. Louis was still dangerous. He hurt Max in the seventh, I recall. But it was one right after another. And there was nothing Louis could do. It was as though, after the first knockdown, he knew what he was in for and was ready enough for it, ready enough not to fall down. Otherwise, he could do nothing. Joe started getting puffy and clumsy. It got bad.

Now, the twelfth round. Louis had been stumbling around and Joe Jacobs was worried he might butt Max, accidental or on purpose. He urged Max to do what didn't come natural. To end it. Early in the twelfth, Louis fouled him. Joe Jacobs was right to be worried. Then Max scores with a right that jars Louis and then another right. The crowd is begging for it. They've been on his side since the fourth. And Louis is ready, too, wandering around, shaky, drunk-looking. Max goes after him, "like a panther," the paper later says. More rights. He steps back and waits for Louis to fall but he's standing right there. Standing is all he's doing. His face is swollen, his hands are at his sides, he's not even looking much at Max. His eyes are open but they're off somewhere. Max steps in one more time. No need for a jab or a left, a bob or a weave, it's one more right, direct hit on the unmoving target. At last, Louis collapses, down on his knees, in a praying position. Donovan waves that it's over, the seconds rush in, Joe rolls over on his back, later they carry him to the corner. At the same time—this I'll never forget—there's Max and he's jumping in the air. Oh, hell, how can I say this? He's not jumping up like a cheerleader. He's jumping forward and upward, like towards something, with his hands at his sides and a huge grin on his face. It's the way people look in paintings when you see them going up into heaven, not flying themselves, wings flapping, but being drawn upwards. But it wasn't God that Max was headed towards. It was his Jewish manager, Joe Jacobs. The invincible had been vinced.

"What time is it, George?" I ask. I'm wrung out. Every time I think about that night, I relive it.

"Ten o'clock," he says.

"God, I'm thirsty."

"We can find a beer back in Strasburg. Or go down the road some more."

"I'm not done yet," I say. "And I don't want to leave here until I am."

"Stay here," he says. "I'll see what I can do." I expect to see him driving out and heading down the interstate to the next exit, looking for a convenience store. Out and back, that should be half an hour. A lot of fuss to go through for a beer. But I appreciate it. I'll finish the story and then I'll be all out of history. Until Florida, at least.

"Here you go," he says, back in no time. He holds out half a six pack, the cans held together by the plastic webbing that'll be around when Jesus comes back to earth. There were some kids parked at the edge of the rest stop, it turns out. Smoking funny cigarettes, listening to loud music, drinking beer and just generally preparing America for the next century of global competition. They were so pleased George wasn't a cop, they gave him the beer for nothing. Old Milwaukee. Free beer. Beer soda.

"Pop," he says. "Earth to Pop?"

"Yes?"

"Finish the story."

"Well, son," I say. "It goes downhill. From the moment Max Schmeling jumps—flies—into Joe Jacobs' arms, it goes downhill. And far. Not just to the bottom of the hill, but into the ground, into the deepest hole that ever got dug, that swallowed millions."

It's funny how folks who came over here from other countries looked for a piece of America that resembled what they left behind. You ever notice that, I ask George? I don't just mean neighborhoods, like Germans in Yorkville and Italians in Little Italy and Chinese in Chinatown. I'm talking about outside of cities. You used to have those Greeks in Tarpon Springs and Basque sheepherders in Utah and even today, Vietnamese down in Louisiana, fishing in the Gulf of Mexico like it's the South China Sea. In South Jersey, even, there were Russian places with onion-steeple churches. I guess those pine barrens and birches and cedar lined rivers reminded them of home.

Well, Germans have a thing about forests. You know that. It shows up in our houses, all that wood paneling, and our gardens, dotted with elves, in our loden jackets and deer heads and cuckoo clocks, our fairy tales and our food. We head for the woods whenever we can. That's what pulled me to New Jersey in the first place. And that's what got me and Mom and my brother Heinz in a car, headed up into the northwest corner of the state, out in the mountains toward Port Jervis. Some of my brother's pals had a "sport camp" there and they were having a picnic.

I hadn't seen much of Heinz in the months since the Schmeling-Louis fight. At first, I figured he was too busy celebrating to worry about his dull old married brother living out in the sticks. Maybe he'd taken a trip or found new friends: I would have welcomed that. It was time he took off on his own, found a wife and a new life, outside of Yorkville. There was more. Whenever we talked, it was all about us going to Florida. "Florida-on-the-brain," Mom called it. It was as if the house I'd built and the garden I put in didn't exist. You should have seen the look on Mom's face, when she heard that talk. It got unpleasant, kind of. Heinz might be the life of the party, the dancer and athlete and charmer, but he needed me more than I needed him and what he needed I couldn't give. We were drifting apart. Sometimes, when we spoke, he got sarcastic. He called me "*brüderchen*" in a mocking way, same as when he asked about "the brand new home, the lovely wife, the well kept garden," and when he called me "*Amerikaner.*" I could hear the pain. Life in New Jersey was steady as she goes, working and saving, a step at a time. Like raking leaves. Heinz needed a place that was an adventure, the gamble, the inside track, the getting in on the ground floor. The next big, bright idea. And, while I stayed in New Jersey, New York City was getting uncomfortable. In New Jersey, I stayed out of politics. We all did. We voted Democrat, paid our union dues, and kept our mouths shut. But in Yorkville there were people out on the streets, looking for a fight.

So there we were, George, an outing into the woods and God, it was beautiful up there in those days, farms here and there and shaky one-pump gas stations and hicks who looked like they'd never been to New York or cared to go. It was a bigger country. It's shrunk, since then. The woods were hemlocks mixed with beech and maples, with sycamores down near the rivers we crossed on rickety one-lane bridges and at the end of it, a turn we nearly missed onto a dirt road that curled downhill, a road shaded by trees that met overhead. It was through the woods to grandmother's house, it was a Grimm fairy tale. There could have been trolls under the bridge, elves peeking out from among the ferns. But those weren't elves that we met down there. We drove to an entrance, with a banner strung over the gate: CAMP DEUTSCHLAND, it said. I think that's what it said. My attention went to the men who were standing there, checking the cars that arrived. They wore dark trousers and tan shirts with sleeves rolled up and, just above their elbows, armbands with swastikas on them. They nodded and waved us in, once they saw Heinz.

I could feel Mom freeze up and Heinz tensed too. He waved his hands and said something like "those guys," in a tone of boys-will-be-boys, we shouldn't worry about it. What I did—or didn't do—next was the biggest mistake of my life. I should have made a u-turn, right then and there, and gone back up the road and not stopped until I had my wife back in Berkeley Heights and my brother on the road to Florida.

Maybe you never heard of the German-American Bund. It was their camp. They were a pro-Nazi group that came out of Yorkville, led by a man named Fritz Kuhn, who later got deported. They had parades, staged a rally in Madison Square Garden and they scared a lot of people. Sometimes what they said was a little reasonable: they were putting out the story that the press wasn't getting, they were organizing just like all foreign groups organized, to lobby for the folks "on the other side." Still you couldn't wear a swastika in New York and expect a reasonable conversation. They scared me, that day. Sure, later on we found out they were pathetic. They were just-off-the-boaters, with no deep roots in America, watched, covered, penetrated every move they made and they were so out to lunch they even embarrassed the German diplomats in Washington. Still, it gave me the willies, getting out of my car that day. Mom put her hand on my arm as soon as I opened the door for her. She was shaking.

Heinz led the way and we followed, wondering about the cost of every step we took. Germans had all kinds of groups.

Hiking clubs—those were the Nature Friends. *Turner-verein*—that was athletes, soccer players and gymnasts. Choral societies—the *sängerbund*. Heinz acted like this was like that, just another club. He was at his most happy-go-lucky, a hello here, a wave there. The day's program hadn't started yet, although there was a little wooden stage set up for speeches. Right now, it was innocent: little blond-haired kids marching around playing soldier, no different from the Boy Scouts. Other youngsters waded at the edge of a pond, their mothers watching out for them. Beer kegs and picnic tables and oom-pah music on the nicest day of the year, and the woods all around us, just like Germany.

Heinz escorted us from table to table, presenting us by name. With one exception they were all strangers to us, from Fritz Kuhn—a puffed up, unimpressive man—on down. But when people saw us there was something uncomfortable that passed between us, a nod, a recognition, as if we were on their side, we'd already joined up. The next thing, I saw Mom walk towards the pond. I started to follow her but Heinz steered me in the direction of horseshoes. He knew my weakness. I looked again for Mom. She was at the edge of the pond, on a walking path that went all around, so you could see people on the far side, sitting on grassy banks where trees hung over the water. She would be okay, I thought. She'd keep. Well, once I played, I got into it. One of our opponents was the only man I recognized, Karl Lobel, a bicycle repairman, lived in Scotch Plains, lost his boy on Okinawa. I met him dozens of times over the years, shopping in Plainfield and we never said a word about that day.

Well, after I won horseshoes, I looked around and I couldn't see your mother. I stared across the lake, I walked from table to table. They were preparing for ceremonies, kids getting ready to march and sing, Kuhn ready to speak and your Mom was nowhere. Heinz sat at a table, the Mayor of Yorkville spinning a yarn. No point in disturbing him. I kept walking around and then I saw her, sitting in the car with the door open.

"How long have you been in here?" I asked. She shrugged. "You want to go?"

She didn't have to answer. She was sitting in the car! Did that mean she was having a wonderful time, she wanted to stay?

"I'll get Heinz," I said.

"No," she said. "Leave him."

And I left him. I left him. That simple. I didn't even argue. I did what she told me to do. I left my brother. On the way home, after a few miles, we talked, but not about Heinz. We scared each other to death. We wondered how many G-men had been out in those lovely woods taking pictures, and whether that yokel fence-mender at the top of the road was writing down our license plate. We worried that we'd wind up on a list, that we'd get in trouble, lose everything. What I'm saying, George, is we weren't so brave, that day. It wasn't about walking out on a hate group, voting for the American way. It was about holding onto what we had. Maybe *that* was the American way. It was the right choice, no doubt about it, but it felt wrong, it felt cowardly and all the rest of my life, to this day, I thought I should have gone back in there for my brother. I should have saved him.

A few months later, Max Schmeling was back in America. In a world that was trading boxing gloves for more serious weapons, Max had one last fight: a rematch against Joe Louis. I didn't go, not to the fight, not to the training camp, which anyway was up in the Catskills. I'd have loved to say hello to Max again—I hoped he didn't think I was turning my back, caving in to all the people who wrote him up as a Nazi gladiator. No matter how many times he said it was a boxing match nobody believed him, and I'm not so sure he believed it himself anymore, because Goebbels told him different, he was fighting for Germany and the night of the fight, they say he was in the dressing room, sweating and trembling. Well, Louis was at his peak and Max was past it. I listened on the radio and not very long. It lasted two minutes and four seconds. Max got knocked down three times, one punch so hard they say you could hear him scream in pain. All he threw was two weak rights that made no difference at all.

After the fight, Max claimed Louis had hit him a kidney shot, illegal, it can practically paralyze you. But no one was listening. He'd won once on a foul already, the first fight against Sharkey. Then, Max said, well, I beat Louis once and he beat me once, and how about a rematch and no one paid attention to that either. He'd had his moment and now it was back to Germany with him. Looking back, I see Max had a point. They each won one, they each knocked the other out once and, measuring those victories, it seems that it was Schmeling who climbed the higher mountain. All in all, they fought thirteen rounds and Max won most of them. But never mind. They were never going to meet again, till years later, when Joe was a guest on a TV show, "This Is Your Life." I read that Max wrote him a check to help pay his tax bills. Paid for his funeral too, out in Las Vegas. So I heard.

I didn't hear from Heinz after the fight and, to tell you the truth, I was relieved. Also—no visits. I should have called, I should have gone into the city, gone the next day and sat down with him and made a plan, Florida or whatever, because the boxing part of his life was over and Yorkville was a good place to be getting out of. But I didn't go in. I waited for him to come to me. He was the one with the problem, I told myself. Besides, he was three years older. He owned me a phone call, a letter. He owed me money.

"Your brother says goodbye," Otto Hofer said. This was two weeks after the fight. Already, Schmeling was back in Germany. And Heinz was on his way. He'd come to Hofer's apartment late at night. He let himself in: he still had keys from the year he worked there. Otto thought it was a burglar. He came out of the bedroom carrying the only thing he could find, a broom. Max laughed at him. Otto was still scared.

"Sit down, Otto," Heinz said. "You're going to be alright."

"I'm glad to hear it. You might have knocked."

"I know what time you go to bed, Otto," Heinz answered. "Also … I wasn't sure you'd let me in."

It's late," Otto said. "Some people work in the morning."

"Otto, I made a bet. My own money and money I borrowed, up and down the street. And it was over in two minutes."

Otto didn't answer. What he thought, he said, is that in many ways, Heinz was the best of us. If you'd stood all his greenhorns in a line and asked, which one makes it in America, makes it big, you wouldn't pick me or any of the others because whatever we did, it wouldn't be big. We didn't think big, we didn't dream big, we didn't take big chances. That one jump across the Atlantic, that was all the gambling that was in us.

"A thousand dollars, Otto. That's the hole I'm in. Up and down the street. The bakers, the beer men, the *wurst-geschaeft*, the *delikatessens*. A family emergency, I said. A problem back home. That was five hundred. And another five hundred, I borrowed someplace else. They look for me already. They're not from Yorkville."

"Why do you come to me?"

"A place to stay. Down in the cellar, maybe. The old spot."

"That you had already. For one year. You know the system. One year and out. There's someone else now. Fritz Kammer."

"Only till I leave."

"You're going? Where?"

"I'm ready to take your advice, Onkel. The ship sails both ways across the ocean, you told me."

"So it's not just a place to hide," Otto said. "It's a ticket to run."

"Yes. That too."

"Well," Otto said. "That's a lot."

"I know." Otto could see my brother was on the edge of tears. When he told me, I asked, did you ever think of calling me, Otto? Or reminding him he had a brother in New Jersey? "He didn't need reminding," Otto said. "He knew." And that was that. Otto gave Heinz a corner of an apartment, where the people were in New England for the summer. And he got him a ticket on North German Lloyd. The next week, being a thorough man, he took Heinz to the pier. And he only asked for one thing in return, one thing only. He put it to Heinz fifteen minutes before they left, handing him paper and pencil.

"The names and where I can find them," he said. "And the amount."

Heinz nodded. He was dressed to go, halfway out the door almost. Now, he bit his lip and sat at a little tap in the hall, jammed up next to a coat rack. Otto went into the kitchen to see Hilde. He was talking about supper that night, he thought rouladen was a good idea and Hilde interrupted, holding up her hand, what's that I hear and it was Heinz out in the hall, crying. Hilde started to go to him. Otto stopped her.

"Let him cry," Otto said. "As long as he writes."

"It's sad."

"Sadder than you think, when we start to pay."

"Sad, also for him," Hilde said. "Going back there. Now." Hilde read the newspapers. She'd been through World War I. "Not a good time to be a German in America," I once said to her. "Not a good time to be a German in Germany," she answered back. Later, by the way, I offered to help Otto with the money. He wouldn't hear of it. We didn't talk about Heinz, after that: he was the one who got away. And I couldn't talk to Mom either. She'd made me leave him behind at that camp. And then, she got sent a ticket by her family, a short last trip to Germany.

And she went alone and came back to New Jersey with a photo of my brother in uniform. Arm in arm with the irresistible Heinz. And years later, she made me leave his picture on the mantel in the living room.

Go figure.

IV.

THREE DAYS IN VIRGINIA. GEORGE AND I TALK at breakfast. Nothing heavy, just whatever we feel like. There's the problem with most family visits. There's always an agenda, reports from the finance committee, the social committee, old business, new business, open discussion, bang the gavel and wait till next year. At breakfast, we just talk about the stuff we used to argue about—baseball, blacks, Israel, labor unions, Japan, acid rain, pre-nuptial agreements. After breakfast, he hits the road, like a salesman making calls, only his stops are at state parks, bed and breakfast places, new hotels and restaurants, scenic vistas, chambers of commerce, roadside museums, historic downtown districts. Meanwhile, I take walks, sit around and wait for my son to come home.

We had a family custom that whenever someone went on a trip alone, they couldn't come home empty-handed. That meant peanut brittle, Indian blankets, petrified wood. The custom continues. From a second-hand bookstore, George brings a novel, *Dead Souls* by Nikolai Gogol. It's about a Russian con-man called Chichikov who goes running around old Russia.

His gimmick is to buy "souls"—the names of dead serfs—that he can use in a swindle he's got going. He travels all over the country and everyone he meets is a little crazy. In between visits, you get a picture of Russia, and the Russia he travels through is a huge, raw, lonely country. And the America we travel is like that too. And George is a bit of a Chichikov, a flim-flam man, a traveling saleman with lots of time between deals, all those miles along the way, all those empty little towns with signs that advertise the most famous people who were ever born there and got the hell out, just like the places in *Dead Souls*.

"We'll eat out tonight," he says, coming through the cabin door. We've got a refrigerator full of food—in memory of Mom—but we always eat out. "So how was your day?" he asks.

"Not bad," I say. "Been reading."

"Are you into it?

"Well, I see why you gave it to me. You're in it. You're the star of the show."

"I guessed you'd make that connection."

"Does Chichikov ever get himself straightened out? If he has a happy ending, then I guess there's hope for you."

"That was supposed to happen in the second volume," he says. "Only Gogol never finished it. Couldn't get it to work. Took it out and burned it, most of it. All that's left are some fragments."

"Great," I say. There's another connection I don't tell him about. I can't read about Russia without thinking of my brother. Another con-man in that land of endless snowy plains. Years and years ago now, but so what? If Chichikov is someone I can feel, then so is Heinz. Sometimes I can feel him standing right next to me.

"I walked all around here," I say. "The leaves are really happening. And I saw two kids on the side of the road, blond-haired kids with fishing rods. One was carrying a bucket and a dog was trailing along behind them and it was just like one of those old Saturday Evening Post covers. And I thought, me, I was lucky to see all this again. And that's how I feel about my whole life in this country. I came to America at just the right time, George. I'm sure of that."

"But it was only a visit?"

"Half a century … that's more than a visit."

"But the important thing is knowing when to come and when to go. Is that it, Pop?"

"You really want to have this talk?" I ask. "Because I have this one figured out."

"Go ahead," he says.

"Okay. Let's face it … most of the people who come to America came … why? … They came for the money. Economic opportunity. They didn't come because they got excited about Thomas Jefferson. They came to make out. That goes for the Irish potato farmers, the Haitian boat people, the Israeli taxi driver, the Korean vegetable dealers in your neighborhood, and the Indians selling newspapers and magazines. That goes for me … let's face it. It wasn't the land of the free that brought the most of us … it was free land. Lots of room. Am I going too far?"

"Maybe," he says. "But I want to hear it."

"So let's at least admit it. Most of the folks who came weren't here because of what they believed … they were here for what they wanted. Being an American wasn't the main thing. And I have no problem with that, George. Everything has to begin someplace. And … let me tell you … it's great being in at the beginning of something. Getting in on the ground floor … of the tallest building yet! I'm telling you, coming to America in the twenties … what a country! Who wouldn't love America? Are you kidding?!"

"There was a Depression in there," he reminds me. "A war too."

"I always worked."

"Not everyone else did."

"They didn't have jobs. But they worked. I'm telling you, it was a different country then. People your age don't know. You've never had your world fall apart. And if it does … what are you going to do? Can you garden? Hunt? Can your women bake? Put up vegetables? Sew? What would your idea of belt tightening be? Cutting back on movies?"

"But that's not the question, Pop. The question is, why you're turning your back on …"

For a minute, he's right on the edge of saying: "me."

"… America. Because I can listen to all the rest of it. I can hear it all over the place. I defend this country all the time. Aging superpower. Coca-Cola culture. I've heard it all. But I never thought I'd hear it from you, Pop."

"I told you before, I feel like a stranger in my neighborhood. Since Mom died. The walls come in on me. I just wanted more around me in my old age."

"What? What more?"

"Let's go eat," I say, getting right up. "No point in continuing. I've got nothing against anybody, believe me. When I go, I'll go quietly. I'll pay my bill. I'll leave my tip. Memories? I've got a million of them, milestones and tombstones all over the place. I trip over them in my sleep. Heinz going back. Closing of the Ballantine Brewery. Dodgers off to California. Mom dying. You changing your name. No big deal. But still …"

The buffet. The old man and I were seated at a table right next to the salad bar. We couldn't see anybody's legs. Those were out of sight. And, since the buffet had a sort of hooded roof over it to prevent people's hair and snot from landing in the food, we couldn't see anybody's face. All we saw was from the belt line to the bustline. A buffet view of America. We studied the different strategies people used. Most started at the beginning, loading up on lettuce and tomatoes, basic stuff that crowded their plate, but then got to the olives, to the Jello, and you could see everything go to hell, plates turning into mishmash, with vinegar and oil slopped over pineapple, bread croutons going on the Jello, jalapeno peppers dancing with the kumquats, and phony bacon bits thrown onto everything, like rice on newlyweds. Some folks tried two plates, juggling, bumping, dropping. Every now and then someone would do a preliminary reconnaissance, working from the back to the front. But what never happened was that someone would make a simple selection, take one or two or three things and leave. Mostly it was a mess. That put us in a philosophical frame of mind. Inhaling Manhattans helped out too.

"You know what I've noticed?" asked the old man. I expected him to say that here, right here, was the problem with America, that buffet said it all, low quality, high volume, etc. I was wrong. "How rare we are."

"Rare?"

"Look around this place. You've got families galore, chowing down. Mom and Pop and kids, all messing around together at the salad bar. It's not, can they have a nice meal together. It's, can they eat enough to run the place into bankruptcy. Or die trying."

"That's called 'family dining,' Pop."

"There's a bowling league or softball over there," he said, signaling towards where a mixed-gender crew of sumo wrestlers were waiting for a tray of nachos and chicken wings. "And ..." A gesture towards a table of seniors dressed in Western garb, string ties, cowboy shirts, jeans on the men and women, all coal miners' daughters, wearing fancy lampshade-shaped skirts and dirndl tops. "I can't say what they do."

"That would be the square dance club," I said.

"And there's some kids. Dates, I mean. Not many." Some young couples sat against one wall, unlikely to get into much trouble, after all that food.

"*Fressen. Nicht essen.*" Another chunk of German popped out of me. Childhood table talk. *Essen* was to eat like a person. *Fressen* was to gobble like an animal.

"What you don't see is a father-and-son. You notice how they look at us when we come into a place? What brings those two out together? And when we tell them, they act like it's the cutest idea in the world, no one ever thought of it before."

"I'm glad we did this," I announced. And then, feeling lucky—it was the Manhattans—I took another chance. "Just bear with me on this one, Pop. Have you ever noticed, on road maps, how they mark the scenic routes? A broken green line, usually?"

"Sure."

"Ever think there's someone who decides those routes? What's scenic? What's not. Somebody has to drive those roads and decide."

"And that should be you?"

"I'd love it, Pop. Forget all this other stuff. No columns, no tips-for-travelers. No words, even! I'd be a writer who never wrote except for the marks I made on a map. *One true map*. A green line alongside a road. That would be my life's work, clean and honest. *One true map*. What do you think?"

"I think the fried chicken looks good. Or the liver and onions."

"Okay ..."

"And the buffet's quieted down some, what's left of it."

We cruised the buffet. He settled for some liver, beets and onions, two German vegetables it's hard to do much harm to. I chose something called Swedish Noodle Bake. The restaurant was emptying out now, with customers who'd ordered off the menu carrying doggy bags. In Europe, they let dogs into the restaurants. In America, they carried the food out to them. I felt a column coming on.

"It's tricky, Pop," I said. "Listen, you've got to find some scenic routes in every state, or else you haven't done your job. So Colorado is easy. But what about ... not to beat around a bush ... New Jersey? And who decides how much scenic mileage a state has? Is it in relation to the size of the state? The population? The total miles of road? There's more. There's the fairness question. You have a road that's real pretty in New Mexico, but not quite pretty enough to make the top of the list. In New Mexico, that is. But it's a heck of a lot better than the best in, say, Oklahoma. What do you do?"

"I see what you mean, son."

"It's a mess. It's affirmative action, quotas, reverse discrimination. And there's more. Just suppose you had a road that's been a scenic route for years. Only, what with this being America and progress is our most important product, it gets ugly. What then?"

The buffet was now a miniature battlefield, with weapons, shells, uniforms and bandages all over the field of combat. Kernels of corn, chunks of onion, little rivers of Jell-O-colored mayonnaise. The waitress slipped us our check which she autographed on the back. "Thanks! Krissie!"

"You know what you do, son?" he said. "I know. It's like when they … what is it? … decommission a church."

"Deconsecrate."

"Yeah. That. You just take the road that used to be marked yellow … and you mark it black."

"I LOVE IT!" I shouted out. And I loved talking to my father. "I can hear the howl going up from the Chambers of Commerce. But I'm gone. I'm down the road!"

"There you go …"

"One true map, Pop …" I said. "That's all I want to make."

We're both wobbly on the way back to the motel, but the thing about being half-drunk is not that you notice things more —probably you notice less—but everything is fascinating. A dog barking somewhere is all the loneliness in the world. Then I hear myself say something he can't quite make out. "What's that?" he asks.

"Don't go," I say, in a little boy's voice that I haven't used since he dropped me off at Boy Scout Camp. Camp Watchung, Glen Gardner, New Jersey, which was my last run at a Physical Fitness merit badge. "Don't go," I say. "You don't know what it means to me, just looking at you. Don't go." Little boy lost. He doesn't answer, but he puts his arm around me and we go back to the motel.

V.

“Hey, Pop,” George says, the next morning. It snaps me out of a trance. I get hypnotized, watching America pass by: an American Legion hall, a lumber yard, a mobile home, a farm—or what’s left of one—a car lot, an ice cream place, a discount carpets place, fireworks, cigarettes. “We went to Florida lots of times. Three or four anyway.”

“That’s right,” I answer. I can’t get over the satellite dishes, like cupped hands waving hello at the universe, begging for an answer, even if it’s video shopping and preachers. Anything that’s out there, please come down and visit me.

“Three days, two nights, I think it was,” George says. “Good roads all the way. Motels weren’t so good.”

“There were plenty of good motels,” I correct him. “But I was cheap. There’s no getting around it. I saw a swimming pool, I’d speed up. ‘Somebody’s got to pay for that, not me.’ Six bucks a night, eight tops and I always sent your mom to look over the room first. Tour of inspection. She liked a place, I worried we couldn’t afford it. George?”

“Yes?”

"I'm sorry I was so stingy with Mom. Always cutting corners. Saving for what?"

"Tell me about your first trip," he says. "First time to Florida."

"That was 1933," I say. "In a Ford I bought for $200 when I was living on Classen Avenue in Brooklyn, a little before we got married. I got up in the dark and got over to Yorkville. Then we headed ..."

"You traveled with Mom ... before you were married?"

"No. That was me and my brother. Heinz. My famous brother." I stop a minute. Sometimes, when you picture the past, you step right into the picture, like a trap door opens right under your feet. One minute you're talking to someone like George, the next you're back fifty years. And when you get back, it's hard to put in words where you've been. You were in the picture. They get the caption.

"So ..." He jogs me. "America. Summer. 1933."

"It was just after the Max Baer fight. Max—our Max—Schmeling got knocked out in the tenth round."

"What's my father talking about?" I can see his expression. One Max knocked out another Max? He thinks I'm losing my mind. That I'm senile all of a sudden. Drooling memories. But, even though he's lost and he doesn't know one Max from another, and all these fights he never heard of, he doesn't do what he used to do, that always drove me crazy. He doesn't yawn, stretch, roll his eyes. He sits and listens. Would you believe it? Are you looking down from heaven, Mom?

"Schmeling was heartbroken after Sharkey. He expected he'd get a fair shake, a re-match. He got nothing. He got Max Baer and the press made it a Jewish-German thing and Baer came into the ring with the Star of David on his trunks, even though nobody was sure whether he was really Jewish. Kind of makes you shudder, wearing that star, when you think of what happened later. Oh Christ ..."

George was bargaining for a Readers Digest yarn about traveling in the thirties, funny stories about flat tires and farmers daughters, but now he watches me tumble into something strange, boxing matches from before he was born. Still, he doesn't interrupt.

"It was an ugly fight. Baer by a knockout. I sat right behind Al Jolson, the singer. 'My Jew-boy beat the German!' Heinz took it hard. So the Florida trip was my idea, to get him away from boxing and out of Yorkville. We had a flat or breakdown every day and it took ten days to cross the Florida line. Waiting for ferries. You never knew what was next. Half the time you never knew where you were and when you asked directions, *they* didn't know where *they* were. Florida was something they'd heard about, way south. A rumor. They asked us to come back and tell them what it was like there. Everything was new to us. Everything was new, period. Buying watermelons right out of the fields. A million times, we said, someday we'll look back and laugh. We were laughing then, already. It was a new country. It's an older country now and I'm an older traveler. This whole neighborhood seems like an autumn kind of place, the same way a beach is summer. The white churches, the post office which is also a general store, the red brick mill-factories, scuffed-up chicken farms trading in maple syrup and apple cider, all of it has a tired-out feeling, hunkering down for winter, just around the corner. No wonder the senior citizens love it this time of year. Who wouldn't want to go out like a maple, flaming red and filling the wind with leaves? Hoping for a glorious resurrection, come Easter? But we don't go out that way. We go like cars, dented, leaking oil, mufflers farting. We go into automobile graveyards, where weeds grow around our axles and mice next to the driver's seat—that's burial. Or we go into one of those pressing machines that can squeeze a Cadillac into the size of a toaster. That's cremation."

Living with George, I write columns in my head.

VI.

"Hey, son," the old man says. "It's none of my business. I'm just wondering." That's his trifecta, I think. When the old man says "son," he pulls rank. It's none of my business suggested disinterested curiosity. Just wondering suggests the idea is scarcely his own; it just popped up.

"Shoot," I said. Now that was what I called straight-forward, as in ready, aim, fire.

"You going to your reunion?"

"It's in ten days."

"That's a yes?"

"That's an 'I guess so.' We may have to hurry back from Florida. I have a date. Maybe."

"How do you go about doing something like that? At your age, I mean?"

"At my age?" He acts offended but he laughs. "It doesn't get easier, Pop. It's just as cruddy and awkward as ever."

"Who's the lucky lady, if I can ask?"

"I knew her in high school. I ran into her again a couple of weeks ago."

"She's been waiting for you all these years?"

"Not exactly. She's separated from her husband. You remember Kenny Hauser?

"You bet I do. Jewish kid. A real crackerjack."

"Well, I want to give her a call. Joan Simmons. I always liked her."

"Okay by me. But you're not rushing your work, are you? Work comes first, I always say."

"Pop, I did Australia in a week."

Then he gives me this sly look, like he's deciding if he can get away with something. "Let me ask you, Pop. After Mom died ... did you ever look around ... for company?"

"We Germans are like pumas, son," I begin to say. Which is as far as he lets me get, before he chimes in. "We mate for life."

It was hard, sometimes, to take my work seriously. Covering autumn? If the leaves fell without my writing about it, it would still be autumn; if they didn't fall, I had a scoop. Meanwhile, I was sharing autumn with the old man, streaks of color in the mountains, leaf raking in a dozen Shenandoah Valley towns and leaf burning and billboards advertising high school football games, bitter rivalries between places I'd never heard of, and Halloween closing in, pumpkins and goblins, spooks and effigies, and that snap in the air, flowers waiting for the first killing frost and, after that, maybe one year in three, the miracle of Indian summer. It was coming into Lexington, crossing over the Maury River, glancing upstream at the remnants of other bridges and an old mill that once drew power from the river. We passed a football stadium and meandered down streets lined with red brick houses, small shops and restaurants, the kinds of places that get murdered when the malls come in, and old houses with porches, gardens loaded with mums, people raking leaves in afternoon light. See, I told the old man, there's still nice places in America. There are handsome towns and fine drives, woods and farms and likeable cities, all here, spread out like the ingredients of a meal no one has quite figured out how to prepare.

The old man worried as we headed south. The brother waiting at the Flamingo Motel was bothering him. The night before, he'd gotten dressed while it was still dark and gone walking. The Flamingo Motel was getting closer, like a police car with lights flashing at the scene of an accident that included him.

We drove north out of Lexington, past horse farms, rolling country around Rockbridge Baths. The car windows were open, the radio off. We passed through Goshen, another crossroads collection of old houses and trailers and what looked like a school turned into a Dollar Value General Store. I divided American small towns into the ones that were waiting for something to happen and the ones that had given up on waiting. I'd have gotten a column out of that once. Now I had the thought and let it go: unseen leaf in an imagined forest.

"We're almost there, Pop," I said, downshifting as we started a serious uphill through George Washington National Forest. "Five miles."

"To where?" he asked. The mountain air perked him up.

"A place I never wrote about," I said. "Warm Springs."

"Where Roosevelt died?"

"That was Georgia. This is Virginia. Bath County. Jefferson wrote about it. Early on, this was spa country. Like Carlsbad and Baden Baden. You'll see."

"How come you never wrote it up?" he asked. "Sounds worth writing about."

"Also, worth *not* writing about." It was kind of a gift, not having to turn places into columns. When you wrote about places, whether you praised or knocked, you were a predator. That was the appeal of one true map to a writer tired of words. We came to the top of the mountain, Warm Springs Mountain. Through a cut in the trees along the road, we glimpsed what we left behind, Shenandoah Valley and Blue Ridge Mountains. Then we headed downhill.

"I don't want to build this up too much, Pop," I say. "You know how it is. You talk up a restaurant, bring a crowd of friends, that's the night that immigration raids the kitchen."

"If you never wrote about it," the old man says, "it must really be something."

"It's a place out of a children's book. 'The Happy Valley.' I always leave feeling ... better. You ever have a place like that, you could count on?"

"Yes," he said. "My back yard."

Now I could see the Warm Springs Courthouse, way down below, and the little town around it. We dropped out of the forest, into uphill meadows. Across, on the other side of the valley, one ridge of mountains followed another, all the way to West Virginia, like mountains doodled by kids who couldn't get enough of them. At the bottom of the hill, the highway that ran into the valley, east to west, intersected the highway that ran through the valley, north-south. The valley was no secret. It had a huge hundred-year-old hotel with a Sam Snead golf course, scores of Jamaican and Filipino servants, and hundreds of rooms that conventions, tournaments and old money couldn't seem to fill. That was a few miles down the road in Hot Springs. This was Warm Springs, one town north.

I pulled to the side of the road. A creek meandered through a grassy field, fenced off from the surrounding pastures, occupied by two rickety white clapboard buildings that the creek flowed in and out of: the Warm Springs Bathhouses. Getting out of the car, the old man stretched and strolled over to the brook, where he knelt on the grass, sniffed the air, and put his finger in the water.

"It's warm," he said. "I think I'm going to like this."

"That one …" I pointed to the building on the left, "… is for women. Mrs. Robert E. Lee. An invalid. They lowered her into the water."

"Let's go," he said, gesturing to the rickety bathhouse on the right. He was impatient, like a kid. Always. Start and finish. Even at Mom's funeral he was impatient, as if life itself were better when you started on time and finished early. So I let him go first, pulling open the bathhouse door. The bathhouse was an octagon, built of wood, white painted and peeling and before every season—April through October—management replaced a dozen of the most obviously rotten boards. That was about it. A building could last, that way. Stone buildings last forever and if they fall, they still leave something behind, a chimney or a wall, a ruin. Old wood buildings were something else again. Stone you respect. Wood you root for. I felt another column, slipping away from me.

Pop stopped as soon as he stepped through the doorway. He found himself on a boardwalk that circled around the pool. Off the boardwalk were a half dozen changing rooms. Overhead, the roof beams converged, like spokes meeting at the hub of a wheel, except where the hub would be, the roof stopped and there was a circle of sky overhead, so light came down into the water and sometimes rain, which didn't bother you at all.

He stared down into the pool, like a kid at the edge of a wishing well. The pool was thirty feet across and five feet deep and you could see through to the bottom, rock-covered, with bubbles, endless bubbles, rising to the surface. Pop knelt down again, just as he had outside, feeling water the temperature of warm milk, and bubbles like champagne. The old wooden building enfolded him, warm water mixing with nippy autumn air, winter just around the corner, and when he looked up he could see a late afternoon sky, pink-tinted clouds scudding by. We had the place to ourselves, except for the attendant who gave us towels and our choice of changing room. End of day, end of season: I liked the feeling. The old man turned to me, puzzled.

"Bathing trunks?" he asked me. The attendant overheard him.

"We don't use them here," he said, over his shoulder. "The women do."

"Is that so?" Pop responded. "Well, how about that?" He looked at me, shrugged and walked into a dressing room. I was the one feeling awkward. I took another room. He was already in the water when I emerged—I gave him time—and he was floating on his back, eyes sighting through the hole in the roof, when I stepped into the pool, going backward down the ladder, not that he was looking.

After that, the place took over, those tickling bubbles from down below, the whiff of lower regions, the changing light that filtered into the ancient clapboard shell and the quiet, the absolute quiet, except for the sound of the water, coursing in and out of the pool. It was baptism, immersion, cleansing, voyage. For the first half hour, we didn't speak. The power of the place was absolute. Sometimes Pop came into view, floating on his back, paddling lightly, or sitting on the steps at the edge of the pool.

"Well," he said after nearly an hour. "You've done good, George. I have to say."

"They close next week," I said. "We're just in time. They open again in the spring."

"I might be back," he said. "And George? Don't ever write this up ..."

"Not much risk of that."

"Just don't write about it till I'm gone. Promise?" Then he looked at me in the eyes. "At least we had this."

When I had toweled off and dressed, I stepped out into an evening that was chilly and found the old man sitting in a gazebo near the woman's bath house, ladling some water out of a well into a paper cup.

"That'll go through you like prune juice, Pop," I said, but I drank the cup he offered me. It felt like communion. "At least we'll be on the same schedule."

"Nippy out here," he said. "It feels good, after those baths."

I sat next to him, watching evening take over the valley, cows in a neighboring pasture turn into silhouettes, a dog barking up the road, a very occasional car coming up the road from Hot Springs, headlights on, though it wasn't quite dark.

"Good sleeping weather," he said. "We have far to go yet?"

"That's the beauty of it," I said. I nodded right across the street where the Warm Springs Inn sat at the meeting of the mountain roads. "Over there. I'll bring the car around. You just cross the street."

"Where do we go from here?"

"A day or two in the mountains, to someplace I can say, this is where autumn stops. That's all I need. After that I was I was thinking about Savannah."

"No," he said. "Please. I want to go to Florida. Direct. I can't dawdle. I can't wait. Please."

"Okay, Pop," I answered. "Whatever you say." Suddenly, something was ending. It felt sad, that our easy traveling was over, zig zagging here and there, stopping a day or a week, moving on when we pleased, following the leaves. The old man picked up on that. Or, it could be, he felt the same way himself.

"What about Germany? How's that looking?"

"Germany?"

The way he said it, it was if Germany were something new, a suggestion he was hearing for the first time. I might as well have said "Portugal" or "Chile." Something had changed, that I didn't want to press. Then, his mood changed. His face was grim. "Germany's waiting for me. Right down the road."

PART FIVE

I.

IT'S JUST PAST DAWN ON A HIGHWAY OUTSIDE OF NEW Port Richey, Florida and George and I are looking in at the Flamingo Motel which we found five miles south of town behind a car lot with prices chalked on windows and a line of plastic flags flapping in the breeze. The motel sits in back of the car lot. Air-cooled, the sign says. And NO VACANCY, though there's only two cars parked in front.

I pull into the lot. No one's around. That's good. I like the idea of getting there early and waiting, of seeing him before he sees me. I drive along the rows of cars for sale, clunkers mostly, till I find an empty space in the row that looks right out at the highway.

"I'll paint a price on the window," George says, "and we could sit here forever."

"It doesn't amount to much," I admit.

"At least it's not called Cheap Adolf's or Crazy Otto's," he says, trying to keep things light-hearted. George means well but it's not working. I feel my calves tensing, tying up into knots and the car's feeling small. I try stretching my legs but I can't.

"Listen, George," I say. "I've got to do this alone. When he comes. Whenever he comes. I meet him by myself."

"Okay by me," he says. "I'll hang back. I'll stay in the car and read. It could be a while, Pop."

"Could be," I grant. But I know I'm close. I can feel it all over me. "Please. Don't argue. I want you to take your stuff out of the car and walk across the street to that Eckerd's Drug Store. I want you to call a taxi and take it to the airport and fly north. Newark, if you can. If not, La Guardia."

"I know the names of the airports," he says. He's hurt, I can tell, and rightly so. It's as if I told him he could stay up till midnight and now it's lights out at eleven.

"I don't know how this is going to work," I admit. "Whether it lasts a day or a week. Whether I like it or hate it. But it's him and me. It's not a family party, 'here's my son, fine looking lad, thank you very much, a chip off the old block, looks like his mother, takes after his father, not his grandfather.' That stuff is for later. If ever."

"I get it. You're dumping me."

"I'm not going with you to *your* reunion," I say.

"Maybe you should," he counters. "I might need you." Still, he gets out of the car. I open the trunk. He pulls out his suitcase and his tote bag. Then we're just standing there, feeling foolish.

"Well," he says. "Good luck with this. If you think of it, pick up a bag of grapefruit on your way north. Indian River's the best." And suddenly he's hugging me. "Bring me some kumquats, too." He backs out of my arms, but we're still touching, his hands on my shoulder, my hands on his arms. We're standing there, looking foolish, but I don't care.

"I'm not done with you yet," he says.

"Well, I'm not done with you either."

"We sound like a couple of kids planning to have a fight."

"I think that's over," I say. "The fighting."

"Well, then ..."

"I'll see you up north," I say. "My boy."

Then I watch my son wait for an opening in traffic, scoot across the street, walk into Eckerd's. The next five minutes, I divide my attention between the drugstore in front of me and the motel in back. Then there's a taxi and I see George pile inside, looking over his shoulder to wave goodbye, like one of those times he went off to college. Hello and goodbye, that's what life is. And love, I guess, if you're lucky. I'm luckier than I knew. But, looking at the Flamingo Motel, I wonder how long my luck will last.

Twenty minutes later—8 a.m. sharp—a door opens on the second floor, a room at the end of the building. A man walks over to the railing, looks into the car lot, like a farmer checking crops. It's Heinz. It's Heinz plus forty years and forty pounds, but it's him alright. I see him. He doesn't see me or notice the car I'm sitting in. He goes down the steps. He walks well and he's nicely dressed for Florida, black slacks and a white shirt that's rolled up at the sleeves. He's not doing any work today. He always dressed sharp. He passes along the front of the building, past flower boxes full of weeds, pulls some keys out of his pocket, unlocks the office. Before he opens the door, I make my move. I slam the car door shut. He turns around—what's this?

I take my time. I sense my brother watching me and I guess he's irritated. We Germans never like dealing with people before we're ready and that means coffee, two cups. Then I step out and walk towards him, just waiting for the moment when he knows it's me, after all. And then it happens. He stares hard—could it be? is it? for sure?—and then, as if one more second of delay is unbearable, after so many years, he's running towards me, running awkward and flushed, Max Schmeling's road work partner, a heavyweight and then some, and he's making a sound that raises goose bumps, somewhere between singing and crying, and I'm suddenly wishing George could see this, how my brother hugs me. I'm losing it a little myself, so I hold him at arm's length and give him a real good look and try to say just the right thing.

"Boy, did you get old," I say. And my brother hugs me all over again. Then, he gets this puzzled look and looks around for my luggage, my car.

"I parked over there," I say, pointing over at the rows of cars. What a place for a reunion. I can't get over it. Two old men in a used car lot. In Florida. George, what would you make of this? Is God piling it on a little?

"It's alright? My parking over there?" How quickly we move to the important things! "They won't sell it while I'm visiting you?"

He waves off my worry and throws an arm around my shoulder. So far, he's said nothing. He just looks at me and chokes up. He takes me into the office, sits me down, and starts fussing with a coffee maker, looking back at me every few seconds so I don't disappear on him.

"I don't know where to begin with you," I say in German. And it's the truth. Do I start with the hard questions, the nightmare makers? Or do we have a nice chat? So, Heinz, how do you like the Sunshine State, the second time around? Things like that?

At the coffee machine, he shakes his head. He doesn't know where to start either, I suppose. He signals I should wait, while the coffee machine starts to drip. Looking around, I see what used to be the registration desk is now a salesman's cubbyhole. Behind it, there's a cork board with hooks dripping keys. The motel's out of business, I decide, but just then a black woman opens the door and sticks her head inside.

"Hi, sweetie," she calls out to Heinz. She's pushing a shopping cart full of sheets and towels, plus those little bars of soap and bottles of shampoo, with conditioner, they put in bathrooms. Heinz points to me, as if this were the opening day and I were customer number one and they'd get me to sign the first dollar I give them and put it in a frame behind the counter.

"Well, how about that!" the woman says. "The long lost brother. Hans, right? I'm Millie."

"Nice to meet you," I say. This place feels strange. Suddenly, I'm back at Schmeling's camp. *Der brother von Heinz.*

"I'll fix up number seven nice," Millie tells Heinz. Then she turns to me. "About time you came." With that, she disappears and Heinz brings over coffee, black.

"So," I say. "How was the voyage back to Germany?"

He laughs, shakes his head, points at his mouth. He shakes his head, no, no, no, and then I understand that funny noise he made as he came running towards me is the only noise that he makes any more, the last note on his scale. He shakes his head back and forth, no can do, no can do. His tongue has gone down for the count. He lifts a pad of paper and a ballpoint pen, like a student showing he's ready for school. I waited too long, I see, or not long enough. This was going to take a while, here in Florida.

Wait, he signals. He pantomimes the lifting of luggage, points out to the car lot. I should bring my stuff in. He points upstairs. Room seven. I get my luggage and I see Heinz walking around the back of the motel, with our coffee on a tray. I find room seven on my own. Millie is inside.

"It's clean alright," she says. "But it needs some airing out. Later on, you can turn on the air con."

"Not air-cooled?"

"That's from years ago," she says. "Heinz put in air-con."

"Millie, I don't understand. Who stays here?"

"Your brother," she answers. "This is how he does it. He starts out in one room, spends a night or two, moves into the next one, works his way down the hall, room to room. He likes it that way."

"And … it's just him?"

"Well, I'm in room four." Millie gives me a warning look. "That one he stays out of."

"Does he … is it a business?"

"He rents out the front, like you see. Those cars aren't much to look at. 'Little shit boxes,' he called them, before his stroke."

"When was that?" I ask. My guess is that the stroke was something that happened in the war. As if that were the only harm in the world.

"A year ago," Millie says. "He knocks on my door and shows me a piece of paper. *Millie, I had a stroke.* You believe it? He's doing okay now."

When I come down, Heinz is waiting at the bottom of the steps. He leads me around to the back of the motel. I expect weeds and a dumpster. You know how it is with motels, you walk around them in the morning, just stretching your legs. Out front they keep up appearances. Out back, nobody pretends. But I'm in for a surprise. There's a swimming pool, left behind from another time, filled with clean water, and a table and chairs underneath a beach umbrella. Heinz looks pleased and proud. He takes me into the garden that fills up the rest of the property, right up to the fence that runs around back. He has eggplant and morning glory and snap beans growing on the fence, like he's trying to see which can get to the top first. Between fence and pool, he's done all sorts of things that Germans do when they have time on their hands, flagstone paths winding around a sort of rock garden, a bird bath grotto with ceramic dwarves fishing in puddles and Roman babies pissing onto pebbles. He watches me take it in. I nod appreciatively, act impressed, even though the whole project is a disaster. He's got no idea what he's doing, no clue about sunlight, shade, watering and spacing, so he just threw a bunch of stuff in the ground and waited by the swimming pool to see what happened. "Nice place you have here," I say to him, still in German. Now he is ready to talk. He jots a quick note and hands it over. "*English, please,*" it said. And then, he starts writing. "*Dear brother. Thank you with all my heart for coming. This is what I wanted, for many years already. I always thought about you and Maria, wherever I was. H.*"

"Yes," I say when I finish. "I understand. I thought about you also. When I thought you were dead, even then you stayed in mind. Heinz, listen. Back then you were wrong. But I was wrong also. Letting you go, like I did. Leaving you. Losing you ..."

He shakes his head in disagreement, taking up his pen. And then something enormous overcomes me. I reach out and stop his hand from writing.

"She died," I tell him. "Our Maria." I watch him, to see how he reacts. When the news of a death reaches someone who hasn't heard, the death itself happens all over again and you're back on the day it happened. But while I watch him—wondering if he'd break down and what it would mean—he's watching me right back. It's strange. Did she send him a letter, while she was dying? Did she have his address all along?

"Cancer," I inform him. It's as if I'm dealing with it for the first time. "A little cough that wouldn't go away. Annoying, that's all. Stop it, I'd say and she hid it pretty well. But didn't get rid of it. So I pushed things. I wanted us to go back to Germany. She didn't feel like it, but she pretended she did. Well, over we went and it was me going out, and her sitting in hotel rooms. When we eat she hardly touches her food. She moves it around, I say it looks like food-arranging is her brand new hobby. Wasn't I a hoot? And I'm mad. I'm mad at her for getting sick and ruining our retirement, canceling out on all those trips we were going to take, all those tours and cruises. Out the window. All the time she was dying I was mad more than sad. Death wasn't cheating us. It was cheating me. She was leaving ahead of time. Skipping out on me. Absent without leave ..."

I stop to rest. I've been talking non-stop. Something is turned around, is backwards. He should be filling me in. Adventures, secrets, crimes and confessions, they should be coming from Heinz to me. Yet here I sit, like a priest on the wrong side of the confessional. Boy, that dead tongue is his secret weapon. Someone can't speak, you think of them as helpless, like a baby or someone very old. But Heinz has the edge. And I see his eyes are still gambler's eyes, taking chances I never took with my life, measuring odds, knowing me much better than I know him. I also notice a kind of valise at his feet, a scuffed-up leather thing, leaning against the edge of his chair. He rummages around and out comes a copy of George's first book about interstate interruptions.

"Where'd you find that old thing?" I wonder aloud. "And how did you know that this guy was your nephew?"

He opens up to the front page and now I see. George dedicated the book to his parents, Hans and Maria Greifinger, from "the little boy in the back seat." I'd forgotten that. At the time, I said he dedicated it to us because, what with the name difference, he could tell anyone who asked that he was adopted.

"What else you got in there?" I ask. It's a regular show-and-tell period. Out comes another book, this one in German, Max Schmeling's autobiography. I didn't even know he wrote it. Heinz has it all over me in the homework department.

He passes me the Schmeling book, opened to a certain page. Maybe he got mentioned, I guess, or maybe I did: how Max played horseshoes on my property. But what Heinz wants me to look at is a photograph. I see Max in boxing trunks, clinging to ring ropes and the ropes are all that holds him up. The caption says it's his last fight, 1948, scuffling for money among piles of rubble, the glory days gone forever, you might as well ask the Hindenburg to try another landing at Lakehurst.

When I hand the book back to Heinz, he points at himself and at the photo, back and forth, as if to say, Max and me, Max and me, the whole story of his life.

"You were with him at the end?" I ask. "You found him after the war?" Heinz nods. "How many fights?" He holds up five fingers. Then, three up, two down. Then he waves the memories away. Next he pulls out a clipping, a business story, and watches me read it: how Max contacted James Farley, Roosevelt's postmaster general and a long-time political operator, and Farley helped Max get set up with a Coca-Cola franchise in Hamburg. And when I finish reading, Heinz makes the same sign, him and me.

"So you went in business together. Economic miracle. Germany comes off the canvas."

Yes, Heinz nods. And then, maybe for the first time that day, I have a thought of my own. I'm not just responding to what he gives me, a piece of the time. "You know, I wrote Max after the war," I say. "About you. I thought you were dead … and I blamed myself … and I thought, well, maybe you got lucky. And Max might know. Max wrote back, too. He said you went to Russia. Twice. That's all he knew. So he said."

Heinz smiles, almost like a kid who pulled off a fast one. He points at himself, pantomimes writing. Now we're doing charades. He folds an imaginary letter, licks a stamp, waves goodbye to it. So the joke was on me. Then, seeing some anger flash across my face, he writes a real note. *So you wouldn't worry about me anymore.*

"But now's the time for us?"

He nods.

"Too late for Maria," I say. He closes his eyes, bows his head. The meaning is clear: I'm sorry.

"So where were you, Heinz? Were you in Russia? Or was that something you made up?"

That's where the curtain comes down. He gives me a look that makes me feel, though we're sitting close, we're miles away. It's like the gap between a healthy hospital visitor and a terminal patient. So near and yet so far. Hey? What do you know about it? He puts paper and pencil back in the valise. Over and out. It's his story. His life. I don't own it. He'll tell me what he wants me to know, not more. I don't think he'll lie to me, although that Schmeling letter was a lie. But then—why contact me at all, if not to tell me the truth? Maybe he just wanted to see me, that rush across the parking lot, that crying, gurgling sound that came right past his tongue. Maybe that was all he wanted.

"She put your picture on a shelf in the living room," I say. "And it stayed there all through the war. You in uniform, with her, that last visit she made before the war. I wanted that photo down. She said no. I thought you'd like to know."

He sits there, taking it in. I have spoken, if not in anger, then with some other kind of feeling, and I can tell it registers. He blushes some, though it's hard to be sure, he flushes easily, big as he is and in this heat. He looks at his watch. He rubs his stomach. He's inviting me out.

His car is a BMW that smells new. He turns on the air conditioner, which I appreciate. He turns off the radio, but not before I notice it's one of those easy listening music stations. "We've Only Just Begun," by that woman who starved herself. Odd, listening to that on the way to lunch. Heinz is a good driver, left hand on the wheel, right relaxing at his side. What's more, he's got that air of ownership people have, driving in their own neighborhood, keeping track of things. I can't get over seeing him, cruising down a Miracle Mile, mall to mall, and pausing at a stoplight across from a "Bagel Bonanza" store, next to a pick up truck full of sun-tanned kids with bleached-out hair and a portable radio blasting music. Florida makes that war I worried about seem far away and long ago. Maybe Florida is right. It was four or five years out of more than seventy, he's lived. What's my problem, anyway?

"How's Max?" I ask. Heinz gives a thumb up. "Still alive," I muse. "That's something. All the others, down for the count. Louis, Baer, Sharkey, Carnera, the bunch, he outlasted them all. Joe Jacobs died, though. I guess you knew that." Heinz nodded. "He was something. Did you like him?" Heinz nods. "Not every Jew would have handled a German back then," I add. It's a leading question. I'm watching for Heinz to make a face or maybe rub his fingers together as if to say, well he got his money. But all I get is another nod.

We're moseying along the coast now, in no rush. It's terrible what they get away with, building on beaches, big houses that look like space stations, other houses in developments—transplanted Levittowns—where one shot could kill a dozen mailboxes. But then it thins out and we're closer to the Gulf of Mexico, more like a lake than an ocean, with inlets and bridges, keys and passes and folks fishing, senior citizens studying the newspaper weather map while waiting for a bite. After twenty miles, he cuts inland into orange groves, and I remember that happy time when I was a greenhorn, the time of oranges. Now he rolls down the windows, so we can catch the smell. He breathes deep and smiles at me. At that moment, he's so loving, it's more than I can bear, thinking in another couple of years, one or both of us would have been gone. We finally got back to Florida. New Jersey was my America. This was his. A paradise of oranges.

"As long as she lived, she wondered about you," I say. "She never forgot. That picture was like a shrine. I never could figure it out."

He nods as if to say, he couldn't figure it out himself.

"Some ways, she was rough on you, Heinz. That last time, at the Bund picnic, she wanted out of there. If it were up to me, I would have gone back for you. We were scared, though. And I guess you made your peace with her. I mean, you were in that photo, side by side."

Another nod. He couldn't be more agreeable.

"After I heard you went back to Germany—Otto Hofer called and told me—I told Mom and she said it was just as well you went. That got me. What if a war came, I asked. At least one brother would be on the winning side, she fired back. That was harsh, I thought. She wasn't like that, usually. Then she calms down. If you stayed in the U.S., she says you'd be a traitor. A criminal. But there were criminals over there, too, weren't there? Or so the whole world thinks."

He nods and just keeps driving. I'm right where I ought to ask: were you one of them? One of the criminals? But I just can't manage it. And he just keeps driving. That speech loss is a million dollar wound.

"One thing I wonder is … whether she loved you before she married me. Whether I was something she came up with on the bounce. Rebound, I mean."

No, no, he shakes his head. Maybe he's saying I've got it all wrong. Or I'm dead right and he doesn't want to talk about it. Or how dare I even ask.

"So," I say. "Was I kind of … number two? I mean, she left you at that camp. She watched me drive away. But later that year, you see her in Germany. You're in that picture together. I had to wonder. But I never asked. Never found the right moment."

He glares at me. He gives me a look I haven't seen since I was small. But none of it works. I plow ahead. "It doesn't change anything … but … I'm sorry … I'd like to know. What was going on with you two."

All of a sudden, he slaps the turn signal and pulls over to the side of the road. He reaches past me, elbowing me a little, and pulls a pencil and another pad of paper out of the glove compartment. He opens the door of the car to catch a breeze, starts to write. Then he sees me, sitting there. Go take a walk, he signals. Go play in traffic.

He's scribbling as I walk away. I stand under an orange tree, at the edge of the grove, thankful for shade. Heinz looks like a student taking an exam, struggling to beat the clock. I step into the orange grove. There are rows and rows of trees loaded with fruit, so close to the road. And dozens of oranges, dozens under each tree, that no one will ever eat. Windfall oranges. I keep walking. Fruit above, fresh as blossoms, marmalade at my feet. And bees everywhere, fat and sluggish Florida bees, too lazy to sting. The car's far away now, a glint of metal at the side of the road. The orange trees surround me. The smell of them could make you swoon, alleys of orange trees, you could walk in circles, you could wander for days. Maybe that's what I deserve. *I'm sorry, Mom*: I say it aloud and my voice is choking. *Bringing you up this way. I'm sorry. I've got a good memory for bad things and the good things I take for granted. I'm sorry.* I've gotten so deep into oranges, I can't even see that zone of sunlight that would mark the edge of the road. Hey, I'm lost. Do I drop markers on the ground, to make sure I'm walking in a straight line? What do I use, in here, for markers? Oranges? They're all over the ground, in all directions. I step on them, left and right, the place is rotten with oranges, I hear a truck go booming by and I head towards where the sound came from. When I come out on the road I'm a quarter mile from the car, on a shoulder that's littered with beer cans and pizza boxes. Heinz is staring anxiously into the orange groves. Then he sees me coming and he waves. As soon as I get back to the car he hands me what he's written, signals me to sit and read. I try putting it in my pocket. Read it now, he gestures. Right here, right now.

Hans, it begins. *I had my eye on Maria from the minute I saw her. I told my friends, she's young, but when she's older, she's mine, you stay away. I was a playboy, in the meantime. She saw that. And then you came in, a complete greenhorn, and she wanted you. So if you think you saw something between us, maybe you did. But it wasn't what you thought. It wasn't about what was. It was about what might have been. That's why she didn't take the photograph down. She was a good woman. Better than we deserved. Either of us. H.*

When I finished reading I sat awhile, wondering why Mom took me and not my brother. I got out of the car and came around to where he was, leaning against the car, looking down the road. There were tears in his eyes. And mine.

"I'm sorry," I say. He nods. "I can eat now," I say. He nods again. We keep driving through the orange groves, which go on forever.

"Your brother's out back," Millie says. It's next day, the middle of the morning and the heat is something fierce. Tar bubbles and blisters, grass turns into straw and that car lot looks like a barbecue grill loaded with lobsters.

"Swimming?"

"I wish," Millie answered. "Working in the garden. You know anything about gardens?"

"Yes," I answer. "A lot."

"Anything you could do, you'd be doing a favor. There's a world of pain out back."

I slip on some shorts and a pair of old shoes and walk around to the back of the building and right away, I see what Millie meant. It's a comedy, a clown show, and a good thing he's working in back of the motel, not in front, because people would pull over to watch, the way they slow down passing a car accident. Heinz as a gardener would be an attraction, right up with the Parrot Jungle and the Circus Hall of Fame. He's sweaty and dirty, sighing and grunting and he's got no idea what he's doing. He waters the flagstones, not the plants, with a hose that gets wrapped around the legs of a chair and garrots some snapdragons. Another thing, he's wearing the same clothes—slacks, shirt and shoes—he wore at lunch, that are covered with dirt and water and green smudges. He's got no clothes to work in—he never did—and if I guess right, he believes that this is all part of it, if you don't finish looking awful, you weren't out there. He can't tell weeds from plants and when he weeds he grabs the tops and yanks hard, leaving the roots in the ground. He's bought himself a tree that he's digging a hole for, huffing and puffing. First time he tries to put in the tree, the hole's too shallow. The tree looks like a statue, up on a pedestal. Next, he digs deeper, dirt flying in every direction and the tree half disappears, its lower branches touching the edge, like the poor thing is clinging to the side of a deep pit. He fusses some and on the next try the tree is lopsided, like something you'd see growing off the side of a mountain. Then he decides, well, time to rest, and he pulls out the chair, which is tangled in the hose, which knocks over the other chair and it goes into the swimming pool.

"Don't move," I shout. I sound like a television cop breaking into a drug deal. But I see a rake right at his side, upside down, ready for him to step on it so he can puncture his foot and—boing!—knock out his teeth. This whole garden is like one of those things they used to run in the Sunday funnies: how many things are wrong with this picture? So he obeys, he stays in his chair, smiling weakly at me.

I motion Heinz to stay: *Don't just do something, sit there*. And bit by bit, I set the place in order. The tools that are all over the backyard, dropped or thrown, I put on the table. I follow the hose, which has actual knots in it to where it's half attached to a faucet at the back of the motel. It's made a puddle that could fill a bathtub and there's black mold on the concrete that National Geographic should photograph. I turn off the water, re-connect the hose, tight, and turn on the water, not full-blast like Heinz had it, but less than half and I set the end of it in his vegetable garden, near the fence where some eggplant have been trying hard to jump to freedom.

It's simple. Heinz loves the idea of having a garden. I love gardening. That's the difference. I take a spade and square up the hole. When it's ready, I motion Heinz over. Like a parent lifting a bratty kid by his throat, he hoists the tree—a kumquat tree, the tag says —and holds it over the hole. It's bombs away, any minute. I stop. I tell him it's a good idea to take the tree out of the pot it came in before he plants it, and to loosen the roots. The survival rate goes up enormously, if you do that. And we don't drop the tree in the hole, like a World War II pilot putting a bomb down the smokestack of a Japanese battleship. We take the tree in our hands—like this, see?—and we put it gently in the hole, fitting and turning it, till everything is snug and comfortable. It has to feel right, I say. Then, while we're kneeling down on the ground, we take soil, a little at a time, and we fill in the space between the earth that the tree came with and the earth around it, we pat things into place, like this, we build a mound around the newcomer, because the soil will settle later. And then—bring that hose over here, brother of mine—we give the lemon tree a drink of water, just a trickle at the roots. Next I lead him over to the so-called vegetable garden, where he's got an acre's worth of tomato plants in a ten by ten plot of ground. It's a jungle out there, survival of the fittest, it's a scene from Our Crowded Planet. I take half the plants out, so there's at least eighteen inches between what remains. I spade the soil between the plants, so the roots get air, and I don't turn over five pounds of soil at a time, this is a garden, not a trench on the Russian front.

He's been watching me, he's good at that. Now I signal he should get down on his knees, please. I teach him how to weed, how to pull gently from the bottom, so that everything comes out, roots and all and I suggest that, though it's fun to throw weeds over your shoulder it's even better if you put them in a pile. That way, we can start a compost pile. I have my doubts about this, that I don't tell him. In New Jersey we had food scraps, grass cuttings, leaves. In Florida, I don't know. Maybe he can get doggie bags when he eats out, add French fries and dinner muffins and Jello to the mix. Now I'm done for the day. I sit down next to him. He nods thanks. I guess I got a little out of hand—it's his garden—and I was bossy.

"I'm sorry if I ..." It's not easy to convey regrets, after I've killed myself while he was mostly watching. Someone should tell him that mid-afternoon isn't green thumb time in Florida. "I know it's your garden." And then, when I look at Heinz, I see I'm wrong. It's all over his face. This garden wasn't for him. It was for me.

"I've been wondering," I start. It's my fourth day with Heinz. We've both cleaned up and we're down in front of the Flamingo, headed out for dinner. To be honest, it tires me out, this long-awaited reunion. Heinz organizes his day around errands and meals and it's always just the two of us, which means that I do all the talking but I can't talk about what I really want to know. Even now, as soon as it sounds like there might be a question coming, I see him backing off.

"... what you live on," I say. "The money side of things down here."

He relaxes, relieved it's not about the war.

"This motel isn't exactly a cash cow," I continue. "You drive a new BMW. We eat where you want and it's always your treat."

Wait a minute, he signals, wagging a finger. You'll see. Off we go, down the coast ten miles and then cut inland. I still can't get over seeing him here. Who are his friends? Heinz was always the heart of the crowd. And what about women? He loved women and they went for him and he still draws looks, when we're out together. Tonight, for instance, he's got polished leather shoes and black slacks, nicely creased, and a light blue shirt that's long sleeved, with the cuffs nicely folded above his wrists. Me, I'm wearing stuff Mom bought for me years ago, a pink polo shirt with some kind of animal, maybe a crab, crawling around the pocket and khaki slacks and open-toed sandals.

After half an hour, Heinz pulls into a line of cars stopped outside the gatehouse of something called The Greens. The guard waves some people through, saluting briskly. Others they check and double-check, making a phone call to warn insiders that someone's coming. They recognize Heinz. More than that, they throw him a salute, an arms-out Hitler salute, that's a running joke, I guess. Heinz waves back—an on-purpose sloppy wave—and gives me a what-can-I-do-about-it look, the same look he gave me at the entrance to Camp Deutschland, years and years ago. It gives me the willies. We head down a curving road that has a landscaped island in the center, with hibiscus and plumeria and grass that looks like an unrolled carpet. Left and right, I see a line of antique lamps and benches. There was a time, I guess, when people grew up—like my son—thinking that, if they made it big, they'd live in Manhattan with a view of Central Park. That was the dream. But dreams go out of style. And America came up with something different to dream about, a place like The Greens, where you live on the edge of a golf course.

At the end of the road there's a gate. Heinz picks up a plastic gadget, like a remote control for a TV, pushes a button and the gate opens, then closes behind us. We head down a crushed coral driveway, towards a house that has a garage that's bigger than our whole place in Berkeley Heights. The driveway curls around the front of the house, showing off the property, which includes a lily pond, a row of palms, a hedge of hibiscus, lots of orange trees and flower beds, well-kept. As we get close to the house, a couple of dogs—German shepherds—come running out to us. They recognize the car, they dance around it. He gets out and the dogs are all over him, jumping up, licking his face, rubbing against his legs. Me, they're not so sure about.

"Ticks and fleas must be something fierce in Florida," I say. Not much of a contribution. Anyway, Heinz doesn't hear me: the dogs have priority. The front door opens and a man and woman come walking down the sidewalk.

"Hi, Pop," the woman says to Heinz. "I wish they gave me that kind of hello." Heinz is sitting down, getting dog-loved. He better wash up before he eats. Hitler loved dogs too, I recall. While he takes care of this important business, he signals for everybody to introduce themselves.

"Hi," the woman says. "I'm Debbie Greifinger Barnes."

"I'm Buddy Greifinger," says the guy.

"I'm Hans," I say. No need to add Greifinger. "Who are you folks, anyway?"

"We're his kids," Buddy says.

"I guess we should call you uncle," Debbie adds.

"Nice to meet you," I say. Once they tell me he's my brother's son, I can see some resemblance around Buddy's mouth —the look of a charmer—and in the way he carries himself. Debbie has more of Heinz, a female Heinz, looking like one of the cable television women who sell exercise equipment, stomach firmers you can put in a suitcase, rowing machines where you can work out and watch television at the same time.

"Were you born here?" I ask. "Or on the other side?"

"Over there," Buddy says. "Right before they came over. Hey Pop, what was the name of the place l was born at?"

"Buddy!" his sister protests. "You know he can't ..." Heinz glances up, gives Buddy a what-a-cluck-you-are look. He points to his tongue, the same as he'd done for me, only then he was smiling.

"Oh yeah," Buddy says. "I keep forgetting. A man talks to you all your life, you forget to adjust. I don't think he had a stroke, actually. I think he just ran out of words. My theory is, you have only so many in you. You run out, that's all."

"Was it Hamburg?" I ask.

"That's right," Buddy says. "I guess I'll go over, check it out sometime. I don't remember a thing."

"About your mother," I say. Heinz is still fussing with the dogs, checking for ticks and fleas, running his fingers through their fur, lifting their ears, taking his time. "When did she pass on?"

"Beg pardon?" Debbie says. "Do you know something I don't?"

"She's in Germany," Buddy says. "She goes back every year, spends a couple of months. Far as I know, she's fine. Anyway, we keep getting credit card statements."

"Could we go in, now?" Debbie asks. "Pop?" Heinz lifts himself off the ground. He and his son head in towards the house. Debbie takes me by the elbow to follow but, when I start walking, she holds me back.

"This all must be a lot for you to take in, Uncle Hans," she says.

"We were out of touch for a long time. We were close once and then we headed in different directions. Then came the war."

"That was … World War II?"

"Yes," I answer. Dumbfounded. It's amazing what you can't count on people to know.

"It's been over a while, hasn't it," she says. And, I guess, maybe she's not so dumb after all. "You stayed out of touch a long time."

"It's hard to explain. I thought he was dead. And maybe he thought it was just as well. Does he … I mean did he … ever talk about it?"

"Never," she says. "It's off-limits. He was in it, over there. Someplace. That's all I know. I'm sure of one thing, though. He's excited about you. I've never seen him that way about anyone. He told us ..." She stops to correct herself. "I mean, he wrote it down, that he tried to reach you."

"By postcard!"

"Well he can't call, can he now?" she says.

"No, but not a regular letter? Or registered mail?"

"He's a funny man," Debbie says. "Sometimes, he's funny hah-hah. Sometimes another kind of funny. But, he let us know. Any day now. The long lost brother ..."

"No," I interrupt. "*He* was the long-lost brother."

Heinz and Buddy stand waiting at the front door. When I get there, Heinz takes me by the arm and leads the tour, with his son trailing along behind, like a realtor commenting on points of quality that might not meet the eye: central air conditioning, controlled in every room, central heating, even central vacuuming, a hose in every room, and the dust shoots right down into the cellar, so you don't have to drag that doodlebug behind you. The house is huge and modern: it has high ceilings and tall windows, a covered porch, an open patio and a restaurant-size kitchen with Mediterranean-looking tiles, six-burner stove, a counter the size of an autopsy table, strings of garlic and tomatoes everywhere, bowls of fruit that looks just like the soap that looks like fruit in bathrooms. There's even an "entertainment center" with a television screen the size of a bed sheet and three little kids camped in front, watching something with rocket ships.

"Those two girls are mine," Buddy tells me. "The boy is Debbie's."

Heinz creeps up behind them and puts his arms around them. He gets a short flurry of hugs and "Hi, Opa," but then the novelty wears off. On the whole, he'd done better with the dogs.

"Kids," says Buddy, "this is your *opa's* brother. He's your Uncle Hans."

Maybe it would go better if he waited for a commercial. When I step around to say hello I make the fatal error of standing in front of the television screen. One minute they're looking at me, the next they're looking around me. I'm in the way. We leave the kids and head through the kitchen, out to the patio, where Debbie is grilling hamburgers. Heinz joins her while Buddy goes for beer.

"I couldn't find any Ballantines," he says. "Pop said you used to work there. Here's a Becks."

"That's good," I say. "Nice place you have here."

"I'm glad it's here. I'm divorced. I live in an apartment. Tiny. The kids like to come here. Debbie's husband is a recreation guy, works on a cruise ship, like the … you know … Love Boat. She did the same thing, till the kid came along. They live in Fort Lauderdale. They like coming over. Hey …" He looked at my beer, which I was holding. "I'll bet you want a stein!"

"I'd like that, yes," I say.

"It's okay, Pop's the same way." In the kitchen he discovers a mug, which he brings out to me. For himself, he pours vodka over a glass full of ice cubes and adds a little tonic water. He smiles when we toast each other. What a funny habit it must seem. Beer in a glass. So Old World.

"So … you don't live here?" I ask.

"Just visit … when I get custody."

"So … the house belongs to …"

"Pop. Mom and Pop."

"His house?"

"Sure. Him and Mom found this place themselves. Designed it too."

His house. I can't resist getting up and walking around, looking at the place more carefully, now that I know who owns it. Looking for him, in the house. And not finding him. When Heinz came back to America the second time around, he did it right, he did it all the way and, if this house is any measure, his first commandment was: never look back. This time around, I'm the disloyal one, he's the hundred-percent *Amerikaner.*

"When he came over he was in beer and soft drinks," Buddy says. "Before long he was into real estate. He's got the gift of gab."

"Always did," I agree.

"A natural. He had a piece of this development. A big piece."

"Then ... what confuses me ... is the motel? The Flamingo? Where does that fit in?"

"Hah! That's a question."

"He lives there. So I thought."

"I guess," Buddy says. "But it's nothing. It's a toy, a hobby is all. People buy old trailers, don't they? Vintage cars? Railroad cars, even? Maybe motels are the next thing. It didn't cost much. Back taxes. He bought it at auction. It's just his hangout. His place to go to get away from ... well ... us."

"It's different when your mother's home?"

"Not so different. He shows up, he eats. He feeds the dogs. Sometimes he sleeps here, sometimes he goes back to the motel. He's like a kid with a tent in the woods. Only there's no parents to make him come in."

Dinner is strange. With Heinz, I'm accustomed to sitting in silence. Now, with Debbie and Buddy, there is something called conversation that has to be kept going, like a ball that can't hit the ground but has to go on bouncing from mouth to mouth. While I get tired hitting the ball, Heinz sits contentedly, enjoying his food, nodding, smiling now and then. Buddy talks real estate. He'd gone into the business, though with less success than his old man. But it wasn't his fault.

"Pop caught it just right," he sighs. "Late fifties, early sixties, you'd be an idiot, if you didn't get rich. It rolled in."

Those were the days. I've heard it before, I've said it myself, but it sounds different, coming from a young fellow. Angrier. George sounds the same way, sometimes. You guys, you old-timers, you got in on the ground floor of *everything*. Cream off the top, high on the hog, fat of the land. Now you sit back and congratulate yourselves and watch us struggle for table scraps, watch us mess with the ... the what? ... the Japs, the Arabs, the blacks, the I.R.S. I wonder who his particular villain is.

"What happened?" I ask. And get five minutes on growth restrictions, building codes and the damned E.P.A. Buddy drinks vodka like water and it starts to show. It's amazing how fast things can go downhill with family. Here's a bunch of blood relations I've never met before. I can see my brother in them, when I look, and my parents too: the nose, of course, the eyes, and the set of the shoulders and a certain impatience, something that makes it hard to sit still for long. We're reunited, just like those reunions you see on television during the day, all the hugs and screams. For about a minute. After that it's some guy you barely know, some version of yourself, wondering what's your position on capital punishment. It's like you recorded an original song—words and music—and you hear a bunch of copycats singing it. But it's not the real thing.

After awhile, Buddy warms up on blacks. Not all blacks are niggers, not by any means, he grants that much, some of them it doesn't matter what color they were, black, white, or green. But some others—he could show me tonight—are. Whole neighborhoods, shot to hell. I look at Heinz.

"Remember Cleveland?" I ask. "And Billy?"

He nods. He probably still owes them money from a bet he lost.

"Ever wonder where they wound up?"

Another nod. Our eyes meet. For a second we link up. Then Debbie calls out from the kitchen, whether we want coffee now or later. At that, Heinz just lifts himself out of his chair and motions for me to follow him. Buddy pops up to trail along but Heinz indicates, no, it's okay for him to stay, maybe help his sister in the kitchen.

"Now you'll meet his real family," Buddy says, a little resentfully. "They weren't here, we'd be down to Christmas and Thanksgiving."

Heinz leads me across the patio out onto the grass, still wet from the sprinklers, sweet smelling. From a far fenced-off corner comes the sound of joyful barking. Now I see a whole pack of dogs. I guess we'll get swarmed, nuzzled and licked to death, Heinz especially. But when he opens the gate he claps his hands, twice hard, and maybe he isn't any kind of gardener and maybe his kids are write-offs, but he sure has his dogs in shape. Except for one who was nursing puppies—he excuses her with a wave of the hand, when she starts to get up—his dogs sit quietly. He greets each one of them, the two German shepherds from out front and the others, a mixed bag, kneeling in front of them, touching them. When he's done, he claps his hands again and the dogs break ranks, some of them playing, others rolling over on their backs, hoping for a tummy scratch, one or two drinking water, making that musical sound while their tags clink against the side of the bowl. Heinz meanwhile leads me over to the puppies, four of them, golden-retriever looking, but smaller and shorter haired. He makes an approving sound, like he's humming. Then he gestures for me to take one.

"No way," I say. "Drive back north with a puppy in the back? Cover the seat with newspapers?"

He's not giving in. Take one, he commands.

"I'm a little old," I tell him. "Puppies are for kids, they grow up together. After maybe fifteen years, the dog dies and the kid gets his learner's permit."

Heinz stares at me, just waiting, listening and not believing a word. And then the moment comes, just like we both knew it would, because we're brothers.

"Maybe if you had something older," I say.

Sure, Heinz signals. Right away, the German shepherds are in front of me, his special pets. Take one, take two, I don't care, he signals. But I can't take them.

"Could I see the others?"

There's a Dalmatian. Sorry. Dalmatians remind me of Budweiser beer ads. There's a collie. I didn't know they still made collies, after Lassie went off the air. And there's a brown something or other that comes over last, with a what-kept-you-so-long look on the face, a mutt, no doubt about it. And smart. Some dogs are all appetite and impulse. Others mull things over. This one's a thinker. I check around back. A male. Sits confidently. Waits patiently. This case is closed. I can picture him next to me in the front seat when we head north to Jersey. And I remember a man who I met in New Jersey.

"Hello, there," I say, "Mr. Jacobs."

Wouldn't you know it? Buddy has a boat that his father bought for him. The next day we go out on the water, there's no getting out of it. At least we don't pretend to fish, we just go streaking up and down the coast, poking into rivers and inlets, sneaking peaks at the houses that millionaires build along the water. Mr. Jacobs likes what he sees, he rides up front like a hood ornament on the top of a car. It's hard to talk when a boat is speeding. The idea, I guess, is that we're all supposed to be speechless with joy. Heinz and I sit on chairs bolted to the deck, while Buddy steers and, now and then, shouts out the price of waterfront footage. Heinz, meanwhile, smiles up at the sun as if he's personally grateful for its appearance today. The Russian front could do that to you. If that's where he was. But I may never know. It's none of my business. Still, it gets to me. There's men all over America who've come back from wars, making it very clear that they didn't want to talk about it. And people respected that. But a German—from that war—you can't cut the same slack. They have so much more not to talk about.

"Heinz," I say, "I've got to go back to Jersey. Not this minute," I assure him. "Not even tomorrow. But the next day. Soon, anyway."

Out come the paper and pencil. He hasn't used them much lately because I've stopped asking questions. We've settled into a pattern, no questions asked, puttering around together, taking Mr. Jacobs to the beach, contemplating senior citizen early-bird specials. We move from room to room in the motel, up and down the hall, a pattern that seems completely sensible and natural. One night, there's just a wall, the next we've got a half dozen rooms in between.

What is wrong, he writes. *Everything you need is here.* "Well, that's mostly right," I say. "But you didn't expect me to come and never leave, did you?" I look again. "Did you?" I can tell that's exactly what he wanted. "Heinz," I plea, "you've got your wife coming back from Germany soon. I guess you timed our reunion so that it would happen while she's away but still ..." *I visit the house every day.* Then he smiles and adds a line. *I see her when I feed the dogs.*

I'll come back again, I promise, I'll come back every winter, I'll spend February and March every year. But he just doesn't want to see me drive away. He was thinking of taking a trip down to Key West, he writes, and he already has Debbie working on a surprise for me, a cruise through the Caribbean. And there was the America he hadn't seen, all those places out West. *The Grand Canyon. Yellowstone. Alaska!*

"I'll come down in winters. I'll meet your wife. I'll come down again *this* winter ... in January. That's what? Eight weeks? I really look forward to meeting her."

He shrugs. He doesn't seem to care whether I meet my sister-in-law or not. I saw pictures of her at the house, an *echt* German blonde, the kind you picture on skis in the alps, bursting with health. Later, she put on weight—you could trace it in the pictures—but she's got that patented German I-am-sturdy look. Some of these women talk a lot and I have a hunch this might be one of them. Heinz can't talk. That makes it worse. Maybe he sits around, hoping his ears will go out next.

Buddy and Debbie and the three kids meet us for a farewell dinner at an Italian place called Pavarotti's. The margaritas come in buckets, the onion soup is a crock the size of a flower pot, with a big gob of Parmesan on top, half melted, so it looks like they dropped a grilled cheese sandwich in it on the way out from the kitchen. The pasta comes in piles, not portions, you get the idea, but thanks to the margaritas, Buddy is lively and for once I don't have to talk a lot. Debbie chats with me a little—I make sure I sat next to her—and she strikes me as a lively woman who's just now discovering she made all the wrong choices. She talks about going to college up north and maybe law school. Every now and then I check out Heinz, who listens to Buddy conspire about some orange-grower who's ready to subdivide. Well, Heinz, I say to myself, looks like you finally made it in America.

It's already late when we get back to the Flamingo. There's a funny peacefulness about a car lot after closing time. The cars sit out like senior citizens on the porch of a retirement home. You can almost hear them talking. *You still here?* asks one and *yeah, made it through another day,* says another and, *I got worried for a while,* comments the third, *they popped my hood and poked around. That's nothing,* says a fourth, *they're turning back my odometer. Oh man, bad news,* adds a fifth, *I got taken for a ride around the block and the son of a bitch kicked my tires when we got back.* Then, they all say goodnight. But not Heinz. He taps me on my shoulder, signals, let's take a swim, which we do often, a couple times a day.

"But my swimming suit is packed," I say, pointing to where my car is pulled around to the front, full of gas and oil, pointed north. So what, he shrugs. He's right. So what. I shouldn't be in so much of a rush. I go up to my room for Mr. Jacobs, who stands at the door—he heard me coming—and I can see the place on my bed where he was sleeping and it looks like his head was on my pillow. We'll talk about this later, I tell him. I go to the pool. Heinz isn't there yet. I take off everything, pile it near the edge, and step into the water. The pool is just thirty feet long so you can do a lot of laps quickly and think you've accomplished something. I start swimming back and forth, Mr. Jacobs running alongside back and forth, until he decides it isn't worth it and flops down on the pile of clothing. I keep going. Full moon. There is glitter on the waves I make and the leaves on the trees are all shining. Now, I see that Heinz has come. He's unwinding the hose—carefully—and watering, just the way I showed him, mainly concentrating on the roots, but he can't resist splashing the leaves, and I can't blame him: they're dripping silver now.

Heinz slips into the pool and stands by the edge, just watching me go back and forth. While I swim, I think about how to say goodbye. Germans go out of their way to avoid emotional scenes: those are for Italians. We shake hands, we nod, we're gone. I want something special that's not corny. I paddle towards him, altering course, catch the ladder and wrap my arms around it. He's in chest-deep water, arms up on the edge, facing me. I stare up at the moon, which pleases me. I've always wished that full moons came more often. I point up, so that Heinz can appreciate it too.

Then comes a moment that will give me goose bumps the rest of my life. I hear something frightening. I turn towards what I hear, which is a voice out of the past, the kind of English—correct, school-learned German English—that I remembered hearing from Hauptmann and Schmeling and Heinz Greifinger.

"Well, *brüderchen,*" he said. "So how do you like your trip to Florida?"

PART SIX

I.

SATURDAY NIGHT—DATE NIGHT, WE USED TO CALL it—was turning into Sunday morning. The bars on Columbus Avenue were crowded, limousines were parked outside Mexican restaurants, a queue of yuppies waited for admission to Steve's Ice Cream. And the Sunday *New York Times*, fat and smug, crowded walkers off the sidewalks. An appeal to conscience, to all the things you're supposed to care about, movies, surrogate mothers, peace in the Middle East, homeless people, the environment, all of it waiting to ambush you at brunch. I bought a copy and thinned it savagely, a section at a time, one for every garbage pail as I walked home. It had felt good, being out of reach of the *Times*.

I missed my old man. The motels, the rest-stops, the random roadside food. Also, his moods, reflections, opinions. The memories that he carried around like luggage. Now my apartment, my exotic, costly, cluttered apartment looked to me the way it must have looked to Joan Simmons. A roost, not a nest. And, for the first time, I felt lonely in it.

When the bell rang, I grabbed my wallet: I'd ordered Chinese takeout and the carryout guy was there alright. And Gooker was right behind him.

"Hey, it's the Flying Dutchman! How you doin', George?"

"You just happened to be in the neighborhood?"

"Something like that. Pot luck. Okay if I come in?"

Five minutes later, we were drinking beer and I was waiting for him to tell me why he'd come. There was plenty Chinese carry-out for the two of us.

"So you followed the leaves south? With your old man? How'd it go? The color nice? Come down on schedule?"

"It was better than I thought it would be," I said. "Relaxed and easy. I was worried he'd get cranky. And we argued some. I got cranky, too. But he was good company all the way. I'm glad we did it. Years from now, I'll be more glad."

"And now ... the $64 question. You coming to the reunion?"

"I guess so."

"Alright! You're coming! Alright! Sucker for punishment!" He went into the kitchen and brought us back some beers, heaved himself back into the hammock. "I'm glad you're coming. Misery loves company, I guess. I'm getting fat. I get up to piss in the middle of the night, most nights. I use Grecian Formula in my hair. Shit ... Well, we're in this together, I guess."

"Listen, Gooker," I said. "I've been thinking about Joan ..."

"My sources say you been more than thinking," he replied. "Better late than never, I guess."

"Do you know ..." I began. Of all the people to find myself confiding in. "What's going on with her? What's she up to?"

"She takes courses all the time, Rutgers, Drew, Farleigh Dickinson. Wants to be a college graduate. Flirting with age forty, who cares you went to college? All these years, they said, you were nothing, you didn't go to college. So I went. They said you gotta have a good transcript, A's and B's, because people would want to see that transcript, like it was a physical, bring in some pee and a stool sample. Well, George, guess how many times I showed my transcript? How many times I had to whip that sucker out?"

He raised his hand, joining thumb and trigger finger to make a goose egg. "Anyway, what I don't get, George, is why bother?"

"With college?"

"With her. I mean, now that you got over on her. There's lots more out there. They keep coming along ..."

He stopped, almost as if wanted to think over what he'd just said, another Gooker-type one-liner. Something came over him. I'd never seen a mood change so quickly. "All that I'm trying to do," he said and I swear that his voice was breaking, "is feel like I'm alive. Is that so much to ask?" He leaned towards me. "You think I'm an asshole, don't you?"

"Gooker ..."

"Well, everybody's somebody's asshole. Forget about it. Question is, what *kind* of asshole am I? That gets interesting. Let me tell you what I think."

He finished his beer, hauled a couple more out of the refrigerator, gestured for more. We could have been doing a downbeat beer ad: well guys, it doesn't get lower than this. Beer ads for bad times. Pop a chilly on your way out of a numbers-crunching tax audit. Have a brew after a gloomy doctor's office visit. Here's looking at you after a lay-off at the steel mill.

"I'm the kind of guy who does things other people don't do and if I don't do them they don't get done. This reunion. Exhibit A. Exhibit B. I've got this slow-pitch softball team. The Retreads. Everybody over thirty and no ringers. Men *and* women. And the other teams, they bury the women at the end of the batting order. One third of the line up is a write off. They call it the women's inning. My team, they bat first, fifth, eighth. So we lose a lot and we lose big, 19 to 5, scores like that. End of it all we go to Two Guys from Sicily and it's my show. Everybody loves it. They talk about it all week, keep charts and stats. But I skip two weeks in a row, it dies. Just like the reunion would die if I didn't have my secretary making phone calls and licking stamps and putting last-known-addresses in a computer. So. Am I still an asshole?"

I raised my hands. "I never said you were. Tell me ... on the softball team ... does Kate play?"

"Does she play? She doesn't even *watch*. She stays at home and ... I don't know ... reads magazines."

"Oh."

"There's no dancing around it, kiddo. The things I care about, I'm on my own. Not supposed to be that way. But it is. Like the reunion." He stopped to finish his beer. "I'm the local bozo. I'm the class cut-up who never left town. People come back to visit their parents—or maybe bury them—and they know where to find me, right on the highway between Coney Island Hot Dogs and Toys 'R' Us."

I saw his point. Whatever we had—of community, of union—came down to someone like Gooker Cerruti. Not me, not Joan or Kenny, not any of the others, but someone like Gooker you could count on to be there. But who could Gooker count on?

"You remember that night in New York, Kate and I got into it a little after dinner? She actually liked the idea of moving into the city and living in one of those loft things ... and I don't know ... going to galleries and museums and theaters. The kids are leaving, she wants us to start another chapter. 'Have adventures.' That's what she says. She wants us to change ... Hold on a minute."

He went down the hall to the bathroom, pissed without closing the door, returned, sat down heavily and found the bottom line.

"Kate wants us to move," Gooker said. "Sometimes it's California, in the wine country. Or Seattle, on the water. Depends on what magazine arrived that day. It's Yankee Magazine, we're running a bed and breakfast in New England. Southern

Living and I'm raking Spanish moss off the lawn in Charleston. *And I don't buy any of it.* I know where I'm from. My grandfather came off the boat from Sicily and dug subways in New York and went home to a place in the Bronx that's a nest of Ricans now and grew tomatoes in a yard that's smaller than the closet Kate keeps her shoes in. My old man lived in Berkeley Heights, worked for the road crew and if it weren't for the U.S. Army and the Monmouth Race Track he'd never of left town at all. Now I've got a company that grosses two million a year. I've got seventeen people working for me, my wife's got a George Washington house and my kids had horses to go riding on, till they got bored with them, and now the horses are gone, the kids are gone and Kate wants us gone. And I ain't going."

"So stay," I said. "To hell with it."

"I might be staying by myself. She's getting worse. Your fault."

"My fault?"

"Not fault, exactly. But she looks at you and … maybe you didn't notice … you had your eyes on Joan, which I don't blame you for … but you start rattling off the places you been to … I could feel her getting itchy."

"Jesus, Gooker. I never knew." Kate, the cheerleader, interior decorator, mother of two. Kiss me Kate.

"Well," Gooker said. "Maybe people do change. Or maybe you got it right. Maybe it just takes longer to figure out what they were like all along."

"It takes time," I agreed. "Figuring other people out. And ourselves."

"You got that right," Gooker said. Then he got up. "I just needed someone to talk to. And you were the guy I thought of. You of all people. And after all these years. Is that a … what … tribute to the past? To what we had? Who we were? Or is it a criticism of the pa-fucking-thetic grown-ups we are now?"

"Beats me ..." I said. "But you're showing up here ... it's okay with me."

"Really?" Gooker asked. I nodded. "And your dad. He okay?" I nodded again.

"He picked up a dog. My father did, I mean."

"They got lots of dogs in Florida. I picked up a whole kennel once."

"He means a real dog."

"These were real dogs, too," Gooker persisted. "Fort Lauderdale. Break out the kibble. Hey ... did he tell you? I drop by your father's place every other week or so?"

"Why?"

"Well, shit, George, I know your old man lives alone and you read these stories about people they don't find for days afterwards and I thought, the least I can do is check on your old man. I always liked the guy."

"Thanks," I said. It would be Gooker, I thought, or someone like him, coming down the sidewalk to check on things, some imperfect savior, some vulgar-mouthed buddy who defined virtuous conduct as "giving a shit."

The next day, I did something I'd never done before. I set the whole day aside to think about my life. Does it sound easy? Try it. People do anything not to think. Balance checkbooks. Clean ovens. I started after breakfast, on a bench in Riverside Park, looking across the Hudson at New Jersey. The sight of broken down railroad piers and half-finished apartments and the occasional garbage scow getting tugged out to sea got me thinking about the past. The old man, first coming into this harbor from across the sea. Mom working as a nanny in Riverside Park, sitting on this same bench, maybe. And then, their beginnings in New Jersey, job, house, family, the whole drill, a story that seemed so old, these days, it could be Little House on the Prairie, it was that far back.

I make these thoughts seem more orderly, more purposeful than they were and omit a dozen distractions which, once overcome, oddly complemented my reflections. Those elderly West Side couples, for instance, tired, cranky, old world Jews who fought their way through D'Agostinos, took their afternoon cake at Eclair, and hobbled down to the promenade along the Hudson when the weather was good. A wounded, cultured folk, and not the easiest to get to know. After all they, or their unlucky relatives, had suffered, these survivors carried a certain entitlement so that, if you beat them to line at a grocery counter, they could make you feel like Himmler's godchild. They were dying out and the City would replace them. Their stuffy furniture, their cherished LP's, their decades of opera programs would go down the river on barges, out past the Statue of Liberty somewhere. Yuppies would romp in their old apartments. Still, they made this the autumn side of town, hurt and melancholy.

At mid-day, I walked across Broadway, on into Central Park, retracing the route I'd covered with my New Jersey visitors a month before. It had been that long since I'd slept with someone. But not someone. Joan. And I wondered if she could say the same. There's a place I like in Central Park, a knoll just north of the Sheep Meadow. I sat there, facing the 59th Street skyline to the south. No melancholy here, no sense of the past. This was the New York of dreams, the magic city, bristling with hope, Mecca for the yuppies who tracked south in the morning, bound to mid-town offices. This was Sunday afternoon, volleyball time, kite-flying, newspaper reading, bicycle riding. Young people, young pursuits. They came to New York as I had come, snapping up $18,000 jobs in publishing and brokerage houses, doubling up in studio apartments, grabbing supper from salad bars at Korean vegetable stands, and mostly, loving it. But it was hard to picture them growing old here or even staying as long as I had stayed and I was beginning to think that I had stayed too long. My work took me through the towns they abandoned, forlorn towns intolerable to kids with looks and brains and heart, towns made even more intolerable by their desertion. Ugly, betrayed places, the more they grew, the uglier they got. Well, maybe we'd all have to go home, sooner or later.

II.

"'WELL, *BRÜDERCHEN*, SO HOW DID YOU LIKE YOUR trip to Florida?' That's what I heard him say. *Brüderchen* means little brother in German. Coming from my brother, it can sound affectionate, even loving. Other times, it drips sarcasm. It's a put down. You never know."

At last I was sitting in Pauline Kennedy's living room in Lakehurst. I'd motored up from Florida in twenty-eight hours. Say what you want about interstates, you can really make time, if time is all you want to make. It's like driving through a tunnel at seventy miles per hour. Sometimes it's night, sometimes it's daylight. It doesn't matter a bit. As soon as I crossed the Delaware Bridge and stood on Garden State soil—at a rest area—I called her. "I got a dog," I said. Those were my famous first words. At 6:30 a.m., it was risky, saying good morning. Then I asked could I come by for breakfast. And she said she'd go out for rolls.

"I tell you about it now," I said, "and I get shaky all over again." I reached down and patted Mr. Jacobs. It hadn't been much of a trip for him. But when we pulled into our last rest area he'd jumped out and gave me a surprised look. Something new in the air, just starting out: winter.

"So the stroke was ..."

"It never happened. A lie. His maid and his kids were in on it. Not much of a conspiracy. But it fooled me."

"I wondered about that stroke as soon as you told me," she said, over her shoulder, on the way to the kitchen.

"So," I shouted after her, "you're saying I'm easy to fool?" Pauline Kennedy was one of those people who figures out Murder, She Wrote before Angela Lansbury stops for the first commercial.

"It sounded very selective," she said. "And convenient."

"It was ... for him."

"Till he decided ... to give it up," she said. She put some plates on a little table, fresh rolls and some cheese and jam, then coffee. "That's interesting. Tell me about it."

"You wonder why?" my brother asked. I stood there in the swimming pool, hearing a voice I thought was gone forever. "And why now?" It felt as if he were reading my mind, just like I'd been reading his, all week. Our roles were reversed. Now I was speechless, wondering if I was facing the brother I used to know, or my anxious host of the last few days, or a stranger I was only meeting now.

"I thought about you a lot," he said. He went on. His life was settled, his money was made, his family all around him. And in Florida! The same state we'd blundered into and broken down in, a pair of greenhorns in America. I was his unfinished business. It's just that we were brothers and it didn't feel right, that we should live so long and not see each other again. Sometimes it seemed that was the only reason we'd both been left alive.

He liked odd projects, hideouts, hobbies, stunts—the old gambler in him—and the motel was one of a long list that had included antique cars, a home brewing kit, a fish-smoker, since disposed of, a German pork butcher shop, prospering, volunteer work at the local animal shelter, now replaced by his personal kennel-of-last resort. As soon as he saw it, he sensed that the Flamingo Motel was perfect. It would be as if we were picking up where we'd left off, on that 1930's trip to Florida. Meeting there would be like traveling through time, as if nothing had come between now and then. Neutral ground on memory lane. A rest stop.

"I knew that you would come," he said. And then he'd started to worry. It wasn't whether I'd come. It was *how*. But he knew that I'd come down with a load of questions. "Like a doctor checking a tumor," he said. "Malignant or benign."

He knew what I deserved to know. He could put it in a sentence. He'd entered this country legally on a Lufthansa flight from Frankfurt to Philadelphia, with a continuation to Miami. He hadn't paddled to land in a rubber raft launched off a U-boat. No one was looking for him, in Germany or Israel or anyplace, that he knew of. Visiting him wouldn't get me in trouble. That much he could tell me, that much he would volunteer. But he knew me. He knew I'd want the whole story, in order, from the beginning.

The stroke. No problem. A stroke of genius, no? Well, maybe not. Millie and the kids. In the words of Buddy Greifinger, "Whatever, Pop." And, let's face it: "You weren't so hard. Was I on the Russian front, you wanted to know. Hans, don't you know that *every* German veteran who speaks to an American was on the Russian front? It was almost a joke, right after the war. An American couldn't find a single German who fought in France and Italy. Not one! They were all in Russia! Where were the other ones, they wondered. The answer was, in East Germany, telling the Russians how they'd fought the Amis."

"So," I asked, now that we'd established I was gullible, and better late than never, "Were you there? In Russia?" But he didn't respond. He just waved it away, as if he were waving it to the back of the line. *You tried that once already*, he seemed to say.

"You gave up so easily, Hans, you let me go. On the first day, a few questions. You were eager to get it over with. It was hard to believe. You were too good to be true. You took what I gave you. My scribbles. You believed what I told you."

"No," I said. "I wanted more."

"Of course. Every day, you tried. And when you failed you said to yourself—well—what did you say? Tomorrow is another day?"

"You want to know?" I said. I'd had enough, the way he was talking down to me. "I said, maybe this Heinz of mine is a monster who should be shipped to Israel. Or maybe he was a hero who did what he could to save people. A good German. I wondered about you. Who is he, this eager-to-please motel owner, this clumsy gardener, this heavy-tipping Florida senior citizen? Good German or bad? I wanted to know alright. But no matter what he is … he's my brother."

"Are you sure you want to know?" he asked. "Really sure?" There was no missing it, his tone was menacing. "Are you sure? Brother?"

"Yes." One word. But it was hard getting it out. Maybe I wasn't so sure.

"Well then, let's try. I'll tell you a story. And … *brüderchen?*"

"Yes?"

"There are many other stories besides this one," he said. Then … funny thing … he swam across the pool and back, using a breast stroke, slow and careful, that kept his head above the water, like the periscope on a submarine.

"So," said Heinz. He was back in the corner of the pool. "Let me tell you how the war ended." He glanced at me. "That's not the part you want to hear is it? But you'll take it won't you?"

My silence said he was right. The end of the war? Not what

I would have chosen. But he wasn't a waiter, offering a menu.

"I was in all the cold places, Hans. Norway. In the Lofoten Islands, for nearly a year. And Russia. Forever in Russia. And then, Belgium. End of 1944, beginning in 1945. The Battle of the Bulge, the Amis called it. The war was already lost, of course ..."

Now it was his turn to get quiet. I studied him, wondering if he was organizing his testimony. What to leave in, what to take out. But maybe not. He looked the way I guessed I looked, when I studied an old picture, talking about it with someone who wasn't there, George maybe, and one minute I'm explaining the when and where of it, putting names and faces together, and then I'm gone, I'm back there.

"Some say it was over before it started. So I read. But it didn't feel like that. As close as we came. But by 1942 I knew. And it didn't make any difference, that we would lose. Think what you want, but you still fight. You still want to live and you want the men around you to live. You understand this, Hans? Whether the tide goes in or the tide goes out, you still try to swim. The things we did! All in a losing cause. All for nothing. Agreed. But I saw brave things. I had my life saved by men who died. I gambled my life, that men would live. I was a hero, they said. Tell me, can a losing side have heroes?"

He no sooner put the question than Mr. Jacobs, shifting position on my pile of clothes, let out an enormous groan, the way dogs do at the end of a long day. I couldn't help laughing a little. Heinz shook his head, smiled.

"The south ... in America ... plenty heroes among the Confederates. Gone With the Wind! And the first World War. This silly business about the Red Baron and ..." He gestured at Mr. Jacobs. "Snoopy."

I was surprised he knew the name. America had this way of getting its paws all over everything.

"Forget this hero business," my brother said. "I only wondered. And you're leaving in the morning." He sounded back in control. How-the-war-ended. He had kept it locked away in a trunk, I guessed, and when he opened the trunk, this was on the top, neatly folded, the last thing that he'd put away. So I thought. But his first sentence ended that.

"I hated shooting prisoners, Hans," he said.

I must have flinched. This was going to be awful. And I was sure he hadn't said that he'd hated *the* shooting of prisoners, like it was something that happened he had nothing to do with, the way I hate television commercials that are louder than the rest of the program, but it's got nothing to do with me personally.

"The war goes bad," he said. "And then this comes along. Who started it ... Did you see what they did to ... did you see what he looked like when they finished with him ... animals ... take no prisoners ... a see-saw battle ... us or them ... no one available to guard ... take them back of the lines ... a waste of time. A group of unarmed men, huddled together. Standing. Kneeling. Sometimes facing forward, bravely, other times, turning their backs not caring anymore what we said or did ... all of it ... Disgusted ... Praying or pleading sometimes, in broken German. Cursing. That they did in their own language. Once, I heard some singing. Not so good, but it was there. And then ... one minute it's a group of men. As many as forty ... I saw forty ... and then it's a pile of ..."

He turned away from me, pounding his hands against the edge of the pool. He'd had things nicely under control, at the start. Made in the shade, wrapped with a ribbon. I was practically out the door. Then he decided he should talk to me. His brother. The easiest of audiences, takes what you give him, believes what he gets, but it didn't matter how easy the audience, it didn't matter about me, because his memories were as out of control as the war itself. You didn't come to them on your terms. They came to you.

"It wasn't only us, Hans. The Russians and the partisans ... you should see what they did. Once, we recaptured a village and found a group of our boys who'd been captured by the Russians. And executed. Maybe that doesn't bother you so much. Things happen in the heat of battle. But listen, *brüderchen*, they hadn't been shot. They'd been tied up and then they'd been strangled, one by one. And you could say ... someone did say ... maybe the Russians were saving bullets. Maybe. Then again, maybe they were having fun. Also, the British. 'Too late, Fritz,' they shout at some men with their arms in the air and then they shoot them. The Americans—the Amis—at Anzio. And in France. And all over the Pacific, I hear. Piles and piles of Japanese. Both sides. Both. That was how it was with us and the Americans, that last winter. Fighting back and forth and finding bodies in the snow. Don't fool yourself about the Americans. They made their piles.

"So, January, 1945. Already, our push is over. The last great effort falls short. Of course. The end is coming. Why do I say that? The end was always coming, coming from the beginning. But it was close now. Still, we kept dying and killing and sometimes murdering. The war didn't end, like a storm passing, fading away. It kept getting worse. As if, now, it knew. It was in a rush. Things to do, before peace came.

"So. Snow. Forest. Bitter cold. Someplace in Belgium. Not Antwerp and Ostend. We'll never see the Channel. No second Dunkerque. It's not orderly. In defeat there are these little victories, these temporary things that no one writes about afterwards, not as long as winners write the history. This was one of them. We took a farm-house back and there were five Amis sitting inside. So Lieutenant Greifinger is ordered to take charge of the prisoners, along with Private Beck and Corporal Peyser, and march them to the rear. Where they would try to escape and we would shoot them."

The Americans were worried at first, he said. But the more they walked, the less they worried. Every step took them closer to a safe captivity. That was what they thought. The further you got away from the front lines, from the heat of battle, the better your chances. That's what one of them was saying, reassuring another captive who was extra scared. Heinz understood. The worried one looked left and right, looking for a chance to run. The others relaxed, waved at jeeps and ambulances coming up the road. The more traffic, the less likely their murder in a lonely place. Only one stayed worried and Heinz knew why: he was a Jew. And the Jew's name was Tauber. The others had to keep him from bolting. *Every step we take, we're closer. We'll sit behind the wire and wait this baby out, Tauber. Won't be long now.*

Then, they turned off the road and took a path into the forest. The Americans turned ashy, turned silent. Tauber had been right, not only for himself, but for all of them. They were going to be shot in the woods. Off the road a little bit, out of sight a little bit. That was all the modesty that was left in the world: like motorists pulling off a road to piss, the murderers took their business behind the trees.

Beck led the way, an anxious little scout, a *Hitler Jugend*, recently arrived. Peyser and Heinz followed the prisoners. He'd been with Peyser in Russia, from the start. Two left out of two dozen. The rest, dead or prisoners, missing or wounded. Those weren't separate categories: they were synonyms. Through all of Russia, they kept their distance, the outgoing Hamburger and the dour Bavarian. But, as the others dropped away, the survivors drew closer. Waiting for their turn to come. *And then there were none.* But when they moved west, when they faced the Amis, things changed. In the deadliest of winters, Heinz talked about Florida. In bitter snow, he blended fantasy and memory. Heinz furnished Florida in incredible detail, nuances of weather and water, tin roofs and leaking porches, orange groves and fishing piers, one-lane roads through palmetto swamps, pelicans and stone crabs. He tested Peyser and he probed and finally the Bavarian said yes, he'd take a chance on Florida. And now the moment had come: to make themselves the prisoners of their prisoners. It was simple. "Florida?" Heinz asked. And Peyser nodded.

Peyser joined Beck at the front of the prisoners. Odd, it came to Heinz, that prisoners never—almost never—ran. What was it that kept them together till the end? Was it courage or discipline or something else? Lack of imagination? But that, he decided, was the wrong question for a German to ask.

"The war is over," he said. Beck was standing in front of him.

"You really think so?" Beck was a kid, dressed up in a uniform that seemed too big for him. His helmet almost covered his eyes. A teenager!

"I mean for us," Heinz said. "You know what we're supposed to do here."

"I think so," Beck said, swallowing hard. "We have orders." Beck was scared every minute. He rushed through everything, jumped when you spoke, ran when you called him. He obeyed orders, though. That was the problem now. He should never have been there, Heinz thought, but saying that was saying nothing. "It ends here," Heinz said. "We're going with the Amis. We're giving up."

"Giving up?" he asked. His eyes welled with tears. For years, Heinz regretted saying it that way. He should have said, we're taking the Americans across the lines. Or, there has been a change in orders. But when he said *giving up*, Beck took it to heart. Heinz could see him picturing his family and playmates, everyone he was betraying.

"You can come with us, Beck." Another error. He was giving Beck a choice. "Or, you can go back and tell them what we're up to and they'll send a patrol after us."

"I won't tell them." Beck said. And he probably meant it,

Heinz thought. But when he came back alone, they'd ask him why. And he would tell them. This was a fine and truthful boy, ready to save lives and sacrifice his own. Innocent and ignorant: they came together.

"You don't want to come with us?"

"No," he said. "I'm sorry."

"Well, then, off you go," Heinz said.

Beck turned and ran. Peyser raised his rifle, aimed, hesitated, looked at Heinz.

"Yes?"

"Yes."

Peyser fired, hit Beck as he was running, hit him in the back. With a huge final effort, Beck turned over where he'd fallen, looked up at the sky, lay still. Heinz walked over. It was the least he could do, making sure the boy didn't need another shot. When he reached him, he was relieved: no need. But as he looked down at the young face, the blonde hair, the gentle hands, he knew that he'd remember this forever. You'll try to forget it, he told himself, and you won't. Fair enough.

The Amis didn't know what to make of it. But they knew this much: a moment ago there were three Germans guarding them. Now there were two. Heinz could see them getting restless. Then, the Jew—Tauber—saw that Heinz was staring at him. Heinz could have approached any of the Americans. Some of them looked reasonable. But he approached Tauber, whose face was full of fear and—because he was also brave—hate. He thought he would be the first to die. To him, to all of the Americans, it looked like Beck had protested against their execution.

"You want to get out of this, Tauber?" Heinz asked. Tauber was startled hearing English. Yes, he nodded.

"You, especially, I suppose." Heinz studied Tauber. Among Germans, it was well known, the Jews had an extra score to settle. Stay away from the Jewish soldiers. Heinz could have talked to him some more, felt him out, what kind of man was this. He might have asked where he was from, maybe New York. So how's Joe Louis?

"Ernst," Heinz shouted. "*Komm mal her.*" Peyser was standing next to him.

"Give him your rifle," Heinz said. Peyser looked at Heinz, protested. "Not him!"

"You used it enough," he said. Peyser passed the rifle over to Tauber. He put his ammunition on the ground in front of him. And some grenades.

"What …" Tauber didn't want to touch it. He suspected a trick, a way of provoking an incident. He was sure the rifle was empty. And Heinz was standing in front of him, fully armed. And that moment—facing each other, studying—lasted until Heinz took his rifle, his pistol and put them on the ground as well. Then he stepped away, unarmed, hands in air, wondering what would happen, curious in that indifferent way you are curious when you watch the ending of a movie that doesn't involve you, all you know is that the film is ending, no matter what. Oh, so that's how it turns out.

Two days later, Tauber walked Heinz and Peyser into the prison stockade, spoke to the officers in charge. Heinz didn't know what was said but the next day the two Germans were working in an American officers' mess. At the end, Tauber walked over to Heinz. They didn't shake hands—that wouldn't feel right. They never considered it. But they nodded at each other.

"My lucky day, back there," Tauber said.

"Mine also," Heinz responded.

"You should have seen him, when he finished talking," I told Pauline.

"I see you," she said, "if that's any indication ..."

"He looked terrible. That was all the stories for one night, he said. He told me, I should go upstairs and get some sleep, I had a long drive in front of me. I don't have to leave tomorrow, I said. Seeing him the way he was. Knowing it was my fault. I don't have to leave tomorrow. I repeated it. Expecting him to be delighted. Just what he wanted. Then a third time I said I don't have to leave in the morning. 'Yes, you do,' he answered."

I stop. Give myself a break. Breathe deep. Feel shaky. Not just tired, shaky.

"You ought to rest," Pauline says.

"In a minute," I answer. "Sorry I'm dumping all this on you."

"Well, it's a lot to hold in. To have to yourself."

"That's it. That's exactly it. That's what I realized when I left him down there. I went upstairs. I put some water in a dish for Mr. Jacobs. Heinz was still in the pool, easy to see in the moonlight. I took a shower. He still hadn't come in. Only moved to the table. I crawled in bed. And here's what came to me. I admit, it's odd. Just listen. You know that I believe in ... in remembering things. It's important. But my memories that I play with are puppies. They roll over on their backs, wanting their tummies scratched. His memories are wolves. They go right for the throat. And in this country ... we make a big brave deal out of facing up to the past and how we got treated when we were kids. That's what shrinks do, no?"

"That's part of it ..." She balked but decided not to correct me.

"Talk it through, work it out. Come to terms with it. Heinz did something else. He put it away. He went on with his life. And he was doing alright, until I came along. Even then, he handled things. Until that last night."

"That was just a beginning," Pauline said.

"I know. And now I'm in it too. I'm with him."

"He needs you."

"God knows where it's headed. God knows where it's been ..." I say. Then I finish the story. The story so far.

"That last Florida morning I got up early. And it would have been alright with me if I just slipped away. But first, I had to take Mr. Jacobs around the car lot, pissing on tires, taking care of business. And when I got back to the car, Heinz was there, all red-eyed and wrinkled and this was a man, mind you, who doesn't just get up in the morning, he sails out into the Florida sunshine, he drinks at the Fountain of Youth, pink cheeked and spiffy dressed and smelling of aftershave, up for another perfect day."

"'You're ready to leave?'" he asked.

"'Heinz,'" I said. I wanted to offer to stay. I said I was sorry for coming down and starting all of this.

"'I'm the one who sent the postcard, no?'"

"'I hope you don't regret it. I hope I don't, either.'"

"'I didn't tell you half of it last night,'" he said. "'I didn't tell you ten percent.'" Then he looked at me and for the first time in our lives, *he's* the little brother. "I did the best I could," he said. And it was unclear to me whether he was talking just about last night—that he'd done the best, talking to me—or whether this was about the war itself, *I did the best I could.* I repeated the phrase to myself, driving north, driving against the current of snowbirds headed south, all those New York, New Jersey, Pennsylvania license plates and Canada too. I did the best I could. Say it one way, it sounds fine. Did the best you could? Who could ask for more? Or ... the best you could ... too little and too late.

"'So here,'" Heinz says. Another eloquent German farewell. He opens up a plastic bag from Eckerd's Drugs. It's a hairbrush for Mr. Jacobs and—this I never heard of—a special toothbrush with special paste. Also, from a local vet, a vaccination card and some heartworm pills. 'Once a month,' he told me.

"'Thanks,'" I said. At our age, I might not see him again, I thought. You never know. There's something crazy about the way our lives arrange themselves. All the time we spend on people who are just so-so. Still, none of this stopped me from getting in the car. The last I saw of him, he was standing in the rear-view mirror, already watching for my return. I lifted the coffee, which had gone from warm to cold. "You have this look on your face. What is it?"

"Your brother pointed it out himself. You didn't interrupt his life. He initiated this. He wanted to see you. And he knew what it would involve."

"I know. I know what it involves."

Pauline sits there, just waiting. She knows what's coming.

"It involves me. That's what I've been thinking. In that Belgian forest, what would I have done? Would I have been Peyser, aiming to execute a scared kid? Or my brother, ordering it? Or was I Beck rushing off in the wrong direction, all for nothing? This much I knew: the story wouldn't have changed one bit, if I had been there. I was no stronger than my brother, no braver and no better. Smarter? Maybe so, but it was nothing to brag about. Luckier. That I was. Luckier for sure. But that was nothing to brag about either."

"You'll see him again, won't you?"

"Yes. I'm in it. His wife doesn't want to hear about it, I'm sure. His kids ... forget it."

"Good ... it's good you went. You've got your brother back."

"I just don't know what I'm letting myself in for. And if I stayed up here, he wouldn't push it. He wouldn't come after me. He'd fade out, all over again."

"You left him behind once," Pauline said. "And regretted it for years."

"Sure ... but Pauline! ... I keep telling myself, what I don't know ... won't hurt me."

"Wrong. And you know it. Why are you even talking this way. You're going back to Florida. Period."

"Yeah. Would you go with me?" That stops her. Stops us both. We just stand there looking at each other. "Are there any presidents buried down there?" I ask.

I was staring at the sunlight on the wall, which was late afternoon sunlight, getting more golden by the minute. That took all my attention, that sunlight, it soaked me up. Then I heard a whispering outside. The door opened just a crack and Mr. Jacobs shouldered his way into the room, saw me, jumped up.

"Two paws on the floor," I said. "That's the rule."

"You slept all day," Pauline said. She'd made me take the bedroom. "You can stay in bed if you want, but if you want to get up, do it now. Your dog wants a walk."

So we walked. South Jersey has never been my favorite place. To me, it spells sandy soil and scrubby trees and abandoned farms, chicken farms mostly. South Jersey is pancake flat and I go for land that rolls. Still, that walk restored me. There were trails in the woods around the edges of the retirement community ... although, before long, another subdivision would swallow them. Mr. Jacobs went rushing ahead, disappearing, running back to make sure we were coming. The cold air made him younger and it revived me too, all those cells in your skin that go into a coma south of Jacksonville. And the sunset was a winter sunset, sharp-edged and bright, colors holding their own, not melting together like five flavors of ice cream, Florida style. After a while we came to a lake—well, more of a pond—and though by now it was dark in the woods around the shoreline, the water caught the colors of the sky, splashes of orange, red, and purple.

"George and I figured it out," I said. "You should never judge a sunset till it's dark."

"Meaning what?"

"Only this. People watch the sun slip under the horizon and they say, well, that's it, we saw the sunset. Let's go home and eat. They miss the best of it. The deeper colors. The reflections, not just in the west but all over the sky, if you're in luck." We walked around the pond to a culvert and sat down. There were bullfrogs croaking out on the pond and ducks, or silhouettes of ducks, paddling through the lit-up water. Mr. Jacobs patrolled the edge of the lake, finally satisfying himself, and joined us. Cattails, sunken logs, it all got dark now.

"What day of the week is this?" I asked. "Down in Florida, it's not just the seasons you lose hold of. It's the day of the week too, unless you watch television a lot."

"Thursday. Your son's got a reunion Saturday. So do I."

"I'll bet he's at the house," I said, wondering if he liked it there. An odd question. It was his home. "I've got a problem up the road," I said. "This master plan of mine just bottomed up. Heinz screwed it up. My big project. Research, travel, the works. I was going to find out what happened to him. There's veterans outfits all over Germany. I could maybe find some of the men he was with and put the stories together and maybe even go where he went, in the same season, and go where he died, if I could find out. That was the least I could do. Also, the most. My master plan. Only now, up he pops, my long-lost Heinz, up he pops in Florida! So it's goodbye *bierstube* and fish market and promenade along the Elbe. And it's hello, Flamingo good-as-new cars and my choice of tapioca or Jello, if it's before 6 p.m."

"He's alive, Hans. You came out ahead."

"I know that. But meanwhile I talked George into taking over the house and now ..." I stood up, turned in front of her, threw up my arms. "I'm homeless."

I was piling it on some, I admit. Pauline laughed at me. Mr. Jacobs yawned. I got no sympathy from the one, no respect from the other.

"They don't take dogs down here, do they?" I asked. "Not many places do."

"Not as a rule," she said. "That is, you can't purchase one after you move in. But if you have one before then, you can bring him along."

"Is that so?" The silence that followed gave me a chance to think. Which I declined. I just walked with Pauline, back towards the village, through a collection of garden plots that some old-timers had put in at the edge of the woods. Nothing much left in November. Some cabbage leaves and carrots nipped by frost. Almost every garden had a bench or chair, so you could weed and sit, weed and sit. Pauline turned towards me right there, near where the trail meets the road. Ahead of us, Mr. Jacobs stepped onto someone's yard, lifting his leg against a birdbath and a light snapped on. He looked surprised—no regard for privacy —and I called him back. Pauline was facing me, studying. I had no thoughts of my own, honest, only this feeling of trust that comes to you when you're very young or kind of old and no time in between, the feeling that you're in good hands.

Back in Berkeley Heights the next morning, Mr. Jacobs and I explore the property, sit out on the stoop, watching cars go up and down the street and, later, we sit in the living room doing the same thing. George is camped out here. His things are in the bedroom. But he's not at home right now. And I am. Waiting for company. Waiting for Pauline Kennedy, following me up from Lakehurst.

Even now, she's probably on the way here, every second is subtracting from the distance between us. I haven't told George that she'll be coming or that she'll be staying the night with me. I can't live alone. I've tried it and I can't. I need people around. When I retired from Ballantine's, I swore I'd never go back, the way some old timers do, coming back to see the gang and tell them how great it was, having nothing to do but sleep late. Lying about how much they loved it when you knew they were just sitting around the house driving their wives crazy. Get a hobby, get a hobby, I could picture those women saying, like parrots. When I was gone, I was gone for good. But I missed having someone to argue with about unions and politics and television. I missed the World Series betting pools and having a couple dollars down on boxing matches, even though I made a point of betting against the guy I wanted to win because that way, if my man lost, I'd have some money for consolation, and if he won, I wouldn't mind paying up. Then Mom died and I got seriously lonely. And I was drawn to this schoolteacher woman who wasn't lonely. I wondered how she managed that. I saw her a time or two at the library, always asking me about George and me always saying he was making out fine, the way parents do, even if their boy is in prison, until one day after an extra dumb piece about Six Flags over Texas amusement park, she asked and I said, "you really want to know?" After that we talked, we met for coffee, she got me to join a book discussion group. When she was facing retirement, I set her up in Lakehurst, I helped her move in. No hanky-panky either, back then, not even a thought about it. Pauline Kennedy saw that I knew about gardening and hardware stores and lumber yards. I wasn't helpless. I was Old World stock. So what brought me down to Lakehurst were questions about storm windows and bird feeders and such, then it was sitting around afterwards, going to movies, drives to farms for corn and tomatoes and sometimes blueberries that you pick yourself and it's so much fun you wind up with twenty pounds of blueberries you don't know what to do with. It took a while, I'm saying, before I felt comfortable, sitting in her house when work was done. It felt like I needed a reason to be there. Help that I was giving. Or getting. Maybe that's why I started talking about selling the house and moving back to Germany. I wanted to start something, test something. It's as though I were saying to Pauline, you think you're smart, let's see you talk me out of this one.

The next car that comes down the street, it could be hers. I'm sitting at the window, watching cars, the way George used to wait for company, betting me whether five or ten more cars would pass before our company came. And I'm thinking about Mom. I'm feeling guilty about Mom. You. Who I walked with in Riverside Park. Who, pregnant, steadied the saw horse while I cut the lumber for this house. Who owned this kitchen and fussed over hollyhocks and kept track of miles per gallon on the way to Florida and always made us wait until dark on Christmas Eve before we opened presents. You. Whose ashes I scattered around the hemlocks, you ghost now, looking over my shoulder as I watch for cars down the street. Company's coming. And you. I'm all full of you, in these last moments alone. I guess this means I don't believe in heaven. If I were sure I'd be catching up with you in a couple years, or that you'd be waiting up for me some place, this wouldn't happen. I guess this means I loved you. Love you. Will love you. How am I supposed to put it? And could I just say I'm sorry I didn't say it more often, while you were still around to hear it? I'm sorry I didn't spend more money on vacations. I was too damn tight! I had a stroke, whenever we pulled into a hotel that had a swimming pool. I made dumb wisecracks about not being able to see the food, whenever we passed a restaurant that was a little nice, with candlelight. I'm sorry I talked you into that last trip to Germany, when you were already sick, and the way I glared at you when you were coughing, like your cancer was spoiling our retirement and I'm sorry—what a list I could make —I'm sorry I was out in the garden spreading peat moss and feeling cheated, the morning you died. I'm sorry we never got to say goodbye. At least I think I am. People check out of motels and say more. I'm sorry I was in such a hurry to clean out the house after you died, your clothes out of the drawers, your shoes out of the closet, everything you wore or touched, your soap and perfume. I didn't know what I was doing, I still don't, putting boxes of things you cared about out on the curb, or offering them to neighbors—take what you want—forcing gifts on relatives, emptying out our house as though somebody new would be moving on in. I wish you'd warned me about that. You could have said, take your time, let these things linger, these bits and pieces, let them keep you company awhile. Maybe I'm wrong, but I think that if I'd gone first, you'd've stayed here and been okay and not needed someone else, the way I do. You. Stay with me. Even if you don't forgive me … don't forget me. We Germans are like pumas. We mate for life. At least we try.

III.

Snuffy's Restaurant sits off Route 22 in Scotch Plains. It was our family place. We went there every Sunday, the old man always there when the door opened at 12:15, anxious to beat something called "the luncheon rush" from "the church crowd" and be in on something he called "the first sitting." What pleasure he took, glancing around an empty dining room, waitresses still slipping on aprons, and forecasting what a "madhouse" this place would be by the time we finished our fishermen's platters. I hadn't been to Snuffy's in years and it had changed while I was away: more Greeks. They'd turned a road house into a Parthenon, with columns, fountains, function rooms, piecemeal additions that surrounded the old place without quite obliterating it. But Joan was waiting for me at the bar.

"Hello, lady," I said, hopping on a neighboring stool next to her.

"George." She took both my hands and held them and what I felt in her hands wasn't eagerness so much as a gathering of nerve, the way people take your hands at a funeral and urge each other to be strong, hang in there.

"You're looking good," I said.

"Is that a tan?" she asked.

"I got what I needed," I replied.

"What was it like, traveling with your father?"

Once I started talking about the old man, I relaxed. I told her about how, when we checked into a motel, the first thing he would do was strip the room: of stationery, visitors magazines, an extra roll of toilet paper. And while we used one bar of soap he'd brought from home and carried from place to place in a wet washrag, he collected dozens of little bars. How he insisted that we always pump our own gas, even when it was raining. And—the classic old man moment—the afternoon I'd picked him up at a laundromat where he'd insisted on doing our wash, even though many of the places we stayed at offered laundry service. I found him pulling stuff out of the dryer. When he was finished, he peeked into neighboring dryers, the way a bum checks a row of coin returns in phone booths, and sure enough he dug out somebody's orphan sock, white with a red band. He lifted it, scanned it, sniffed it. "It's clean enough for my foot," he said.

"But I'm glad we traveled together," I told Joan. "You can wait too long to do things like that. Before you know it, you've missed your chance. That's what I've been learning lately."

"Just what's that?"

"You're the kid, they're your parents. For years. You're in the house together. Then you move and you figure it's over. The longer you're gone, the more over it gets. But it's not over. At least, it doesn't have to be."

She nodded. She got it. And she knew I wasn't just talking about getting back in touch with my old man. She came into it, too. And I could see that it made her uncomfortable. It was time to back off.

"So how have you been?"

"There's good news and bad news," she replied. "I went on a trip myself, George. Out of the blue, I flew down to Miami and I took a cruise."

"Where to?"

"You probably think it's dumb. It was one of those cruise-to-nowhere things you read about. You go out in the Caribbean and sail around in circles."

"That's the good news?"

"I knew you'd hate it," she said. "What could be dumber? Sailing around in circles."

"Everybody sails in circles," I said. "The world being round."

"It's still stupid."

"Look, if you liked it …"

"I did like it, George. Not just the meals and stuff. They feed you to death and it's all B, B plus, tops. But the ocean … I mean … you're on vacation all year 'round. But I'd never been on a ship before!" She went on. The smell of the sea, the empty horizon, the motion of the waves, the stars at night. The blue of the sky and sea. She loved it all, without reservation. Sunrise, sunset, stars, horizon. She reminded me of how I was when I'd started out. She reminded me of my early columns.

"What's the bad news?" I finally asked her. "There was some bad news, you said."

"Maybe," she nodded, pushing away her plate.

"Now you're back in New Jersey." I said. "Is that it? Eating at Snuffy's? With me? Your high school reunion coming … which by the way, I want you to attend with me."

"I went with Kenny," she said. "On the cruise."

"Kenny …" I said. "As in …"

"That Kenny," she answered, nodding.

"I thought," I couldn't help saying it, "you learned that lesson." It was as though I'd slapped her, not that she winced and turned away but she looked as though I'd hit her, like she was discovering that one of the things we shared was the ability to cause pain.

"I'm sorry," I said. "Christ."

"Hey George?" She managed to smile but it was the kind

of smile you get from someone who's ahead of you. "You were just philosophizing about how nothing is ever over."

"But Kenny wasn't what I had in mind."

Coffee, when it came, felt like a ceremony of departure. In no time, we'd be gone.

"I was thinking about you all the way to Florida," I said.

"About me?" She seemed surprised at that, that she'd been in my mind when I was so far away—as though, when people get beyond a certain range, they couldn't occur to you anymore.

"Yes," I said. "I thought ... we could work something out." I faltered, the whole edifice tumbling to pieces, everything that had seemed logical and inevitable. A great idea, last night. Maybe I'd been right, maybe not, Kenny had finished his examination ahead of me. "What's Kenny got in mind?"

"Something's come over him," she said. "He says he wants to take me to the reunion ... I don't know. He talks ... like you talk." She reached across the table and took my hand. "Something's happening to all of us right now. What is it?"

"We're all looking around and measuring how far we've come."

"Or haven't," she added.

"And whether we like it. Whether there's anything we can do about it. In the time that we have. The reunion has something to do with it too. It makes you look at yourself and wonder if there's a second chance ..."

"Last chance?"

"Could be."

"I don't want to make the same mistake again, that's for sure. I don't want to assume that if you do the normal things you get married, have kids, stay home ... you'll be alright. Because it wasn't alright. And if you're right about second chances well I might make another mistake but I'll tell you one thing, George. I want it to be far from here? Also ... far from Kenny."

Twenty minutes and one hug later, she left. And I lingered at

Snuffy's, considering the picture I made, sitting alone at a bar in New Jersey, wondering what next. Joan was gone, I was pretty sure, outward bound and wherever she found herself, the interest she'd felt in me, the attraction that brought us together for a night, would seem way behind her. I was just another something she'd left behind in New Jersey. Just a guy she went to high school with. So I had some beers, just looking around the room, remembering the hundreds of Sunday dinners I'd had here with my parents. Seafood special with fries and coleslaw, vanilla ice cream for dessert. When I got up, I knew I'd have to watch it, driving home. I could feel the beer. Most of the way home, I drove carefully, begging the roads not to betray me. And I made it, almost all the way. Turning into Hilltop Avenue, I snapped off the headlights and ignition ... the way I used to do ... and coasted slowly down the street. At the bottom of the hill, the trick was to turn into the driveway with enough speed so that I could roll all the way to the garage. That way, not seeing the headlights, my parents might not know when I'd come home. I took the corner fast, crunched onto the gravel and, halfway toward the garage, saw a dark square something right in front of me. I slammed on the brakes, veered to the side, smashed through the forsythia hedge and skidded out onto the grass. Sweating, trembling, all the cockiness drained out of me, I backed onto the driveway and got out. The car looked alright and I'd managed to go between, not over, the forsythia. Still, there were deep ugly ruts in the lawn, which would look awful in the morning. Like a drunk pulled over and made to walk the line, I marched back and forth, stamping the upturned grass, trying to get the sod in place. "Oh, shit," I muttered. The old man was going to have me now. An angry glare, maybe, or a crack about how I just missed the For Sale sign. Or maybe one of those hard, fatherly stares I got when I struck out in Little League. Jumping up and down on divots of grass, I glanced at the vehicle that blocked the driveway. What do you call those things? Recreational vehicles? Mobile homes? Trailers? I'd seen them by the hundreds, driven by elderly nomads who moved from national park to national park, like migrant crop workers following the harvest, but the crop was sunshine. What the hell was it doing here?

I walked across the grass, behind the garage and pissed long and luxuriantly: something else I used to do, coming home late, avoiding a trip to the bathroom, where my parents would hear me, even though we never flushed after dark. But you could never fool your parents. As I walked back around, the lights snapped on ... garage lights, houselights, and the front lawn lights the old man put in after someone sawed off one of his hemlocks just before Christmas twenty years ago. And, when I walked towards the house, ready to face the music, I saw what was waiting for me at the door, and I stopped dead.

There were two people watching my approach. It could have been Pop and Mom, together. And a dog. It could have been them and something in me choked. Who hasn't wondered what it would be, the ultimate reunion, if you could see your parents standing together, one more time, and go rushing towards them?

The old man came out onto the doorstep, walked across the lawn in bathrobe and pajamas. He glanced at the mess of grass and shook his head, not unkindly.

"Backyard Adventure, George?" he asked.

"Hello, George," Pauline Kennedy said.

"Mrs. Kennedy!" I said. "Hi ..." I turned to the old man. No, he wasn't mad about the lawn. He was worried about other things. He was worried about this. I turned towards him and saw tears in his eyes. "It's okay," I said. "Never apologize, never explain."

"That's what Henry Ford Junior said when they caught him drunk driving with a bimbo."

"It's okay," I repeated. "I love you." He took my hand, half a handshake, half a squeeze. These things come hard for us.

"Me too," he said. And we walked into the house.

In a neighborhood where houses are huge and lots were

small, our house was tiny, our yard was large. If you liked vacuuming carpets, you lived one way, if you liked cutting grass, you did something else, the old man always said. Our house was small, with my bedroom upstairs, and Mom and Pop's downstairs. So Pauline Kennedy wasn't upstairs. They were together. They were a couple. We stood around a while. Then we went into the living room where Pop sat in the chair that I always checked for lost coins and Pauline Kennedy sat beside me on the sofa. It was my house but I felt like company. Three's a crowd, and I was third.

"So," I began. "How'd it go in Florida?" The question seemed odd and that was because I knew he'd already answered it. Pauline Kennedy had gotten the story first.

"Well, I found him," he said. "Twenty minutes after you left." And ... I heard his voice trail off. He needed prompting. "A dozen times, I thought of you," he said. "I needed you. Your way of asking questions. I needed you to check things out. Tell me how I was doing. I needed you, George." Now he found my eyes, then looked away. "Missed you too. We talked, but not until the last night. Till then he said he had a stroke. I mean ... he acted that way."

"Hold it. You're telling me your brother faked a stroke?" I couldn't help laughing. It was funny, it was sit-com premise. Wait forty years for a reunion and fake a stroke! "So ... what happened then?"

"He didn't want to have to deal with all that stuff in the past. So ... yes ... he went mute. I asked a few questions that he answered with paper and pencil. Then I sort of threw in the towel. But, the night I left, he opened up."

"And?"

"I got a piece of story, anyway."

"What kind of story, Pop?"

"I don't know yet. I've got to go back."

"You don't sound so happy about it."

"He's my brother. I can put up with him. I put up with you."

"Is that so?"

"And I'm glad I did." With that, he got out of the chair, gestured towards the bedroom. "I'll see you in the morning. I'm tired."

"Okay, Pop. But what's that thing in the driveway?"

"Ask Pauline," he said. "We've got a long day tomorrow. I'll need you to help me roll the lawn."

"Yes, Pop."

"Well, then ..." He got up and headed towards the bedroom. The dog—I'd barely looked at it—followed along. Pauline Kennedy and I were left together. She watched him leave, shaking her head.

"I wonder how your mother put up with him sometimes," she said.

"Actually, he's mellowed," I said. "Years ago, he wouldn't be able to go to bed with the lawn looking that way. He'd be out there now. The times I saw him out in the middle of the night, raking leaves. Four a.m., I mean. 'Leaves aren't garbage,' he'd say. He'd sweep them onto a blanket and pull them towards the compost pile. Later ... Sunday afternoon ... he'd have that blanket over his legs, when he sat out in the sun. He was something. You won't have as hard a time ... as Mom did."

"I thank her for that," she said. "If he hadn't had her ... missed her ... he wouldn't want me."

"What did he find in Florida? I know he told you."

"At length," she acknowledged. "He needed to get it out and I was there. I hope you don't feel that was out of order ... or out of place."

"No. But he was having nightmares on the road about meeting his brother. So I'm wondering ..."

"He sees himself in his brother. What happened to one brother could happen to the other. The life he didn't lead ... all that. Maybe it's why we have brothers."

"How bad is it?"

"He heard a story it was hard for his brother to tell. Hard

for him to hear. And that was just an overture. George, I don't know what kind of testimony he got ... or is going to get ..." She broke off, thinking. I looked around the living room. It was still Mom's room. The plants were gone, those African violets, but you could tell where they'd sat, because the wood was darker there. I wondered how long a person stayed around a house after they died. Not forever, certainly. But for a while.

"And now ... you're part of it," I said. "Of us."

"Yes. Do you mind?"

I was surprised she asked. Teachers weren't supposed to worry about what their students thought.

"Well, I wouldn't have pictured you two as a couple. I'll go to bed tonight wondering how it happened, how it works ..."

"*That*," she said, "is none of your concern."

"But I'm glad you found him. That you're in his life. And mine. God, he's a handful. One of a kind ... But I like your showing up ... that pleases me. And not just for his sake."

"I don't think you'll be hearing much about moving back to Germany."

"One question, Mrs. Kennedy." I hope she wouldn't ask me to please call her Pauline. And she didn't. It would be Pop and Mrs. Kennedy, to me. It wouldn't surprise me if he called her Mrs. Kennedy too. "What's that thing in the driveway."

"It's rented."

"That's how you get to Florida?"

"Not right away." She walked to a shopping bag that was just outside the bedroom door, pulled out a map and spread it out, like a chef presenting a special dish. Her dish was the United States—her gift to my father—the states all speckled with stars, dozens of them, red and blue, each one numbered.

"What's this?"

"Figure it out," she said. She was smiling, pleased as punch. The initial tension was gone. Most of the stars were in the east, most of them in Virginia, some in New England, some in the Midwest. Ohio did pretty well. After that it was slim pickings, until California.

"It's the presidents, isn't it? Where they were born ..."

She nodded. "And ..."

"Died ...

"Well ... are buried."

"And this is a trip you're taking. Cradles and graves. But not in order."

"Does it sound ... daft?"

"It sounds terrific," I said. And then it was like school days, caring teacher and game student, taking an idea for a ride. We went at it for an hour, talking about the mythic, monumental presidents—the Mt. Rushmore quartet and a few others—and the notoriously bad ones, the mean and the obscure, the part-termers, the not-reelected, the ones who were right on the edge of oblivion: no visitors at the museum, grass growing over their graves.

"I'd go with you in a wink," I said.

"I'd like that. But your father's going with me, you see."

"So ..." That wonderful German word, which could be the beginning and end of everything, the start of a question, the tail of an answer. There it was. The old man had gained a dog and girlfriend. I got a house. I was happy for him. Not so sure about myself, but happy for him. "How long will it take?"

"Oh ... months at least."

"After that?"

"Well, this is between us. I haven't told him yet. And I won't be telling him for a while. Alright?"

"Yes," I replied. We were co-conspirators. The old man was our mutual responsibility. She lifted the map of the U.S. How many people visited Grant's Tomb? How many dropped in on Millard Fillmore? Beneath the first map was a second, and a whole new set of stars. I looked at it and at her and couldn't help laughing.

"The vice-presidents."

IV. Le Bistro was a quaint place, by North Jersey standards, columned portico entrance, a neon sign that welcomed the Class of '64, and a parking lot that was about the size of a football field, and I was hiding in a corner of it, sitting with Pauline Kennedy, watching arrivals. We didn't want to be the first. And, besides, I was nervous. I could feel it in the palms of my hands. I watched cars pulling in and couples stepping out, classmates and spouses, but it was too far away to be sure which was which. I wondered if this was what the old man had felt down in Florida, sitting in another parking lot, waiting for his brother to show. Wondering, how far have we come? How far apart are we now? How close together? What remains of what once was? Sticking your hand in life's grab bag, that's what it was.

"I'm a grown up man," I said. "I make good money. I travel wherever I want. I don't have anything to apologize for to these people."

Pauline Kennedy glanced at me and smiled. "Of course you don't," she said. My teacher was wearing a black dress with silver threads in it, severe and classy. She looked readier than I was. When I'd visited her in Lakehurst, I had wondered whether being around students, year after year, made you old ahead of time or … the opposite … somehow kept you young. I had my answer now. She had come to see if her students were aging as well as she had … and knowing that they hadn't.

"It's revenge, isn't it?" I asked.

"Pardon me?"

"Now I get it. Revenge. Year after year they sit in front of you, those ripe little cheerleaders, those athlete studs, those wise alecks like me … and they think they've got it all coming to them. Time and tide. Their lives in front of them. And they think of you as a schoolmarm. So you wait a couple of decades and then bingo."

"Bingo?"

"You've lapped them. You're coming up behind them. Yes. Bingo."

"Well, I wouldn't call it revenge."

"What would you call it?"

"We don't live alone, George, even if it feels as though we do. There are others all around us, going through the same things. We tend to forget that. And then, true enough, people move, scatter, lose touch. You should know that. You of all people."

"Do you ever wonder … you must … if we'd all stayed in the neighborhood?"

"That can't be," she said. "But I've thought about it, yes."

"Would it be a better place? Would we be better people?"

"Yes," she said. "I think so. People move. That's how the country began. And grew. Freedom of movement. It could be in the Bill of Rights, at the top of the list. I'm sure it means more to people than all of the rest of it." She paused and lit a cigarette. The secret vice of teachers. "What's missing is something else," she resumed. "Roots. Commitment. Community. Love of place.

You need them both, the moving and the staying. It's like breathing, inhale, exhale. It's the beat of a heart, systole and diastole, in and out. Leaving and returning. It's out of balance now. That's why tonight's important. It's a reminder of what we need. Tonight ... tonight it's as if every one of us had kept on living here. For one night, a community that doesn't really exist reconstitutes itself. Can we go in now?"

"Mrs. Kennedy? I'm just asking. Did you ever go to any of your own reunions? High school? College?"

"Good Lord, no!" she answered. With that, we stepped outside the car and walked across the lot together, her hand around my arm. Her walk was brisk, mine nervous. Coming to the reunion with a teacher! That takes the cake, I could hear Gooker saying. What a brown noser! And he didn't know the half of it, that the same woman escorting me to my reunion would be accompanying my father to his. He didn't know how lucky we were.

You never meet the people you want to meet, at least not in the order you want to meet them. Otherwise, Joan Simmons would have been standing there in the lobby, right where members of the reunion committee were making out name tags, and Kenny Hauser would have been with her, along with maybe a dozen others—out of four hundred—that I'd wondered about now and then. But reunions were random occasions ... pot luck Pauline Kennedy called them ... and the first person who shook my hand was Doug Russo. I hadn't wondered about Doug at all but as soon as we touched hands I remembered him pinning me in twenty seconds in wrestling, I remembered the smell of his sweat and the feeling of a sweaty plastic mat under my shoulders.

"Where'd you come from?" asked Doug.

"I'm at my father's place," I said. "Same as always ..."

"Too bad. We were talking about you the other day. A

cinch for the traveled-farthest-to the-reunion award ..."

"Oh."

"But five miles won't do it."

"I can hack it," I said. We'd gone through twelve grades together, plus Boy Scouts and summer camp. Now he told me he ran a U-store in North Plainfield.

"U-store?" I asked. "You store?" I forced myself to focus on him, because I hated it, when the people I was talking with searched the room behind you for better company.

"Storage buildings," Doug explained. "People rent out their houses. Or maybe they sell one place and they buy another but it's a while before they can move in. So they come to me, with everything that used to go in attics and barns and garages. I've got a hundred units." He pulled out a card, wondered if I might want to "do a write up."

"People keep buying more stuff than they know what to do with," he reflected. Already, he was feeding me quotes. "Trampolines, mountain bikes. Things their kids have to have. Then they lose interest."

"Maybe you should store the kids," I said.

"That's what school was for," he snapped.

"Is it Greifinger tonight?" someone asked. There was a woman labeled Sandy Parks Cowan. Sandy Parks anywhere, we used to say.

"Hi, Sandy. Better make it Greifinger."

"Okay." She wrote the name under my picture, as it had appeared in our high school yearbook. She slipped it into a plastic sheath that had a pin on back, tossed it into a box, and gestured for me to reach in a brown paper bag she held out.

"What's this?"

"Just take one," she ordered. I was holding a picture of Sue Hoover.

"Oh boy," I said. There she was: blonde hair, teasing smile, slightly slanted Slavic eyes, all presiding over a sweater and a crucifix.

"Oooh, you got Sue," Sandy said.

"Yeah," Doug interjected. "Lucky you."

"You're supposed to look for her," Sandy explained. "And meanwhile, whoever picks your picture is looking for you."

"Everybody mixes and mingles," Doug said.

I moved from one person to another, handshakes, hugs, stares, exclamations. Pauline Kennedy had gone her own way, joining some other teachers Gooker had found. I was on my own. I hadn't been sure what it would be like, "going stag." It didn't matter, though. The people we'd married were along for the ride—polite representatives of a country we hadn't traveled to yet, when we were in high school together. We were all stag. And lots of us. I'd forgotten how many of us there were together, back then. Four hundred in our graduating class: a gigantic enterprise, bigger than anything else I'd belonged to. Memory had shrunk those long, waxy, disinfected halls, the cave-like steamy cafeteria, the high school auditorium that could match a Broadway theater. It had been a regional school, drawing on grungy enclaves that staffed oil refineries and old colonial enclaves where genius scientists went to work at Bell Telephone Laboratories. There were Portnoy-ish subdivisions within commuting range of Wall Street and the garment district. There were nests of Old World Italians and Germans and moderately left-wing Jews besides. And everybody sent their kids to school. Amazing, when you thought about it.

Things sorted themselves out quickly, college prep from vocational ed. It was a cliquey place. Still, you walked the halls, ate in cafeteria, shared home room and at least a few classes—phys ed was a democratizing experience—with people you'd never meet again. So there we were: snobs and sluts, A-students and ass-men, science fair winners, Boys Staters, home-ec majors, detention hall recidivists, beatniks, rope-climbers, cheerleaders, auto mechanics: we were virgin, pregnant, promising. How could I ever have even contemplated not coming back? How could anybody *not* wonder how it all turned out?

"Guess who?" someone said, slipping hands over my eyes.

"Give me a hint," I said. "I wasn't into hands."

"We were in Foundations of American Culture together."

"That brings it down to thirty people."

"You lusted for me."

"Hi, Sue," I said, slipping my hands around her wrists, moving them away from my eyes, turning to face our Kim Novak.

"I heard you were looking for me," she said.

"I got your name," I said, flashing the yearbook picture I'd gotten at the door. No connection at all, no help at all. I could have looked all night and never matched the yearbook starlet with the heart breaking heavyweight before me.

"I set that up," she confessed. "I heard you were coming. I said to myself, no way does he get away without talking to me."

"That's good," I said, staring at her the way everybody stared at everybody else tonight. She hadn't needed to slip her hands over her eyes. I'd never have recognized her.

"It's okay," she said. "I know I'm big."

"We all change," I said.

"Sure, George. Gray hair. No hair. Some wrinkles. A little pot. Everybody changes. Not everybody doubles."

"I'm glad you came. Anyway."

"I was going to skip tonight. It's not easy to go around in a crowd of people who remember me when I stopped traffic. Now I block traffic ..."

"Don't do this to yourself, Sue." I hated hearing this. It took courage to come out looking the way she did. I'd been around the party long enough to notice how many suits and haircuts looked new, how many women had been at the beauty parlor that day. And when Gooker and I got around to our inevitable post-mortem, it wouldn't surprise me if the classmates we marked absent looked or felt like Sue Hoover. Failure stopped them, age and weight and divorce: they figured they had nothing to show, nothing to report, they weren't worth seeing.

"I'm here because of you, you know," she said.

"You are?

"I wanted to talk to you," she said. She was studying to see how I'd take that announcement. How appalled I'd be. How I'd look to escape. She was shrewd, alright and I wouldn't be getting away except on her terms, which I didn't know yet.

"Well ..." I said, spreading my arms. "Here I am."

"I have a favor to ask. Not a hug."

"Sure."

"I'm a writer, too, George. Not like you. I have a bunch of ... I don't know what you'd call them. Maybe you think it's silly. Maybe people come at you all the time, showing you stuff."

"Not so often, Sue. My coat tails are short."

"You're from here. That's what I tell myself, when I want to quit writing. And if you did it ..."

"Yeah. How hard could it possibly be?"

"Maybe you never noticed. I was smart. Now ... maybe you'll notice."

"Okay, everybody," a voice I recognized announced. There was Gooker at the center of things, at the podium. I wondered why he dressed the way he did. His wife had taste, lived in a colonial estate, dabbled in interior decoration, yet she had a husband who dressed like Rodney Dangerfield: maroon sport coat, white slacks, white shoes. Was that by accident or design? Her revenge or his rebellion? I told Sue Hoover to send her stuff to Pop's address, that I'd look it over. I promised I would. And now a couple of hundred reunion goers were headed towards dinner tables.

"If you'd all take your seats, we'll get this show on the

road," said Gooker. "Anyway, the bar's closing for a while, but there's wine on the table." He grabbed a carafe and hoisted it in the air. "Says it's got to be sold by Thursday." He poured a glass, gulped it down. "We're in for a hell of a night."

I found Pauline Kennedy chatting with former coach Art Moynehan, who nodded hello to me before rising to get a drink before the bar closed down.

"How's the old coach?" I asked.

"Fascinating," she said. "He thinks that dodge ball should be an Olympic demonstration sport. He belongs to something called the U.S. Dodge Ball Association. You catch the ball someone throws at you, he's out. If it hits you and you drop it, you're out. That's life."

"It's an American game," I said, joining her at a table with Kate and a seat for Gooker who was at the microphone, starting things off.

"People ask why I put this thing on," he began. His jacket made him into a game-show host. "What's in it for me? Am I looking to show off or what? People ask me all the time. My wife asks me."

I saw Kate stare at Gooker, and not kindly. Leave me out of this, her look said.

"So I've got an answer. Listen up. HEY! Can you hear me in back?"

They could hear him alright. The trouble was, they weren't listening. There were shrieks of recognition at the door, when late-comers appeared, there were parties at every table, drinkers four deep at the bar, which showed no signs of closing. Everyone who walked across the dance floor drew a roomful of stares. Now it was Joan Simmons and Kenny Hauser, headed for our table, where Kate had saved seats for them.

"The delegate from Israel," Gooker muttered into the microphone. "Fashionably late." He knew his act was bombing.

"Let's give him a big hand."

I glanced at Pauline Kennedy. Call this class to order, please. Mediate. Instruct. Discipline. But she just sat there, unsurprised, taking it in.

"So, anyway," Gooker continued. "You start out together. Kindergarten on up. It's classes and field trips and locker rooms and stuff after school, which would be sports and clubs and in my case, detention. There's summers, those old summers that stretched out forever, like one long sandy beach. Baseball games after supper, 'member those, when daylight savings time kicks in, you get maybe five innings before sunset and then when it's too dark for grounders you're still out there, so only fly balls count. It's dating too, sweaty palms and proms and corsages and making out in cars and stuff. What it is, is you grow up together ... sort of."

He'd gotten carried away and now he choked and still, only half the room was paying attention. And they mostly didn't understand. And his wife was leaning back in her chair, talking to a woman at the next table. Gooker was talking to me.

"This isn't about bringing anything back," he continued. "But I think ... this is maybe half-assed ... I think you can keep it together a little. Stay in touch. That's what tonight is for. That's all. Okay? Okay."

Stepping out from behind the dais to a scattering of applause, he moved our way. I clapped for him and so did Pauline but the others, Kenny, Joan, Kate were otherwise occupied.

"Well, that's that," Gooker said. I was the first one he looked at. I died up there, his face said.

"Here we all are," Kenny said. "Delegate from Israel? That's what I hear you call me? All in good fun, right? In keeping with the spirit of the evening?"

"Forget about it," Gooker said, the fight drained out of him.

"Forget about ... that speech?" Kenny asked. I could see

Joan place a hand on his arm, the way women do, when they see their husband headed for trouble. They were separated, but some gestures remained. And didn't work.

"You said we 'grew up' 'together' 'sort of!'" Kenny wiggled his fingers to put quotation marks around each phrase. "You're deep. You're an orator."

"You got a problem with any of that?" Gooker asked.

"Questions. About the growing up we did. About how together we were. And about ... what on earth did you mean ... by 'sort of.'"

"It's always 'sort of,'" Thank God, Pauline Kennedy had spoken. "It never ends. Thank God, it doesn't. I'm still learning. And making mistakes. New mistakes. That 'sort of' is just fine, Mr. Cerruti."

"Me too," Kate said, although the mistakes she was making might not have been what Pauline Kennedy had in mind. "Sort of, all the way."

"I'm another 'sort of' too," Joan said. And then to Kenny, "As you know."

"I'll be damned," Kenny said. "It's rally around the Gooker time. I can't catch a break around this table."

"That's because we grew up together," Gooker said, his good mood returning. "Sort of."

"Sort of," Kenny repeated. He turned to me. It was my turn. "How about you champ?"

"Sort of. I'm moving back here."

"Here?"

"Right back here. I can work from here. And there's other things I want to do than run around the world rating beaches and buffets."

"Besides," Gooker said, "we got plenty of beaches and buffets right here in Jersey."

"Now listen up," Gooker said, back at the microphone. The meal had ended quickly. People were too excited to eat. First one, then another, then dozens started table hopping. They'd be eating three meals a day for as long as they lived. But the chance to check out flames and rivals, to inventory spouses, came once every five years.

"This is the program," Gooker said. "We got about half our class came back tonight, we have to move along. I'm going to call everybody up, one at a time and they're gonna say something about themselves that I hope is true ..."

"He's had a few," Kenny remarked.

"He's worked hard on this," I said.

"I'm sure he did," Kenny said. "I don't doubt it for a minute. Nostalgia is probably the strongest emotion he feels."

"You can say anything you want," Gooker proceeded. "Dumb stuff about your swell wife or husband or your wonderful kids. Your job or your house, all that stuff. But stick with that and you'll sound like a bunch of game show contestants being introduced ..."

A little nervous laughter around the room, but Gooker had a point. This wasn't about spouses and children, about the cards and pictures you kept in your wallet, or the cash.

"Anyways," he said, "you're all gonna come up here. Stand up and let us all get a look at you at least. That'll do." He glanced at a list of names in front of him. "Hey, George Greifinger, George Griffin, come on up here. You're the first."

I got up out of my chair and headed for the microphone. At least it would be over soon.

"... one of America's most beloved travel writers," Gooker was saying, "author of the Faraway Places/Backyard Adventures column that appears all across the country ..."

What did I say? Something about how, much as I traveled, I often found myself thinking of settling down and, although it hadn't happened yet, the place I pictured settling down in was the place I came from, which was here, and if it ever came to pass, I hoped that I would find some of my old classmates around, the way we were tonight. Something like that. It started easily, just words, the way my writing was just words, most of the time. Automatic pilot. But something happened along the way. I was ambushed. I all-of-a-sudden knew this was a bunch that mattered and that seeing them again provided, not closure, but a kind of completion. I would always wonder about them and would want them to wonder about me. We were in it together.

"Atta boy," Gooker said when he retrieved the mike. "Not a dry eye in the place. I'm gonna call on the fellow who led out basketball team to an unforgettable four-and-seven season, Ronnie Napolitano, where's he hiding?"

"That was fine," Mrs. Kennedy said as soon as I got back to the table. I nodded thanks and looked at Joan, wondering what she thought. I got a friendly nod; maybe she was nervous about Gooker getting around to her.

"You really believe that?" Kenny asked. "About settling down? Come on George! There's more to life than the rediscovery of New Jersey Maybe it feels right, coming back here. Maybe you think it makes a satisfying pattern, a circle or maybe a spiral. The prodigal returning ..."

"So what about returning to Israel, old buddy?" I asked, more sharply than I wanted. "You're telling me that's not a circle too?"

"Let's put it like this, George," Kenny said. "I walk on the Via Dolorosa. I pass the Wailing Wall. The Mount of Olives. What have you got? Route 22 and Two Guys from Sicily?"

"Hey you two," Joan interrupted. We were missing the parade of classmates to the podium. Even then, we might have kept on, but Mrs. Kennedy leaned forward with a look that silenced both of us.

Tom Atkinson, our black class president, was career Air Force in California and close to retirement. Sandy Delia, the sexiest woman outside the Ronettes, was married to an Amway representative and Sharon Witherspoon, introverted and poetic, wrote steamy x-rated potboilers under the name Lucinda Whippet. Maybe we were all cliches: the hot rodders become local cops, the radicals who were worried property owners, the science fair winners doing brilliant though anonymous things with transistors and genes. The class nerd—how refreshing it had been to find a mediocre Jewish student!—now incarnated as Marty Singer Inc., a platinum merchant bristling with conviction that people who complained about South Africa just didn't have all the facts. Maybe there was nothing that happened to us that television hadn't anticipated. But that was before Gooker called on Kenny.

"You called me the delegate from Israel when I came in tonight," Kenny began.

"Oh shit," Gooker sighed, holding up his hands. "I'm in for it now."

"We all are," Joan said, speaking to me for the first time that night.

"... The delegate from Israel," Kenny began. "It makes me sound like an alien ... like one of those foreign exchange students who wandered around for a year before they went back to wherever on earth they came from." He paused and leaned against the podium, as though mulling over what to say next, but I knew better than that. Kenny figured things out from beginning to end.

"It won't take long. You don't come to reunions to talk. You come to stare, to check people out, size them up. I've been doing this as much as anyone. But sorry about this I've been thinking too. I've been asking myself a question. I mean, here we are, American kids, public school graduates, New Jersey products. And I've been asking myself, what defines us? What identifies us? What holds us together?"

At the side, Gooker yawned, audibly, and made a sawing motion with his arms as if he were playing a violin. "Hey," he asked, "could we put this to music?"

"What holds us together? The place we live in? The place we used to live? *New Jersey?!* What else? Memories of prom night? Convertibles? Rock and roll? That's our history?"

Gooker had heard enough. He got up and stood behind the podium. In a minute, he'd jump forward and shove Kenny aside. I didn't want to see that. In the end, I was rooting for him to finish.

"Call me the delegate from Israel," he said, raising his voice. "But there's politics in my life. And religion. And history every minute." He looked like there was something else he wanted to say; he almost decided against it. Later, I wished he had. "The world's an unsafe place. I'm sorry. I'm sorry for you, I'm sorry for me … Sorry." He walked back through the tables, where everyone sat quietly.

"Thank you Kenny Hauser," Gooker snapped. "In New Jersey, call Bigelow 6-5800. Operators on duty, waiting for your call …"

Kenny came back to our table, but he didn't sit down. "I'm going now," he said to Joan "You can come with me or you can stay here. Want to come with me?"

"No," she said.

"You'll get someone to drive you home?

"Or I'll walk."

Kenny started to leave. I jumped up and joined him. I put an arm around his shoulder, an unwelcome arm. Maybe he wanted to be seen stomping out in protest. When I joined him, it looked like we were going out to the parking lot for a smoke.

"It can't end like this," I said. We were out among the cars. There'd been a shower. The parking lot was wet. A whoosh of spray accompanied the convoys of trucks headed into the city. All that wasted rain.

"I can't believe it!" Kenny said. "I lost it! I never lose it! You saw me on television I let everyone else lose it. Then I take my shot. But in there ... I really screwed up. And that half-assed Gooker! He's a magician after all, isn't he? Bringing us back like this. I didn't know what I was getting into."

"But you're not sorry you came. Not really."

"I don't know George. Hell ... There's something to it. God knows ..."

"Maybe this'll sound stupid, but it's late, we've had some drinks and ... it seems right now that the saddest thing is that there are classes that ... don't have reunions."

He didn't say that he agreed. But he took my point. So I pushed my luck.

"Come back in."

"No ... it's alright ... you and me ... everything ... it's alright. But I'm not going back in there." Still, he lingered, leaned against his car, not opening the door. "So ... how's your father?"

"He's planning on exploring America in a mobile home. You believe it?"

"No!"

"There's more. He's doing it with Pauline Kennedy."

"Amazing." Somehow we were close again. Those old conversations. Who said what. Who was in love. Confidences and confessions. It's kind of neat.

"Come on back inside," I said, signaling back towards the restaurant. Someone opened the door and we heard music from inside, Maurice Williams and the Zodiacs singing "Stay." God the D.J. was on the job. "I guess they're dancing now."

"Or they could be watching American Graffiti," Kenny retorted. "Which this whole evening resembles. Watch out for 'Smoke Gets In Your Eyes.' Your old man really traveling with the dragon lady?"

I told him about the presidents. And the vice presidents. We played with it for awhile: it was that kind of idea. Once you heard it you were hooked. We laughed about it. Then he stepped into the car, shaking his head.

"Well," he said, turning the key. "God bless America."

"Excuse me," someone said. It was Pauline Kennedy. She was the one who'd let the music out into the parking lot. "Would you mind driving me home, Kenny?"

"No problem." He shot a glance at me, just a quick one, and I stifled a laugh. He was riding home with the woman he'd just called "the dragon lady." He got out to open the door for her. But we kept standing there on the edge of the party, the three of us, close enough to catch the music that drifted from inside, and to hear it mix with the sound of the trucks barreling down the highway to New York. It was a rain-wet parking lot outside an overpriced "family portions" New Jersey restaurant in the Phil Rizzuto style. But no one was ready to leave.

"I have something to say," Pauline Kennedy said. "Before we go, a benediction. This is for both of you. It's a funny thing about reunions. When you see a group of people go through high school, you say to yourself, here are the brilliant ones, here are the promising ones, here are the problems and so forth. The stars. The dunces. You attend a five-year reunion and you say to yourself, I'll see if I guessed right. And then, you realize you need more time. Ten years—that's when all the returns are in. But when ten years are over you say, maybe not. These things take time. Twenty years, at least. Well, this is twenty years and it seems to me that'll take even longer to sort things out. Forever, perhaps. Anyway, more time. I'm giving you all more time. I hope you use it well. And that you keep in touch. It's not so lonely then. Never lose touch."

Inside, God had arrived. God the disc jockey, the heavenly sender, who traveled from party to party, from era to era, big band to acid rock, thirties to eighties, whatever we wanted, and tonight we wanted the sound of the late fifties and early sixties, when we were young and music was good. The golden age, it seemed to us that night, and God a.k.a. Eugene Moretti obliged, from "Why Do Fools Fall In Love" to "Since I Don't Have You" to "Smoke Gets In Your Eyes" and in no time the bar was open, the dance floor was crowded, and a couple hundred people were back where they wanted to be. And yet, even as harmony prevailed, even as I led Joan out onto the floor for "Daddy's Home," especially then I wondered about where Kenny Hauser had gone.

"An asshole," Gooker had said, meeting me at the bar a moment before. "Okay, I know it. I'm drunk. But that doesn't make me wrong. And I say he's an asshole. He stank out the place." Gooker gulped his drink—it looked like he'd shifted to scotch by now. It smelled like scotch, even though he drank it like iced tea. "What did we all do to deserve that kind of lecture? Is this so bad? So stupid? Old friends coming together?"

He gestured out towards the dance floor, where crowds of our classmates shifted from fast dance to slow, all of them pawns of Eugene Moretti, unmoved mover who presided over everything from a portable sound system at the side of the bar.

"He made it sound like all we do out here is date and marry and breed and die and the only adventure we have is a little bit of action on the side ..." Gooker drank and, as he swallowed, thought of something funny, so that he spurted some scotch and a half-chewed ice cube out into space. "He forgot softball."

"You should get out and dance," I said.

"Yeah, well, a funny thing happened on the way to the reunion. Seems my wife is leaving me." He stared at me and maybe he was remembering when he'd asked me for my apartment key, brushing away the chance of Kate making the same sort of request.

"A hairdresser," he said. "The whole town thought he was a fruiter. You believe it?"

"I'm sorry," I said. Kate and Gooker weren't a honeymoon couple, that was for sure. That didn't stop me from hoping they'd last.

"You know something, George?" Gooker asked. "I thought I was the ringmaster of this particular circus. Maybe I'm the clown. That's not all. These months ahead are gonna be rough."

"I'll be here," I said. "You know where I live."

It ended like all the dances I remembered, Jesse Belvin's "Goodnight My Love," benediction and prayer sounding over a dark dance floor, and then it was time for God the disc jockey to pack up his records, load up his van and drive back to Fort Lee. Brought back together just long enough to wonder about what might have been—all those delectable "ifs"—now it was time for my high school classmates to file out the door and into the parking lot, where our cars awaited us and then, honking and shouting, hugging and waving, leaving almost as if we'd all be back in school comparing notes on Monday morning. Out onto Route 22, out and away, probably—let's face it—forever: people from New Jersey can't kid themselves. Not Joan and not me.

"You said you wanted to talk," she reminded me.

"In a minute," I said. "We're almost there."

I pulled off the highway near Snuffy's, uphill past the Blue Star Shopping Center—God, those vast malls were odd at night, those plains of asphalt, those dark buildings that went from Two Guys to Korvettes to Caldor, recycling themselves forever—and up over the speed bumps onto Johnson's Drive and the turnoff

I was looking for, a yielding in the darkness, softness between the trees, and then we were at the secret height from which we could see the lights of Manhattan.

"Top of the world," I said. "Never fails."

"That's a movie line, isn't it?"

"Yes. A Cagney movie. '*White Heat.*'"

"You know what this place reminds me of?" She lit a cigarette and stared out at the lights, at the houselights and street lights that were still and headlights, moving slowly down tree-lined avenues, faster along the highway, some of them our classmates driving home, dispersing into a landscape that ended God knows where. That was the problem—where it ended.

"*Jude The Obscure?*" Joan said. "By Thomas Hardy?" The way she added the name of the author, she sounded like a student answering questions in a classroom. And then, by way of further explanation. "I read it for a course I took."

I nodded, listening. It was alright and then some. She didn't have to apologize for catching up. Or passing.

"And there's a scene where Jude goes to the outskirts of this more or less hick town he's born in and praying to get out of, a high-up place like this, and in the distance he spots the lights of the university town where just maybe, if God drops all his other projects, he might someday get educated and change his life and become a better person ..."

She took a deep drag, blew the smoke out of the window into the night, exhaling luxuriously. Maybe we were the last generation that would smoke this way. "Christminster was the name of the town," she said. "I think. Or Jerusalem. Or Hamburg. Or New York. Anywhere but here. That's what I've been thinking about."

"Listen," I said. "I've been to all those places. And you know what it amounts to? I've been dodging from island to island. Because islands are all that's left. Islands are national parks and resorts and theme parks and beaches and ethnic sections and rich neighborhoods—everywhere else is New Jersey. Believe me, I feel like I've been skipping from one place to another, writing up all these puffy columns while all around me the tide was rising, the ocean rolling in."

"New Jersey."

"You said it."

"And so you figure you'll just … dive right in, huh?"

"I want to come home. To New Jersey. I know there's better states …"

"About forty-nine of them."

"But this isn't something you pick and choose. This is home. And until all this wandering stops, this moving, mine and everybody else's … there's no way America's going to work. That's the message from my father …"

"But you said he was leaving … going back to Germany, you said."

"He's sticking around, but I've got the house."

"So you're the prodigal son, I guess."

"He wants me to have it. And I'll give it a try. As long as he's alive, I won't sell it, that's for sure. I'm coming home. Sinking roots. Taking a stand. Staking a claim." A deep breath. I turned to her. My high school dream, my Jersey girl, with me on reunion night, the cycle, the circle, the pattern, everything was perfect.

"No way," she said. "Just listen, will you …"

Random, lonely reading. Odd little courses at schools that mostly taught tai-chi and cooking-with-a-wok and Spanish For Beginners. Heavier stuff at Drew and Rutgers. She'd only guessed she was smart, but for years, circumstances had conspired to keep her from confirming it. Then, a few months ago, she had taken the U.S. Foreign Service exam. Not telling anybody, not really having anybody to tell, and with no greater expectations than filling out a lottery ticket. She was assigned to the U.S. Consulate in Oslo.

"I was hoping ... I don't mind telling you this ... that I might see you there sometime," she said. I guessed she meant it, but it sounded like a good will offering, because she was going either way. I couldn't stop her. And I couldn't blame her either.

"Congratulations," I said.

"Really?"

"I got wrapped up in my own ... voyage. I see that. I thought part of my coming back was coming back to you."

"Well ... I'm not your homecoming queen," she said. "But what are you going to do out here, George? What on earth are you going to do?"

"I'll give it a try. That's all. It'll be harder. Without you ...

"I guess."

"Well ..." I snapped on the headlights, which lit up the clearing: the overturned shopping cart I'd noticed a few weeks before was still there. I backed out of the clearing and onto the drive, then drove down to the highway, where we joined the traffic. That's what we were now, part of the traffic. In no time, we were parked outside that garden apartment at the highway's edge.

"I guess you feel pretty good," I said, "leaving."

"It's high time," she replied. "You get some of the credit, you know. Just knowing you were out there, seeing your byline from all those far off places, it kept reminding me, 'hey, I went to high school with that guy.'"

"You get some credit from me," I told her. "You got me back here."

"Come in, will you?"

"You mean ..."

"If you don't mind packing boxes." She leaned over and pressed against me. Nothing left to doubt, nothing to say. No wondering about tonight or tomorrow. My welcome home party, her bon voyage.

V.

"Go out and talk to him," Pauline says as George pulls in the driveway. It's not even seven o'clock but we're both morning people, it turns out, like to get a leg-up on the new day. I nod and step out the door and the morning is plain gorgeous, bright cold air that came down from Canada leaving a last blanket of leaves on the lawn. It's as though there are cells in my body, sleeping all summer, which wake up and say, let's get a move on, let's burn daylight, let's hit the road and have breakfast a hundred miles from here.

"Hi, Pop," he says, looking like he'll be needing a nap before noon. His reunion wore him out, maybe, but I've never been one to ask questions about that stuff. His mother dreamed of intimacies and confidences they'd share. She got nowhere. I've done better, just waiting, keeping my mouth shut. Now he's glancing at this mobile home that's sitting in the driveway.

"Gets maybe six miles a gallon," I tell him. "But it's nice inside. Come on, I'll give you the tour." So we go up these tiny folding steps I don't trust yet and you bend to go through the door, which looks to me like one of those flaps that dog owners put in their screen doors so their pooch can get in and out on his own, but inside, I have to admit, built-in kitchen appliances and all. "I stocked it up yesterday," I say, opening the refrigerator door. "I got creamed herring, dill pickles, limburger cheese and pumpernickel bread, because once we're out on the road ... God knows what we'll find."

I gesture to the two berths, upper and lower, the shower, the chemical toilet.

"It's even got a television," I say. "I was wondering what to name this thing. Dun Rovin? Heaven on Wheels? Faraway Backyard?"

"Say, Pop?"

"Yes?"

"I think I'd like to try to live here for a while and see if I can make things work."

"What'll you do for a living?" I ask. I'm frowning, but inside I'm turning somersaults. "I mean, guidebooks to New Jersey? Is there much call for that kind of thing? Seems to me, people want to know the fastest way through, is all."

"I don't know what I'll write," he says. "Or if. It won't be easy. I might fail. Big deal. Maybe I'll borrow your trailer sometime, work on my scenic map."

"It's not a trailer," I correct him. "A trailer is something you pull. This is something you drive. A recreational vehicle, they call it."

"Hard getting to Germany in this."

"We put that off," I tell him. "Pauline talked me into knocking around America some more ... visit your uncle down south ... head out west ... spend the winter in the desert ... and so on." I gaze around the inside of this contraption and wonder how it'll work. All my bad habits. My way of dripping all over everything, when I come out of the shower. Also, I bend paperclips and dig out earwax with them. Sooner or later she'll catch me doing that. I'm not such a prize. "Anyway, Germany will be there. I haven't forgotten it."

"She talked you out of it, didn't she?" he asks, gesturing towards the house.

"She … I don't know … she got me to consider whether what I was missing wasn't the Germany that used to be, but the America that …"

"You hoped would be?" George looks up at me and takes my hand and suddenly I get the oddest feeling, it's like we're in business together, me and him. "Still hope."

I nod. "Something like that."

"Oh boy," he says. "Travel writer who knocks around America comes home. Travel writer's father hits the road with his new partner. Pop, you're really something. Did you have all this planned?"

"I'm not that smart," I say, in a way that suggests he's not so far off the mark. Take credit where you can. "In the end … I'm an *Amerikaner.* I traveled. I found something I loved. Found it again, I should say."

"What's that?"

"You. And Pauline. She dances rings around us both."

"Yes. She does. I'm glad you found her. Or she found you."

"Anyway … we'll go out and knock around some … see what's out there."

I see Pauline coming out of the house. Leaning towards him, I whisper. "Could be I'll be in Germany yet. This gallivanting around … it's no sure thing."

"Neither is this New Jersey thing," he answers. "I'll give it a try."

"That's good, son. That's fine. Don't rush things. Don't expect too much. This isn't the neighborhood for miracles." Then I think—but I don't say—maybe it is. He's home. That's a miracle.

"Audience, subject, self," Pauline Kennedy says, stepping inside.

"Huh?"

"The big three. George knows." Then she says, "Good morning, George."

"Kenny got you home alright?" he asks.

"Eventually. We went to a diner on the highway and we talked for a while." She glances at me. "We have an invitation to the Holy Land."

"Maybe we'll take him up on it," I say. "But see America first, they say."

He stands there, my son, watching us pull out the driveway. I take my time about it. This thing drives like a cement truck. He follows us out the driveway and then, as we back onto Hilltop Avenue, he walks across the yard waving. I see him pulling the for-sale sign out of the grass in front of our house. And I picture him walking over to the beer-party table to pay his respects to the old timers.